# A TRACE OF RED

*Other books by*

# Edward Hannibal

*Chocolate Days, Popsicle Weeks*
*Dancing Man*
*Liberty Square Station*
*Blood Feud* (with Robert Boris)

# A TRACE OF RED

## Edward Hannibal

AN AUTHORS GUILD BACKINPRINT.COM EDITION

iUniverse, Inc.
Bloomington

# A TRACE OF RED

AN AUTHORS GUILD BACKINPRINT.COM EDITION

Published by iUniverse, Inc.

For information address:
iUniverse
1663 Liberty Drive
Bloomington, IN 47403
www.iuniverse.com
1-800-Authors (1-800-288-4677)

Originally published by The Dial Press

ISBN: 978-1-4759-8184-1 (sc)

Printed in the United States of America

iUniverse rev. date: 05/13/2013

As always, for Maggie.
And this time with gratitude also
to Mary Ellen, Edward, Eleanor,
John, and Julia Hannibal.
Plus special acknowledgment to
Wendy Lipkind, Joyce Johnson, Juris Jurjevics,
William W., and Colonel Roger P.

Fancy gloves, though
Wears Macheath, dear
So there's not
A trace of red.

"Mack the Knife"
*The Threepenny Opera*
by Bertolt Brecht

# ONE

# 1

The call caught him at the end of a workday. He was alone, staring out at Manhattan through his office windows, watching the city turn dark with night. He saw one of the clear plastic buttons on his phone light up, and expected the buzzer to sound. Instead his secretary appeared in his doorway. She was already dressed to go home and said, "Mr. Burke, there's a Colonel Joel Kelsey on hold for you. Says you know him. I've gotta run, okay?"

He was too stunned to answer her. He grabbed up the receiver and shouted, *"Kelse?"*

"Yeah!"

"Holy God!" It was Kelsey's voice! After twenty years, practically! "I can't believe it—where the hell are ya?"

"I'm in New York! At this here Yankee Hilton! Waitin' for you to get your ass on over here!"

"You're not!"

"The hell I ain't! How are ya, Nick?"

"Jesus . . . well, all right! Don't move, I'm on my way!"
He hung up, then ran along the hall to the next office and told his partner, "Grant? Listen, I can't stay tonight after all. Tell some lies for me, will you?"

Grant, an art director, had been studying transparencies on

his light box. His face immediately filled with worry. "What is it, you got bad news, Nick?"

"No—God—just the opposite," Nick said. "I just heard from my best friend, this guy I was in the *Army* with!" He knew that he didn't need to explain the significance of this to Grant, who was only a shade older than himself and had seen combat in Korea. "He's still in, a fucking full-bird colonel, and we haven't seen each other since! Since freaking Germany!"

"Fantastic!" Grant said. "And he's in town?"

"Yeah!"

"So go already, Nickie—and don't worry about here, I'll cover for ya, and take notes and everything, and fill you in in the morning—*mazel tov!*"

"Thanks, babe." Nick took off. The building he worked in was on Third Avenue in the fifties. Trying to flag a cab in the clog of rush-hour traffic, he ran up to the next corner. The crosstown traffic was just as thick and slow-moving. He decided he'd make better time walking and began crossing the avenue, darting between cars. His excitement abated just long enough to let his sense recover and send him toward Fifty-third Street, the closest subway stop.

The days had been staying remarkably warm for the end of October, but the nights came on more and more chilly. Threading the mobbed sidewalks, Nick enjoyed the feel of the cold air breaking against his face and hands. He kept nursing the foolish question, How could Kelsey be in the Philippines and here at the same time? Underground, he boarded the first train that came, an E. It shot him under the five blocks to Seventh. Outside and hurrying again, he slipped into a liquor store and bought a quart of what would mean the most to Kelsey.

He walked back one long block to Sixth and turned north. Inside the hotel the lobby was jumping. A crowd covered the main desk, so he darted to the house phones on the wall. When Kelsey answered, Nick yelled, "Clear the women out, I'm coming up!" and hung up. He stepped into an elevator filled with men and women wearing laminated name tags on polyester clothing. The closing of the doors seemed a signal for them to cease their laughing and chatter.

By the time he reached Kelsey's floor, Nick was alone, and when the doors opened, there stood Kelsey himself, waiting in the foyer. For an instant each of them assumed the same crouching position of recognition, like two sumo wrestlers addressing each other before contact. Nick jumped out of the elevator, and Kelsey jumped up and down in place. Then the two old comrades threw their arms around each other and danced the dance of reunion long thought impossible, laughing and hollering and pounding one another.

"You sonuvabitch!" Joel Kelsey sang.

"You bastard!" Nick Burke answered. To him, Kelsey in his forties seemed the same as he had in his twenties. His hair was more brown and less blond than it used to be, that was all. Nick raised the paper bag into the air, like the Statue of Liberty's torch.

"What you got there, son?"

"What else?" He pulled the bottle of Jack Daniel's into the light.

"That is my man!" Kelsey took it, swung his arm across Nick's shoulders, and led the way down the corridor to his room. There, he tore off his suit jacket, pulled his dark necktie loose, and began unwrapping hotel drinking glasses.

Nick was wearing a suede jacket over a turtleneck. He took the jacket off and said, "You look great, Kelse."

"You too—regular long-hair, huh?"

"Should've seen me a few years ago."

It seemed necessary for them both to keep walking around the room, still kind of circling each other. Then Kelsey poured some Jack Daniel's into both glasses. This seemed to call for them to come close again and shake hands, hard and seriously.

[ 5 ]

"It's great to see you, Kelse."

"Gawd, it's great to see *you*, Nick!"

"Cheers."

"*Prosit!*"

They clinked glasses and drank.

"I liked all your letters."

"Yours too, Nick."

There was a sofa against a wall, and two barrel-back chairs facing a small, round coffee table. Each took a chair, Kelsey standing the bottle on the table between them. They grinned away at each other for a while, sipping. Then Nick lit a cigarette and said, "What in *hell* are you doing here anyhow? I thought you were in Manila."

"I am," Kelsey said in his same old Kentuckian lilt that Nick was used to hearing from the pages of his letters. "I get pulled back to the flagpole from time to time. This is—"

"Well, thanks a lot, prick!"

Kelsey also lit a cigarette. "Naw . . . gimme a break. If I ever got a chance to see you up here in New York, you think I wouldn't?"

"I was only kidding."

"I've thought of giving you a call on the horn once or twice, but I always figured that'd just be bullshit."

"Oh, God, yeah," Nick agreed. "I hate phones."

"Right. Fact is, I been doin' quite a bit of jet-settin' around on this new job, but most times it's been in the opposite direction."

"Hey, James Bond himself, huh?" Drinking gingerly, Nick realized that he was neglecting to ask about Bibs and their kids. But he decided it was better to let it go. He was already up to date in Kelsey's family department anyhow, from their correspondence. The shock of Kelsey's presence was beginning to pass. "This is fantastic, Kelse!" he said, and sank with pleasure into the moment.

[ 6 ]

Kelsey curled forward and poured more whiskey into their glasses. "What do you say, old partner, we gonna go the distance?"

Nick picked up his drink. "I will if you will."

Kelsey drank. "That's my man. You're sure, now. I don't wanna make you do anything you're not up to anymore."

Kelsey's lip curled, but not fast enough to distract Nick from catching a fleeting glimpse of a strange look that passed across Kelsey's eyes. It was there and gone, too swiftly to be identified.

"Tell you what." Nick grinned. "Since I can see you're worried about making a fool of yourself drinking in front of a civilian, I'll get us some high-price chow. Help you tamp your tummy down." Saying this, he went and brought back the room-service menu from the dresser.

"Well, I can't very well let you eat alone."

Reading the menu, Nick said, "I'm going to have a four-dollar, a nineteen fifty, and a seven ninety-five."

"Same here." Kelsey nodded. "Very rare. And how about a bottle of something, oh, twenty or twenty-five?"

"Excellent idea. Oops, we're out of luck. They only have fifteens and then fifties."

"A fifteen's fine by me, just so long as she's very red."

"You got it." He picked up the phone and called room service. Nick said seriously, "I'm assuming this isn't your own money I'm about to spend, Colonel."

"Have no fear, Mr. Taxpayer. It's as much yours as anyone's." Nick ordered their meal and hung up.

Kelsey said, "Shit. No African lobster tails from Bremerhaven?"

"No," Nick said, "John the Hawk couldn't get DeSimone to fly up this week." He marveled at the intensity of the warmth that coursed through him with that remembrance.

"Oh, God, poor old D."

[ 7 ]

And so they plunged together into reminiscence. De-Simone, whose death in the helicopter after setting the steeple on the German church previewed, they agreed, the Vietnam carnage. The Duke, Scotty, J.J., Billy Hogue, all those crystal evenings on the terrace of the officers' club in Germany.

"When you think about it," Kelsey said after a while, "we both had a way of making defiance look like obedience."

"You lost me."

"No matter, just something I've seen from time to time in certain guys. It's a good thing. It's making their will your own."

A waiter knocked, then rolled their dinner in on a wagon. He began to set the table by the window, but they told him to just lay it all out on the coffee table between them. Kelsey signed the check and passed him a folded five-dollar bill, so he stayed a moment longer and uncorked the wine. Then they ate, talking, drinking the wine, and sipping at automatic intervals from the ritual glasses of the warming Jack Daniel's, not breaking the rhythm of the steady, measured, army drinking.

Nick found he was listening longer than he spoke, and eating more bread than he would have normally.

The Kelse belonged to it all, had shared with him practically every moment of every year of it—if he glazed his eyes, he and Kelsey could be again anyplace back there: at Grafenwöhr on cots, in mess tents, at kitchen tables in their apartments, leaning on jeep hoods on forest roads at night, waiting for an alert to be called off. Remembering, they would laugh to coughing, or resume old arguments.

"God damn it, Nick, if I've told you once, Honk was in the *same* class at West Point as Pete Dawkins!"

"Nossir. The year behind."

"Use your head, dammit, he used to say so himself. If he hadn't been the same year as Dawkins, *he* would've been the superstar hero in all the papers and—"

"One way or another, Kelse, they lost him. A *great* soldier. The absolute best, and they—"

[ 8 ]

"Aw, he asked for it."

"Bullshit, he asked for it."

"Honk asked for it! It was his own pigheaded—"

"Kelse! Look—am I the goddamn one on the goddamn direct radio line to him, or are you? *I* am. You're off sawing zees, and I'm in that APC oven, and the man *penetrates the enemy's goddamn regimental command post!* Does he not?"

Kelsey snuffed. "Fucking Honk! Go!"

"All right! The man not only gets in, he goddamn well gets out again, with the fucking operations map in his pocket! We went nuts in that tin can! He—"

"He *also,* Nicko . . . Honk the asshole also, and you *always* leave out the insignificant detail, that he also took the time to snatch their goddamn *boots* while he was at it, and threw them into the woods! The damn—"

Nick roared. "Hah. You can never tell it without laughing, can you, you bastard!"

"Okay, it seemed funny at the time, but—"

"It's still funny!"

"I don't care, Nick. I don't care who you are, or how great a soldier you might be, you do not . . . take . . . a *full colonel's* map! *And* his boots!"

"Even if he's nighty-night?"

Kelsey wouldn't be pulled off into hilarity again. "You just don't do it! Even if it's only Red army–Blue army games. Unless you're looking to be reprimanded. Honk was a fool, Nick. He was West Point, and a son of generals, but he was asking for it. He saw too many asshole movies!"

"In real combat," Nick pointed back, "in actual war," he said, trying pleasurably to remember exactly where and when he and Kelsey had had this sheer bullshit, steel-helmet dialogue the last time, "the man would have been given the Silver Star. And you know it."

"In the real thing he would've been dead before he ever even found their perimeter," Kelsey put in, cool as always. "As it was, he got his hotdog ass kicked royally, as well he should have. He fucking asked for it."

They lapsed into silence here, as they always used to. All that was left was for Nick to get in the last, childish word. "Oh, yeah?" Instead he found himself quietly saying something new, he wasn't sure why: "They let him resign, Kelse. That's all I'm mad about. Honk was a fantastic soldier. He would've made general officer before he was thirty-five, and over some grab-ass stunt they allowed him to resign! They shouldn't have. That's all. Honk was a serious loss."

Immediately Kelsey said, "In the real thing that kind of John Wayne mentality would've got Honk and probably you and me and his whole Long Range Patrol wasted, Nick. Fucking *killed*, man. Serious loss, my ass. He . . ."

Suddenly Kelsey's face seemed to slide back behind his words. Perhaps it was only the room shadows, but that glint snapped back into the pupils of his eyes, staying and filling them with a sharp-pointed fullness Nick couldn't remember ever seeing there before.

It quickened some deep-down wariness in him, but his body stayed sprawled and lax as he held his drink.

". . . and nobody made him resign," Kelsey was finishing. "A man who resigns his commission over a little well-deserved ass-kicking couldn't have done much with it after that anyhow."

"Honk was right," Nick said as lightly as he could. "If they held some fat-ass colonel's wounded pride more important than—"

"*You* wouldn't have stopped for those boots, Nick," Kelsey cut in hard, "and you damn well know it!"

He sat up a little, smiling. "I don't know. I might have given the idea some serious thought and—"

"Not with an ops map in your pocket, you wouldn't! No way."

"What size boots were they?"

Kelsey didn't even pretend to laugh. "Don't try to smart-mouth yourself off this. I'm serious. Would you or wouldn't you?"

Nick shot a glance at the bottle: there was still too much whiskey in it to explain this sudden squall. *Oh, God, don't let one of us spoil this. The one guy in all my life!*

He shrugged and grinned. "All right, Kelse, I probably wouldn't have. So what?" He was about to add that they were talking about Honk, not him here anyhow; but now he wasn't so sure that was true.

"So I just wanted to hear you admit it, that's all."

"Then I take it back," Nick said. "I sure as shit *would* have grabbed all those idiot boots, and pitched them in the woods just like Honk did. Christ, without the boots there wouldn't even be a story!"

Kelsey grinned and made peace signs with both hands.

It must be just the booze after all, Nick thought, and said, "And I don't care what you say, old Honk was a serious loss."

Then the Kelse was making his old hillbilly hoot and saying, "Oh, yeah? Oh, yeah?" in his lilting voice.

"Yeah," Nick said. "Christ, we both must be getting blitzed."

Kelsey leaned forward and took the bottle again. "Shoot, we've hardly begun to put a dent in this sucker yet!"

They took turns using the toilet. Nick didn't let himself glance into the mirror, afraid the sight of his face would confirm that he and his long-lost best friend had just come close to real hostility, and over nothing. Over that stupid, hoary old Honk story. He returned to see that the Kelse had cleared the low table of all but their bottle and glasses, and was semiprone in his chair again, feet up and face looking even friendlier than it had when he'd first arrived.

Nick sat back down and said, "So here we are, anyhow,

huh? We held to our bargain, at least—I've kept you briefed on how it is on the outside, you try to—"

But Kelsey was having none of that. "I still don't have a clue to how's it like outside, Nicko. Still seems all jerkoff Disneyland to me. I don't see how you can stand it. To me, it's—"

Feeling defensive, Nick spoke without thinking: "It's recruitment for your fucking wonderful *inside*, right now," he said, and found himself telling Kelsey about the latest project the agency was assigning him to—soliciting the Army's advertising account. "There's a bit of irony, huh, Kelse? We might be jerkoffs, but it seems you boys need us to do something you sure can't pull off by yourselves."

Kelsey crooked an amused eyebrow, lit a fresh cigarette, and said, "Shoot, that's a bit like ending up in Postal Service or *Finance*, seems to me. That's woman's work, Nick."

By now Nick had suspected that Kelsey knew exactly where he was going with all this. Inside his shanghaied system his plain curiosity seesawed with his real dread of what it might be.

"By the way," Kelsey said, "you know that Artillery full bird you had the showdown with that time?"

"Yeah," he said, quickening. "Ewing."

"Ewing! By God, you're right, that was his name. Jesus, what a memory you got there."

"What about him?"

"Nothin' . . . just, I thought you might get a kick out of knowing what happened to him. He's a three-star general now."

"Good for him," Nick said gingerly. "All those *real* nukes to kiss all day."

"I happened to spot him at this War College seminar a while back. I didn't go over and say hello."

"Well," he shrugged, "that answers one thing, anyhow. If I did stay in, I wouldn't have run into him, after all."

"Oh, I don't know about that," Kelsey drawled. "This was only me. You, I think that motherfucker would've made a point of tracking your ass down, somewhere along the way."

"That's comforting."

Kelsey grinned across at him. "You still don't like to take anybody's shit, do you." He scissored his legs to the floor and sat forward so intently that Nick in response brought his glass up fast to his mouth and drank a full mouthful of the Jack Daniel's, then put it down like a hot coal.

"But, Lord, Nick, seein' that son of a bitch almost knocked me over, I mean it! Will you *ever* forget that fuckin' night in that TIC? Ol' General Night Train ridin' that chair, an' spittin' tobacco all over? Jesus!"

"No," he said quietly, "I'll never forget that night."

Then Kelsey came to the place he'd been heading. The points filling his eyes seemed to soften and glisten like sparks as Nick watched, mesmerized, fearful and oddly anxious. "Nick," he said hoarsely, "I just want you to know a couple of things, about the inside, in case you don't. . . .

"One's this: Our first years back there in Germany? You never missed anything after them. I never quite told you this in writing, but every stop I made after that was never better than like a faded negative of Baker Barracks. Nam was a whole other thing—forget Nam. But I understand now that I was always lookin' for the life to be like it was for us then, and it never was. You had her in her prime, Nick."

*We were young, that's all,* Nick thought.

Omnisciently, Joel said, "Didn't have anything to do with us being kids, either. I watched guys just as young at every other post I hit, and they just weren't having it as great as we did. Must've just been one of those magic times, I guess. Some kind of peak. . . . Just so you know, that's all, Nick. . . .

"And the other thing's this," Kelsey said, placing his drink on the table so it was touching Nick's, and looking straight into

[ 13 ]

his eyes. "I just want you to know, my friend, once and for all, that even after all these years . . . the way you faced down that Colonel Ewing that night, in front of that general . . . that was the most honorable and bravest act this old soldier has ever witnessed another soldier perform, man or boy. The Service—"

"Aw, shit, Kelse, are—?"

"At ease, now, dammit. I came to say my piece, and I'm gonna by God say it. The Service I love still suffers from your absence in it, Nick. I consider it an honor and privilege to know you, to have served with you, and to still be considered a friend by you." He retrieved his drink and curled back into his chair.

Nick just stared, dumbstruck by a resurgence of his old guilt: *I should have stayed in!*

But Kelsey wasn't done. He followed his salute of regard with a slight slap of rebuke: "And let me tell you this, too, partner—I *know* that that candy-ass civilian dreamworld of yours out there has never let you come even close to doing anything like that again!"

Nick poured a splash of whiskey into his glass, spilling some onto the table, and brought it to his mouth, not to drink but to inhale the fumes and try to force some clarity into his mind. Had old hotdog Honk started all this? Honk seemed a thousand years ago. He decided Kelsey must merely be drunk, and said, "Oh, yeah?"

"Yeah. It hasn't, has it?"

"No, Kelse," he sighed, "it hasn't. Thank God."

"Never mind your thank Gods—it must eat you up, being out there."

"It's . . . a living" was all he could manage. To try to get away from it, he lied, "Christ, the whole room's spinning on me. Guess I can't drink the way I used to, either."

Kelsey smiled. "Shoot, you could *never* drink worth a hoot, Nick."

"You don't mind me bunkin' with you tonight, do you?"

"Hell, no. I was about to suggest it myself. There's a whole other bed."

"Great."

Kelsey rose, reading his watch. "Hey, not even two yet. That wasn't so bad at all, was it."

Like so much of what else Kelsey had said, Nick couldn't tell if it required an answer or not: his questions seemed like proclamations, his statements seemed to hang in the air like questions. He chose to stay silent, and went to bed that way.

# 2

Morning came and he woke. He felt the same as he had felt falling asleep: thoroughly beaten down, yet strangely elated at the same time. He looked across and saw that Kelsey's bed was made. He heard the shower running. That was the Kelse all over. Always up like a shot, bed made and in the shower before anyone else was even near waking. He sat up and lit a cigarette, realizing that he was still wearing his jeans and socks and had slept on top of the bedspread. Perhaps Kelsey had also just crapped out? No, he somehow was sure Kelsey had folded his clothes and slipped between the sheets, properly. He scratched his back; it felt as corrugated as his soul.

He walked to the still uncovered windows and looked out.

The sky above was clear and blue, the city below seemed very clean. He turned back into the shady room, realizing how badly he needed to pee. He went into the bathroom. Kelsey was lathering his face in the mirror and said, "Feel free to use my shaving gear."

"*Danke.*"

"*Bitte.* . . . Hey, get the door, will you, Nicko? That'll be breakfast."

"I'm pissing."

"God, have to do everything myself, you surely haven't changed one bit!"

He stripped and got into the shower. Kelsey came back in and finished shaving. Nick shaved, threw on his sweater, and joined his friend at the table. Pewter hoods were lifted to reveal plates of pancakes and sausages. *What a commercial for coffee,* he thought: guy careens about, bleary and numb, takes one sip of hot coffee and suddenly his whole immediate reality snaps into crystal-clear focus for him, practically with the sound of a *boing!* For that was exactly what had just happened to him. He put down the cup and leaned back.

"Eat!" Kelsey urged him, chewing. "Not that hung over, are ya, son?"

"Okay, Kelse," he said. "Let's have it."

Kelsey's eyes came up, eager but not surprised. "Eat your breakfast while it's hot, Nick. You're gonna need your strength."

"I'm not just imagining things, then, am I."

" 'Course not."

Keyed up as he was, Kelsey's eating sounds made it impossible for Nick to resist the food any longer. He dug in, glad for the excuse to keep his words to himself. From the maelstrom of all last night's talking, only one diamond-sharp piece of speech still sounded in his memory, and it was Kelsey's final, startling tribute. Could he have really meant it? Could it even be true? Had it actually been such an *honorable* act, and *brave?* Kelsey wouldn't flatter, nor would he lie. *My God!* he marveled, feeling something like a genuine thrilling sensation course through his system.

He stole a look at Kelsey eating, and identified another sensation he'd been feeling: how good it was to be with a friend again. Drinking, talking, smoking, eating, sacking out, shaving and showering together. He knew now that the Kelse did have some reason beyond affection for being there, but that didn't take anything away from the pure, relaxed enjoyment of it for him. And how far he had wandered away from such simple, human contact, too, come to think of it. Even all his relations with women had been so side-eyed and left-handed, so brief and ginger, so rife with mere conquest or relief from loneliness. Never *toward* anybody.

He cut a four-tiered, syrup-soaked wedge of pancake, speared it and half a sausage link onto his fork, Kelsey-style, and fed it into his already jubilant mouth. How had he ever forgotten how much he loved pancakes? He hadn't ordered a pancake in a hundred years; it would never even cross his mind to. Even in an International House of goddamn Pancakes, he'd always have eggs. Yet . . . ah, because it was such a boyish breakfast, that's why, such a—such a soldier's morning meal. Christ, he thought, how even the tiniest details of your life co-operate so insidiously in the conspiracy against you. How they support your denial system, the little sons of bitches.

Cheeks bulging and moving, Kelsey went, "Mrm? Good, huh?"

"Mrh!" he agreed. And all his so-called civilian friends and constituents, he saw now: he'd hang out with the plain, gray, earnest souls so that he could feel hip, free, and colorful. Then he'd hang out with the glamorous, bizarre, fast-burning zanies, in order to seem the controlled, respectable one. Mostly, of

[ 17 ]

course, he hung out with nobody. Mostly he worked. But even there, what a dodger he was, always choosing the sweatshop over the decent place, to be sure he was the only quality around. And even then never staying more than four years.

High school, college, the Service, business, even his marriage hadn't lasted much longer than that enigmatic four years. For the first time ever, he looked at that now and felt only puzzled—what did *five* mean to him anyhow? Forever? A long, slow dying? Or did he just get too bored at four to go on? He dropped the whole line of thought. For one thing, he'd read somewhere recently that "Boredom is only hostility without enthusiasm." And if he'd been hostile, then at what? For another thing, his four years at this latest agency was coming up in a month, and while he sure felt the old urge to start looking around, what new outfit would buy his precious new four-day-week deal?

But, damn, in Kelsey's presence, even his four-day week suddenly looked like such a feeble gesture, only pointing up the spectacular unimportance of what he was doing in the rest of his life. For a second he almost regretted having committed that single brave and honorable act of his youth. But he couldn't. It was, after all, the only ledge of significance he'd had to hold on to down all the years.

"So." Kelsey grinned, leaning back and lighting a smoke. "Give it a shot."

He felt like a kid asked to guess what's in the beribboned package. He said, "I'll feel like such a fool if I'm wrong."

"Say it, Nick."

"I'm being recruited?"

Kelsey nodded, winked, and said, softly and seriously, "Son, I believe you've *been* recruited, no?"

It hit him like news of a birth or a death: so unbelievably *real*. "My God," he breathed. "Yeah, I guess I have. But what—"

"Hang on," Kelsey said quickly, and made a small circle in the air with his finger. "Time to step out into God's great outdoors, huh? Walk some of that chow off."

Automatically Nick looked at his watch.

Standing, Kelsey said, "No fear, son. This part won't take long. We'll get you to work on time."

They stood next to each other against the rear wall of the elevator. As always, Kelsey seemed to be so much *taller* that he felt compelled to retaliate and cracked, "Geez, what a waste of height." More people got on, so Kelsey could only laugh.

Outside, the morning air was much cooler than it had looked from the window. They walked east. Kelsey said, "Ready?"

"Probably not, but go ahead."

"Okay. First, I guess you know how much public flak the CIA's been taking the last few years. They're not exactly gone out of business, but one spinoff from their troubles has been a kind of lateral shift of power to us. The CIC's been operating in a lot bigger arena than you might remember, Nick.

"Anyhow. Make a long story short, we've got a very special assignment that needs to use somebody totally off everybody's map. And I've recommended you as that somebody."

Nick threw a sharp glance up at his friend's face, but Kelsey kept telling it to the city: "I want you to just take it in for now, Nicker—let it stay as simple as you can. I know from your letters over the years that it all still means a lot to you, and nothing you said last night makes me think you've changed. You don't have to say anything today. I'll give you some time to think on it. Not much, but enough. Then you'll tell us yes or no, and that'll be it. Either way will be fine."

"Jesus, Kelse, I—"

"You'll be doing us an incredibly great service if you go with it, but I won't push that too far with you, either. You already know better than anything I can tell you. That's one reason why you're the one we're calling on."

Listening, he thought, Christ, that *we* again—he's talking about the Country! Intelligence. The Service. He felt a chill that didn't come from the morning air. They crossed Park Avenue.

Kelsey said, "One more thing for now—you'll be having a visitor drop in on you one of these days. He'll be from us, but I don't want you to let on that you know anything about anything."

"That'll be easy, I *don't*!"

"Not even that you've seen or talked to me. I'll explain why later. If you go with it. Roger?"

"Roger."

"Good." Kelsey looked at him now, and smiled his slightly twisted smile. "And I think you'll be surprised when you see who I'm sending to you."

"Why—do I know him?"

"You'll see." Having finished talking, Kelsey stopped walking. They had come to Lexington.

He put his right hand onto Nick's shoulder for a moment; it felt good. All Nick could think to say was "I don't believe it—I remember when you couldn't get out more than three hillbilly sentences in a row without gagging on your tongue. Now the man swamps me with speeches!"

Kelsey grinned. "It weren't easy. . . . You okay?"

"I don't know. I'll let you know."

They shook hands again. Kelsey gave him one more long significant look, then turned and walked away up the sidewalk, heading back west. Nick went on toward Third, feeling drunk. He looked up at the skyscrapers standing dumb and innocent against the silvering sky, and couldn't understand why it wasn't still yesterday. When Kelsey was on the other side of the earth. And the Service was still nothing more than a memory.

Walking, he tried to remember what he might have done to prevent this from happening. But there was nothing. He guessed that because this was certainly happening, then somehow it had to have happened to him, was meant to happen to him.

# TWO

# 1

Memories.

He had just arrived in West Germany, and was about to fly for the first time from Baker Barracks to Grafenwöhr.

It was 1959, summer, and dusk.

The plane was small, an olive-drab L-20. He was buckled into its copilot's seat, with Lieutenant Joel Kelsey wedged in right behind him. The young Negro captain seeing them off stood against his red MG over by the closed gray doors of the Aviation Company's main hangar. Just as the L-20 lurched forward, Nick had seen him smile, raising his hand in an honest-to-God wing-and-a-prayer thumbs-up sign.

Only twenty-two, he'd returned the cocky, corny gesture and thought, *It is, it's all a war movie, and I'm in it!* The plane moved off then down the tarmac, the roar of its engine drowning out the sound of his and Kelsey's laughter.

Static and word-crackle leaking in from his earphones, the pilot taxied the small plane away from the complex of old wooden airstrip buildings, past the newer, low, yellow brick Division Headquarters building, and out onto the runway. "Here we go, guys," he yelled, "your ass is now in the heroic hands of TWA—teeny, weeny airlines!"

There had been a couple of Army Air officers with them in

[ 25 ]

the nine-month Photo Interpretation course back at "The Bird"—the U.S. Army Intelligence School (USAINTS), Fort Holabird, Maryland. From them Nick had learned the difference and now asked, "Hey, Wheatley—you a pilot or a flier?"

"Shoot, neither one anymore, just another airplane driver, just movin' brass, mail, and cannon fodder like yourselves from A to B."

They had paused at this end of the short runway to rev for takeoff. Suddenly they were shooting forward, then off and up into the air like a stone from out of some giant sling. Side-eyeing Wheatley's technique, Nick decided he was merely a pilot: he had learned what to do and did it, but he still had to think. "A flier's a natural," the aviator at The Bird had explained. "He just fucking *flies*. He don't have to know what he's doin', because he's already doin' it." One of Nick's fears was that he'd never find anything at which he'd be more than a pilot.

Climbing high above the Swabian Alps, Wheatley began banking the plane to the right. They were high enough now to see the sun setting a second time, this time somewhere west of France. Below them the Fils Valley ran away deep and narrow for miles between two side legs of the low Swabian mountain range.

Nick knew the names from studying the map on their long, slow MATS trip across the Atlantic, but not even the color photographs in the travel brochures had suggested how excitingly *foreign* the place would seem. Of course the very notion of his being there at all, in *Europe,* for God's sake, was still at least a double beat beyond his ability to believe it.

With his new best friend not only assigned to the very same outfit, but right now jackknifed behind him in the same rickety-ass Esquadrille flying machine . . . and his new love, no his *wife* now, Christ, on her way to join him . . . it was all too much yet to swallow whole. All he could do was keep moving and let it happen.

"How long a trip is it?" Nick asked.

"Oh, three hours, give or take, see what kind of winds we get—no matter, you'll wish it was longer once you get there."

"So we're told. Real boonies, huh?" For a tall man Kelsey had an unusually light voice, so by habit yelled slightly when he spoke. The engine was a steady drone now, easy to talk over.

"Graf? Ol' *Gravamore*?" Wheatley smirked. "Goddamn hemorrhoid on the ass of the universe, that's all. Makes Texas in a drought look like rain forest. Fine for tankers, of course, they just love it to death."

"General Rommel trained his Panzerkorps at Grafenwöhr," Nick said. Funny: he felt a strange urge to defend this Graf. Until yesterday he hadn't even known it existed.

"Did he, now. Say. If you don't mind me asking—what're two Seventh Army engineers doing being stationed with a tank division anyhow? Something new?"

"No," Nick said, "we're with the 504th MI."

"Uh-oh, better mind my mouth, huh? Got a couple *spook* types aboard!"

"Naw, we're combat types," Kelsey yelled, leaning forward into the cockpit between them.

This was still a semitender spot Wheatley was touching. Both Nick and Kelsey had applied for Intelligence with visions of spending their active duty years in civilian clothes chasing Reds as Counterintelligence Corps agents. When fate, in the form of the Army's quota needs for raw second lieutenants, dictated otherwise, they had accepted their less mysterious lots without showing too much chagrin. Nick wasn't used to not getting what he tried for, though, and still felt vaguely rejected— not that he'd ever admit it outright, even to Kelsey, who he was sure felt the same.

He looked out his side window, wishing the entire plane were made of glass so he wouldn't have to miss one detail of this new, exotic landscape rolling slowly past so close beneath him. The photo interpretation course at The Bird had been nine months of staring down through the lenses of a stereoscope at overlapping aerial photos, trying to make images rise up in 3-D. It had felt very much like looking down from a low-flying airplane like this one.

He kept reading the West German terrain beneath them until it finally floated out of sight into the night. It was all small farmland and scattered tiny villages, a living jigsaw puzzle of mostly greens, yellows, and browns, straight out of a *National Geographic* magazine. Only themselves, and occasional TV antennas, railroad tracks, electric and telephone wires, reminded him that it wasn't the Middle Ages; he had not been moved centuries back in time, merely a world away in space. He could hear the Kelse's breathing changing gears for one of his famous crapouts, and thought, *How the hell could anyone possibly sleep at a time like this?*

Some long, droning hours later Wheatley spoke again, first into his headset, then to Nick: "Slight pucker-factor coming up now—we're going on automatic, let them land us from the ground. New toy they're playing with. Be nice if it works."

Nick laughed, and sucked in his breath. His stomach went up, his legs went down, and then they were suddenly touching the ground with a bump and a little yelp from the wheels. The pilot took back control and steered the craft off the strip and up to the open doorway of the low shed that was the Graf airport. He killed the engine.

Inside the shed Brian Galgay entered Nick's and Kelsey's lives for the first time. The unsmiling guy came up, introduced himself, and announced, "I'm with Security Section. Jeep's outside."

This Galgay appeared to be perhaps a year or two older than they were. Like them, he wore fatigues, but the insignia on his collar wings and on his stiff-blocked, slanted-topped cap were the plain U.S.'s of the CIC agent. He hadn't let a "sir" slip, but that didn't necessarily mean that he was not an enlisted man. Those were the types that chafed Nick and Kelsey most: the Pfc.'s and the Sp4s whose agent status let them live in BOQs, work in civilian clothes, and wear U.S.'s on their uniforms—it was bad enough to get that oblique glance of snotty superiority from another officer or a warrant, but to get it from an EM or a noncom doubled the irritation. They followed this Galgay outside to his jeep, waiting in the shadows with its top down. Kelsey said, "My turn to ride shotgun, big fella," so Nick climbed into the back with their bags.

Moving, the night air turned cold in Nick's face. "No roof for this heap?"

Galgay talked in a slightly arrogant monotone. "Grafenwöhr's considered a combat situation. The only reason we can keep even the windshield up is the dust."

The Kelse confronted the man directly: "What's your rank, Galgay?"

"First lieutenant."

This only made Nick feel all the more intimidated by him. The truth was, he and Kelsey were trying to pass for first lieutenants—they had burnished their bars until they looked more silver than gold. They'd also had their fatigues tailored and bleached to fit snugly and appear long-used and sun-faded. He said, "You're CIC, right?"

"Right."

Kelsey cracked, "Catch a lot of Reds in a tank outfit, do you, Lieutenant?"

Galgay kept his eyes ahead, turning off the airport road's paved blacktop onto deep-rutted dirt. Nick's bottom left the metal seat, and the jeep started shooting off billows of dirt in their wake, some of it whipping in at them from the sides. "Tank trail," Galgay explained, as if he were coining a new phrase. Then: "Okay. There's no room at the Detachment for

[ 29 ]

you two now, so we field-requisitioned you some bed space for the night here in Algiers. It's not much, but there's running water. Got you a couple sleeping bags, on the floor back there, under your feet."

From the narrow doorway where he left them, Nick and Kelsey watched Galgay disappear into dense pine woods. No moon shone, but they could make out the forms of other long, low, concrete-block buildings across the flat, empty fields of dirt around them. Theirs was the one light shining in the whole desolate-feeling place, and it was only a single, unshaded forty-watt bulb dangling on its cord from the middle of the ceiling. They went back inside and opened their canvas cots on the cement floor under the bulb. "*Algiers!*" Nick said. "Terrific name for the place, huh?"

"Yuh, I don't know what I was expecting anyhow."

"*I* do, dammit," Nick cursed. "I wanted a bunch of guys around tables in the officers' club, or at least a mess hall, with steaks and wienerfuckingschnitzels all around, and big, cold steins of Löwenbräu, and—"

"Sissy."

Nick unrolled the sleeping bag on the cot. "Shit. No air mattresses, even."

"You're in the *Army* now, soldier!" Kelsey opened a fresh pack of Camels and lit one. "This is *it*, where we separate the men from the boys!"

"Wouldn't mind separating *Mister* Galgay there from his fucking eyebrows. Pompous ass."

"Yeah, real serious stud, wasn't he? 'Course, those Notre Damers, they gotta be careful who they talk to, you know. Hell, the secrets he's carrying around, you can't go mouthing loose with any old green-ass second johns that pop up in the middle of the night." Kelsey unzipped his AWOL bag and produced two Milky Way bars and a pint of Jack Daniel's.

Nick grinned. "Ah, so that's where I put it." He washed

his candy down with a swig of whiskey and passed the bottle back. "How do you know he went to Notre Dame?"

"Looks it, don't he?"

"Yeah, he looks like every black-Irish cop's son I ever met." Nick walked the length of the barracks to the latrine door and snapped the light switch: nothing. "Unless you've got some serious business, Kelse, might as well just go outside."

Joel was already inside his bag. "Fartsack's quilted, anyhow. Better than them woolly mummy bags. Last one in gets the light."

"Oh, Jesus, another fraternity rule." Nick snapped the wall switch beside the door and followed the path of dim night light back to his cot. He stripped to his skivvies and socks, piled his folded uniform into a pillow, and crawled in. "No explosions yet, anyhow."

"Maybe there won't be any, according to Mr. Lieutenant Galgay."

"Some master spy," Nick said. "*I'd* goddamn well know if there was or not!"

Kelsey chuckled. "How do you know—we might be *inside* that impact area, instead of just near it."

"That's right, maybe Sir Galgay was one of *them*, and this is all a plot to have us blown away."

"And replaced by our doubles."

"Yeah." Nick closed his eyes, thinking, then asked, "Hey, Kelse?"

"Yo."

"Do you . . . feel married?"

Kelsey stayed silent for a while. "That's a hard question, kemosabe—do you?"

"I asked you first."

"Well, how do you mean? All the time? Or just now, way the hell out here in the middle of Czechoslovakia?"

"Now. Out here."

"Oh, I got you—you want to go find a town and get laid."

"Never mind."

"No," Kelsey said. "I don't feel married."

"Me neither. It's weird."

The sounds of crickets and night creatures had begun to reach them from the woods beyond. The half-light through the doorway and dirty windows seemed brighter. Kelsey grumbled, "I sure wouldn't mind having her in here with me now, though."

"Christ, he's going to start loping his mule."

"Damn, I wish that goddamn Galgay—"

The first round seemed to explode on the roof.

"Holy God!"

The windows rattled like ice cubes, then stopped. The next time they thought they heard a faint whistle first, arching across the night sky. The second explosion sounded even louder and closer than the first. The windows seemed sure to shatter.

Kelsey groaned. "Christ, that ain't mortars!"

"Hell, no, that's fucking artillery!"

"Or tank guns, anyhow."

They curled deeper inside their bags, covering their heads. The night-firing into the impact area continued until first light, haunting their dreams like violent thunder.

# 2

Up with the sun, they shaved, dressed, packed, and waited.
The jeep came bouncing out of the woods a little before eight.
"I passed somebody's mess hall down the road," Galgay said.
"Let's move it, before they close."

Nick said good morning sarcastically.

Eating, Galgay told them: Major John Pachek, their new
commanding officer, was waiting to meet and brief them. "For
obvious reasons," Galgay added, "he's nicknamed Big John."

A half hour later Special Agent Galgay ushered them into
the field headquarters of the 504th MI Detachment. A clerk-
typist and a first sergeant worked right inside the door of a
building exactly like the one they had slept in, except this one
was swept clean and fully lighted. Nick saw what Galgay meant:
against Major John Pachek's bulk, his field desk looked like a
lap tray. They snapped to and reported in smartly, eyes level
above his head. Big John looked ferocious, but his laugh came
out as a high hee-hee. He didn't remove the cigar from his
mouth. "At ease, gents, relax."

They shifted to a loose parade rest.

The major put his hands behind his head and leaned back.
An ominous creak pealed from his chair. "Now, lemme give it
to yez straight—you both get the battalion briefing?"

They had. Their Top Secret and NATO Top Secret clear-
ances were being processed through. The orientation ritual had
included a general introduction that Nick remembered verba-
tim: "You are privileged to be joining the most combat-ready
fighting force America has ever had assembled in one place at
one time, including World War Two! One half of this splendid
machine—that is, either Fifth Army or Seventh Army—could

have resolved the Korean conflict in about ten days. It's can-do, and it's no-sweat, and it's gung-ho, and don't you forget it!"

Big John Pachek went on, "You're both PI, but I need another photointerpreter like a bull needs tits. Kelsey, you're the history major, you're gonna be the Order of Battle officer. Burke, you're gonna be my MI officer—that's newspeak for something between an exec and an admin officer. Now, these are both captain slots on the charts, so we're giving you a nice head start. There's a slew of other jobs we'll divvy up between yez later, ye'll have about fifteen titles after your names that'll make your résumés look real swell later. Okay, now that I've taken you to my bosom, I'm gonna throw yez to the wolves, hee-hee.

"The Division G-two officer thinks young bucks like yourselves oughta pull some dogface duty before getting to work at the General Staff level. Personally, I think you could just as well read about it, but he ranks me, and I don't have a goddamn thing for yez to do out here anyhow. So tomorrow morning at oh eight hundred you report your asses to the CO of the Forty-fourth Combat Engineer Battalion, one Lieutenant Colonel Philip T. Pomeroy, better known as 'Ax Handle.' Any questions?"

No.

Next morning he and Kelsey reported in and learned that Colonel Pomeroy had been nicknamed for the swagger stick he carried: a full-size, smoothly honed, and stained ax handle. It had "Ever to Excel" burned deeply into it, and he swung it from a leather wrist-thong. His staff officers were permitted to carry similarly engraved hatchet handles, and his company officers got hammer handles—but not until Ax Handle himself declared that the privilege had been earned. From the start both Nick and Kelsey harbored hopes of leaving the Combat Engineers bearing honorary hammer handles.

Ax Handle himself radiated heat through mad black eyes and reminded Nick of the British actor Jack Hawkins playing RAF aces or King of all the Egyptians. He did not command from any spindly field desk in any cinder-block building. His was a real desk, huge and mahogany, and it sat upon a raised wooden platform inside his large, single-peaked command post tent. Surrounding it stood hundreds of other tents of various sizes, together forming a vast, canvas complex called "Tent City," less than a mile from the Graf main post. Unlike Big John Pachek, Ax Handle gave them their choice of duty assignments. Kelsey spoke up first: "I'll take the simulated nukes, sir!"

Dismissed and outside, Nick complained, "You son of a bitch, I really have to hand it to you—you're fast. Now he thinks you're the guts-ball one!"

"Well, what the Christ was I supposed to do? Say I don't know the first thing about putting together any *brochure?* That you're the one who was on the college magazine?"

"Christ, I only wrote shit for the thing, Kelse, I don't know anything about *making* one!"

By their third week there Nick was no longer envying Kelsey his "simulated nukes" detail. The job was to supervise a special squad of men ("Nothin' but goddamn eight-balls, Nick! Retards, niggers, spics, and degenerates! Fucking *dispensables*, every fucking one of them! And dumb? Jesus!"). Their mission was to prepare, conceal, and then detonate on cue caches of explosives, mostly napalm, mixed in fifty-gallon drums to go up in "Little Nagasakis" of mushroom clouds—all to give Armor and Infantry troops a taste of nuclear-warfare techniques.

It was largely night work: five or six times a week, the Kelse and his "suicide squad" would have to be busy on site no later than three o'clock in the morning. Detonations for the first units through "Hell Alley" happened at around noon, then again at around 4:30 for the afternoon outfits. At first Joel would come off duty so strained and exhausted that he'd skip eating and go straight to bed. Later he became able to eat and stay up longer, sometimes as late as nine or ten o'clock. But by then his nightmares had begun.

"*Fire in the hole!*" he'd scream. "*Fire in the hole!*" making his midnight, somnambulistic runs for cover. After the first time, Nick and the other guys sharing the room moved Kelsey's bed from the wall-end of the room to a place beside the wide, open doorway to the hall. But the next night he ran to his left, right over the bellies or genitals of at least four sleeping men, before diving headlong to the bare wooden floor. By the time Nick reached him, he had commando-crawled to a corner and was trying to claw himself into it, "*Fire in the hole!*"

Nick grabbed him by the shoulders, took his head into his hands, and talked him awake: "Kelse! You're okay! Wake up, bud. It's all right." The Kelse was crying. Nick wiped his tears. Kelsey then let himself be led back to bed and slept peacefully until his alarm went off at 0200 hours. He didn't remember it the next day. Nick told him, but Kelsey only scoffed, "Cut it out, I did not. Listen, this kamikaze job's scary enough without you trying to break my spirits."

Then one night he came awake in midrampage and mid-scream, and believed.

Nick was genuinely worried, but only halfheartedly suggested, "Let's go to Ax Handle and swap assignments. We're almost at the halfway point now, and—"

"*Danke*, Cisco, but I'd never give that brass-ass fucker the satisfaction."

Nick was relieved. He was enjoying himself. To gather material for the brochure, he literally had the run of Ax Handle's whole battalion. He spent his days racketing over roads and tank trails in his own jeep, driven by Pfc. Lou Goodman of Canarsie, the Engineers' official photographer and unofficial draftsman. He would write captions for Lou's pictures of, say,

SS-10 rockets penetrating tank hulls, and together they would lay out page after page of the booklet. Nick had named it, and consequently the day it was to commemorate, the *44th Combat Engineers Spectacular!*

This year the Engineers had been taped to stage the day-long demonstration of combat capabilities that would mark the close of the Grafenwöhr training period. Brass would come from all over USAREUR and NATO to observe, as would some senators and congressmen from America, and even, the rumors had it, several sergeants-major. As Ax Handle explained, "The Spectacular will be just that, or you'll wish your mothers never had you."

By the end of the first month Nick, like Kelsey, had all but forgotten the existence of his own unit, the MI Detachment. But then he stumbled upon a reminder.

One morning he and Goodman were occupying a bare hill, ready to catch the action of an Engineer bridge company in support of an Infantry company in the advance. Squad by squad the foot soldiers came seeping out of a woodline close below Nick's position to approach and then cross a small river, now spanned by an armored vehicular-launched bridge. Nick used his field glasses to make sure: yes, by God, it was that stuck-up Brian Galgay guy, running like a bastard down there! Wearing a Pfc. stripe!

". . . or else his identical twin," Nick told Big John Pachek.

"Jesus Christ, what can I say—you've caught us in a real fuck-up, Nick. . . . All right. Nothing for it but the truth, then—we forgot you boys were out there. We also forgot you'd met Galgay." He went to the small safe kept deeper in the building and brought back some posters. "Seen any of these in your travels?"

Nick looked. They showed well-drawn caricatures of Sammy Davis, Jr., wearing a skullcap, his nose grotesquely enlarged and sharpened. He remembered that Sammy Davis had converted to Judaism and had married a white Swedish actress. The messages on the posters varied in wording but carried the same theme: while white American youths were risking their lives and sacrificing their time in foreign lands, the Jews and blacks were idling safe at home, making the money and the girls. "Nice."

"They're coming out of one of our own Infantry outfits. Some weirdos from George Lincoln Rockwell's American Nazi Party, we think. I sent Brian down."

"You can trust me and Kelsey, Major."

Later, Kelsey laughed. "Hoo, ol' Mr. Galgay's gonna hate *your* ass, boy! I can't wait to see if one of my nukes made him chew his tongue!"

Uncovering the condescending Lieutenant Galgay gave both Nick and Joel a perverse, temporary shot in the arm. They felt that both the Corps and the Detachment had been paid back a bit for having rejected and treated them so poorly.

Weeks later something else strange happened to Nick. He flew out of Graf early one morning, carrying the precious rough dummy of his brochure back west to Stuttgart for printing and binding. By the time he and his bundles of some three hundred copies returned to Graf, it was after nine at night. Lou Goodman was waiting with the Jeep and the word: "We got troubles, Lieutenant. Somebody showed somebody at Division a copy of the dummy, and . . . you know the full-page portrait of Ax Handle's puss?"

"Don't say it."

"Yessir, and the colonel says they better *all* be gone before he sees them tomorrow morning."

They used the rear end of the S-3 (Operations) tent. By midnight they still had only about half of Ax Handle's noble-warrior faces torn off their staples, but they decided to break for coffee. They were almost at the mess tent's entrance when the whole grid of clay streets and tents around them was suddenly illuminated as if by flares. The two of them were eerily lifted free of gravity and floated, tumbling, through the air.

Nick saw the ground speeding flatly up at him and managed to get his forearms and shins out before landing, not quite catlike but nimbly enough to save his face and vitals from taking the full impact. Up and running, he saw Goodman awkwardly toppling from the mess tent's roof to the ground. It was only then that the awful noise reached him, a roar so ear-ringing that it seemed the single accumulation of every nocturnal impact area explosion he had heard since arriving at Graf—except this was not the impact area.

Men in white T-shirts and shorts came running out of the dark tents, and crawling out from under those that had collapsed upon snapped poles. He found himself alone and running with them toward the raging fire and smoke, boiling up yellow and white against the pitch sky. It seemed much farther away than he would have guessed. With his boots on he was able to pass many men running barefooted, but it was still several minutes before he reached where the errant artillery round had struck.

Nick heard men screaming and cursing, the crackle of things burning in the flames, and the more distant wails of the Post Engineer fire engines and ambulances speeding to the scene. The inferno itself seemed to have been confined to just four or six huge, flattened tents, but soldiers with fire extinguishers and bucket brigades were dousing everything in sight with foam and water.

Nick stood there gaping at the wall of incredible heat. Robotlike figures in asbestos suits were drifting in and out of the devastated, burning place, carrying things in their arms and on stretchers. His face and hands stung hotly. The rising stench of burning flesh and wet ashes bit the insides of his nose and mouth. He bent at the waist, finally, and vomited.

After making sure that Goodman was all right, he returned

to the BOQ. Kelsey threw his arms around him. "Jesus, Nick, I was afraid you bought it!"

It was officially reported later that nineteen soldiers had been killed and many more injured. Some young officer in some heavy artillery battery was being held, pending further investigation of the accident.

Ax Handle's *Spectacular!* went off as planned to general acclaim.

Their first tour at Graf over, Nick and Kelsey went off post to the Micky Bar and drank themselves stupid on shots of schnapps with beer chasers. They weren't given hammer handles, but by now had forgotten ever wanting them.

# 3

Nick's reunion with his wife, Susan, on their pushed-together beds, and on the carpeted floors, and on the long, soft sofa, and even on the wide, wooden bench of the breakfast nook of their new, first home, reminded him of why he had fallen for her. The girl surely did love to love.

The Baker Barracks Dependent Quarters were long stucco buildings three stories high on a hillside outside the post. Most men walked to work mornings, down the steep street that bottomed out at the main gate, then climbed sharply again through the small, tidy *Kaserne* to the cul-de-sac of "Brass Hill" at the top, above the airfield, where the ranking field-grade officers resided in duplexes.

Nick was delighted to find that Kelsey had been assigned living quarters in the same stairwell of the same apartment house. Bibs Kelsey was enormous with child by now. But Susan still was not showing at all. Bibs predicted, "A girl for sure, she's carrying so small and high!"

By custom the commanding general hosted a dinner dance at the officers' club to celebrate the return from Graf. Big John followed his wife, Nola's, suggestion and reserved the Fireplace Lounge for an hour of cocktails—and to announce a "very special surprise."

All officers wore their dress-blue uniforms. Agent personnel wore dark civilian suits. Women wore semiformal gowns and cocktail dresses over crinoline petticoats. With Brian Galgay at his side Big John rang his martini glass for silence and announced, "Ladies and gentlemen—our young Brian Galgay here has just returned to us today. He's successfully carried out what's probably the most significant peacetime mission in the history of the 504th MI Detachment. The fact is, friends, hee-hee . . . *we* have pulled a doggone outright *coup*, is what *we've* done. And now I'll let him tell you all about it. Take it, Brian."

"I can't wait," Nick side-mouthed to Kelsey, "can you?"

"For about the rest of my life."

Standing tall and frowning, Brian Galgay spoke to the gathering in a proper tone of modesty. "Until less than thirty-six hours ago a cell of George Lincoln Rockwell's American Nazi Party has been operating from within one of the division's own combat commands . . . spreading seditious propaganda, mostly, among our troops. . . . As of yesterday all members of the cell found themselves airborne. They were shipped stateside for trial and punishment. We—"

"*We* were the ones to nail the bastards!" Big John cut in.

[ 41 ]

"Mimeograph machine, correspondence, the works! Lock, stock, and incriminating evidence! And, contrary to our normal policy, hee-hee, feel free to mention this—far and wide, every one of yez! . . . Now, let's hear it, from the bottom of your hearts, to the man of the hour—Mr. Brian Galgay!"

The whole company, even Nick and even Kelsey, applauded.

Nola Pachek raised her champagne cocktail. "To *us!*"

After dinner Nick and Susan were slow-dancing outside. Other couples glided through and around the shadows. Warm, lemony lights spilled from the main hall onto the terrace. A touch of autumn enlivened the evening air, but it was still dry and warm with the memory of summer. Bobby Darin was singing "Somewhere, Beyond the Sea" through loudspeakers. Susan moved both bare arms to around his neck and purred excitedly, "Gee, that was super news! Do you know him, Nickie, that Galahad guy?"

"Galgay. Not really. Just saw him around a couple of times."

"He must be really something."

"Yeah."

"Nickie?"

"Yeah?"

She moved even closer to him. "I've got a secret, too," she whispered. "I'm not pregnant."

He felt a chill. "Did you . . . lose it, or what?" he said. He realized now that their baby hadn't yet even become more than an it to him.

"Not really. Not exactly, I don't think."

He hated it when he couldn't see her eyes like this: it made her sound truly, maddeningly stupid to him. "What the hell do you mean, not ex—"

"Oh, Nick, please." She'd begun to weep. "I don't know! I'm not sure! They said they think I maybe never was. A false

[ 42 ]

alarm, they said, and they said the doctor was probably wrong, but it happens all the time. Or that I *was*, maybe, but lost it without knowing it, even! All that traveling over here in the heat and everything, and moving into the apartment without you, you know, in all that heat and—"

"Ssh, ssh, there, it's okay, doll." He put his arms around her. "Take it easy, there's nothing to cry about."

"Oh, you're mad, you hate me, you—"

"No, no. God *does* that," he said in his mother's voice. "It means there was something wrong with it. It's better this way." He went on comforting her until he almost believed it himself.

"I *thought* I was." Susan pouted. "I really did, Nickie—you know that, don't you?"

"Sure."

Four days after that Thanksgiving, Bibs Kelsey had twin boys. When they were big enough, Nick held one and Susan held the other while Kelsey and Bibs got secretly remarried in the post chapel. In the States they had only eloped to a justice of the peace. Hearing the priest's words, Nick couldn't avoid the thought: if he and Susan had just gone to a JP, they still wouldn't be married at all in the eyes of the Church. Ashamed, he dismissed the notion as unworthy of him, as well as futile—by now Susan was verifiably pregnant herself.

By Christmas the "garrison blues" had set in. Among other duties, Nick had to run the Supply Room and the unit fund. He prepared the Weekly Training Plan and the Troop Information and Education Program for Saturday mornings. And he wrote or edited all official documents leaving the Detachment, including all classified Agent Reports prepared by the Security Section's staff—except Brian Galgay's, whose grammar and composition were always flawless.

Brian also knew Russian and German, it turned out. The

guy was "really something," Nick had to admit, the better he got to know him. He never could honestly say that he liked him, but he did find himself having to defend Galgay's smartness, seriousness, and dedication. Kelsey continued to see him as merely "another goddamn prima donna! If he's so fucking dissatisfied down here with us grunts, why doesn't he just get himself shipped the hell out?"

"He's tried, Kelse. Big John keeps disapproving his requests for transfer. Kind of a compliment, in a way, I guess."

"Balls. Loyalty and morale are more important than technical skill any day."

"Ho, look who's talking—Mr. G-two!"

"I'm talking about the Division, son. If combat level ain't big league enough for ol' Superspook, Pachek oughta fire his ass out!"

# 4

That spring Nick and Kelsey got away from Baker. They left the Autobahn at Munich and cut south onto the thin, dizzy roads that led to Oberammergau, deep in the Bavarian Alps. They wore civilian clothes and drove Nick's racy new Triumph, rather than Kelsey's equally new but unracy Volvo.

The "Special Weapons" school occupied a tiny *Kaserne* tucked into the base of the high-looming mountains. For Nick the highlight of the Advanced Photo Interpretation course was getting to work with actual current photos of the Soviet Union, taken by secret, high-flying CIA U-2 reconnaisance jets.

During the first week they were given a tour and shown life-sized, accurate mock-ups of various Moscow city sites built in subterranean chambers beneath the post, where covert operatives were trained. Kelsey said, "This is where Galgay wants to go when he dies."

In the second week they were broken into groups of four and dispatched to observe a Green Berets field training exercise. Parachutes popped open like silent ack-ack bursts of flak in the postcard-blue air, and floated down to vanish in the lush countryside. Up in the mountains it was still winter. New snow fell upon old.

One night up there Nick's group tramped through the snow to a small farm that had been "occupied." The "command post" was in the barn. A squad of armed Berets guarded a corral. Nick saw a group of men inside it. They were stark naked and huddling together in the center of the open enclosure, pinkish orange against the white. The escort officer explained, "They're captured enemy soldiers. We've had them out there only about an hour or so now."

Inside the barn a kerosene stove provided heat, and light came hissing from several Coleman lanterns. One stall had been cleaned out and converted into an office. A huge old rolltop desk stood against the outside wall. A Green Beret captain sat at the desk, interrogating an "enemy" captain of about his same age, twenty-eight or thirty, Nick guessed. They knew, the escort officer whispered, that he was the leader of the bare-assed men penned outside in the snow, but all he was admitting so far was his name, rank, and service number.

Then the interrogating officer gestured. Two of his aides moved forward and held the arms of the "POW," who was still fully clothed. Without leaving the chair, the Beret captain un-zipped the other man's fly and scooped out his genitals to hover over the desk drawer, now opened beneath them.

In the shadows Nick stiffened back flush against the barn wall in nausea and disbelief. The sudden slam and scream shut his eyes tight. When he looked again, the "enemy" leader was on the floor, folded in half, crying and vomiting.

"This way, gentlemen." Their guide led them through a low doorway into an adjoining milking shed. Steaming cocoa was being ladled into canteen cups from a pot on a hot plate. The shivering prisoners were herded in, single file. They were given cigarettes and Snickers bars along with the hot chocolate. They lit up and began to eat and drink. Suddenly the officer in charge cocked his carbine loudly and ordered them to stop. Then he went down the line, questioning them one by one. All eleven told him whatever he wanted to know. Nick heard one guard mutter, "Fucking pansies."

Outside, the escort said, "Sorry you had to see it turn out that way. The average outfit can take a lot more of it than that, you can rest assured. These were soft, real soft. Of course, you understand we're limited—can't risk real frostbite with your own, can you."

In a candlelit local *Weinstube* in the village later, Nick was still boiling from the experience and snapped to Kelsey, "It's easy for you to be so goddamn cool, you didn't *see* it!"

"Okay—but I wonder what you really saw, way *your* head works sometimes!"

"I didn't add a thing! Honest to God, on my mother's grave, Kelse—it was exactly how I told you!"

Kelsey grinned. "A security violation in itself, by the way, blabbing it to me, in a public place like this—shoot, Nick, you're no better than them kids were!"

"God damn it, it's not the *GIs* I'm pissed about!"

"Shouldn't be pissed at all, Nick. It'd be a hell of a lot

[ 46 ]

worse in the real thing. . . . This way it won't be new to them, and they'll know what to do."

"Hey, Joel," Nick said wearily. "I know the *doctrine*, for Christ's sake. I thought I was just telling this to *you!*"

Susan and Bibs arrived by Volvo that second Friday, the end of the course. For Nick, Susan was a badly needed distraction; he found he simply could not resolve or dismiss his deep ambivalence by himself. The four of them stayed in a *pension* near the village of Ogau. Days, they walked the cobbled streets.

Nick was much amused by the look of the townspeople. With their hair grown long, young boys were virtually indistinguishable from girls. Even men, although most were bearded, had tresses falling to their shoulders or bobbing in long ponytails.

Susan grimaced. "They're disgusting."

He laughed. "Aw, it's just for the Passion Play."

"They should wear wigs or something, like in plays back home!"

"Hey," he pointed, "there's Jesus! No, never mind, it was only Mary."

"Very funny . . . Come on, you said we could go to Garmisch, are we going or not?"

He mimicked Nola Pachek's Louisiana honey: "Wal, shore, chile! Why, they got dollah night at the club theah? And a real lahve ice show? Why, y'all swear yore back in Cincinnati!"

It wasn't exactly dollar night at the U.S. Army Recreation Area in Garmisch, but it was incredibly inexpensive. Chewing on prime ribs, Kelsey chortled, "Not bad on two twenty-two a month, huh, folks?"

"Make that two-five-nine any day now." Susan beamed. "Soon as those silver bars arrive. Plus forty-seven eighty-eight subsistence, don't forget!"

Nick grimly went along, trying to get into the swing of it

[ 47 ]

with them; but his recurring vision of the one American officer slamming a drawer upon the gonads of the other American officer continued to shock him as thoroughly as the Tent City slaughter had.

# 5

It came at least once every month, and almost always at or near three o'clock in the morning: *Alert!*

All-American fire-engine, police-and-ambulance whining, crying sirens would reach deep into Nick's and everyone else's sleep, wrenching open eyes and adrenaline valves. His phone this night rang the minute his feet hit the floor. "Burke on the way," he spat. It was May, but they hadn't changed to summer uniforms yet. In OD wool shirt and trousers-with-shells, field jacket, and helmet liner, carrying his parka and "bunny cap," he joined the hundreds of other dark, moving figures outside in the cold. They clomped in double time down the hill and up again to their units, their utility belts rattling, heavy with full canteens, bayonets, rolled ponchos, first-aid and nerve-gas kits.

On post, men were silhouetted against headlights and lights from doors and open windows, outloading files and equipment from buildings into vans and trucks. Steam came from breaths and exhaust pipes. Nick chewed out the new Supply clerk handing him his carbine: "No *ammo*, Eldert—it goes out in the boxes!"

"Not this time, sir!"

Safes and cabinets holding classified material normally got signs dropped on them reading DESTROYED. But now he spotted Brian Galgay feeding reams of stuff into the firedrum furnace, ablaze outside. Running out, he yelled, "Christ, this ain't for *real*, is it, Brian?"

Even Galgay seemed to have lost his perpetual, unctuous cool for once. "I don't know," he said, "but it's not normal! You better not come too near this fire with that magazine of rounds on you, Burke!"

They thundered in convoy down out of Baker and up the high hillside road around the center of the town. Then they turned east, shaking awake one small village after another. They reached their first assembly area, a road-looped stand of pine woods in sprawling farmland, right on time. But instead of dismounting and lining up for coffee and bacon on white bread as usual, they immediately moved out again. Nick rode shotgun in the Supply deuce-and-a-half, but ran back to ask Big John in his jeep.

"It's a Red Alert," the major said, "that's all we know."

By morning the villages on their route began turning out schoolkids, but today their cheers and waves and yells of "Ami!" and "Gum!" went answered only by grim, unsmiling, scared faces rumbling past. The children, and the sight of shawled old grandmotherly women driving tractors and "honey-wagons" into the fields made Nick finally think of Susan. Christ, had she paid attention at the NEO briefings? Would she remember to take the emergency kit with her to the car? Would they be actually made to drive all the way to France? CIC Major Scott's wife, Louise, a veteran German hand, had told of an actual NEO (Noncombatant Evacuation Order) move-out having been tried once, years ago: "They finally found one hysterical woman three weeks later in Portugal. She'd lost one of her kids somewhere along the way."

Oh, God, he worried. Susan would have another miscarriage. He hadn't even said good-bye to her. He kept smoking and fingering the carbine magazine of live rounds in his hand. Only the solid feel of it and the steady, erection-making vibration of the truck's engine let him seriously believe it was happening to him. He thought it very stupid of the countryside to look so serenely lovely while they were piercing so frantically and mightily through it.

Night found them gathered waiting in yet another assembly area, this one a dense, newly greening forest somewhere north and east of Grafenwöhr, near where East Germany's Iron Curtain meets Czechoslovakia's. By now they knew why they were there: a U-2 reconnaissance plane out of Turkey had gone down in Russia. Its CIA pilot had not died or committed suicide—he had been captured by the Reds. Nick couldn't look at the landscape around him without seeing the aerial photographs he'd studied at Ogau. He mentally went up to look down and try to read the story he was suddenly a part of himself, and what he saw was himself dying in defense of his country and the free world.

They were outnumbered ten to one. The best they could do was to hold long enough for America to retaliate, ideally with ground forces, at worst with intercontinental ballistic missiles. Two days at the outside, if it stayed conventional man-to-man, tank-to-tank combat. And if they were as superior as they thought they were. And if it was God's will to make them get lucky. Three days at the very most.

He came back down and clicked the magazine into his rifle.

First Sergeant Charlie Hardt, playing solitaire on his jeep's hood, looked up and cautioned him, "Just don't go cocking that thing! Safety on?"

Nick, embarrassed, removed the magazine, poured himself more tepid coffee, and ate some more of Scotty's fig bars. In a way, he thought, it wasn't as bad as waiting for a street fight to start. He only hoped it wouldn't be some anonymous shell, like at Tent City. He wanted to at least see some bodies, if not faces. He knew for certain that he would take at least one enemy soldier with him. "One, at least," he vowed to himself. He fired expert with the carbine, and also with the M-1, the grease gun, the .38, and even the .45. As did the Kelse, whom he wished was with him here now, instead of miles away with the G-2. Nick didn't exactly *want* them to actually come now, through those trees, up that road, down out of that sky—but the tactile reality of its possibility made him realize a major truth about himself: He could imagine no better place or time or way to die.

It was why it was called The Service, he reminded himself, and he felt prouder than ever to be in it. "Ask not what your country can do for you . . ." their new, young commander-in-chief had challenged. Living away from America had helped him see just how beautiful she was, how free and good.

For the first time in his life he felt important.

It was only this goddamn waiting, he told himself, this goddamn not-knowing that made him succumb to his periodic spasms of utter dread and fear.

But the Soviets did not come this time. After forty-eight hours the Red Alert was terminated. They moved out and returned to garrison duty at Baker. He felt enormously relieved, and at the same time terribly disappointed.

# 6

That summer not even going to Grafenwöhr relieved his garrison blues. But then, in August, he was flown out to join Susan at the Bad Caanstadt hospital, where she had the baby, a boy.

Stunned and abashed by the miraculous event, he let her will prevail over his twice in a row—instead of naming him "Nick the two," they called him James, after Susan's daddy. And instead of going to the jazz cellars of Paris to celebrate, they used the money to hire a nurse.

In the fall he began teaching nights at the Education Center, basic "bonehead" English for dropouts wishing to earn their high school equivalency certificates. Susan was desperate to start buying more bargain crystal and china and things, and to travel more. The teaching paid five dollars an hour. He told her he was doing it for the money.

His class was an even dozen GIs, nine black. They met in a Quonset hut in a pine grove behind the provost marshal's office. Those evening hours became the high point of his days. As some line officers came to love their platoons and companies, he came to love his night class. He felt like an older brother to them, the one who had been given schooling and brought it home to share.

At night school he also found a kind of older brother for himself: Walt C. ("Waltzie") Cooper. Waltzie was a captain and the Division psychiatrist. In the other half of the hut he taught a psychology course, mostly to wives and bachelor officers and GIs with some college credits. He and Nick began driving home together nights.

Waltzie was a skinny little guy behind big eyeglasses. He was in his early thirties, had a wife, Julia, and five kids. Nick was amazed: the Coopers had dared to personalize their QM-issued quarters. They had painted the beige walls white and had covered the drably upholstered furniture with bright fabrics and imitation furs. A Navajo rug hung on one wall, and the quartermaster prints of trees had been replaced by huge mounted blowups of photographs Julia had taken of French coal miners at work. Waltzie had dodged military service until he couldn't, and now rationalized his stint in Germany as "invaluable fieldwork." He said he owed the University of Pennsylvania some four years of teaching in return for his graduate studies, and that he intended never to pay them if he could get away with it. Besides teaching, Waltzie saw patients privately in his off-duty hours. The extra income helped finance their frequent junkets around Europe. "Whenever Julia gets the blues," he told Nick, "she has to hear good music, live."

"And I get the blues a lot," Julia added.

Waltzie wasn't so antimilitary as he was amused and bemused by Army ways. "They send this hillbilly kid three hundred miles to see me, because every time they ask him if he's homosexual, he says yes. And it takes me five minutes to find out that he thinks it means *homesick*! What are they *afraid* of?"

Waltzie wouldn't listen when Nick confessed that he was seriously considering making a career of it, going Regular Army. Nick wanted to explain to him that they weren't talking about the same Army anyhow. But he couldn't, and not only for security reasons: it was hard for him to express in words to anyone outside it what Intelligence meant to those inside—the promises, the commitment, the ideals. Even the American Nazi Party thing Galgay had pulled off—where on the outside would you ever get a chance to do something like *that*?

One night Julia Cooper finally intervened: "You know, dear," she said, "I think Nick knows a lot more about the Service than you do, and than I care to. Since we're all in it for the moment anyhow, you should stop playing chaplain. Besides, what do *you* know about the outside anyway, aside from campus life and the number of patients big business sent your way?"

Nick's secret lech for dark-eyed Julia turned to pure, eternal adoration. After that he and Waltzie talked very little about the Army.

After the first few times, he had stopped bringing Waltzie home. He would always go instead to their place, where there was no Susan to act upset and chilly. She called Waltzie "an egghead," and thought both the Coopers were "queer. And they're phonies! Going around with just the teachers and Special Service types, as if being in the Army's something low class! And if I were you, I wouldn't let myself be seen sucking up to them so much, either!"

This only made them all the more attractive, and he continued to stop in for tea or a drink with the Coopers nearly every night they had classes. He couldn't explain, even to himself, exactly what made him like Waltzie and Julia Cooper so much. He knew that they were no re-creation of family life for him: their rooms were bright and loud with games, music, the din of children. Those of his own youth he remembered as empty and silent—his father had been killed at Anzio, his mother worked.

Nor would he accept Susan's accusation, that the Coopers appealed to some "yellow-streak" antimilitary inclination in him. He thought the opposite was true: they were proof that you could be offbeat and a good soldier at the same time. Knowing them, he felt, gave him all the more hope of finding a role for himself, in the Army, at which he could prove to be a "flier."

In time he barely even heard Susan's flak about the Coopers. But when Brian Galgay entered his office one day and broached the subject, he was amazed at how violently he reacted. He said, "Is this an official warning, Brian?"

"No," Brian said, "just a personal word to the wise, huh?

I'm sure Cooper's probably a real fine guy, if you like the type. But if I were in your position, I'd think twice about being associated with someone too many people see as a weirdo. You're not just some Armor or Engineer officer, after all, Burke. We both know you're prime Counterintelligence Corps material, and that you want it. So I'm just trying to remind you—their screening process is mighty tough. What seems innocent enough to you might not look so—"

"Hey!" Nick cut him off. "I'm much obliged for the advice, Lieutenant, but if you don't mind, I've got a lot of work to do. Go someplace and spit-shine your fucking cordovans, why don't you."

"Don't say I never told you, Nick."

"Listen, Galgay, it's your problem, not mine. If you feel the need to see Captain Cooper professionally, let me know. I'll get you a discount."

When even Kelsey started making grumbling noises, Nick chose to feel more flattered than insulted. He suspected Joel was just a little jealous, that's all, and told him, "I'm having an affair with her, all right?"

"Come on, Nick—you going to him as a *shrink,* or what?"

He laughed. "No. You want to know why I really like to go there, Kelse? Because they never play 'Mack the' fucking 'Knife,' that's why!"

Bobby Darin's "That's All" album, and especially its lead cut of "Mack the Knife," had hit Baker Barracks like the Hoola Hoop and rock and roll had hit America. "Mack the Knife" played so often in all the clubs, the snack bar, bowling alley, *Rathskellar*, PX, barracks, and apartments that Nick thought it ought to be named Baker's official theme song. He liked the tune as much as anyone else did. It was hard not to. The beat was contagious, the lyrics infectious. They seemed somehow to express perfectly the kind of flirting-with-danger, sexy jazziness of attitude everyone there in that place at that time was feeling.

[ 55 ]

Actually he had lied to Kelsey: Waltzie and Julia played "Mack the Knife" as often and as loudly as any GI in a dayroom or young louie in the BOQ . . . the main difference being that the Coopers would talk about Weill, Lenya, Brecht, and that whole Berlin-Paris *Threepenny Opera* world—all new and fascinating territory for him.

He never did resolve the conflict caused by his relationship with the Coopers in the eyes of observers. In his own heart the friendship was no conflict at all. It at least yielded him nothing but fun and affection and stimulation—so why risk analyzing it to death? His instincts told him that the Coopers were good for him, and for once he trusted his instincts.

# 7

The news broke that Big John Pachek had been promoted to lieutenant colonel. The Detachment received the event with rejoicing: they all loved "the Old Man," and for him to be passed over would have been disastrous.

No one was happier than Special Agent Brian Galgay. In a burst of magnanimity Big John finally endorsed his transfer and within a month orders were cut on high assigning him to a choice unit in West Berlin, the Big Apple of the intelligence world.

By tradition the going-away party for any officer had to last until sunrise. In Mr. Galgay's case, however, by 0400 hours, the number of well-wishers gathered in his BOQ room had dwindled from fourteen down to just himself and Nick. The one remaining half-quart of Cutty Sark sat on the coffee table between them.

"Know something, Brian? I faked it," Nick admitted blearily. "I could never really drink that much and live. I'm pretty blitzed as it is."

"Me too," Brian said, looking as groomed as he had at dinner.

"Blitzed?"

"No. Faked it."

"Tongue in the bottle?"

"Of course. Kelsey did too," Galgay added sourly. "I saw him. He faked having to leave, too, because he doesn't like me much. The same as the rest of them. Thanks for staying, Nick."

"That's okay, Bri. Somebody's got to keep the legend alive. 'Course, you are pretty much of a pain in the ass, you know. It's the way you stay *off*, you know? With your snoot in the air all the time. People just think you're superior to them, that's all it is."

"You probably ought to start heading home now, too, Nick."

"Sun's not up yet. Rule's a rule. I love the Army for its *rules*. They're so *easy*. And they're also *all* they want of you. So, *inside* them, you're *free*! . . . Get it?"

"Yes," Galgay answered solemnly. "I do. I guess I see it pretty much the same way. Yes, there is great personal freedom inside duty, if that's what you mean. It . . . centers you. It concentrates you. It simplifies your life."

Nick nodded in total agreement. "I mean, as long as you do what they require of you, by the book . . . they don't care what *else* you do!"

"Well, of course, they do require a lot of you, Nick, they—"

"But it's the *accidents*, Brian," he insisted, having lost all

track of it now," "and the certain *individuals* that pop up every
now and then. That kind of screw up the works and make you
wonder if there really is anybody in charge . . . up the line.
Behind all the regs." He was thinking of the Tent City slaughter
again, and of the Special Forces "games" he had witnessed.
"They're what worry me."

Galgay stayed looking perplexed for a moment, then
yawned and stretched melodramatically. "Well, sun's up,
Nick."

Nick knew it wasn't, but he was eager to end it now, too.
He got up. "Do great in Berlin. Glad you got it, if that's what
you wanted." At the door he turned back. "By the way—you
going to stay in, Brian? Now that MI's a branch? Go RA, be a
lifer?"

"I think so. I hope to, yes."

"Me, too. I fuckin' love it. I majored fine arts, you know?
Ha. . . . What'd you major, Brian?"

"I . . . I, uh, went to the Maryknolls for four years."

"Ah-ha!" He had known this from Galgay's file, but wanted
to see if the spook would admit it. Now that he had, Nick felt
free to tell him, "I thought there was something priesty about
you. . . . You've got the whole God *and* country high mass
going for you then, huh, Galahad?" It had come out sounding
much more hostile than he meant it, but he let it go.

"If you say so, Nick," Galgay finessed it. "Listen—thanks
again for staying to the bitter end. And good luck to you too,
huh?"

Nick nodded and smiled, lingering, taking a last look at the
strange guy: Christ, even the tie was still knotted tightly into
the top of his shirt collar. He suddenly felt struck sober, and
was moved to say, "You know, Lieutenant—you're *not* a priest.
I love it, but it's only the Army. Why don't you try coming
down off that high horse of yours, huh? You might have a better
time of it. We're all just people, Brian."

Then he left, and until the unnoticed moment when the pebble of that sad farewell party landed on the muddy bottom of Nick's memory, he always reassured himself that he had spoken out of sympathy, not hatred, for Brian Galgay.

# 8

Aside from feigning interest whenever Big John or Scotty mentioned some news of him, Nick never again thought of Brian Galgay until a dreadful day in the following August. Once again they were in Grafenwöhr, and again they had spent so many long days in the hot dust of the place that it was hard to remember much of their lives prior to arriving.

Then the Berlin Wall happened, and they were called to the Curtain again on their second Red Alert. During the all-night vigil, with Susan pregnant again, Nick once more had miscarriage to worry about as well as the baby, Jim. This time he and Kelsey waited it out together, in the G-2 armored personnel carrier.

Berlin was a lot closer than wherever the U-2 had gone down, so it all felt even realer to them than it had before. The word was right, Nick sensed: this time it was really coming. And this time the part of him that wanted it spoke louder and clearer to him than the part that wasn't sure.

"Damn that bastard Galgay anyway," Kelsey said.

"Why?"

"He's right there, where it's happening!"

"Yeah," Nick said. Then: "Kelse, we gotta fish or cut bait."

The Kelse agreed, "I know it."

From the start both of them knew they were all but certain to get Regular Army commissions if they applied for them. Each had been a DMG (Distinguished Military Graduate) of his college ROTC program. With MI at last a separate branch of service, the Department of the Army had actually sent them both letters stating that duty tours in one of the combat branches would no longer be required, and that their records to date showed them to be "highly desirable" candidates. . . . It was theirs for the asking.

That night on the border Nick and Kelsey vowed that, unless this was the real thing, they would do it.

In the morning G-3 Major Billy Hogue announced the call-off with fury: "Another goddamn false alarm! God damn it, one of these times they're gonna pull us up here and we're not gonna fuckin' stop! Roll right the Christ to fuckin' Moscow, once and for all! George S. Patton was right then, and he's still right now, goddamnit! We oughta just take 'em and get it over with! Just fuckin' *take* 'em!"

Nick and Kelsey put in their paper work that same morning, and went back to work. Field training exercises resumed. Nick was on duty in the G-2 APC when the current Long-Range Patrol Platoon leader, First Lieutenant Warren ("Honk") Hennebury, succeeded in penetrating an "enemy" command post and in absconding with their tactical situation map, plus several pairs of sleeping officers' boots.

At the end of that September the Burkes and the Kelseys went on leave together, *sans* children, to Spain. There, Nick knew it was not just Kelsey's presence that was making him continue to feel like a soldier, even so far away from things military. On previous trips, to Vienna and to Venice, he had reverted to his civilian self within alarmingly short distances from Baker. But this time he stayed feeling clearly the U.S. Army officer, traveling in mufti. And this new sense of solid identity came to Nick with a rush of relief. Waltzie Cooper was wrong about him.

Upon their return they learned that they had been accepted into the Regular Army.

That last winter they went into the field on "Operation Snowsword."

# 9

War games.

On a map, a line was drawn across West Germany, corresponding generally to the course of the Main River, to simulate the Iron Curtain. North became east this year, and south became west, making Fifth Army the Soviets, leaving Seventh Army a NATO force.

"Combat" would begin and last for some six to eight weeks, in a make-believe World War III.

Commanders at all levels on both sides took the games most seriously. Promotions and assignments were known to bear very close correlation to performance displayed under these simulated battlefield conditions.

The MI Detachment became part of the 4th Armored Division for the duration of the maneuvers. Nick was made officer in charge of the "TIC," the Target Information Center. He would split twelve-hour shifts with Major Fred Tillwell, of the G-2 staff.

The alert came at three in the morning, and Baker Barracks emptied of fighting men and equipment in record time, despite a snowstorm and icy road conditions. As on a Red Alert, all elements roared right out of normal assembly areas, heading hell bent for leather for their prescribed Snowsword combat locations.

By dusk that first day Nick was watching his first Division Command Post being assembled. The five Division HQ staff vans, all customized five-ton trucks, went crashing into a forest clearing. "Big Lou" Clark, the sergeant major, picked a spot, stood on it, activated his stopwatch, and yelled "Go!" The trucks screamed into reverse and backed straight for him, not stopping until he yelled "Yo!" At his command running men brought up an enormous wooden center pole and raised it upon Big Lou's boot prints in the snow. A great canvas roof was unfurled from the pole to extend beyond the fronts of the five staff vans. Not until this "Circus Tent" had been camouflaged and long coils of barbed concertina wire had been laid around the whole complex did Big Lou click off his watch. He looked at it, and began bull-moosing his foul curses at everyone in sight for their laziness, slowness, and universal deficiencies.

By then Nick was already running into the Circus to set up his TIC—a cramped, floorless cave roofed by a small, extra star-point of canvas.

No sooner did everyone have their maps, charts, tables, and radios ready for action than the call came to break down and move out. They lumbered on in convoy farther north and east, for another fifteen hours.

The 4th Armored Division nearly washed out of Operation Snowsword altogether only two days later. The master plan required an actual river crossing. It began as a field day for Ax Handle Pomeroy's Combat Engineers. But when the first forward elements moved to approach their crossing sites, a freak piece of April weather suddenly struck the brittle February earth: the sun came out and turned the frostbitten ground to soup. Frustrated tankers cursed the maneuver damage strictures to high heaven for forbidding them to end-run the muck and mire by striking out cross-country. The Division had to start again, with a lot of catching up to do. The atmosphere around Nick in the Circus Tent was not serene.

They moved, set up, operated, broke down, and moved again, by day and by night, until soon there were no days or nights anymore, only the moving, the setting up, operating, breaking down, and moving more. Caught up in this dayless, nightless cycle, Nick found himself at one point inside a sleeping bag on the frozen ground, churning hastily into his tubed, spit-moistened hand. He'd thought it would help hurry the knockout into sleep he craved, but it didn't. The jerking off only left him depressed.

It was only a physical slump, though. His spirits were all right, considering the last call to move had come just two minutes before his twelve-hour duty shift in the TIC had been due to end. He had spent all of his sleep time huddled in the back of Major Fred's jeep. By the time the Circus Tent was again pitched and activated, it had been his turn to take the duty again. Luckily the action had been slow to resume, so he had let his driver-clerk stand the watch, with orders to come running should the "war" start again before he was back.

But now he gave it up. He unzipped the bag enough to find and tug on his big, rubber Mickey Mouse boots. He put on his pile-lined parka, strapped on his equipment belt, and retrieved his carbine from inside the bag. He put on his steel helmet and stood in the dark outside the tent for about seven minutes, pissing against a tree and letting his eyes get their night visual-purple, so he could see in the dark. Then he followed the treeline path over the snow toward the Circus. No moon shone this night. At the hole in the concertina wire, the sentry slapped his M-1 to port arms. "Halt! Who goes?"

"Friendly."

"Red Rider."

"Little Beaver."

"Advance and be recognized."

Nick trudged forward and showed the guard his laminated ID pass. "Cold, huh?"

"Shore is, sir, ah'm about to dah."

Inside the Circus, Nick stepped up onto the pallet floor of the arena. Men were running up and down metal stairs from the opened backs of the mammoth staff vans. Smoke hid the tent roof, and radio crackle permeated the blue-and-yellow air. He looked up into the G-2 van, saw that Kelsey wasn't there, and passed on to enter his TIC, stepping down onto its boot-dirtied, squeaky snow floor. Sp5 Albertson was tidying up their grease-pencil markings on the acetate face of their situation map. "Still nothing, Bert?"

"Nossir, you could've stayed sawing zees."

Nick undressed down to his wool shirt-and-trousers layer. "How about making a coffee run before you knock off?"

"Roger. Best make the most of the moment."

He scanned the boldly marked field phones on the tables. "We in business?"

"Yessir, all but the Cowboys, of course." These were the "Long Rangers," the Division's special Long-Range Patrol Platoon, a kind of miniature Green Berets unit trained to operate behind enemy lines and no longer under the command of Honk Hennebury. The TIC was prepared to receive information from them, as well as from all Divisional S-2 sections, attached Air Force reconnaissance, and the various MI Detachment sections.

Nick blew on his stiff hands. "Bundle up, Bert, it's the witch's tit out there again."

"Yessir . . . but after the river, I wouldn't go criticizing the cold too loud around these parts."

*Waiting for calls,* Nick thought testily. *The story of my life.*

He moved to the target status chart. He saw with dismay that there were still more symbols entered under the POSSIBLE column than under either the PROBABLE or the CONFIRMED. TIC regulations were conservative, specifying that a single sighting of an enemy unit made it only a POSSIBLE target for action. Reports from two separate sources were required to make it a PROBABLE. And for a target to be CONFIRMED, the TIC needed three separate reports of its existence, size, nature, and location.

"Still nothing but chickenshit, huh, Burke?"

Nick spun. It was Sergeant DeFalco again, down from the fire Coordination Center van. Again he hadn't heard, seen, or smelled him come in. "I'm going to tell you this just one more time, Sergeant—you can call me by my First Lieutenant!"

The older man just leered at him. He looked so much like Ernie Kovacs as a musical comedy villain that Nick wished he were a likable guy, but he hated him. The arrogant prick happened to be the Division Artillery Officer's fair-haired boy, and virtually had the run, in the colonel's absence, of the whole FCC operation. "Get out, DeFalco. When I get something, you'll get it."

"When's Fred come back on?"

Nick started redrawing blurred symbols, times, and coordinates on his chart. "Major Tillwell died in his sleep. I'm on all the time."

"Too bad. Fred gives us a lot of action."

"He gives you one-report bullshit, and I'm thinking of telling the G-two about it."

"Well, something better get cooking down this rathole and quick. We're sitting on our thumbs up there. My colonel comes back, he's not going to like this."

"Your colonel's your problem."

[ 65 ]

"Yeah, you wait till he gets here, then you'll—"

"Tell him to keep his eyes peeled on the way. I could use a lot of second and third reports."

Alone, Nick lit a smoke and fumed. He knew that he could start fanning the fires by calling out to his various sources. He was eager to do just that, but it might seem that he'd been intimidated by DeFalco . . . and that would be the goddamn day. He had to laugh at himself, though, for preaching the two-report, three-report regs at that greaseball. There had been plenty of hours earlier when he himself had been rushing one-source reports straight onto the CONFIRMED column for immediate Artillery response, just to keep it a party.

Suddenly the TIC exploded into action, all phones ringing. He sent a runner for Albertson to help him handle the rush, and when Major Fred and his man came back on duty, he declined to be relieved, unwilling to quit the excitement of running from phone to radio to map and chart.

Now one of them was handing target slips up into the FCC van faster than DeFalco or anyone else could run down after them. Copies went to G-2, and whenever Nick delivered a batch, he could see that Kelsey was just as lost in it all as he was, just as exhilarated.

The Circus Tent stayed operating at full tilt for four days, their longest stay in one place yet, before the call came to again break down, mount up, and move out.

The weather was holding viciously cold. Nick rode the backseat of Major Fred's open jeep. No snow fell today. The clouds had breaks in them here and there, revealing a sickly blue of sky. Everything was black and white or gray to him by now, grainy and dim and harshly lit.

The stress and fatigue had done it, he assumed. He supposed too that the various tricks were beginning to work on even him: umpire teams had taken to firing off live rounds, at all hours of the days and nights, in the forests around their working and sleeping areas. Through concealed loudspeakers, tapes of frighteningly real-sounding mortar and artillery explosions were constantly being broadcast, and the sounds of tank treads crushing through brush. He realized it was only the Psychological Warfare units at work, but knowing made it no less unnerving. Nor did the increased reports of actual casualties lessen the scraping of everyone's nerves: GIs being run over by tanks as they slept; the accidental decapitations by revolving turrets.

He carried in his pocket an air-dropped leaflet explaining that they were only being *told* that these were war games. Because, after Korea and aware of the odds, "the rich men" knew that no American was willing to fight well anymore. So they all were *"being tricked! This war is real! Every third round of ammo is live!"*

For every artillery battery not pulling the lanyard that fired the round, the next one over was *"going all the way."* The attack had come through the Fulda Gap. Fifth Army wasn't facing south at all, it was facing north and being creamed. They were next, right behind them. The time to stop and run was now. Before it was too late. *"Go ask the handful of leaders at the very top—at Corps and at Army! They know! But of course you can't! They'd silence you fast! So, stop! Now! And run!"*

At the moment, Nick was more than willing to give in and believe it. *Just shove Fred out and tell Bert to hang a sharp left. Fuck it.* Instead he slept.

Later that day in a gray dusk the Circus was built yet again, within black trees against gray snow. Nick felt sure he'd been here before. Someone had come in and covered the markings, fresh snow had done the rest. Moving like a zombie, he helped get the TIC operating, then left it in Major Fred's unsteady hands. He met Kelsey at the big sleeping tent. They walked off

[ 67 ]

into some woods, pissed, rubbed snow on their hands and faces, lit smokes, and passed Nick's fifth of cold Ballantine's back and forth a few times. It wasn't his favorite brand of Scotch, but its flat bottle traveled better than round ones. "Nearly out, Joel."

"No problem. I got Jack Daniel's o.t.a."

They slogged back to the big tent. The cots closest to the stove were already claimed or occupied. They found their stuff among the huge pile of duffels and sacks in the corner, took their air mattresses outside and inflated them on the airbrake-release valves of the nearest truck. Like a Halloween skeleton, G-4 Lieutenant Sidney Cohen was standing on his cot naked, taking yet another of his obscene whore's baths. Nick and Kelsey made do with soaking their feet in water warmed on the stove in canteen cups, then poured into their helmets. Nick tiredly watched the snow melt around the bottom of his helmet. Some soggy grass started to show through, gray. He changed the water and shaved without a mirror. He ran his deodorant stick under his arms and across his chest beneath his thermal undershirt, then zipped himself into his bag. Through a gap in the wall of blankets he could see Sp5 Albertson sucking his thumb in his sleep.

Suddenly Albertson's enormous face was above his, whispering "Scare you, sir? I'm sorry. It's time, though."

In the TIC, Bobby Darin was singing "Was there a call for me?" on Bert's transistor, and Nick had to smile at the coincidence. Their map showed all enemy locations only. If he wanted to know where they themselves were, he'd have to go check the G-3 map. But he didn't; he'd rather live with the eerie feeling of being lost. "Okay, Burke, now what chickenshit you got for us?" It was DeFalco again. Nick grabbed the sheet of paper out of his hand. "Get the fuck out of here."

Storming out, DeFalco mouthed something.

"God damn it—what did you say?"

DeFalco turned. "I said, one of these days, hotshot, I'd like to take you outside and teach you the—"

"How about now?"

"No rank?"

"You got it. Go ahead. I'll be right behind you."

DeFalco left. Albertson giggled nervously. "Gonna let him stand out there and freeze his balls off, right, sir?"

"Watch the fort," Nick said. He stopped at the G-2 van on the way. "Hey, Kelse—give me the gloves for a while." Knowing the GI gloves-with-liners would be too cumbersome for the work, Kelsey had brought a pair of civilian dress kid gloves. Nick put them on now and left the Circus.

DeFalco was waiting by the sentry. They walked away from the compound and entered the woods in silence. Air heaved in and out of the other man's nostrils loudly. Nick knew it meant rage, but also fear, age, cold, fatigue, and excess weight. In a clearing they leaned their carbines against a tree trunk and dropped their helmets near the butts.

DeFalco removed his equipment belt. Nick didn't. He didn't want to make any too noticeable marks, but knew that all the layers of clothing would make any clean body punching useless. So it would have to be the face: the nose bone and the ears. He knew the barehanded boob would be compelled to say something first, and then rush and try to wrestle him down, so he watched only the mouth, and when the lips opened he shot his left fist straight into the nose. The surprise and pain made DeFalco whip his head to the right, so it was his left ear that caught Nick's second, right-handed punch. To his credit, the man swallowed his cries. Nick stepped back and waited, crouched and protected, fists and arms cocked, praying to God that the guy was not a fighter.

He wasn't. He stayed a bent, whimpering statue, both hands up to his face. Nick retrieved his rifle and helmet and left. It was still about the only thing at which he was a flier, not

[ 69 ]

a pilot, and now that bumptious clod behind him knew it too. Walking, he wondered if DeFalco might be feeling as good about it now as he was. He hoped so, anyhow, because at least it had been real. Realer than these endless, masochistic chess games, anyhow.

He threw the gloves back up to Kelsey, and took with him into the TIC a haunting vision of the Circus arena he'd just swaggered through: they had finally plateaued, all those senior men holding the power. They had burned down to a strange state of relentless exhaustion, their skins gone gray as fish. Many were taking pills openly now. All their eyes looked to Nick now like the eyes of aviators, of sailors, of cowboys, of anyone used to glaring into far distances. They could keep it going forever now, he realized, if they had to, into an infinity of remote-control warring, if somebody told them to. Nick answered Bert's asking eyes with a quick wink, and stripped down to his working layer. "Let's go," he sang. "Let's get those mothers humping out there!"

Albertson said, "Your CO called you, sir—he's gotta see you right away."

Nick found Big John waiting in his CP tent. "Sit down, kid. We just got some terrible news."

Nick sat, sure it was about Susan or the baby. Big John's face looked green in the eerie light of the Coleman lanterns. He told Nick: "Our friend Brian Galgay is in some very serious hot water, I'm afraid. Berlin twixed us—Brian's already on his way stateside. . . . You know about the tunneling under the wall? Well, I still can't believe it, but it seems Brian was in on it! They say he had taken up with a Russian girl—actually, I knew about that, he mentioned her in a letter to us. Anyhow, he was trying to bring her out. There was a trap, and he got caught. I guess we can just thank God it wasn't the other side that got him."

The news about Brian Galgay's downfall certainly surprised Nick that night, and even shocked him. Yet its impact on him was oddly short-lived. Its imprint in his memory was shallow, and quickly covered over.

Watching Big John's aggrieved face, he felt mostly relief and some bafflement. He had known how fond Big John and Nola had been of Galgay, and he'd been aware of their shifting some of their affection onto him after Brian's departure—but why was Big John telling *him* all this, as if the world had ended? He said, "What'll happen to him now, sir?"

Big John sighed bitterly. "Well . . . he's young, and with his record—they'll probably just put him pushing doorbells in someplace like Omaha, Nebraska, until they think he's learned his lesson. If he's fool enough to stay in after this, which I think he is. Christ, I still can't believe how he could have done this to himself!"

Nick truly didn't know how he was expected to react. At the moment, he was having a hard time remembering even what Galgay had looked like, much less feeling crushed by his fucking up in some tunnel! Big John gave him a brief, hard hug around the shoulders. "I just wanted you to hear it from me, Nick."

Back at the Circus he immediately told the Kelse, who only snuffed, "Fell for a girl! Well, that's excellent. Now we'll pass that sanctimonious bastard's ass in a year!"

Nick threw himself back into the workings of the TIC. Gradually memory images of Galgay came back to him in clear flashes—husky, erect, rosy-skinned, black-browed, son-of-a-cop Galgay . . . Galgay in fatigues, as a GI, in civvies . . . Galgay frowning and preaching down his snoot from his high horse. But priesty Galgay down a tunnel? Trying to rescue a *girl*? Nick couldn't begin to imagine it. Maybe he was trying to save her soul from communism. Hell, even at club functions Galgay's idea of a date had always been some older, absent officer's wife!

It wasn't that there was ever anything even close to *queer* about the creep, it was just . . . *Galgay falling for a girl? With tits and everything?* Negative. She must've been a nun.

In a tie between Big John's affection and Kelsey's loathing for Galgay, Nick admitted that he'd have to lean toward Kelsey. And with that he gave it up altogether, and let Galgay vaporize away.

Into the third week, the fourth, into the fifth. They moved, set up, operated, broke down, and moved, again and again. Chaplains jeeped in and held services on portable altars in mess tents or pine groves. One night, off shift, Kelsey said, "Enough!" and disappeared with his carbine. He came back later carrying a collie-sized roebuck, and they ate two meals of fresh venison; it tasted gamey, but all the more delicious for its being *verboten*, and a change. Nobody asked Kelsey where he'd got the ammo, and they called him "Davy Crockett" for a while.

The pace and the strain picked up. In the midst of the next rush of action one caller reported to Nick sighting traces of "a Red Army headquarters." The transmission came by radio from the Long Rangers' base camp.

He wrote down the map coordinates and replied, "Red Dog One, Red Dog One, this is Coyote Four, over."

"Coyote Four, this is Red Dog One, over."

"Red Dog One, this is Coyote Four—do all in power to confirm. I say again—continue tracing. Do all in power to confirm. Most critical. Over."

He drew the symbol on the map and then under POSSIBLE on the chart.

Major Fred noticed. "My God!"

Then Albertson did. "Holy shit!"

Nick drew Fred aside. "Sir, listen—do you know how big this might be?"

"Well, sure, it's—"

"It's a possible nuclear. Nobody's thrown one yet, and those FCC yo-yos up there are going out of their skulls to be the first. We can't fiddle-fuck around with this one—we get an umpire zero on this, and we can all kiss our pensions good-bye, you know?"

"I know, Nick, but my God, we—"

"We gotta get three reports on it, is what we gotta do. Two more real ones. All I'm asking is, let me take it down off the boards until we do, okay?" He was sorry now that he hadn't just pocketed it on his own in the first place, but he'd been on automatic.

Major Fred was chewing his lips. "I see what you mean, I can see your point. They might. But, Christ, the—"

"*Hot dog!*" DeFalco again.

"Well, that's that," Nick said and went over. "Take it easy, Sarge, we just got it, we don't—"

"Don't you realize what this *means*, Lieutenant?" DeFalco was only excited, not hostile. Sharing their secret, Nick and he had been enjoying a certain peace and mutual regard since their showdown.

Nick sighed. "Yeah, I know, and I've got our guys breaking ass all down the line already; Bert's still on the horn now. We have to do this one by the book, though you—"

"How about I send some forward observers!"

"Great! That'd be a fantastic help. Code the shit out of it, though."

"Right, right."

Nick cranked up Big John. ". . . yessir, and if maybe you can go crack some whips, they'll— Right. Thanks a lot."

From the doorway Kelsey hooted, "Hey! Hear you hooked a whale, huh? Where is she?" He walked to the map. "Hey, right near Hof."

"Yeah—you guys got anyone that far forward?"

"Christ, no, not unless they're POWs. Well, good luck,

son, I'm going to bed, drunk. Goddamn Army headquarters, whooee! That'd be a feather in your cap!"

"If it's there."

"Yeah. . . . Would they go into a town like that, you think? Seventh Army HQ is out roughing it like the rest of us, I know that."

"They could," Nick said. "In fact, that might be a good reason to."

"Us figuring they wouldn't."

"Right."

"Nagasaki time, huh?"

"Don't even think it."

Kelsey left. DeFalco returned. "Hey, do you realize how long it'd take my FOs to get anywhere near that—?"

"Yeah, forever. Our Detachment's sending a couple guys up undercover—they probably got a better chance of making it. Listen, Sarge, we're flying air, we're doing everything. We want it too, you know."

"Good. One more thing, though—I just had my colonel on the horn. He's hauling ass in for this. He says to remind you, don't go upstairs on this, okay?"

"But Corps *is* supposed to be one of our sources. You oughta see the TIC they got, like an airplane!"

"Just don't, okay?"

"Don't worry," Nick said. "But listen, blabbermouth, go tell *all* the vans that, not just me."

"Jesus, you're right. Okay."

Nick and Albertson could make only so many calls so many times, and they made them. After that they could only go on with business as usual, and wait. Just wait for the call, if any, on the big one. Nick went off shift. By the time he came back on, nothing new had happened, except for the arrival into his life of Colonel Nathan S. Ewing, Artillery.

Ewing's own first star was reputedly in the next mail. Directing the FCC by phone and radio and messengers, he had been spending all his time out with his guns, "shooting and scooting" over the countryside. But he looked now as if he'd just arrived from garrison—or else had his own barber and valet in tow. Even his branch insignia, the double-crossed cannons-and-missile "spider," gleamed like gold. He entered the TIC and fixed his gray, stony eyes on Nick's name tag. "So you're the young man giving us a hard time."

"Sir?"

"I want that Soviet HQ, Lieutenant."

"So do we, Colonel."

"Then why don't we have it?"

Nick explained, needlessly he knew, feeling that he was lying. He couldn't get over how young this Ewing was, and how . . . cruel, somehow. The man scared him.

Ewing cut him short. "Tiger, if the Long-Range Patrol Platoon says it's there, it's there. I *know* it's there"—laying a clean-nailed finger over the village of Hof—"it makes absolute sense for them to be there. Lieutenant Burke, write us out a target slip for that baby, and you and I will end this engagement tonight!"

It sounded tempting, but Nick said, "I can't do that yet, sir."

Ewing's eyes pushed into Nick's like fingers. "Have you been such a purist all along? You've been rather, ah, inconsistent, couldn't we say? Where is your superior officer?"

"He's off shift, sir."

"Fetch him."

Nick jerked his head. Albertson went running. Nick relaxed: he was off the hook now. A phone rang behind him and let him escape Ewing for the moment. It was the IPW compound. A POW had just placed his unit somewhere north of Hof. It had been traveling the last time he'd had word of it, in a southerly direction. It was an element of Fifth Army HQ

Company. Nick moved his symbol from the POSSIBLE column to the PROBABLE.

Colonel Ewing carried a swagger stick of wood and shell-brass. He cracked it hard against a chair back. "Splendid!"

*Still only two,* Nick thought. Remembering the POWs in the Oberammergau snow, he privately gave the snitch's word less credence than the Cowboys' initial report. He looked now where Ewing was looking, and his heart split painfully: Major Fred was reporting in, trying desperately to look and act sober. His hands shook, his eyes were those of an injured Saint Bernard.

The shocked colonel hissed, "You're on report. Dismissed, Major!"

DeFalco had slipped in and stood meekly beside Albertson.

An otherworldly calm in his voice, Ewing ordered Nick, "Ask Lieutenant Colonel Trotter to please step down here for a moment." Nick wouldn't have been surprised to feel the stick whip across his face.

"He's traveling with the General, sir. Lieutenant Crane is senior man in the G-two right now, sir."

"And who ranks, Burke?"

"I do, sir."

"Put your name on that target order, Lieutenant."

He felt physically dizzy. He knew the reasons he was prepared to give for being unable to cooperate with Ewing's will—but he couldn't say that they were his true motives. Did he really give a rat's ass what they did or didn't do? It was only a game, after all, only make-believe. The Davy Crockett missiles out there were real, but they weren't going to be really *fired.*

"We can just take it, sir!" DeFalco whined.

"Go ahead!" Nick snapped, careful to look away from the colonel when he said it. He realized now that he wasn't the only one trying to stick somewhere close to the book: so was Ewing, by insisting on getting a signature.

"This should be done right, Burke."

"I know that, Colonel."

"Damn it, boy!"

"I'm sorry, sir, it's still only a probable." Nick regretted the gratuitous remark at once, but inside he felt reassured: right was right, and he didn't see why he should be the one to capitulate.

Colonel Ewing swung a chair around on the snow floor and straddled it. Even sitting, he seemed taller than Nick. "Do you understand, Lieutenant Burke," he said, "that in the Commanding General's absence, and without need of his approval, the Division Artillery Officer holds the authority to direct nuclear fire against an appropriate target?"

"No, sir, I didn't know that."

"You *are* aware, I assume, that an assembled enemy army-level headquarters complex constitutes a legitimate nuclear target?"

"Yes, sir, I'm aware of that."

Ewing stood up and stepped closer. "What's your first name, son?"

"Nicholas, sir. Nick."

"Nick, where are your guts? You look like a pretty tough young fella to me—let's *get* that bitch!"

Up close, Nick realized that the colonel was wearing a cologne. The fact befuddled him oddly. He could see that an audience had formed at the TIC's opening. "The regulations . . . my orders, sir, specify three separate reports for confirmation, sir."

"God damn it to hell, boy, you're not—"

"What for Christ's sake is going on in here?" demanded a new voice.

DeFalco and others in the gallery shouted, *"Ten-hut!"*

Fourth Armored Division Commander Major General James "Night Train" Miller advanced through the cluster of men. "As you were, as you were!" he barked. "And clear the

[ 77 ]

fuck away from here! Buncha gawkers, who don't have something to do?" The TIC door and the arena behind it emptied instantly. "Sounds like a goddamn catfight in here. Hello, Ewing. I said as you were, Lieutenant."

Nick let go of his anxiety: G-2 Colonel Trotter stood right behind the General—he could sign the target order.

Trotter frowned. "What's up, Burke?"

Ewing stood. "I'll tell you what should be up, Trotter!" and gave his version of the situation.

General Night Train Miller squinted at the map. "So why haven't we taken them out of there? Hell, then we could all go home!"

Silence.

Ewing sneered. "Speak up, Lieutenant, you had enough to say before."

Nick explained as succinctly as he could.

Colonel Trotter ordered, "Well, get the goddamn third report on it!"

Night Train had taken Ewing's chair. He spread his legs, unzipped his jacket, lit a Chesterfield, and looked around the TIC. "Where'd we get this brown shoe shithouse, anyhow? It's cold as sin in here!" Then, to Nick, he said, "Being kind of a tight-ass here, ain't you, Lieutenant? What's your fucking problem?"

"It's . . . nuclear fire, sir. Hof's a town."

The General nodded curtly. "Kid's got a point. Must've gone to school. Don't know what this army's coming to, heh. Okay, so what's *your* problem, Colonel Ewing?"

"We can pull the pin on the whole show, sir. We should hit it immediately." Glancing to Nick, he added, "In the real thing, we'd be saving more lives than we'd be taking."

Night Train nodded again, coughed, hocked a lunger of phlegm, and spat it into a far corner of the cavelike room. "Guess someone could give you an argument on that one, if they wanted to, Nat. . . . What say, Jason?"

[ 78 ]

Colonel Trotter teetered, then fell: "Well, I, uh . . . um, I believe Colonel Ewing's correct, General."

*Kiss-ass!* Nick thought.

Ewing handed Trotter the pad of target slips. "Give us your John Hancock there, Jason, and we'll—"

"Hold your horses now, fellas," Night Train growled. "Nat? Let's say for the moment that, heaven forbid, we didn't have your new little monsters to help us—how long would it take to move enough conventionals within range? Not on paper, on the ground."

Ewing looked to DeFalco, who said, "Three hours, sir— maybe five, max, depending on the roads and the—"

"Let's do it that way, Nat. For old times' sake, or something. Good chance to see how hot your boys are."

"Begging your pardon, General, isn't it a better opportunity to test our—"

"Look, Nat," the General prevailed, "you can always push that button. The minute G-two comes up with a confirm, we halt the move and shoot the nukes. Because, damn it, what if it *isn't* there, man? Jesus, if these bozos"—looking at Nick—"are as good about getting the two reports as they are about getting the third . . . we could be sending Crocketts in on some goddamn QM supply depot or something!"

Trotter agreed, "The General's right, there, Nat."

Ewing snapped, "Get on it, DeFalco!"

Nick took the phone from Bert, listened, hung up. He didn't go to the map.

Trotter asked, "What was that, Burke?"

Nick felt feverish. "The CIC agents we sent in, sir. They got captured."

Night Train let out breath wearily. He looked around the room again, then across at Nick. "What the fuck does your almighty chart have to say before I can get a cup of coffee in here?"

Albertson flew.

Ewing said, "Sir, wouldn't you be more comfortable up in the FCC? We've got—"

"Naw, this'll do. If we're gonna do this the hard way, might as well go for broke."

The little TIC, then, became the whole Division's seat of power for the next four hours. Nick wished he could appear more busy, but his network stayed maddeningly calm. Coming back on duty, Kelsey stuck his head in, popped his eyes, and vanished. Nick had to piss but held it in. Night Train finally instructed his aide-de-camp to waylay all messages and visitors outside in the arena, then chatted quietly with Ewing and Trotter. The Old Man looked very tired. It felt inappropriate, but Nick wished he had a cot to offer him. Once, he overheard the General saying ". . . on the way up, and I'm on the way out, but I still wouldn't want to have to go face Jack T. and tell him . . ." and the phrase *on the way out* sent a jolt of quick terror through him: all at once, right as he felt, he sensed very clearly that he was on the wrong side in this mess.

Their long, tense vigil didn't end well. The crucial call did come, but it came from the Corps TIC, reporting "A Soviet Army headquarters in the town of Hof has been destroyed by Corps Artillery, using nuclear firepower."

The General rose, stretched, and yawned up at the tent roof. "Well, it could have been worse. It could have been five hours." Then he was gone, Trotter in his wake.

Colonel Ewing sent Albertson outside and came over close to Nick. "Just for your information," he said, "I'll be sending a special letter for inclusion in your permanent record, Lieutenant. I have found you surly almost to the point of insubordination. Wrongheaded, uncooperative, and incompetent. You showed gross misjudgment in a matter of the gravest importance to this command. . . . Are you Reserve or Regular?"

"Regular, sir."

"Then, sweetheart, say every prayer you know that you never cross my path again. I'll ruin you."

[ 80 ]

Alone, Nick marked the target destroyed on the chart and map. In self-defense he had kept repeating *Fuck you!* and *No!* to himself while the strangely scented nuke colonel berated and threatened him, and had stared back at him with all the straight defiance and scorn that he could manage. But the menace had got through to him anyhow, and left him shaking.

Major Fred's wracked body relieved him on time, and Nick retreated to his bag, this time getting a cot close to the stove. He conked out for nine hours, dreaming dreams of dark tunnels and women, of fights in which Ewing was DeFalco, and of guns . . . guns aimed at others, and guns aimed back at himself.

# 10

Back at Baker, the best Big John had to offer was: "Listen, Nick, one letter's really not worth getting your balls in an uproar like this. You know you're getting an Army Commendation Medal when you rotate, your efficiency reports are all maxes straight across the board. . . . In no time at all that Two-oh-one file of yours will be bulging with so many songs of praise that one combat-type colonel will—"

"It's not *fair*, sir! That Ewing's a freaking psycho!"

First Sergeant Hardt poked his head into Big John's office. "You're gonna be late, Lieutenant."

"And that's another thing!" Nick complained. "I'm not home two days, goddamn it, and I have to pull their goddamn

OD duty for them! We're Seventh Army troops, goddamn it, and we—"

Big John drummed his fingers madly. "Give me a break, will you, Nick? Go take it out on the GIs."

"Shit!" He grabbed his polished black plastic helmet liner and stormed out. He went to the arms room and checked out a .45 and a clip of five rounds. He forced the clip into a starched-shut side pocket of his pale, tight field jacket, slipped the pistol into his black patent leather holster, signed out, and walked uphill briskly, across the long, sloping playing field, toward the guardhouse.

Normally he found Officer-of-the-Day duty a welcome relief from the grind of garrison blues, an escape from desks and offices and greens to the outdoors and men and fatigues. This afternoon, however, he was supersaturated with combat life. Mentally, in fact, he was still more away in the field than he was home.

Kelsey's Volvo intercepted him by the movie theater. "Hey, partner, how about doing me a favor?"

"Hi—what?"

"Let me take OD tonight?"

"Why?"

"Aw . . . Bibs got her damned period, and—"

"Cut the shit with me, Kelse—this Big John's idea?"

"No, mine."

"Thanks anyhow, bud, but I'm okay."

"Sure?"

"Yeah."

"Well, just keep your finger on it, son." Kelsey winked. "It'll all blow over."

The guardhouse was in the cellar of the Finance Building. With the off-coming OD, Nick brusquely inventoried the office and the dank rooms crammed to the ceilings with bunks, and signed for it all. They jeeped to Division Trains, where a clerk told them, "Major Sprague's not here. Said there's no special orders for tonight. . . . When'll classes be starting up again, Lieutenant Burke?"

"Another week, Bones," Nick said. "Some of the Signal guys are still out picking up wire after Snowsword. I'll get the word to you."

Three reliefs of eight men each stood at parade rest on the tarmac behind the guardhouse. The sergeant of the guard turned out to be Albertson. He brought them to attention and reported them ready for inspection. Nick returned his salute. "Glad it's you, Bert," he whispered. "We'll be hard-ass at guard-mount, then nice guys later." Then he conducted his guard-mount, inspecting each soldier individually.

His and their good luck ran out on the last man in third relief: the kid looked sprayed with filth, and obviously hadn't even washed, much less shaved; his rifle was no cleaner. Albertson ticked the offenses off on his clipboard as Nick impatiently defined them, ending with "Any excuse, Private?"

"No."

Nick sighed. "No what?"

The soldier sighed. "No, sir." He was a flagrant: he wanted off at any cost. He knew that to be relieved meant getting company punishment, but he didn't care.

"Okay—you're relieved. Sergeant, inform the Signal Company to get their standby up here *schnell*. . . . And have the drivers fall in outside the dungeon, in case they thought they got away with it—and do it loud, Bert, so all these guys hear it."

His next task was his favorite. He rode to the main flagpole outside the HQ building. The MP color guard was there, their glossy black jeep parked by the preserved World War II Sherman tank that stood on the lawn, its muzzle pointing east. They wore white caps and gloves and epaulets-with-braids, the trousers of their greens bloused over their wet-looking boots. At his

[ 83 ]

command they marched across the flagstone walk through the carefully landscaped shrubbery to their places at the pole's ropes and at the lanyard of the small, wheel-mounted, polished brass cannon. He gave them parade rest, and thus began the most beautiful part for him, the wait.

Even on a cold and misty March day like this, he found these moments of formal pause had a calming effect on him. Gazing past the whole plateau before him at the valley and mountains beyond, his anxiety and anger blew off. He felt aware of himself standing there, fixed exactly where he was supposed to be in time and space, as in a photo clicked from a low-flying plane.

Inside the HQ building, the duty officer's hand pushed the PLAY button on the tape recorder. Static rushed through the outside speakers. Nick ordered, "Color Guard, ten-hut!" Then, "Hand-salute!" . . . "Retreat" played. The cannon was fired. Men all over Baker Barracks froze in place and turned toward the sound, holding their salutes until the music died away. The flag came rattling down, to be folded away for the night into its three-pointed envelope. Nick released the MPs, then lingered there a minute, hearing the cannon's roar and bugle's call still just reaching the mountain walls far away down the valley. His driver gunned the jeep around, then drove him off post. He had a half hour for supper.

Jimmy was bouncing in his high chair, tight-lipped. He saw Nick and laughed. "Da!" Susan slid the spoonful of pink paste into his mouth.

Nick said, "Sorry, pal."

"Don't undress, hon, they just called."

Nick dialed Albertson at the guardhouse. "This might not be anything, Lieutenant, but I don't know what to do. I think you'd better come up here."

He parked the Triumph behind the Rod and Gun Club and hustled across the tarmac. It was dark already. The stocky soldier waiting in the hallway stiffened. Nick read his name tag. "As you were, Desmond. . . . What's the problem, Sergeant?"

Albertson rose from the duty desk to the open top of the Dutch door. "It's Private, uh, Desmond here, sir. He's the standby from Signal? And he checks out just fine, I inspected him outside myself, but . . . Well, speak up, soldier—tell the OD what's your problem."

The boy remained silent. His face wasn't averted, but it was hard to tell where his eyes were looking: they were magnified to near invisibility by the thickness of the lenses in his GI, pink-plastic-rimmed glasses. Their smudged surfaces seemed to be the only parts of him that needed cleaning. Nick felt the urge to just take and polish them. "Didn't you hear the sergeant, Desmond?"

"Yes, sir."

"Then answer him, please. This is screwing up my schedule. What's your problem?"

"Ask him his name, sir."

"What's your name, Private?" Waiting, Nick thought he could see physical pain pass through the anguished boy.

Finally: "I . . . I don't know. Sir."

Albertson boiled over. "Now, what in the world am I supposed to do with that, will somebody tell me? I've got logbooks to fill out in here! Watch this, sir—is your name Desmond, boy?"

Nothing but the same eyeless stare.

Nick took out his cigarettes. "Smoke, soldier?"

"No, thank you, sir."

As Nick lit his own, something brushed across his mind as lightly as a bird's wing. There it was again, the night of the Green Berets' cowshed interrogation of the naked "prisoners." He cringed a little inside. Then the obvious struck him: "Let me see your ID card, Private."

The soldier passed Nick his horse-engraved wallet. Nick read the ID. "I see. Now, open your field jacket, please."

The kid obeyed. The name tag on his shirt read FINCHER.

"Sergeant Albertson," Nick said, "unless Private Fincher says different, I believe he's taking some Private Desmond's duty for him—how much did this Desmond pay you, Fincher?"

"Ten. Ten dollars, sir," Fincher said.

"Wal, jeezebeezle, Fincher, why the fuck didn't you just say so?" Albertson demanded inanely.

Nick said, "I don't think Private Fincher wanted to lie. Is that it, bud?"

"Yes, sir."

"That's nothing to be scared or ashamed of. Okay, Bert—strip some tape across the name on his jacket and—" He stopped. He felt a kind of fluttering inside, and then it became a voice that cried, *Relieve him! Send him down!* He stared again at the kid, trying to penetrate the clouded lenses. "Have you stood guard on this installation before, Fincher?"

"Oh, yes, sir."

"Man knows his stuff frontwards and backwards, sir!"

Nick wanted to speak and end it, but the instinct persisted, and now he recognized it. It was now saying, *Relieve him!* but it was that same, sharp-pointed, unreasonable impulse of sixth sense that had pushed him to go against that Colonel Ewing in the TIC.

"Lieutenant Burke, you okay, sir?"

"Yeah, I'm just thinking." He was about to tell Bert to check Fincher out with his company, but then his instinct went abruptly silent again, and he felt reality return. He said, "Fincher—they keep more than one standby ready down your outfit?" but it was only words: he wasn't about to obey *that* self-destructive call again in a hurry.

"No, sir, they—"

"Shit, no, sir, we go calling down there now, some dumbass CQ'll just lay it on the first clown fool enough to be hanging around the barracks! This one's *fit*, at least. God knows what meatball we'd get us if—"

"Okay, Bert, okay. . . . Make the changes, and correct the log, so Fincher here gets credit for the duty. Then notify his outfit of the change. I'm going on first rounds. Call my driver at Headquarters mess and tell him to catch up after he eats—he know the route?"

"If he don't he soon will, sir!"

It felt good to be outside in the cold again. He walked uphill under dark trees thickening with new leaves. He swung up the walk to the Baker Barracks bowling alley. No snow remained on the ground now, except for scattered remnants going gray beneath bushes and between the toes of trees, but he felt that he was still out there at "war" in the no-time snowy wilderness, on shift yet again. The Psy. War propaganda had been right: it was real, and without end. This was a new phase, that's all, the home front. Inside, the bartender put down his *Army Times*. "Evening, sir, you look beat—cuppa coffee?"

"No, thanks." The four lanes were loud with teams. Nobody was at the small pool table. He left and walked back down the hill. In the snack bar he passed through the smells of burgers and fries, returning the German countergirl's brazen glare. He then ushered his armband's presence through the EM club, then through the *Rathskellar* downstairs. He slipped in and out of the movie theater. Most ODs killed at least two hours in here; he never did, even if it was something he wanted to see.

He walked downhill past the dark chapel, across the playing field. Rain was beginning to drizzle. At the bottom he jumped down to the small parking lot between the Detachment and the Service Club. Through the barred glass door of the orderly room, he could see that Lying Francis, the mechanic, had CQ duty. He rapped on the glass, making Francis drop his *Playboy*. "Francis, call the guardhouse and tell my driver to be down here in three minutes." Downstairs in the Service Club, the American Express office and all the classrooms were dark and locked. Upstairs a few soldiers were shooting pool, writing letters, playing chess and "nice" cards. The SS girl on duty was

[ 87 ]

fat, mustachioed, cheery Beverly. "Take some doughnuts, Nick, they'll just go stale."

"Dead all over, huh? Lucky for me."

"Well, half are downtown getting drunk or laid, the rest are scrubbing barracks—war games is hell, huh?"

"I . . . can't talk about it yet, Mom. Listen, I'll have somebody call down later, if you still got the doughnuts, we'll take 'em."

The driver was just pulling up. Nick slid up onto the seat. "Hold it," he told him, "you've got it backwards—put the top up and shut the heater off."

The kid did so. "Supposed to go below freezing tonight, sir."

"Guys on post don't have heaters."

He found the first sentry deep inside the dark Transportation motor park. Without sneaking, he came right up on the soldier's heels without being challenged. Then he saw why: the wire ran from the radio in his pocket up to his ear. Nick picked up a handful of pebbles and peppered the man's helmet liner.

"Fuck!" the kid yelled. "Halt! Who—?"

Nick held out his open palm. The boy surrendered the transistor sheepishly. "Campbell, if some kraut was siphoning gas off in here, could you hear him?"

"Nossir."

"Want this on the report?"

"Nossir."

"So?"

"It won't happen again, sir."

Nick pocketed the radio, returned the salute, and left. He proceeded, making his rounds, checking his guards walking their dark, lonely posts at the QM, HQ, and Signal motor pools, then out at the airstrip. Then he started out the scythe-blade road that followed the edge of the plateau off into black darkness. Out here the rain in the headlights looked large as snow; the wind was sharp with winter.

Post Six was a fuel dump enclosed by high, wire-topped fencing, patrolled from the outside. Nick didn't hunt here; he only parked with motor and lights off and waited. Tonight the soldier came running up after five minutes and challenged him properly. Nick told him, "Stay alert now, you've got a DP camp down there, you know, they come under that fence like snakes. Let's move it, driver."

Post Seven was a long row of five-ton trucks, vans, and tankers, parked noses-out along the road's shoulder like a herd of prehistoric beasts waiting silently in the gloom. He always stayed and chatted with the guard here a while longer than at other posts; the trucks had a way of spooking even the healthiest young soldier.

Then he rolled on the quarter mile to his final stop, Post Eight, the most remote and isolated post on Baker Barracks. This was the ammunition dump, a rectangular wire box blunting the very tip of the scythe-blade. The road changed from hardtop to dirt inside the gate of the steel-mesh enclosure, then ran its last hundred yards to dead-end at the back wall of high fencing. The ammo was stored inside twenty-odd olive-drab, metal huts that flanked the dump road like the buildings of a western ghost town. If the dump was ever blown, the word had it, the whole mountain would go with it, and bury the town below in the valley like Pompeii. The sentry here was the only one issued live ammunition for his weapon. He was charged with patrolling the outsides of each hut as well as every inside foot of the fence, and with phoning the guardhouse every twenty minutes during his four-hour tour. If he failed to call in, it was the sergeant of the guard's duty to call him.

Nick strictly followed prescribed OD procedures for checking Post Eight. He had his driver lower the jeep's headlights to yellow cat's-eyes just before clearing the rise in the road some fifty yards from the gate. At the top of the rise he said, "Kill the engine," and they coasted the rest of the way in silence. Properly halted, challenged, and recognized, he dismounted. The guard unlocked the gate, let him enter, then relocked it.

Nick made encouraging small talk as he inspected the wooden phone booth for contraband magazines, food, books, or radio, then accompanied the sentry on his next full circuit of fence and ammo storage lockers. Done, he watched the guard again lock himself inside the dump. Then he returned to the guardhouse, back to civilization.

Rock and roll was blaring from the bunkrooms over Radio Luxembourg. In the office Albertson was intimidating the corporal of the guard and the three-quarter-ton truck driver with lies about life and strife at the Circus Tent during Snowsword. Nick hid his smile of pleasure at the naked awe that greeted his entrance.

"Get the OD a cuppa coffee, Parsons!"

"Never mind, Bert, I'm going to grab something at the snack bar."

After eating, he returned to the Service Club and took the doughnuts from Beverly. Back at the guardhouse he told Bert to have them passed through the bunkrooms. "I'll be in Solitary if you need me," he said and went down the hall to the cell-size OD's room.

He stretched out on the narrow cot, his head and shoulders against the wall, regretting now that he had bothered to eat at all; the burger lay in his stomach like charcoal, sending up fumes that burnt his throat. He was sorry that he hadn't hidden out in the movie for a while, after all. He had brought his night-school guidebook, and a paperback, but couldn't get up enough interest in either to even take them from his bag. War-game hangover and adrenaline made sleep impossible. Even later, he knew from experience, when he was exhausted and the bunkrooms were quiet, the relentless phone calls from Post Eight would keep snapping his mind out of whatever nodding-off he could manage anyhow.

Nick lit a smoke and studied its gray curls homing up to the lone, bare light bulb. Outside and far away it seemed, "Taps" sounded across Baker and the valley, and made him yet again see Montgomery Clift as the movie Prewitt playing it weeping for dead Sinatra-Maggio. The vision helped respirit him enough to fly out and up over the whole Baker Barracks in his imaginary glass reconnaissance plane. But he had forgotten that it was night, black and raining. So he had to switch his mental film to infrared, which showed him only outlines of heat-emitting objects. There was no telling whether the objects were still there, or merely their warm impressions.

At a quarter after one he woke his driver, drank some stiff coffee, and went out again to check his charges on post. The word of his schedule often leaked, but tonight it obviously hadn't. He found the Post Two guard inside the canvas back of a QM three-quarter-ton truck, then surprised the airstrip sentry sneaking a smoke on the dark side of one of the helicopters that were straining on their guy wires in the wind like angry monster grasshoppers. He chewed ass as needed, but on these later tours he tried to leave even the goof-offs feeling more supported than harassed. The Kelse always claimed that he put himself in their place, then judged them against how he'd walk guard, but Nick had learned by now that that was too much to expect of the average GIs. He had come to feel a lot older than most of these men than he actually was.

Driving toward the herd of tankers, he looked out to his left past the driver's back: nothing but rain-furred lights. They were the string of rhinestones falling from the castle-crown down along the mountain road; the larger, brighter pearls of the airstrip's hangars; then, along the ground, the straight rows of pale blue lights marking the edges of the runways crossing the plateau. "Slow down," he said, not to grow any quieter, but because he suddenly dreaded going back to the confines of the guardhouse. The cellar rooms had somehow fused in his mind with the TIC.

He wished that the row of tankers and the ammo dump beyond would begin receding at the same speed as the jeep's, so he'd never have to reach them. He would stay forever on his way to inspect their security, fixed exactly, as at the flagpole, where he was supposed to be in time and space.

The frail young private at Post Seven acted so comically terrified by the behemoth trucks that Nick gave him a stick of gum and stayed talking with him until he calmed down. Moving on toward the ammo dump, the driver said, "Cat's-eyes going up, engine off at the top, right, sir?"

"You got it." The ammo dump appeared dimly at the end of the long, slow slope, and it did seem to be moving—only toward him, instead of away. "Stop about ten feet this side of the gate," Nick said. "As soon as we spot him, put on—" He suddenly heard the phone ringing from inside the shack ahead, and checked his watch: it was nearly five minutes past the call-in time. "He must've missed his—"

"There he is, sir!"

The guard stood just inside the gate, practically touching it with his face, facing them in a smart, legs-spread position of challenge, his dull-metal, .45 caliber grease gun at port arms. He wore no poncho. He shouted then, *"Halt! Who goes?"*

Leaning out the open side of the stopped jeep, Nick yelled, "The OD!" He peeled off the seat slowly. "Low beams and engine." He stood on the road, awaiting the call to advance and be recognized.

But the soldier stayed silent. He seemed not to be hearing the ringing of the phone. His eyeglasses glinted in the headlights now and Nick remembered who he was, but couldn't recall either of the names. Abruptly the guard with the glasses moved the magazine of live rounds from his pocket, and clicked it into his machine gun with a clean, loud, terrible sound.

"Jesus Christ, sir!" the driver gasped.

The sound of the gun being cocked came loudly and harsh.

*Fincher!* Nick remembered and whispered, "When I speak, you roll out and get under the jeep. . . . *Fincher!*" he yelled. "It's the OD, Fincher! May I advance?"

Fincher neither moved nor spoke. The phone continued its steady, shrill pealing. Nick risked a quick look to make sure the driver had got out. He had. The jeep had stalled, dimming its lights and deepening the silence. Nick heard a voice at his feet: "My God, Lieutenant, he's—"

But Nick already saw: The deep, black eye of the machine gun now protruded through the gate, resting solidly in the bottom V of one of the steel diamonds. The phone stopped. Nick could hear its echo pinging down the valley. He could see Albertson bouncing into the guard truck to come out, and wished he was there to shout, "No! Get some MPs!"

He gingerly lifted out his pistol, fed in the clip, and coughed to cover the sound of his cocking it. He dropped down upon his left knee, pressing his side into the jeep's frame.

The grease gun's huge, bottomless eye followed him down.

Nick's left hand gripped his right wrist to steady his right hand, propped upon his right knee. Closing his left eye, he tried to align the front sight of his automatic to obliterate the sickening image of the machine gun's eye. "Fincher!" he called. "Port arms! Clear that goddamn weapon now, boy!" He was about to add, "It'll be all right!" but the machine gun suddenly jumped out of its perch. The whole gate rattled, and the night all over the plateau, mountain, and valley exploded with fired shots, one of them Nick's.

Nick plunged forward then, running headlong into the gate. He tried to climb it, but the rain-slicked diamonds kept rejecting his boots, and it was too high to make with only his hands, his right still clenching the .45. He hung there, finally, the skin of his face pushing itself into the steel.

As his breathing calmed, he realized that the strange, soft

[ 93 ]

sounds he was hearing were being made by pieces of Fincher, still falling with the rain against the top and near side of the first ammo locker on the right, and upon the muddy ground between it and the soldier's back-pitched corpse.

# 11

Major Archie Sprague, the investigating officer, said, "You did shoot to kill, then, did you not?"

Nick sighed. "I fired to hit the man pointing the machine gun at me, sir."

"I see. Not to wound him, then?"

"Not to miss him, sir. It was a forty-five pistol, sir, and that weapon just—"

"Just answer the questions, Lieutenant."

Nick wasn't being cool. He was numb. The investigation had been going on for four days. This was his sixth appearance before Sprague. From J. J. Kirk, the special agent who had replaced Brian Galgay, Nick knew how Fincher had been struck by the fired rounds. The first, from the grease gun, got his cock and balls and probably killed him. The second went in his belly. The third went up his throat and out the back of his head. The gun had climbed, like a sewing machine. They found Fincher's right thumb still on the trigger. His left hand was still holding the end of the barrel. "The round you got off," J.J. said, "got him in the chest, Nick. But he was most likely dead already, so don't worry about it."

J.J. also informed him: "Sprague's got no goddamn right in the world to conduct this investigation. He's Division Trains, he's the same officer who failed to brief you on your tour of duty. That makes him, one, ineligible for conflict of interest, and, two, subject to investigation himself! Informal or not, it's totally illegal. You don't even have to answer the calls to testify, if you don't feel like it."

But he answered all the calls, and testified as honestly and intelligently as he could. The whole process, in truth, seemed academic to him at best. His heart, soul, and mind were still focused elsewhere—on dead Fincher . . . on the fact of his still being dead, forever.

On the night of the morning it happened, he had tried to express to Susan what confusion and shock he was feeling, but the moment that he choked, she bristled as in fear and clapped her hands twice near his face like a teacher. "Stop that! You're . . . crying! I can't believe I'm seeing you like this, Nick!"

To escape her and Kelsey, Big John, J.J., Scotty, Sergeant Hardt, and all the phone calls that started coming as the word spread around Baker, he walked out of the apartment and down the hill two tiers to find Waltzie. Julia opened the door and said Waltzie was away on a conference in Dusseldorf, ". . . but come in—my God, what's happened to you, babe?" He told her, and she took him into her arms. Her kids were in bed. He was ready to tell her the rest of it, the secret part, but he felt his breathing turn odd, and took it as a signal to get out of their house.

Julia said, "You're still in mild shock, Nick—didn't they give you anything at the dispensary?" They had. "Well, take them and just go to bed. Don't talk to another soul until you've slept."

[ 95 ]

He went home and did just what Julia told him to. He would have run off on foot into the mountain forests, if that's what she said to do.

Major Sprague sat behind his desk, rarely looking up from the papers and folders under his hands. Nick sat erectly in a metal folding chair that had been placed in the center of the open floor, half-expecting Sprague to tell him to hold his balls out over an opened drawer. The room, as always, was almost unbearably hot, the radiators clicking and sissing irritably. From time to time he wondered whether one of the folders might be his own 201 file. Did it contain the damaging letter from Colonel Ewing?

A clerk-typist, Bones, sat in a corner taking shorthand. Sprague went on, "Now, tell me again—exactly what happened when Private Fincher reported for guard duty?"

Again he replied, "I was at home. Specialist Five Albertson had phoned before I arrived there. I called him, and he . . ." He had told it so many times that he didn't have to give it his whole thought. Growing warier now, he concentrated on resisting the urge that always came at the end, to confess the whole truth and accept full blame for the boy's death, and end it.

"Did you *see* Albertson cover the name tag reading DESMOND with the tape reading FINCHER?"

Nick sighed. "No, sir. I had my rounds to make."

"And you failed to notify Desmond and Fincher's unit?"

"I instructed the sergeant to call their unit, sir."

So it went for another two hours, pretty much the same as it had gone all the times before, except today Major Sprague finally looked up, removed his half-glasses, rubbed his eyes, and relit his pipe. "Lieutenant Burke," he said, "we still have a few more witnesses and documents to check out, but we think it only fair at this point to prepare you . . ."

He accepted Sprague's unofficial forecast of results the way

a novocained jaw feels a finger tapping it. In the vestibule outside he passed it on to the waiting Kelsey, who flared,
*"Bullshit!"* Nick only grinned. The Kelse, he knew, was as confused, scared, and powerless as himself, except by proxy:
"Christ," he'd said, "I almost took it for you, Nick, remember?
It could've been me—I would've done the exact same thing as
you did!"

"Except hit him," Nick had said. "You suck with a forty-
five."

Nick went home this day and told Susan of Sprague's pre-
diction. She made her defeated cheerleader face. "Oh, no! Oh,
God, that makes two letters of reprimand in a row, Nick! It's so
unfair! . . . Did you expect anything like this?"

"No," he said, and went back inside his head to the ob-
scure, almost infrared image he'd been nurturing, of himself
being spooked away stateside overnight, as Brian Galgay had
been delivered after his Berlin tunnel escapade. Why, he
wanted to know, weren't they doing the same for him? Did
something have to be off duty or personal for them to back you
up? *The Service takes care of her own,* the word went, leaving
him to conclude that, regular commission or no, he must somehow not be one of her own.

Later that evening Susan breezed off to her Great Books
Club meeting with Nola Pachek at Mrs. Major Scott's house.
Nick dug out his last half-bottle of Ballantine's left over from
war games, and began sipping it neat from a beer stein, listening vacantly to Sinatra on their new Grundig.

Just after nine Waltzie Cooper called and came over, upset
and excited. "I just got in! How are you! Julia's a madwoman
over this! Sit down! Gimme a drink. Never mind. This can't
wait—I *know* about Fincher, Nick! You're free and clear! Listen—the poor bastard wasn't even supposed to be here at all!
Never mind on guard duty! He was a certified Section Eight,
Nick! I myself signed him home on a medical five, maybe six

[ 97 ]

months ago, I'll have to look it up. If he was still hanging around, somebody was letting it happen, and it'll be their ass, not yours!"

"What was the matter with him?" His instinct was screaming wildly inside him, *I knew it! I told you!*

"Ah, the poor kid," Waltzie said, "how he was ever let *in's* the real question. Paranoid schizophrenic, basically. Manic-depressive with . . ."

Numb, Nick listened to Waltzie's psychiatric profile of the boy, some of which he understood. At the end he said, "That's horrible. Thanks a lot, Waltzie."

"This'll *spring* you, Nick! You're—"

"Nah. It's not going to make that much difference."

"What are you saying?"

"It's still my fault. I—"

"For shooting?"

"No. That doesn't bother me, Waltz. That was right. That was correct for me to do. But it never should have gone that far." Then he told his secret: "See, I *read* him, Waltzie. I knew he was mental, and I still—"

"Nick. Stop. . . . Have you said this to anyone else?"

"No, not yet."

"Well, don't. Ever. You didn't know baloney. How was he acting?"

He described Fincher's behavior at the guardhouse accurately. "But I knew it anyhow. I got a message from that kid, Waltzie. And I ignored it. I chickened out."

"Do you truly believe it was your fault, Nick?"

"Yes."

"Wait, now—do you think you were guilty or remiss in *their* terms? The Army's?"

Nick thought. "No. The fucker acted saner than half the kids out there. You should've seen the one I relieved."

Waltzie laughed and took the stein away from him. "Welcome back, then. Do you know enough to stick to just their terms, or do I have to—?"

"I love their rules, Waltzie."

"Does that mean yes?"

"Damn right."

"Okay—now, who do I have to call to testify?"

Within two days Waltzie was able to report: "It was the Signal Company CO himself, Nick. Didn't want it on his unit's *record*! He was keeping Fincher on his morning report, but excused from all duties. Had him running coffee for the orderly room, and confined to barracks nights and weekends, like a prisoner. Waiting for his normal rotation date, the first of April."

"April Fool's," Nick said. "Poor bastard almost made it, didn't he."

He wasn't called again for another six days. This time he entered Major Sprague's hot chambers clearheaded and confident—only to get struck between the eyes: "This is a rough draft of the letter, Lieutenant," Sprague said, "and unofficial. Let me read it to you. We're trying to make it as general and, uh, harmless as we—"

"Excuse me, sir," Nick said. "Do you mean I'm still getting my ass kicked, even after Captain Cooper's testimony?"

"You said it, mister, and I'd be cautious if I—"

"May I request a short recess, Major?"

"Make it quick."

Outside, he asked Big John, "How the fuck can they do this? I know Waltzie testified, and I know they've had the whole Signal crew through here at least twice!"

Big John, worried, nodded knowingly, muttering, "Obviously somebody wants something on the books, just in case. If they go after the company commander, well, that might get too big. But somebody's got to fall. They've already busted the CQ and Desmond, now they need an officer, that's all."

"And a letter's supposed to be nothing, right?"

Big John shrugged, forlorn.

"I'm not taking it," Nick decided. "They're not taking me that easy. What can I do, Colonel, go to the Judge Advocate and get a lawyer, or what?"

Big John coughed nervously, thinking, then he told Nick his options.

Back inside, Sprague said, "May I continue, Lieutenant?"

"Sir, I have a statement to make," Nick said, all numbness gone for the moment.

"And what is that?"

"I wish to exercise my right as an officer to demand a general court-martial . . . sir."

Almost immediately upon leaving his last confrontation with the investigating officer, Nick's numbness set back in. This time it felt deeper and closer to total than before, no longer having the obsession with Fincher's insanity to give it focus.

Numb, he didn't wait for the outcome of the suicide incident to submit his resignation. Soon after, he numbly received his release from active duty and his travel orders; his honorable discharge would follow. This, Big John bleakly informed him, at least meant that no charges, hence no court-martial, were pending.

He canceled his night-school classes, then drove the Triumph to the port at Bremerhaven for shipment home, returning by train. After a while he seemed not to even notice Susan's tears, threats, tantrums, sulks, or supplications. He would tell her only, "I'm sorry, but I can't help it." Neither Big John nor J.J. nor Scotty—not even Kelsey could reach him with his earnest and sensible protests and counsels. All Nick would say was, "It's done. I'm fujigmo," Army for *Fuck you, Jack, I got my orders.*

Susan went again to Bad Caanstadt and gave birth to their second child, a girl. The arrival of new life thrilled Nick, and gave him a small cave of hope within the numbness.

He never was officially informed as to how the Fincher incident was resolved. He learned it by accident, when he was in the PX one afternoon, buying a fresh "That's All" album to take home. Bones, his former student and Division Trains clerk, came over and said, "Congratulations, sir!"

"Hi, Bones, what for?"

Bones told him: He had been cleared. Both the CO and the first sergeant of the Signal Company had been relieved of command, temporarily frozen in rank and pay, and given letters of reprimand.

"Thanks, Bones." It meant nothing to him now. He felt like a guy in a fight who has passed the pain barrier: all hope of winning was gone, but there was no longer any danger of his going down. He could take all they had to throw at him and more. So long as he stayed erect and moving, he was invincible.

One evening near the end, after another strained, silent supper with Susan, he walked down the hill to seek refuge with the Coopers. The door to their quarters was open, and it sounded as if a party was going inside. Major Scott, who lived in the same building, intercepted Nick on the stairs. Scotty's normally flushed face showed white as he said, "Didn't you hear, Nick? They're dead."

"No."

"Yeah, an awful thing, just terrible. Sitter says they were just going up to Stuttgart to have some dinner and catch some concert or other. You know Julia and her music."

"My God."

"MPs say it was one of them frigging piggyback trucks! Came barrel-assing around a turn on the wrong side, as usual, and the trailer jackknifed. Waltzie had no place to get out of the way. Kraut driver bought it too, but small consolation that is now."

"Right."

Unable to think of anyplace else to go, Nick climbed back uphill home. He sat back down at the kitchen table, lit a cigarette, and relayed the tragic news to the salt and pepper shakers.

Susan crimsoned and cried hysterically, "Oh, my God! Oh, God, no! No! I can't believe this! This can't be happening to us! Not them! Oh, God, why them! Oh, dear God, no! They—"

"You didn't even like them," Nick said.

"You *bastard*, how can you say that? I did too! And what difference would it make? They were so young! They had so much to live for! My God, what a waste! And, oh, my God, all those kids! Those babies!"

*You're crying for yourself,* Nick thought, but kept silent.

"And look at you!" she burst forth again. "What's the matter with you, anyhow? You shit! *You're* the one who was supposed to be so buddy-buddy with them! And especially her, oh, I know. But I can see how much you really cared, now, all right! Oh, yeah, you could pretend to get so creepy-weepy over some moron GI! But when it comes to your so-called friends— *nothing,* right? You can't *use* them anymore, so the heck with them! You can throw away your own life like it's nothing, so what do you care about somebody else's!"

Jimmy had been calling out from the nursery. By the time Susan heard too, Nick was already going in to see what he needed and calm him, so he wouldn't wake the infant. Within the dark, warm aura of oil, powder, and Similac, he thought, What did she want of him anyhow? He knew this much: He'd be goddamned if he'd ever cry in front of her again, even if he could.

*Even this, now,* he marveled painfully to himself, *even this!* Even Waltzie and Julia had been thrown at him now, and still he stayed erect and moving. He picked his small son up out of the crib, held him strongly against his chest, and crooned to him, "You're okay, bud, Daddy's got you."

As usual it seemed to be the words, more than the holding, that comforted the child. Soon he was relaxed and dozing again. Nick tucked him into his fluffy blankets and left the nursery quietly. In the hall he let himself feel the panic, went straight out of the apartment and up the stairs to Kelsey's.

He said, "I need to see you, okay?" and Bibs left them alone in the kitchen. Kelsey began to speak his shock and sympathy over Waltzie. "Scotty just called, I—"

Nick cut him short. "I know. Thanks. Listen—I've got to dump something on you, Kelse . . . and full security, right?"

" 'Course."

"Thanks." He lit a cigarette.

"You want a drink, Nick?"

"No. Just listen. The kid on Post Eight, all right? Two things. One, I read him as a psycho and let him go out there anyhow. Two . . . I'm pretty sure it was my round that killed him. No matter what the technicians say."

After a long, unblinking wait for more, Kelsey broke the silence. "Aw, bullshit, Nick. In the first place—"

"Save it." Nick got up. "I know what you want to say. But I don't want to hear it." At the door he turned back. "You're all I got now, Kelse. I wanted you to *know*, that's all."

Kelsey nodded, still staring at him. "Whatever you say, son. What you want I want."

"Thanks, Kelse." The moment he reached the stairs he knew he felt better. He prayed: *Thank God for Kelsey.* Their friendship, he sensed, had suddenly become something else. Something deeper. Something that would keep them connected long after they went their separate ways.

# 12

The early-morning train to Frankfurt turned the curve and slipped toward the *Bahnhof* precisely on time. Kelsey had driven them and their hand luggage down, and waited with them on the platform. Both he and Nick wore their pearl-gray officers overcoats, with belts cinched tightly and wide collars pulled up. Nick cracked thinly, "Electric! What's the world coming to? Foreign intrigue trains are supposed to come in hissing steam all over the place."

He and Kelsey had vowed to stay in touch forever. He was curious to learn how life in the Service would go, especially with this Vietnam thing starting to look real. Likewise, the Kelse was curious to learn how life would go on the outside. Alter egos, they would keep each other briefed, all the way. It was as good a way of putting it as any, Nick thought, and intended to keep his part of the pact.

After Susan and the children had been settled into the roomy, old-world compartment, Nick followed Kelsey back outside. Both removed their right black leather kid gloves. They shook bare-handed.

"Well, I got no competition now, son."

"Go for it, Kelse. Fucking kill them for me."

Kelsey said, "You're making a big mistake, Nick."

Then it just came out: "I know it."

A whistle shrieked and the train moved.

"Guess it's too late now," Nick said. He spun and leapt up the metal steps into the train.

Joel Kelsey stayed standing on the platform until the train turned out of sight, holding his hand raised in the old cocky, corny thumbs-up sign.

# THREE

# 1

Brian Galgay moved along First Avenue and turned into the apartment house, nodding good morning to the doorman, crossing the lobby to the elevators. He let himself into 11J, then, one step inside, dropped his keys onto the carpet. He had caught the duty agent, Shippers, sneaking a hit from the vodka bottle. Rising with his keys, he saw that the evidence had vanished. From the man's tone in his greeting Brian knew he believed he'd got away with it. He half-sighed inside: it had got so he practically couldn't avoid getting things on people; he didn't even have to try anymore; they seemed to all want to *give* him their secret sins. "You didn't call," he said. "I presume we struck out again?"

"We-el, it depends . . ." Shippers left his place at the wall-mounted two-way mirror that showed the bedroom in the next apartment. He flipped on the film projector's warmup switch.

Brian said, "Wait. If we didn't get him, I don't have to see it. Is it just the General and his wife again?"

"Yessir. Mr. Higgins was on."

Brian mulled it. The agent was dying to see his little film again. Brian wasn't sure he'd let him. He did not feel like seeing it himself, and didn't wish to indulge the lesser agent's prurience. Yet there just might be some detail in their subject's latest night work that Brian could use somehow. Shippers's spoken version was bound to be useless. "Run it," Brian ordered.

This was the twenty-seventh consecutive day of their twenty-four-hour surveillance of the General's bedroom. Brian had personally written the lead off as false, but his instincts wouldn't let him cancel the stakeout yet. He watched the film: as usual, the lovemaking of the General and his wife suggested some noble *combat à deux*: she nearly as aggressive and active and transitive as he all the way to the end, loud, laughing, and enthusiastic; then the General, always overpowering her, winning, taking her finally like a goat. Brian watched it reenact itself on the latest reel. Like some soft-porn home movie produced by amateurs, he thought once again, watching once again.

Later on Shippers said, "Shoot, sir, ah believe we oughta fold our tent and evacuate and leave the gentleman to just go on fuggin' his head off, what harm?"

"Not yet," Brian said.

"Psh, you must be seein' somethin' ah'm not, Major."

Brian didn't answer but thought, No, it's something we're not seeing—and anything, as opposed to nothing, often turns out to be something. "Kill it," he ordered, and turned away. He scanned the suspected General's dossier again, and reconfirmed the decision he had made days earlier: to activate Plan B and approach the Subject, per his instructions, from a new and different angle.

He went to the logbook and wrote his initials and the time, 8:45, in the proper squares. Swooping up his attaché case, he said, "Shippers, I'll check back with you later. I'll let you know where you can reach me," and left.

# 2

*Give us twenty-two minutes,* the radio promised, *and we'll give you the world. New York wants to know, and we know it!*

Shaving in his bathroom mirror, Nick thought, If you're all-news-all-the-time, give us some news. All he really wanted was some weather. The newscast resumed. He rinsed his razor, splashed some cologne on his face and chest, and went to dress in his bedroom. It was the second Thursday in November. Still naked, he opened his shutters and looked through the gritty panes of his French windows. A flash of the Stuttgart he had known passed again across his mind.

It appeared to be gray outside, but his Greenwich Village street was very narrow, and he had to open the windows, lean out over the fire escape, and look up to see enough of it to tell. The sky above the brownstone roofs opposite turned out to be blue, running with swift white clouds. Glints of gold were hitting the windows of the high-rise apartment tower west of him. The radio confirmed it: cool, dry, partly sunny. He took his suede jacket from his closet and switched away from the news to music. Carly Simon was singing the theme from *The Spy Who Loved Me.*

The woman in his bed, Honey Epstein, had sat up and was trying to blink the sleep out of her eyes. Seeing her made him begin to come erect again, and seeing that made Honey grin, lie back, and open her arms. She had a habit that amused him: Whenever he entered her slick little socket, she'd cry "Why Nick Burke!" as if she were astonished by his bold presumptuousness. Another thing he liked about Honey was that, being a free-lance fashion stylist, she had no morning time clock to punch. So with her, unlike most of his other night visitors, there was never any running down to the streets at daybreak in search of taxicabs.

He left her again, and this time got fully dressed for work in jeans and a cashmere turtleneck. He kissed her forehead and said, "Love ya, Hon. Hit the lights and close the shutters before you split, okay? I'm getting out of town tonight."

Honey said, "Sure," and lit a cigarette. Then she added, "Funny thing about you, Nick—even in your own place, your feet are always pointed toward the door, know what I mean?"

He set his leather shoulder bag and canvas overnight bag on the landing floor and closed the door behind him. Assuming he got away with the escape he had planned for tonight, he wouldn't have to open it again until next Monday night. Behind his back now, the apartment ceased to exist for him.

He descended the four flights of narrow stairs as quietly as the ancient wood allowed. It was a different apartment but the same building that he and Susan had found when they had first hit Manhattan.

He paused outside on the stoop now, waiting for the heavy door to click closed behind him. The little street looked pretty to him. Locust trees grew along both curbs, the base of each enclosed by wrought-iron fencing about three feet high. His watch said five before seven. He headed up his little street, away from the river toward Abingdon Square. The mornings were getting chillier; fewer winos and junkies were to be found sleeping on the benches in the small park. He reached Eighth Avenue.

On normal, sane mornings it would be an hour later, and

a small band of other professionals would be heading for work uptown right along with him. But this was the seventeenth consecutive, abnormal, insane morning, and he trudged ahead alone. He felt as if he hadn't slept at all.

He picked a *Times* off the stand outside the small magazine and candy store and went inside to pay. The whole left wall lunged at him: lurid magazine covers flaunting breasts, tongues, ass clefts, and pussy innards, with and without fingers strumming clitorises. He left, heading for the subway.

Riding the still empty E train, his day ahead began to seep into his thoughts: first, the Jingo pitch again—the goddamned blind, manic, early mornings, late nights, and weekends push to solicit the forty-million-dollar Army account. He himself had code-named it "Jingo" for them, off the top of his head, at the start, weeks ago. But he had been unable to have another utterable idea on the subject since, and it was killing him. After the first few days of struggling he had had to give up and admit it to himself, if not to anyone else: he was totally blocked, ice cold, empty—a dangerously vulnerable condition for a writer at his salary level. Kelsey's mysterious proposition, still hanging, only made matters worse.

The train swept into the Fifth and Madison station, and the current Marine Corps recruitment poster slid across his window: three uniformed paper boys stared at him proudly. In the white space around their heads one subway artist had scrawled "killers." Another had printed "fools." A third had altered the headline to read *Jesus is LOOKING FOR A FEW GOOD MEN.*

As usual he found Ira Schenker sitting and drinking coffee alone in the empty, dimly lit reception area on the twelfth floor. The receptionist, when she arrived at 8:30, would turn on all the lights and move the stacks of magazines from her locked desk to the white plastic cubes between the black leather chairs and sofas. He dumped his gear on the desk and opened his coffee container. "Hi, Studs."

Ira's small eyes twinkled even when he wasn't laughing. Rotund and balding, he was a Jewish Santa Claus without the beard. Nick had known Ira since his first year and first agency in the business. He had been a trainee and Ira had been what he still was at this place, a group creative director. Finding Ira ensconced at this place years later had felt very reassuring to him somehow. It let him think that there might be some sense of continuity to life after all, at least some connections that endured. Ira smiled like a baby. "Studs—you remember that, Nick?"

"I remember everything. Hell, I even remember when you were thin."

"Then you're smarter than my mother," Ira chuckled phlegmatically, "because I was never thin."

One of the eight elevator lights flashed on to the bing of a bell.

Lemon-haired, mink-coated Madeline Donavan, overloaded as always with shoulder bags, purses, a briefcase spilling papers, got off and bustled straight to her right, toward the conference room.

Ira said, "Poor Maddy, she needs to be on Jingo like she needs another hole in her head." Madeline was a supervisor in the fashion division, notoriously harassed and overworked. "What's she supposed to do, redesign the uniforms?"

Nick laughed. "Yeah. She told me Sam Katz justified it by saying, 'You got two sons at home, don't you?' And, of course, he said how there are a lot of women going into the military now, too."

At precisely eight, young, dark Sam Katz, creative director of the whole agency, stood waiting at the head of the conference-room table, which glistened like twelve feet of solidified bourbon. Pinned on the cork wall behind him were long, white cards. On them were lettered the half-dozen concept lines surviving out of the hundreds presented. In Nick's estimation only

one of them was a possible contender. The group was still nowhere near having any real ones. Katz proceeded. He went
around the huge table, each person reading off his or her lines
or possible directions, each open to the floor for immediate reaction. Theoretically the group was there to eliminate. Instinctively, nobody killed anything, sagely going for quantity, and
leaving the weeding and, too often, the blending of themes for
Katz and Jerry Resnick, DYT president, to do during the day.

At six o'clock that night, when "Task Force Jingo" recon-
vened, the surviving themes or amalgams would be presented
by Katz and distributed to one or another team for development. They would hand their new stuff in by the end of the
night, at eleven or twelve. What Katz and Resnick liked would
appear on the conference-room wall the following morning,
either joining or replacing the previous selections. Unless the
originator of a selected theme insisted, or unless he, she, or
they were already in his group anyhow, the responsibility for
development fell to Ira Schenker, group creative director in
charge.

When Nick's turn came this morning, he read from his
typed list. As usual he gave a few to Grant to read as his own,
just to intimidate the other art directors. He did this whenever
he was dealing in ersatz ideas in "gang bangs." At nine they
broke. On the elevator going down, Ira said, "Hey, Nick, you
know the *skills* one? Did you write that?"

"No."

"I don't remember hearing it in the mornings, do you?"

"Nope."

"Then where the devil did it come from?"

Nick didn't have to say it to the wise Ira, but did anyhow:
"Either Sammy baby wrote it himself, or Resnick, or they've
got somebody else on it they haven't told you about."

After a long pause, punctuated only by his ever-present
wheeze, Ira only said, "Hell of a way to run a railroad, ain't it,
kid?"

[ 115 ]

"Don't worry," Nick said. "We'll just outlast the bastards, that's all."

Katz and Resnick were forever trying to get Ira to leave. They treated him as old, over the hill, burnt out. Their real reason, Nick knew, was that Ira neither liked them nor feared them, and showed it. He was fifty-eight or so, and could in fact have retired already to his country home in the Hamptons, but "What am I going to do—fish?" He loved the business. He was a salesman with good luck and controllable demons. He reminded Nick of Colonel Big John, and it gave him some modicum of hope to know that if he came to it, he could just go to Ira, confess his paralysis, and not be betrayed.

Nick's office was on the thirty-ninth floor, second from the top. It was next to a corner, three windows wide, and faced east. Just as his Village place disappeared for him when he locked its door, the rest of Manhattan vanished for him when he gazed out his windows from the round wooden table he used as a desk. He knew that the water and land he saw in the pewter morning haze were the East River and Long Island Sound, The Bronx, Queens, much of Brooklyn, and, on the horizon, the first hills of Nassau County. But he preferred to view it all as strange, foreign land: London, Prague, Copenhagen, whatever, all blended and displayed for him—busy, crowded, alive.

These, his daytime windows, held cacti and coleuses on the ledges, maidenhead and piggyback ferns and spider plants hanging from the ceilings. Besides his wildly leafy bulletin board, his only wall decoration was a huge, framed blowup of Steinberg's *New Yorker* cover showing everything between Ninth Avenue and Asia collapsed into skinny horizontals: a bush for Las Vegas, a rock for L.A.

Facing his imaginary city and Europe, he lit a cigarette and scanned his day's calendar. The entry for 11:30 stopped him: "CIC?" His secretary had made the appointment, not catching the caller's name. He figured it was another background investigation of somebody he knew being considered for some kind of government job. He'd been interviewed before in such cases, a TV producer going to work for the Carter campaign, a research analyst involved in some hush-hush think-tank operation.

This time, though, the coincidence of it made him wonder. Did it have anything to do with the Jingo pitch? Could they be running security checks on everyone participating in the solicitation? He doubted it, but, connected or not, it affected him the same way as Kelsey's sudden appearance and the military recruitment pitch itself did: it threatened to turn his mind back to face that part of his past life, and he didn't like it. He stamped the whole thought out with the cigarette in the ashtray and went next door to his partner's office.

Grant was on the phone. Nick studied the rough sketches spread across his drawing board. The two had been a team since Nick came to the agency more than three years before; by now he could automatically decipher the other's every squiggle. Grant hung up and said, "Like?"

"Very classy. The print's gorgeous—they can't go for double-page spreads, though, can they?"

"Nah, but I thought we'd do some for the meeting anyhow, get their juices flowing."

"Okay."

"Television's not there yet, I don't think, huh?"

"No, not yet." That was what was really being said: Had Nick begun speaking of the commercials, Grant would have worried about the print.

So they set to work together, speaking in a kind of code, an esperanto that worked in single words as well as in streams of talk. It panicked many a would-be participant because it often seemed to have nothing whatsoever to do with the subject at hand. This morning it was designer sunglasses and Grant suddenly interjected, *"The President's Analyst,* Nick?"

"Yeah!" The movie came back in a rush. "What about it? Which?"

"I don't know, it just—"

"Yeah! Coburn, Harrington, The Phone Company!"

"TPC! Chopper snatches the whole phone booth!"

"Right," Nick said, "and everyone in the CIA's tweedy. Ivy League. Smoke pipes leaning on the mantel. All FBI agents are four-foot-seven, named Sullivan . . . *Gotta do this fast, Maggie's waiting supper.* Pow, pow, pow! Guns the size of toasters. Ha, they . . ." Nick stopped.

"What, Nick?"

"Nothing. Just something personal, and nuts. Sorry. Go back to the whole lookalike part—maybe the shades could do the opposite, somehow."

"Yeah! Yeah! You got a whole herd of people, absolutely identical. They walk at you out of limbo."

"All foggy . . . or, no—*glary!*"

"*Glary!* Right! Then you—"

"You guys got one minute to get back to the twelfth-floor conference room!" Erica, their secretary, yelled from her desk outside, sounding Grant's buzzer like a fire alarm. "It's with Mr. *Resnick!*"

Walking to the elevators, Nick asked, "What do you think, bud?"

"New direction. Ass-chew. Or pep talk."

"Balls."

"Yeah, just what we need," Granted muttered. "Haven't got enough to do."

Passing reception on twelve, Grant was still thinking sunglasses and said, "I don't think it was Sullivan at all, I think it was Murphy."

"It was Sullivan."

"In the movie, I mean."

"Me too."

"No, it was Murphy, or Rogenstein, or something like that."

"*That* was Max Shulman!"

"Oh, I didn't know what?"

"And they had all their hair, too."

"Faggots."

"And I'm splitting tonight, till Monday," Nick added.

"Yeah, I saw your bag."

"I saw you see it."

"You're a suicide."

"I've got to."

Jerome Resnick, president and chief executive officer of the agency, entered the nearly filled room. Resnick had polar-bear hair and a perpetual tan. Seeing to business, he played a lot of golf and hoisted many a drink on terraces and boats in the sunshine. At the head of the table, he removed his pipe and got right at it. "Ladies and gentlemen, I won't take much of your time. I just want to remind you that the deadline for this project is still mid-December. That's still enough time, but I don't want you to think it's plenty. It's not. I know how hard you've all been trying. And the horrendous hours you've been putting in.

"But we're talking of billings in excess of thirty million dollars, and, brother, I don't think you have to be told that we sure as hell haven't seen any *magic* starting to happen around here!" He paused until the flush had left his cheeks. "Maybe it'll help if I repeat the nuts-and-bolts of this thing for you, as simply and clearly as I can.

"It's basically this: There's no draft, but the inflation and hard times are helping the Army fill its quotas, so far. But that's only quantity. The problem is quality. They're being forced to accept too many goldbrickers and animals. So . . . after Vietnam and Cambodia, how do you get the normal, good, bright kids to think of the military, and particularly the Army, as a viable career or experience option?"

[ 119 ]

Grant went for coffee. Nick returned to thirty-nine, and when he stepped off the elevator, his heart quit. He kept walking toward the man waiting on the couch beyond the receptionist, and the closer he got, the surer he was. The man was flipping the pages of a *People* magazine, and still hadn't looked up. Nick felt his mouth break involuntarily into a wide grin. "Brian!"

Brian Galgay's body seemed to move before his eyes did. He came up, saying, "Mr. Burke?" before his gaze met Nick's face.

"Brian Galgay! Holy shit!" Nick's arms had opened and his hands were slapping Galgay's arms near the padded shoulders of his suit.

Ruffled but smiling, Brian still held his credentials up. "Hi," he said, "long time no see. I wasn't sure you'd remember."

Laughing, Nick grabbed the hand holding the case and looked at the laminated card. "Yup, that's you, all right! Good God, man. Wow! A hundred years! Well, so—come in, come in."

He led the way into his office. Just as he reached his chair, and Brian Galgay had begun to sit in the one opposite, Grant burst in behind them carrying a bag with the coffee. "Oh, Grant," Nick said, "say hello to Brian Galgay—Brian and I were in the goddamn *Army* together! First time we've seen each other since! Far out, huh? Brian, this is Grant Evans."

Grant was overjoyed and shook Brian's hand as if he had been Service buddies with him himself. "Isn't that wonderful! A real pleasure to meet you, Brian. Any friend of Nick's! I'll go get another one. Nickie, I'll get back with you later, after lunch, huh? Brian, I'm pleased to meet you, a real pleasure. I really mean it."

Nick set out the two cups of coffee.

Brian said, "None for me, thanks."

Nick felt immediately resentful: how could Galgay refuse Grant's largesse? He left the lid on it, and poured sugar into his own.

"Big view," Brian said in that same flat voice. Holding his attaché case across his lap, he released its two catches in a single, small explosion.

"Yeah," Nick agreed. "What—are you stationed in New York now?"

"No, but I come here often."

Eyeing the case, Nick said, "Not to pry, but they can't still have you running backgrounds, can they? You don't have to tell me, heh, but you must be a lieutenant colonel or colonel by now, right? Or at least close to it?" He was judging by Kelsey, who had made full colonel the year before. He was dying to learn if the Kelse had somehow indeed passed this old nemesis, as he had so ardently hoped to at the time. If so, it would give him great pleasure. Then it clicked—Galgay was the "visitor" Kelsey had said he'd be sending!

Brian said only: "This isn't a background investigation."

The reunion glee seeped out of Nick. "Oh. What is it, then?"

Brian removed a fairly thick folder, then shut his case but kept holding it, like a lap desk.

"Feel free to use the table, Lieutenant."

"This is fine," Brian Galgay said. "In a sense, I don't know what it is. For me, it's an assignment, to question you about certain people and certain events. I myself have no need to know either why the questions are being asked or by whom, or what the answers might mean. And you can decline to be interviewed, of course."

Nick sipped his coffee warily. He remembered Kelsey's warning not to tell even the "visitor" of their meeting at the Hilton. "Well, is it personal, or what, Brian? I can't very well refuse anything until I—"

"The brunt seems to cover your years on active duty."

"Do you mean Germany? Do *they* mean Germany? Hell, you were there the same time, Brian, you probably know a lot more than I do." A faint memory flickered, of Galgay and a tunnel and something about a girl.

"They aren't asking me," Brian said. "But anyhow, ninety percent of the references in here mean absolutely nothing to me. We hardly traveled in the same circles. I mean," he said, "you were there a lot longer after I left."

"Um, Berlin." Nick caught a light flare briefly in Brian's otherwise blank blue eyes. He drank more coffee and lit a cigarette. "Well, okay, then, I guess—shoot. My heart is an open book."

Brian opened the folder and looked at the first entry on the top page. He said, "All right, it seems that when the Fourth Armored Division participated in Operation Snowsword war games, you were given a special assignment by the G-two to supervise—"

"Whoa!" Nick coughed. "Jesus, wait a sec here—what am I getting myself into? I take it this isn't going to be true-or-false. Listen, Brian, I got a job to do here. Is that whole stack for me?"

"Yes. Maybe we can at least get started. It's your lunchtime, isn't it? Then we can set up another—"

"Oh, Christ, not today, man," Nick protested. "No way. Jesus, you have no idea what madness you've walked into. Look. Here's my situation—" He found himself leaning forward, conspiratorially. "Since Labor Day I'm supposed to be on a four-day week around here. I took an outrageous pay cut to get it. Fridays I split. Okay, but no sooner do I get this little fiddle going for myself, than the fucking roof caves in here!

"We're coming in at dawn and going till midnight, and we've worked every single weekend for the past three weeks. I mean, everything you've probably heard about this business is true. It's a bitch, and I do it. Only now it's starting to jeopardize my personal gig, see? And I don't want that to happen. I agreed . . . it was part of my deal that I'd go full time for crises, except

[ 122 ]

I never thought there'd be one this soon. So I'm going AWOL tonight—it's most likely my last chance to get away with it. And to pull it off, I've gotta really scramble my ass off today. I just don't have any time, Brian."

Brian Galgay's face seemed to have turned to marble. "When is the earliest you can make some?"

Nick looked at the stone face and thought, Christ, you're the same old Galgay, all right. He sat back and tried to speak as if the last three minutes hadn't happened. "Say five thirty Monday? There's usually a dead hour or so in there before the night shift gets going."

Returning the folder to his case, Brian closed the catches in double shots. "That's four whole days away. Are you sure you can't spare us some time before that?"

"Look, I'll be more than glad to tell you whatever I can. But hell, we're dealing with ancient history now anyhow, right? I mean, Christ, anything that's been sitting there this long can't be that red hot, can it?"

"I can't say what's been sitting or not," Brian said. "I do know there's a lot of material to be covered, I've got a suspense date on it, and the sooner we start the sooner we finish. I've got a job to do too," he added with a smile.

Nick gave in. "Okay," he said, "tell you what—do you mind working weekends?"

"Not at all."

So Nick set a time and place for them to meet in Derby that Friday night.

# 3

By five thirty Nick was finishing up his second-last chore of the day: he was deep inside a building on Fifth Avenue, watching, over and over, on a large screen, a thirty-second commercial to which he was trying to add sound effects.

In silence he and the sound man leaned forward and listened together to an evenly spaced succession of door slams: aluminum screen door with air valve whoosh . . . immense iron castle door . . . average house front door, solid . . . Finally Nick caught his tired mind being mesmerized and said, "Jesus, is this weird! Two grown men, sitting here like . . ."

The sound man hit the rewind. Nick knew that when voices speaking English were played backward they sounded like Russian, but these door slams now gave out a sound unlike any he had ever heard before, prompting him to say, "Okay, I got one for you, Bob—why don't doors slamming, played backwards, sound like doors opening?"

Bobby said, "For the same reason doors opening, played backwards, don't sound like doors closing . . . stupid."

"Oh. See? If you don't ask, you don't learn."

"Where are you going?"

"Out of my mind," Nick said. "Just pick one, Bobby."

Luckily, his next stop was between the sound studio and where he garaged his car. It was what market research people called a focus group interview and it was scheduled to run from six to eight—he intended to stay no later than seven.

Outside, it was rush hour on the streets and sidewalks. Long cool shadows fell where they were supposed to, and the spires of St. Patrick's were amber with the setting sun. There were also great slabs of greenish light in odd places, thrown off by the glass facades of new skyscrapers, so it seemed that here and there the sun was going down in the east. Walking fast, he thought November should always be like this in New York. He turned west onto Forty-fourth, crossed at the Algonquin Hotel, then turned left, down Sixth to the address.

He entered the emptying building and found the door on the seventh floor. A receptionist held back the heavy curtain to let him step into the hushed observation room. Here, agency people sat in the semidark, around three sides of a long table littered with a deli-catered, green and red cellophane supper of sandwiches, coleslaw, Tabs, Pepsis, beer, and coffee. A serve-yourself bar was set up on a side table.

Eating and drinking, the agency people were watching, through a wide, rectangular two-way mirror-window before them, another bunch of people sitting around another large table, on the other side of the glass, in the other, brightly lighted room. Tonight the people being observed were being paid to speak their minds on liquor. Computer-selected for their various age and income brackets, they had been informed that they would be videotaped and sound-recorded. But they had not been told that they would also be observed by other people, beyond the looking glass. Nick knew that this omission was not meant to deceive, but only to prevent the participants from either clamming up or showing off. Still, he hated it, just as he hated his even being there.

He whispered hello and leaned against a wall. He noticed that Jackson, a management supervisor perpetually dressed in double-knit polyester and known as Unctuous Al, was the only other male on this side of the glass. The rest were "research gals." Nick would rather have studied them, but forced his attention upon the action starting in the room beyond the mirror.

Following the moderator's instructions, the group of inter-

[ 125 ]

viewees was introducing itself one by one, with consumption preferences.

The first said, "Hi, I'm Norman, and I'm a Scotch and vodka man. Scotch in winter, vodka in warm weather."

"I'm Irene," the next said, "Seven and Seven, or rye and ginger."

"Fred's the name, and martini's the game."

"Hello, I'm Joan, and I'm a screwdriver drinker."

Nick didn't hear the next one, or any of the others. He decided he couldn't take another minute of it, and made for the door.

Unctuous Al began to rise out of his chair.

Nick told him, "Send me the verbatims." At the door he paused long enough to light a cigarette, purposely not shielding the light's flame, hoping one of the people on the other side might spot it and catch on.

He still had his red Triumph. After Susan finally took the kids and left him for good, he'd drained it and stored it on blocks in a friend's garage. He knew if he'd left it there it would be a collector's item someday, but when he bought the Derby house a year ago, the car seemed to fit his fresh new dream too perfectly not to put it back on the road.

The garage jockey punched it out of the elevator for him, and he headed for the tunnel. He had installed a tape deck and speakers that turned it into a moving music capsule. He inserted a cassette and sang along with the Stones, "You can't always get what you want . . ."

Heading for Derby, Nick was always going north, not from Manhattan but from his imaginary European city. North nearly three hours through the night, speeding for the sea, his North Sea, where he had a house and what he chose to consider, if not his "real" life, then his new, primary life. After "Let It Bleed," he played the Beatles' "Let It Be," and wondered once again, Which album had come first? Which was point, which counterpoint? For himself, he was tempted to make the "Bleed" sing of his city life, and the "Be" his life in Derby, but it felt too neat to be true.

His weekly night runs to Derby contained definite, recurring checkpoints for him, both mental and physical. The first came about an hour out of the City: his Oberammergau memory. He still wasn't sure what triggered it, whether the opening and leveling of the land into fields and woods after all the factories or houses, or perhaps just the sudden darkening of the night road. Whatever it was, it never failed to happen. It would interrupt all broadcasts streaming through his brain, and whisk him back nearly twenty years in time, to the night he and Kelsey had sped through the strange German night, south from Munich. In particular, he would always recall Susan's reaction to the long-haired boys and men preparing for the Passion Play, and he'd laugh.

One of the few regrets he ever had over splitting with Susan was not being around to see how she reacted to the hippies later in the sixties. In her Detroit suburb, did she ever get to see *Hair*, and if she did, did she think of him? Not likely, he supposed, either one. He gunned the Triumph up to sixty-five and rolled down the window to let the cold, fumey air rush over his head. He had begun again to hear little kids making engine sounds from the rear seat behind him. The thought of losing them still pained him as fiercely as when it had happened.

When they had first arrived in New York, he had tried to get credits for all the teaching hours he had accrued overseas, only to learn that they weren't acceptable. If he wished to teach, he'd have to attend some school of education for a year. Susan, still in shock and furious over his abrupt resignation, had wailed, "Anyhow—if you think I'm going to try to scrimp along on a teacher's stupid pay, you're crazy." Then Ira Schenker hired him, but he lost her anyhow.

[ 127 ]

After a year he even promised to try to get back into the Service. He meant it and she knew it. But, "It's too late, Nick," she said. "They're all way ahead of you now."

"So what? I'll be an older captain than the rest, that's all. Christ, I'm still only twenty-six."

"Yes, and I know you, you'll put in for Vietnam the first chance you get! And what am I supposed to do for thirteen months alone, twiddle my thumbs?"

"How about holding your breath?" he'd cracked, starting one of their last major quarrels before the end. The inevitable break came soon after, when she announced that it was time to quit the Village apartment for a house in New Jersey or Westchester. Nick remembered Waltzie Cooper's dour warnings about suburbs and refused to even consider it. Susan had been forever taking the kids "home" to visit her mother. When she went this time, she bought one-way tickets. Two seconds after the divorce became final, he received an after-the-fact announcement of her remarriage, to the man he still thought of as Melonhead. In his thoughts Nick also called his children's new "father" Dagwood of Detroit, and Major Poople of General Motors.

By now even he had to admit that the longtime estrangement that existed between him and his kids was his own fault. In the beginning Susan and Melonhead had opened their house to him for visits. Every time he had shown up arrogantly juiced. He knew he was a lousy drinker, and didn't even like the stuff, but somehow found himself unable to pull it off without taking several stiff hits of something first. Susan had radiated outrage, but Melonhead always remained nauseatingly pleasant, understanding, and scared stiff. Nick still loathed him for it. After a half-dozen disastrous attempts, he had finally withdrawn and kept his distance, metamorphosing for them not into a cockroach, but into a check in the mail.

Once, somewhere down the years, the prospering, up-and-coming Melonhead landed what Nick thought of as a colonel's slot in his corporation, and phoned him in New York to clubily declare ". . . so you're off the hook, guy, really. Those payments must be keeping you strapped."

"If it's all the same to you," Nick said, "I'll keep sending my share."

"But it's not all the same to me."

"You want me dead. I can't give you that."

"We'll stop cashing the checks."

"The money's not yours or Susan's to cash—open trust accounts for them."

"Why don't you do that, there?"

"Listen, Dagwood, do you want to wake up some morning and find them gone?"

"My God, are you threatening me, sir?"

"Apparently. You made the call." That had been the closest the nerd had ever come to making an emotional stand, but for Nick it was too little too late. He thereafter countersank the nail with a letter informing Melonhead of his intention to bear the full expense of the kids' college educations, when the time came, and if they chose to go. He had received no acknowledgment in return; nor any further protest, either. There came times later, of course, particularly when work situations grew oppressive, when he'd had to regret his earlier bravado.

The cold wind snapped him to, and he rolled up the window, realizing he'd sped past several of his usual checkpoints, absorbed by his thoughts. His next major one now was his favorite anyhow, his bridge, some two and a half hours out. Strangers didn't notice it even in daylight, but he knew that those certain bumps in the highway were a bridge over a canal that separated his sea place from the rest of mainland America, Steinberg fashion.

Beyond the secret bridge he'd leave the highway for the warm, narrow, dark winding country roads that the Triumph could traverse practically by itself. The old milkhorse would take control, and he could finally begin to relax and feel safe. He held the high speed steady, making for his bridge. Spotting the orange November moon, he took it as a reassuring omen. The risk he was running was worth it. If he had let them hold him locked in that mad city for yet another weekend, he might have gone under.

Over the bridge, with his directional signal clicking and its light blinking at him from the dash, the Triumph's wheel turned, and Derby's soft road opened and took him in.

He kept his wine and liquor in a rack set upon his kitchen counter. He slid the bottles of gin and vermouth out of their slots and made himself his traditional, necessary-for-decompression Thursday-night martini. Sipping it, he prowled the downstairs of his house, trying to calm down.

What in the 1870s had been some farming-and-fishing family's dining room, parlor, and porch, Nick had opened up into one large living room, ending in a glassed-in, heated sun porch. There, he watered his plants. He could see through the hundred tiny panes of glass that, rising, the moon had drained from orange to white. The bay waters beyond the dunes rippled with silver, like strings of floating mercury.

He put his finger to one windowpane, and knew he was home.

# 4

Deborah Ormay's phone rang before seven that Friday morning. She ran naked from the bathroom, carrying the jar of moisturizer in her slick hands. Morning light was breaking through the tortoise bamboo blinds of her east windows. It was like stepping into a huge page of sheet music, she thought, lined in sunshine. Her long, tawny legs glistened; the rest of her, still dry, only brightened. Enrico sat flipping pages of an *Elle* magazine on the sofa. He said, "I'll get it."

"You look it. Hello?" It was a French phone. The porcelain grip slid in her palm. "Oh, goddamn them. All right, Monday then."

"They canceled the booking!" Enrico said.

"Right." She walked back out of the light.

"Did you tell them I am here with you?"

"Yup." She closed the bathroom door behind her. Enrico was booked on the same job, to do her hair and makeup. A pal, he had come over before six and prepared her black, thick hair so it could be styled quickly later, at the photographer's studio.

Enrico wasn't doing him or Saks Fifth Avenue any favors. Deborah was one of his two favorite models and he took personal pride in how she looked in magazines, on television, or in this case in the lingerie mailing piece. He was, he felt, doing Deborah the favor, though he would never so much as hint at it to her. She was twenty-eight. In the business this was imminent to becoming long in the tooth.

The phone rang again. This time he answered it on the first ring. It was his service, informing him of the job's postponement. He called, "Deborah? I thought you said you told them I was here!"

"You *heard* me on the phone! For Christ's *sake*, Rico!"

Hurt, he let out a sibilant *tch!* and put his short, leather bombardier's jacket on over his collarless shirt and silk indoor scarf. "*Ciao!*"

"Oh, stay, Rico. I'm sorry." Realizing she had balmed her legs a second time, she also realized it was unnecessary to do them or anything else at all now, and that she was being cranky.

"We'll be paid anyway, darling," Enrico sang, "you should be glad! It's a long weekend! A gift!"

"I know. But they piss me off." She'd spent all yesterday at Elizabeth Arden's, having the whole wax number, the facial mask, pedicure, manicure, massage. She'd been up to *work* today, damn it, and felt let down. No, she felt put down. She knew it was senseless, but couldn't help it; never could.

"Want to hang out?" Enrico called. "Get ripped and go someplace or something?"

"No." She slumped. "I don't know. I think I'll go back to bed."

"Anyone *I* know?"

"I take it back, Rico. Go away."

"Okay. *Ciao!*" He sang it cheerily this time. "I know where to find *lots* to do!"

"Pig!"

"*Merci!* Same time Monday, then?"

"All right, Rico. Thank you." When she heard the outside door slam, she dropped her leg down off the tub and put the jar back onto the shelf over the sink. She rested the palms of her hands on either side of the enamel basin and stared at her face and bare shoulders in the mirror, idly wondering, Were gays really more highly sexed than straights? If so, wouldn't it be interesting to turn one around someday. No, he'd probably leave the oversexedness behind him with the rest, on the other side. Not that you could, anyhow, she reminded herself. She'd known enough girls and women who'd tried, God knows. Poor babies. Jerks.

She turned and regarded herself in the full-length mirror. What the hell, she thought, and retrieved the moisturizer. Then, watching herself, she smoothed it creamily into the velvety skin of her hips, belly, shoulders, arms, neck, saving her breasts for last. She remembered when they had been considered too full for fashion and she'd had to bind them. She and they were lucky that the soft, feminine, nipply look had come back in when it did.

She moisturized them now, in the mirror, nipples coming promptly taut. They had always intrigued her by not being dark; pink, they seemed to belong to some blond Swede. Her father's side again, she guessed, the Irish, them and her eyes. Exotically, and profitably enough for her, her eyes were nearly lilac. The lilac eyes had been what got her her first major break years ago, the Nefertiti cover and feature in *Vogue*, over the dark-eyed full Egyptian or Egyptian-looking models.

When the sweet tingling began, she stopped. She knew what she was doing and what it would lead to; she'd be back into the bed in a minute, alone again with herself and the now boring old fantasies. Then she'd sleep sleep that she didn't need and when she woke she'd be sweating clammily, depressed and morbid.

Something white broke her stare. Her gaze shot to her unwaxed, self-trimmed dark venus; two slender strings of unabsorbed moisturing cream hung in her hair. She walked closer to the glass. It looked like something in a pornographic magazine. Depressed, she whisked it clean with a towel and fled the bathroom for the kitchen, wondering, Why do they always come on the outside anyway, into the hair, onto the face? To prove something real had been happening, or what? She turned the radio on to music and poured a cup of coffee, trying to change her mood, trying to move her mind onto something cheerier, like nothing.

Her belly squeaked and growled. Her parakeet, Joe, didn't notice. When her cat, Joan, had been alive, she used to give

[ 133 ]

her such a condescending look whenever she heard Deborah's stomach roll. She sorely missed that cat, but wouldn't replace her; she had to leave her apartment for too long, too often. The bird could stay alone without harm indefinitely, it seemed, fed by the cleaning woman.

She hadn't eaten anything but ice cream since last Sunday. She took a frozen waffle from the freezer and dropped it into the toaster. There was another way she could get through this abortive day: she could eat her head off. Maybe fudge, like Glenda Jackson did in *Sunday, Bloody Sunday*. And maybe she'd cry and weep big tears while she gorged herself, too. The waffle popped and she yelled aloud, "I have to get out of here!"

She could dress up and go shopping, or dress down and go wandering the streets. Nobody came to mind whom she felt like meeting for lunch or drinks or anything. She was booked full for the next two weeks, so there was no point in seeing if her agency had any calls to send her on. Or maybe she'd just flee to someplace near the beach. That was bound to be better than staying here. The slats of light reached deeper into her living room and she glistened all over.

# 5

Brian Galgay was dialing his home in Maryland. Mr. Higgins had come on to replace Shippers as Friday duty agent on the stakeout. Spooning yogurt into his mouth, Higgins stood near the looking glass, watching the General's wife sleep. The General had been up at six, jogged his mile along the river, put on his greens, and gone to his duties. The camera stood quiet and blind; the tape recorder still and deaf. The heavy drapes were pulled to keep out the bright daylight. "Hello," Brian said.

His wife had answered on the second ring. He asked to speak to the kid.

Evelyn said, "He's in the tub."

"Oh, he's that much better, is he?"

Evelyn said, "I think so. His temperature's almost back to normal."

Brian complained: "Well, I know Weber's supposed to be the best, but dammit, it seems he just always writes out penicillin or some kind of antibiotic for anything! And all they do is take away the symptoms, you know, they don't cure! Christ, he's only six, you know, and kids can build up immunities, so if something hits later on, they . . ."

She let Brian finish, then began saying calm, unworried, reassuring sentences in reply.

He interrupted, speaking as flatly as he could. "You in the den, are you, Ev? Oh. No, I thought I could hear the television, that's all."

She was in the hall outside the bathroom, she said.

Which she probably was: no matter what she thought of him by now, Brian was pretty sure she would never endanger her own child. He had to admit that this time he was probably only imagining the other man's presence in the house.

[ 135 ]

To end it he said, "Uh, listen, dear, I'm not alone, you know?" He couldn't bear to endure the helplessness any longer. "You just keep doing what you think's best, and . . . I'm really sorry about this weekend. You know. But not too much longer now, I hope. Yes, I am kind of tired, I guess. Okay, then, you too."

Brian hung up, carried his suitcase into the agents' bedroom, and shut the door. He changed his white shirt for a blue polo jersey, his suit pants for cuffed khakis, his suit jacket for a tan MacGregor windbreaker, his black dress shoes for white, low sneakers.

He gave Higgins the number of the Derby Inn, then paused at the phone, considering whether to call Evelyn back. The damned penicillin had stuck in his mind. Those labels always warned of causing drowsiness. The kid could be in deep sleep from it all day. She could be in the kitchen with her lover right now, in the living room, on the Castro in the den, anywhere she damn well felt like.

"Enjoy your trip, Major," Higgins said.

Without answering or even looking, Brian left. This was a *case*, he had wanted to say. This was *duty*. How dare you imply I am somehow getting anything for myself out of it!

# 6

At the Derby Inn, Deborah Ormay followed Leola Gates's stick-thin legs up the steep, narrow staircase. The room was small, had a slanted ceiling, gabled windows, wallpaper ablossom with faded roses, and a delicate, high four-poster bed. Leola stooped and gave the radiator valve a few turns. Heat came hissing. "If it don't do the trick, dearie, tell me and I'll come bleed it again."

Deborah said okay. Her room looked down on Elm Street, which seemed to be the main thoroughfare. "Tell me, do you say it, 'Derby' or 'Darby'?" Enrico had recommended the town to her; his pronunciation was no clue at all.

"It's got an *e* in it, don't it?"

"All right. I know you rent bikes—would you have a map of the town?"

"Fifty cents at the desk."

Where I bet you hawk Maxwell House coffee, Deborah thought, waiting for the old bat to leave. When she did, Deborah closed her door, softly but pointedly, then opened her windows wide. The screens were still up, so she couldn't lean out. A classic, soaring-steepled old church stood white against the blue sky directly across the street. The sight of it and the sudden wash of salt air against her face made her want to go out and find the sea at once.

On the rented bike Deborah flew smoothly down the long, pretty street. She had changed her skirt and blouse for jeans and a sweat shirt, tied her hair back with a bright yellow scarf, and put on her new burgundy suede hooded parka. The collar-less dog, a golden retriever, picked her up the minute she reached the beach. Within ten minutes her arm was stinging from throwing the stick into the cold, creamy surf for him. She walked for at least two miles along the swirling tide line. By the time she turned back, both her parka pockets jingled with collected sea glass, mostly whites and greens, but a few browns as well, and even one blue: Phillips Milk of Magnesia, she guessed. She'd put them in alcohol in a small clear apothecary jar and set them on the sill of her bedroom window, where the sun would shine through them and remind her of this gleaming, healing afternoon on this soul-clearing, windy ocean beach.

Halfway back to the parking lot lookout where she had left the bike, she again picked up the soaking slat from a lobster trap and sent it seaward with all her might, the dog's leap going nearly as high as he plunged in after it. She was glad to see a double row of waves ready to break between it and him, thinking, You'll have to work for that one, Bozo! She crossed the beach then, first the damp sand and then the dry, and knee-climbed into the compass grass atop the front, flat dunes, heading for the deep V-scoop she had spotted in the higher dunes farther inland. The one house she could see back in the scrubby woods wore wooden blinders for the winter, but still she stepped into the shady side to squat. The sudden lack of breeze felt warm, then chilly.

Pulling up her jeans, she decided, That was the best pee I ever had, and kicked sand over her little spot of mud. She looked up to see the real dog, slat in teeth, wagging approval from the grass. She laughed, "Oh, hold your horses, Swifty!" She sat in the sun on the other wall of the deep dune, still out of the wind and wholly warm. She worked her tiny vial up from beneath her cache of sea glass. The little silver spoon was attached to the cap by an inch of chain. She unscrewed the cap, dipped the spoon into the vial, shut her left nostril with a finger and snorted the cocaine briskly up the right, then reversed the procedure. Some spilled but she didn't care. The taste in her throat always reminded her of some pleasant medicine given her when she was a child. She leaned all the way back and the dog lay down, too.

To prevent squinting into the camera, photographers had her stare into the sun with her lids closed like this, then look away; her eyes, seeing darkness, would stay wide open. It felt good, she decided, to be in the sun without being on a job.

The dog began to whine. She sat up. "All right, all right, I'm coming, you!" She ran long-legged and full out after the dog, leaping off the dune to the beach, then across it to the surf, swooping up the slat and hurling it before she stopped.

She had jogged to within sight of the parking lot lookout before he caught up with her again. She threw it one more time for him, then headed for the bike. As before, a few men in Scouts and Jeeps and Cherokees sat peering over steering wheels at the sea, fishing reels ready on their roof racks. None even gave a glance in her direction until the dog came skidding up at her heels. "That's all, boy," she said, patting his wet head. "No more, you stay here, now, that's a good guy." He galloped beside her wheels halfway across the big, empty parking lot, then turned back to the sea without a good-bye.

Where the sky dropped down behind the brambly tree-tops, a fierce red seemed to be rising up like vast, wide, flame-less fire. Was it really so beautiful, she wondered, or merely the cocaine? She shifted the gear lever and pedaled harder, dropping her hands to the lower grips and bending forward over the handlebar, racing now, the wind behind her, vowing to let herself feel cleanly happy.

# 7

Leola Gates told Brian, "Just up these stairs. You'll have to carry your bags yourself, no help off-season, you know. Dining room's in the cellar, breakfast eight to ten, no lunch, supper six to eleven but the bar and the fireplace keep goin' past that, tonight and Saturdays."

As she began to bleed the radiator, he said, "There's no phone in here?"

"Nope. Pay phone's downstairs in the vestibule. You passed it coming in."

"That doesn't allow for much privacy."

"Derby's full of phones, mister."

He left the Derby Inn and drove the gray motor-pool Plymouth into the town. He spotted a row of phone booths on the sidewalk in front of the VFW hall, and pulled over. First he called Leola—no, she said, there had been no calls for him. Then he dialed the stakeout, and Mr. Higgins reported, "Nothing much, sir, except the lady of the house, she's been on the phone, she's heading for her sister's in Albany for the weekend. Sounds like she means she's going by her lonesome, but that's not been confirmed as yet."

"Why didn't you notify me of that?"

"Just came about now, sir! And I was waiting to see, if the

subject's going to accompany, did you want us to take the show on the road or—"

"No," Brian said. "We'll stay stationary, in either event." He hung up, but stayed inside the booth, gazing out through the glass panels. The big, bare trees of the town looked like so many pen-and-ink drawings against the horizon, outcroppings of delicate black lacework, first against a sky of pale pink, but suddenly, as he watched, of vivid, raspberry red. The sun was beginning to set. Jet streams drew long, white finger-streaks across the sky. He focused his gaze on them and tried to calm his mind. He felt the dull pain of personal dread rising in his stomach, and was both surprised and relieved to find himself admitting, for once, the truth—he did not want to go home to Maryland. He loathed the prospect of seeing Evelyn in person. Contradictorily, he felt duty-bound to call her. He knew that if he went and saw her physically, he would see, too, the deceit and infidelity in her eyes; then he might succumb to his rage and try to beat a confession out of her, hurt her, and so lose her for certain and for good. The phone was so much safer. He dialed. When she answered, he said, "Evelyn? Hi."

"Hi! Hold on, I have something boiling on the stove."

He waited. It was 5:15. He could believe that she was indeed in their kitchen cooking supper, alone with the boy, unless he was still bedridden.

"So—you okay, Brian? Is it going all right for you?"

"Yeah, SOP. For a minute it looked like I might be able to get away after all, but now it's turned around again."

"Oh, too bad."

"How's Tim?"

"Almost good as new. I'll probably let him go back to school Monday."

"Great."

"Let me get him, he's dying to talk with you."

Brian dropped two more quarters in.

"Daddy?"

"Yeah! Hi, Tim, are you—?"

"You coming home now, Dad?"

"Uh, no, not yet, Tim, I'm—"

"You gotta work more again? For the country, Dad?"

"That's right, Tim, but I'll be home real soon, the minute I'm finished." The boy couldn't quite yet put it together how Brian could be in the Army but go off all the time dressed like "real" fathers. It helped somewhat that a few other military men lived in the neighborhood and went to work, mostly at the Pentagon, also in civilian clothes. It was policy that Washington not appear a city of uniforms. What didn't help was that the others could reveal their true ranks, while Brian couldn't. At a loss for what to say to the kid, he said, "You watching Tom and Jerry, are you?"

"No."

"Is it funny?"

"What?"

"Your mother says you're all better, huh?"

"Dad?"

"Yeah?"

"Uh . . . I had a real bad cold, Dad."

"I know. I wanted to talk to you last time but you were having a bath." He nearly added, "Were you?"

"Oh. Here's Mum. Bye, Dad."

"See you, Tim . . . Evelyn? Well, okay, then, guess I'd better get back to it. Just wanted to—"

"All right, then, And we'll be fine, Brian. Don't worry so much."

# 8

At seven Deborah went downstairs to find a man who looked to be Leola's twin brother manning a whirring blender behind the inn's cellar bar. He didn't seem to notice her come down the spiral stairs, nor did the man, apparently another guest, who was sitting stiffly in a low chair and staring into the small fire burning in the large, stone fireplace.

"Ahem."

Brian looked up awkwardly, suspending his glass of beer in midair. He forced a smile. "Hello."

"Hello. Am I intruding? These seem to be the only seats in—"

"Not at all. Please sit down."

She turned to the barman. "Could I have a Perrier, please? With vodka on the side?" She dropped her handbag on the table and sat. "My name's Deborah Ormay. Beautiful town, isn't it? I had a marvelous afternoon."

"Great. My name is Brian Galgay."

"How was your afternoon, Brian?"

He was too weary to lie. "Lousy, mostly."

She was too pleased to be brought down by a stranger's melancholy. She appraised him and almost said, "Unbutton two more buttons on your shirt and let your collar fall outside your jacket, would you?" She looked him over again: he wasn't all that unattractive. In fact he'd make a pretty fair catch for someone—if this were 1954 and Dayton, Ohio. She dropped it.

Be kind and decent, she told herself, having decided she had had enough solitude for one day and was going to pick him up. At least he might be a relief from the platinum-thatched stockbrokers, the internists, the gays, the married cheaters, the rock stars. She'd try not to be too snotty. "What's your line of work, Brian?"

"Government," he said. "Washington. I'm in the Army, actually."

"I grew up in the Service," she said. "Classic Army brat."

"How was that?"

"I don't know. Compared to what? Got to live in a lot of different places, learned how to make friends fast, and forget them fast."

"It must have been interesting."

"Oh, for sure," muttering the latest Californian inanity, which she winced to hear, especially from her own lips. One afternoon out of Manhattan, and she was falling to pieces.

"Yes, the Service can be great, if you pull the right duty."

"You been around a lot, Brian?"

"No, not really."

She waited, but that was apparently all that was coming. "Where you from, Brian, originally?"

"St. Louis," he said, pronouncing the s, then going silent again.

So much for chitchat, she thought. Amused and resigned, she recrossed her legs, lit a cigarette, and gazed at the fire. Absently she began whistling the tune of "Songs Sung Blue."

Brian swallowed dryly, suddenly seeing not Deborah but Anna again. In that secret Anna tunnel of his mind. Anna: so young and wild and so often . . . whistling. This remarkably good-looking stranger across from him was the first woman he'd

[ 144 ]

heard or seen whistle in a very long time. Plenty of men were whistlers, but none of them ever reminded him of his beloved, lost Anna.

He stole a swift glance at Deborah. There was nothing similar physically, besides the breasts. Anna had been blond. It was only the whistling. Watching the fire, he let himself believe for a moment that it was Anna there with him, that life had happened differently. But then the whistling stopped, and he looked and saw again that it was only this dark woman, dragging on her cigarette. She blew smoke out and resumed the soft, sweet fluting. It began to hurt, but Brian couldn't bring himself to ask her to stop.

Her drinks were delivered. She took a swallow of vodka and chased it with Perrier. Out the side of her eye she caught him looking confusedly at her. She felt the impulse and acted on it: "Olé!" she sang, drank off the vodka, and tossed the empty glass into the fireplace. It broke against the bricks behind the fire.

Brian's eyes and mouth came open. "What in the hell're you . . . ?"

The barman came charging.

She halted him with a hand. "Go get a broom and dustpan, I'll sweep it up! And pay for it, too."

"I don't care, we don't allow no—"

"Well, you do now. It's an old custom for newlyweds." She smiled, childlike. "We're Russians, and we just got married today."

"You don't say! Well! Congratulations!"

"Thank you."

"And to you, too, sir!"

Brian sat mute and beet-faced.

"Well, least I can do is sweep it up for ya—don't do it more than the once, do ya?"

"No, just the once," Deborah said.

*"You're a madwoman!"* Brian said, feeling scandalized, and, at the same time, utterly charmed.

"Thank you," lilac eyes twinkling.

His eyes fell upon her naked throat, just where it turned to shoulder skin and ran hiding beneath the brown-flowered silk of her translucent blouse. He suddenly wanted, badly, to place his mouth there and suck her, softly. Sexed by her, he felt ashamed, excited, and afraid.

She read it all in his eyes and considered moving her neck across the space between them and up to his mouth. Instead she asked him seriously, "Can you tell me any of it, Brian?"

"What?"

"Are you in trouble? On the run?"

"No, no, not at all."

"You look like you are."

Something spinelike in him seemed to bend, and go soft. "Not really," he told her, looking away at the fire. "I . . . I'm not in trouble, but . . . well, I guess I'm having some troubles. If there's any difference."

"Fuck it."

"Excuse me?"

"Screw it. Open your hand and let it fly away. At least for a while. If it's serious and bad, you can be sure it'll be there waiting for you in the morning, or whenever."

He sighed. "That's easier said than—"

"Oh, bullshit. Try it."

"Could I have a cigarette?"

She lifted her Benson & Hedges from the table and handed them to him.

"First one I've had in seven months," he said.

"What I'm saying isn't meant to be corrupting, you know."

"No?"

"No. It's selfish of me, really. I don't feel up to catching anybody else's blues tonight."

"And I'm boring."

"You've got me interested," she flirted, batting her lashes.

"I'm not boring?"

"I didn't say that," she smiled. "I'm hungry. Can we get out of here?"

He gawked at her. Something in him longed to just get up and leave with her, to be as natural, swift, and direct as she was. But his years as an agent reawakened his guard. Could she be trying to set him up? He couldn't tell; he had heard and read about it, but it had never happened to him personally. He hid behind his immediate realities: "I have to meet somebody for dinner in a little while," he said.

"Here?"

"No, in the town."

"A woman? Your wife?"

"No. A man. It's a business meeting."

She shrugged and smiled. "Okay, Brian, I know when I'm beat. Some other time, maybe. Do you know this burg, by the way? Are there any decent restaurants *not* in this inn?"

"I don't know, really, but the man I'm seeing, he lives here, and he told me that the place we're going is the only one, off-season."

"Then do you mind if I follow you there, at least?"

His heart was dancing. His instincts had already assured him that she was safe. He feared that she'd find somebody else. *Open your hand and let it fly away.* "How about this?" he asked her. "Come with me. You can have a drink or something while I deal with this guy, then we can have dinner, all right? It shouldn't take me very long at all." He'd make sure it didn't. He knew he needed his interview with Burke less than he needed being with her.

Following her up the stairs, Brian tried to keep his eyes off her legs but couldn't. He was sure she'd noticed his wedding band. He was also sure that if he tried to mention it, her reply would scald. Her scent flooded his head and diluted the pain there. But almost in the same moment he felt a new pain blossom somewhere in his chest, some black, poisonous thing opening like a vein or an orchid and saying: *Evelyn.* How can you let yourself feel this for this strange woman, and still feel wounded by Evelyn? The answer came in Deborah's voice: *Let the Evelyn pains go too. Stop hating her. Trust her.* It was then that he learned that his jealousy tasted too sweet to quit—which only made him hate himself all the more.

In the foyer he opened the door for her. She stepped through and he followed her into the keen night sea air. Crossing the sidewalk to the car, he had the urge to put his arm around her shoulders. *She's beautiful and fun and good and I am here with her now, and there is no other time but now, and I have nothing else to think about beyond being with her.*

He saw only darkness and houselights to the right, so he made a U-turn and drove toward the village. She said, in a southern accent, "Throw some glass in that hole, will you?"

"What?"

She smiled and said normally, "Roll up the window, Brian, it's cold."

He rolled it up, but not all the way. He left a crack opened at the top. He felt that he was releasing something awful and harmful from inside himself, and he wanted to make sure it all escaped. He had not done anything this bold for a long time. It felt wonderful. He kept his eyes on the road, wishing she'd start whistling again.

# 9

Perry's Publick House sat out over the spotlighted harbor water like a lobster shanty. Inside it felt, smelled, and looked like some barny inn plucked whole from the English countryside. The far end, beyond the bar and pool table, was divided into several small dining rooms.

Nick sat in one of them, at his usual table by a window. Hortense Perry brought him his second Molson's Ale. He had come early; he still wasn't sure why. Smoking, thinking, he idly turned his head and spotted Brian Galgay coming through the front door. He had a woman with him! Nick flung his napkin from his lap to the table, stood, and headed for them. There, he laughed. "Why didn't you tell me, Brian? We could have double-dated."

Brian nearly reeled. He had not expected Burke to be there yet. "Nick," he said, "really, this is just a coincidence, I'm not—"

"Say, I know you!" Deborah sang.

Nick looked at her again and recognized her. "Oh, yeah, hi," he said. "You did that eyeshadow spot for me once, right? You're the fabulous Deborah Ormay."

"Yes. I never did get introduced to you."

Brian did the unavoidable: "Uh, Deborah, this is Nick Burke."

Nick took her hand. "Sure, Nefertiti," he smiled. "Sorry I haven't given you any more work since then" was all he could think to say. "But I was just visiting on that cosmetics thing."

"Don't worry," she said. "I'm still getting paid from it."

He looked back at Brian with new regard. How could such a square-looking guy, in an off-the-rack three-piece suit, carry-

[ 149 ]

ing an attaché case, end up with a stunner like Ormay on his arm? She must know what his job is, he guessed; maybe she's turned on by the old spook mystique. Well, more power to him. "I've got a table in the back," he said. "Let's go. There's no checkroom, you hang your coats on the chairs."

Brian started to follow him, then stopped. "Uh, Nick, just a minute. I thought Deborah might have a drink at the bar or something, while you and I talk."

Deborah said, "If I don't eat something pretty soon, I'll faint. A drink would put me out where the buses don't run."

"Me too," Nick said. "Come on, let's just sit down and have a nice meal first. I'm not going to run out on you, Lieutenant."

Brian went along, fighting a faint sense of vertigo. At Nick's table they gave the waitress their drink and food orders. Deborah attacked the basket of French bread with both hands. She and Nick fell at once into streams of shoptalk, then caught themselves and apologized to Brian for it. They all ate and ordered espresso and liqueurs. Throughout, Brian stayed on edge. He felt acutely aware of time running out, wasted on chatter. He began to suspect Burke of deliberately evading their agreed-to interrogation. Maybe he was even making subtle advances toward Deborah. He found it irritating that he couldn't observe Burke's and Deborah's eyes at the same time. At last he leaned back in his chair and said, "Well, what do you say, Nick? If I don't get some business done tonight, I won't be able to put in for this meal."

Nick, too, had had a different idea of how the evening would go. He had intended to give Galgay whatever he was after as quickly as possible, and send him on his way. He knew it was the presence of the woman that had thrown him off, and couldn't tell which intrigued him more, herself, or her unlikely liaison with Galgay. Truthfully, he sighed, "Ah, God, Brian, I'm too beat to be of any use to you tonight."

"It's not even eleven o'clock."

"That's way past our bedtime in the country. Besides, what are we going to do, make your lovely lady go wait in the car?"

"I wouldn't mind shooting some pool," Deborah said, "but there's still a line for the table. Can't you just have at it, and pretend I'm not here? I'll be quiet as a mouse."

"No," Brian said.

"What's the matter, Deborah, aren't you cleared for top sacred?"

"Oh, that's right, you said 'government,' " looking at Brian. That made Nick quicken. She *didn't* know what he was?

She said, "Listen, no big deal, let me just take my schnapps and go watch the game; do they have side betting?"

Nick and Brian stared at each other in indecision. Nick thought, Don't look at me, you brought her. Then he ended it: "I'll tell you what. This has been too nice to spoil, huh? You and I can meet by ourselves in the morning, Brian, and get it done—then, why don't we do a cookout? The weather's supposed to be gorgeous, and I know some places that—"

"You told me how much you value your private time," Brian said a bit flintily. "I wouldn't want to intrude too much."

Nick smiled quizzically. Did the guy mean it, or did he just mean that he didn't want to lose too much lovey-time with his girl friend? He stuck with the truth: "Hey, what's one day after twenty years? I've been thinking about you, Brian. In fact, I've remembered the last time I heard anything about you—it was on those war games you started to talk about yesterday. What the hell happened to you after Berlin, anyhow? We never—"

"Let's leave that for tomorrow too, okay, Nick?"

"Oh, hell," he said, "*old times* aren't classified information, are they?"

Brian told Deborah, "Nick and I served together in the same unit for a while, many years ago."

"I see," she said. "Sorry I missed the reunion." She wanted

to ask them if it had been anything as raucous as the ones she remembered her father having. But she was surprised then to see Nick stand and abruptly begin to say his good-nights. In two minutes he was gone.

Back at the inn they had nightcaps by the fire, again the only ones there besides the bartender. Brian seemed so distracted that she finally said, "I feel like I might be only adding to your problems here, Brian, so just say the word, all right? I can bow out just as fast as I barged in."

"Oh, gosh, no, don't think that at all. This'll work out fine, don't worry."

"If you're sure. I mean, I'm just up to have some fun, but if you've got—"

"I'm sure, really," he said. "The opposite's true. I'm . . . I'm delighted that I met you."

In a little while she shook his hand good night and left for bed. He waited ten minutes, then followed. He called the stakeout on the vestibule pay phone: the General was not home at the moment, but he had not accompanied his wife to Albany.

The upstairs hallway was dimly lit. A line of yellow light on the floor told him which room was hers. He lingered outside his own door, feeling his heart pounding. Then the line of light went out. He entered his room silently and undressed in the dark.

Sleep, as usual, was a long time coming. The stomach spasms returned. Inside he was divided. One side wished that the Burke contact had been carried out as planned, and was behind him; also, that Deborah Ormay had never happened. His other side was actually looking forward to tomorrow. Deborah was so exciting, and not just in her looks. She did remind him warmly of Anna; he realized that he had not thought once all evening of calling Evelyn in Maryland.

Nor could he deny feeling a certain, unexpected fondness

for Nick Burke. Regardless of what help he could or couldn't
give in the General's case. He remembered how Nick had always been straighter and friendlier with him than any of the
others even then, way back in Germany. Surely less hostile
than that Kelsey character. And, yes, he finally had to admit, it
had to be the same Joel Kelsey on the signature block running
the case on the General. The bastard. A full colonel already.
Yes, and if it was the same Kelsey, then Kelsey no doubt knew
it was the same Brian Galgay way down here, on the receiving
end of the orders, and how he must gloat over it!

Brian sat up and reached for cigarettes he didn't have. That
was foolish thinking, he told himself, and destructive. It might
not be the same Kelsey at all, and even if it was . . . well, all
it meant was that Berlin had happened to *him*, not to anybody
else. And he didn't need Kelsey's name or Nick's face to remind
him of that dismal fact.

He wondered how Deborah might react if he woke her up
to ask for a cigarette.

# 10

Next morning Nick left early, driving fast into the tunnel of dirt
road that careened through the scrubby woods between his
house and Bittersweet Lane, the hardtop road to Derby. Bittersweet Lane cut through the woods and fields between Old
Swamp, by the bay, and Derby itself, near the harbor. The road

was named for the climbing vines that permeated the branches high and low of all the wild-growing trees.

He saw that the bittersweet was showing through the bare limbs. Its yellowing leaf and red-and-yellow berries made it look like gold necklaces festooning the otherwise drab, low, scrawny forests. But the vine was a killer, he knew, a boa strangling the branches it decorated. It fed the wild birds, local and migratory, but it had to be slashed at the roots and yanked to the ground periodically if the woods were to live. A Derby fact of life. So close and low to the sea, Derby's falls and winters were usually never as intense as those inland. Except for the occasional maple, the foliage turned only to subtle, paler shades of browns, reds, and ambers. He took the extra bright foliage this year as a sign that they might be treated to a real winter for a change, with skating on the ponds and sledding on Electric Light Hill.

Most fields were lush with the green of the ryegrass, sown as ground cover until spring. Some fields stood tall with rows of dead cornstalks, like armies of scarecrows. Others spread flat and wide and dark brown, spilling with frostbitten pumpkins. As he got closer to Derby itself, more and more houses began to appear. In almost every yard tarpaulin-shrouded boats rested high and dry on trailers on blocks, letting him fancy Derby a village of Noahs, ready for the Flood.

Nearer to town the homes grew larger and older and farther back from the road, aproned with well-tended lawns. Downtown Derby, called "upstreet," was essentially the intersection of Elm Street with Everett's Lane, each erect on both sides with a few hundred yards of storefronts. He felt saddened to watch Elm Street too rapidly assume a sardonic air—more and more big, black X's were appearing on the majestic, doomed trunks: the mark of blight. The air upstreet was seldom clear of the buzz and whine of chainsaws, or the sight of hard-hatted workers perched high and busy among the dead limbs.

He swung the Triumph into the curb in front of the Four Corners Luncheonette. Brian Galgay was already there waiting, and they went inside. Cops, farmers, merchants, and tradesmen mixed in the smell of bacon with young, bearded workers whom Nick thought of as "counterculture carpenters." Four baymen in black waders were vacating a booth, off to resume their pursuit of scallops. After the waitress cleaned the table, Brian ordered just coffee and opened his attaché case upon the cracked leatherette seat beside him. Nick ordered pancakes.

He let Brian go through the motions of reading from his sheets, but felt the orientation was unnecessary. From the moment Galgay had said "Operation Snowsword," he had been fairly certain where it all was heading. When it got there, he again said, "Ewing," without having to think.

Like Kelsey, Brian looked surprised.

"Total recall," Nick said, and resisted the urge to volunteer what else he already knew, that the man was now a three-star general. Nobody was to know he had met with Kelsey.

Unlike Kelsey, Brian seemed to know nothing about Nick's confrontation with Ewing in the TIC that night. His queries all had to do only with the General himself, as an individual. Nick could answer virtually none of them. Finally he said, "You might as well quit, Brian. All I knew about the guy is what I told you. He was a West Pointer, very young to be a full bird at the time, the Division Artillery Officer, home-based in Nuremberg. And I'm not sure about the Nuremberg part. Whether he was married or had kids or fought in Korea or any of that . . . zip. *Nada.*"

Visibly perplexed, Brian said as much to himself as to Nick, "I knew this was a shot in the dark, but I assumed you'd know *something* more about the man than what you say." He flipped through several pages. "Forgetting his biographical data—how about his personal profile? How would you rate his leadership qualities at the time? Was he fair? Did he—?"

"I never even worked for him, Brian. I came up against him just the one time, on the war games."

"Against?"

"Well, yeah. I thought that's what this must be about. Is there anything in there about him putting a letter into my two-oh-one file?"

"No."

"Then forget it. That was my one and only connection with the guy. Maybe your computers fucked up or something."

"What sort of letter was it?"

"Why are you running the check on him?"

"I can't tell you that, Nick."

"Then why should I tell you?"

Brian returned his papers to the case and closed the lid. "Old times?"

Nick smiled back. "Well, that's different."

They got more coffee and Nick told him an abbreviated version of his and Ewing's clash over the use of nuclear weaponry in the cold Circus Tent that night so long ago.

Brian said, "I see why you can remember it so well. Was there anything . . . I don't know, anything strange, or off, or odd about him, that you recall?"

"He scared me, I know that."

"Physically?"

"Sure. I was a kid and tough, but I wouldn't have wanted to go at it with that prick even then. There was something Green Beret about him, all right."

"Nothing else?"

"No. I don't think so. Tell you something else that's weird, though, Brian—you're kind of connected into all this for me."

"Me? How?"

"I just remembered this since the other day, but it was around the same time, while we were out in the boondocks on Snowsword, that the word came in about you getting pulled out of Berlin. Old Big John called me all the way down to the Detachment one night to tell me. What the hell happened to you, anyhow?"

"What did he tell you?"

"Just that you got your ass caught down in one of the tunnels under the Wall. I remember looking for your name in all the *Time* magazine articles after that, but—"

"No, I never made *Time*, thank God. They deleted any of us who were CIC or FOI or, you know, sensitive personnel."

"What the hell did you think you were doing?"

Brian shrugged. "Trying to help people who wanted to come out, come out." Strangely, it felt good to have someone ask him about it all again, and to tell someone some of it. "It seemed like a good idea at the time, as the saying goes."

Nick grinned. "Ballsy, anyhow. I remember—Big John was afraid you'd get screwed for it, or quit the Corps. I guess you didn't quit, how about the screwing?"

Saying "May I?" Brian took one of Nick's cigarettes and lit it. "Yes, I guess you can say I paid the bill for it. I thanked God for Vietnam when it happened, Nick. It was the only thing that got me out of all the stupid, backwater assignments they threw at me. But then they got me anyhow, I suppose."

"How?"

"Passed me over. I'm still only a major."

That convinced Nick to never mention Kelsey at all to the poor bastard, even casually.

Brian added, "There's a new list due out soon, though, so I still have some hope."

The best Nick could manage was "Hey, shit, a majority's better than a stick in the eye, Brian, huh? And when you think of all the ones who came back in a goddamn plastic bag—"

Brian smiled. "I think of them a lot. Don't get me wrong, Nick, I try not to make a high mass out of any of it. I take it as it comes."

As a reunion it was surely not in the same league as his and Kelsey's had been. But then Galgay was still only the same old Galgay, after all, doing the best he could with what he had. Nick maneuvered him out to the cars and then to the Derby Inn, where Deborah pranced into the Plymouth. Keeping them in his rearview mirror, he led the way out the serpentine length of Bittersweet Lane, then onto the nameless gravel road that cut across the marshlands and joined the ocean highway near the remote dune area few travelers ever found, even in summer.

There, Nick announced proudly, "My secret grove!" and began unloading his hibachi and bags of food.

"It's beautiful!" Deborah said. "And so warm!"

"Climb that dune and you'll change your story."

She took it as an order. He and Brian followed. Together they stood and beheld the winter sea, a pale green, fierce with whitecaps all the way to the horizon. The surf was high and five or six tiers deep, raging like white stallions. Tiny rainbows curled when the mists caught the sunlight. Yelling, Deborah bounded from the crest and ran toward the water. Brian hesitated. Nick told him, "Go get her, kid, the chow'll be a while."

He set the charcoal blazing in the hibachi, then gathered armfuls of deadwood from the ground underneath the scrub pine trees that hunkered low and close all around. These he quickly turned into a large, jagged pyramid of fire, for warmth, and spread his picnic blanket out before it. He had brought steak, bread, wine, salad, metal plates and utensils, plastic glasses. Busy, he realized that as much as he loved doing this in itself and for itself, having some company to share it with was a pleasant change.

As soon as Deborah and Brian came down and in from the beach, a black Labrador appeared out of the woods.

"I'm a bloody magnet for dogs!" she cried and told them of her yesterday's companion on the town beach. This one, she noticed, tried to nuzzle her crotch and went poking at Nick's thighs near the stove, but stayed clear of Brian. Nick commanded him to go home and he did; he went away at least. Brian and Deborah were also sent off for a while, to collect more firewood. "A ton," Nick called after them, "it gets cold fast here after noon."

When the meal was ready, they sat close to each other and to the campfire, cross-legged, and ate from the plates perched upon their laps. This food got loftier raves than the restaurant's did the night before. Satisfied, they scattered their leavings for the seagulls, bagged the plates and stuff, and returned to the fireside to smoke, sip wine, and continue talking. There was an easy feeling among them. Time passed gently. When Nick felt the first chill on his own back, he knew it was time to move, and told them, "Up and at 'em, folks, or you'll catch your deaths." He banked the fire with some large logs and led them back over the dune to the beach. The three walked the tide line for a long way. Deborah found two more pocketsful of sea glass.

By the time they got back, the hibachi was cool enough for Nick to lift bare-handed back into the rear floor of his car. Brian stirred the fire alive with a long stick, and Deborah poured the last of the second bottle of wine into their glasses. Handing Nick his, she said, "Where do you live from here? Don't we get to see your house?"

He didn't know why the question surprised him, but it did. He rarely brought anyone to his house. Normally his excuses came more quickly, but with Deborah he was hesitating. Maybe it was her sudden closeness to him; he felt vaguely guilty and stole a glance at Brian's back. At last he said, "It's a mess, I wasn't expecting company."

"Is it far?"

"Yes and no. It's back on the bay side."

"Wherever that is. Can you see the water?"

"Yes, from one end. There's a sunporch."

"Is it big, your house?"

"No. Just big enough to keep me penniless. I'm still fixing it up."

"I'd love to see it, Nick."

"Next time, maybe."

She turned her body even closer to him and whispered, "Please?"

He answered even more softly than she had asked, "No," and walked away, carrying his wine, to join Brian by the fire.

Ready to leave, he yelled out his car window, "When you see me wave my arm, keep going straight. I'll be turning off. You'll end up right by the inn. Just follow the signs."

Heavy cloud cover had rolled in, blocking the already waning afternoon light. By the time they saw Nick wave and leave them, it seemed like the middle of the night, and the coming rain had turned from a drizzle to a real downpour. On high beams the GI Plymouth was wall-eyed, its right headlight scanning the overhead trees like a spotlight. Brian, still feeling a rush from the wine and the fresh salt air, drove with what he thought was extreme caution over the strange night roads.

Deborah said, "You're on the wrong side of the road, you know."

"Sorry." He corrected it. She was sitting scrunched, her knees up on the unpadded dash. He was sure he could hear the silky rub of thighskin against thighskin, and felt his cock beginning to fill. If he had a third arm, he mused, he would reach over and gently stroke her legs, all the way up; he felt sure that she would either not notice or not mind.

She said, "Did you and Nick get your business done this morning?"

He tapped her shoulder, pointed to his ear, and to the ceiling of the car. He doubted that it was actually bugged, but it could be. At least it gave him a smooth way to end this line of talk with her—*enough about Burke!* He was feeling nearly faint with need for her now. He said, "Would you like to . . . when we get to the inn, should we have a drink by the fire again?"

"Sure." She wondered if he was dreading or hoping that she'd start pitching glasses into the fireplace. Her mood toward him had changed completely now. *Here I am again,* she sighed with regret, *going with one man while I'm thinking about another one.* Pretty sure he wasn't seeing the sign, she said, "Left to the village."

Inside the inn Leola sat bent like a bird over her small lectern of a desk. She handed Brian a piece of notepaper without looking up. "Call came for ya."

He read the number. It had come, he saw, just an hour ago.

"Go ahead," he told Deborah. "I have a call to make."

He hoped it wouldn't be Shippers, but it was: "Hey, yessir, glad we gotcha, hate ta interrupt yor—"

"What is it!"

"It's the jackpot's what it is, sir!"

"Be careful now!" He wanted to also tell him to talk lower, but realized the desire for quiet was only at his end of the phone conversation.

"Yessir, wellsir . . ." He was sure the fool was hitting the vodka again. "We got it all, video and audio. Subject, ah, finally got around ta changin' his battin' stance, heh. Yup, switched over and hit from thuther side uv the plate! It's all dark in theah and the game's over now, but—"

"All right," he whispered, "reactivate to cover the night game and--"

"Oh, hellsir, we got enough in the can now to—"

"*Did you read me?*"

"Yes, sir."

"Then do it. I should be there in three hours, maybe less."

She saw it at once: the man standing in the doorway of the

cellar bar and looking at her was again only the man she had first found sitting here alone. The man who had found the courage to make a play for her had gone and not returned . . . and she felt relieved that her damned body was for once not going to get its way over her after all.

He said, "I have to go back. Now."

"Okay," she said flatly, smiling. "Nice meeting you, Brian."

"Uh, can I call you sometime? In the city?"

"For sure."

# 11

At just before nine that night Brian let himself into the stakeout apartment. He looked through the open door of the duty agents' bedroom: they were playing cards. He stalked through the dark living room to the wall mirror. The bedroom on the other side of the glass was brighter; the window drapes in there were not closed. Still, the occupants of General Ewing's bed were only vague shapes in the gloom. He went into the bedroom reserved for him, and straight into its bathroom. He swallowed two GI APC tablets and a Benzedrine. Then he stripped, showered, and shaved. Work. How he thanked God for work.

When he came out, Mr. Higgins was in the kitchen. The gas was burning blue under the coffeepot. Checking camera and tape recorder for readiness, the elderly agent said, "Evening, Major. Shippers's taking a shower." Then he added wryly, "Here for the finale, I see?" Higgins could pass easily for some gentle, neutral biology professor at some small southern college, yet the man, he knew, had been tortured by the Chinese in North Korea and lived to not talk about it.

Higgins adjusted his footage counter once again. Brian said, "Subject due up soon?"

"Hard to say, sir. They talked about going out for dinner later."

"Any make on his companion?"

That didn't deserve an answer and Higgins didn't offer any, just: "There's Polaroids on the desk there, sir, from this afternoon, and I'll be setting up the still camera again in a minute. Got a man on the street for when he leaves."

"Good. Thanks, Ralph." He checked the Polaroids: certainly nobody he recognized, of course, but chilling in another way. The man could have passed for the General's twin brother. He was the same size and age, roughly, and wore his same pewter-gray hair just as closely cropped.

"Anybody you know, Major Galgay?"

Brian said, "No," adding, "There's always more to learn, isn't there." He went over, poured two cups of coffee, and took Mr. Higgins his.

"Thank you, sir—more?"

"I was about to end this," Brian said. "A couple nights ago. Then I changed my mind."

"Lucky," Higgins said and set the camera rolling, slating it with the case number, date, and time. Then he turned the recorder on, and slated it verbally. The Nikon waited on a tripod under a black hood. He uncovered it, adjusted its framing, then stayed crouched behind it, his hand on the long-cord trigger.

"Trying to break your back?"

"No, sir, we got reveille starting to happen."

[ 163 ]

Brian peered closer through the mirror, but still didn't detect the slightest change. It took the definite raising of a hand and forearm to show him that Mr. Higgins was right. The hand was the General's. As if on its own, like some slender bird that had been sleeping between the two men, the arm rose gracefully from beneath the covers, hovered lightly and steadily, then eased down to gently caress the ear and the hair and the neck skin behind the ear, of the other man's sleep-stilled head.

Brian had watched, live and on film, the General wake up before. It had never been like this. Either he bounded straight from sleep to the floor to shadowbox vigorously around the room before dropping for push-ups; or, if he wanted a wake-up, it was always of the roll-you-over-in-the-clover variety, the roll-over of the wife nearly always being onto her stomach. "Thet ol' boy don't like his eggs any way but sunnyside up in the mawnin'!" Shippers had observed, more than once.

They had kissed on the mouths and were embracing now, more a hugging, really, close and tight, muscular arms wrapped around muscular, hard-looking shoulders and backs. If they were standing and dressed, he thought, it would seem to be the heartfelt welcome or farewell between two brothers or comrades-at-arms. But it was prone and nude. At least he assumed it was nude, for the sheet and quilt stayed pulled up to their chests. *Kashik . . . kashik . . . kashik!* Mr. Higgins's Nikon was operating with the automatic electronic frame-advancer. In another life, Brian mused silently, this might be a tasteful photographic book in the making, *The Joy of* something or other, taking the photographs from which tasteful illustrations would be drawn, in charcoal or sepia.

Watching, he sipped his coffee and thought, If I were the Soviet, General, or if I were the Chinese, or the Cubans, the Palestinians or practically anyone else—you would be mine. You would have to do anything and everything I told you. Or suffer disgrace. Imprisonment. Or worse. As it is, you'll be forcibly retired, with rank, with pension and benefits, without dishonor or too severe a blackballing. If you're lucky. But you're not lucky anymore, I don't think. After all, I am here, am I not?

*Kashik . . . kashik . . . kashik!*

Like a dolphin in the sea, the General rolled massively but lightly onto his knees. The back of his partner's head nestled between the two pillows. The covers slid off the General's back in a small, slow avalanche. The missionariness of it touched Brian almost humorously. If he blurred his eyes slightly, he realized, the men looked really no different than he and the Ormay girl would have looked to a mirror; much, really, the same as his wife Evelyn and her lover would look, right this very instant possibly, in her and Brian's own bed in Maryland, the boy innocently asleep and unaware two solid walls away in his own little bed. *Kashik . . . kashik . . . kashik . . . kashik . . . kashik! . . .* Brian looked away in shame and rage.

"Jesus, no *lube*? It's right there on the end table, for cryin' out loud!"

Brian spun. But he couldn't even speak.

Shippers checked the Arriflex and the tape machine, then got himself coffee. "Damn if you didn't call this one right, sir, damn if you didn't. Thet ol' cocker sure as shit had *me* fooled, I'll tell the world."

Brian muttered, "Quiet!"

Mr. Higgins whispered, "Shippers, man the Arrie."

Brian turned to look at them again. The General and his accomplice-double had cut short their mutual resting by starting to wrestle, then to throw sharp, playful slaps, which promptly turned to a boxing workout on the spacious floor of the General's bedroom. They were about evenly matched and frolicked in it. Shippers had released the lock on the film camera's stand and was working the focus of the lens with his left hand while following the action with his right, on the handle.

It went on through their dressing and leaving. Their con-

[ 165 ]

versation was trivial: personal and jovial. The General put on a
civilian suit. Mr. Higgins reached to his trouser belt and sent
the street man bleeps of alert. Shippers put his raincoat on. Mr.
Higgins said, "If they split, you stay with the General. Just to
destination, then scramble back here. You got a lot of packing
up to do."

Shippers turned to Brian and said, "Hope to work for you
again sometime, Major Galgay . . . an' ah'm sure real sorry
'bout that lieutenant colonel's list, too." Then he left.

Brian wanted to go kick him through a window. What hurt
most was not being passed over for lieutenant colonel, although
that hurt very deeply—it was hearing it secondhand, and from
the mouth of a retard like Shippers. He hadn't even received
his copy of the promotions list yet, hadn't even known it was
out yet.

He looked once more through the mirror into the empty
bedroom. His eyes fell upon the set of shoulder stars the General had left on the bureau. He suddenly felt pity for the man
who would be ordered to confront the General personally with
the news of his defeat. He would be an officer of equal or superior rank, of course. But still, he would have to take upon
himself the General's outrage and fury, the sense that he was
bound to have of being betrayed by his own.

Mr. Higgins was unloading the cameras. "There'll be other
lists, Major."

"I know. Bad news sure travels fast, doesn't it?"

"Yessir. Grapevine's a mysterious animal. Always has
been."

*Work!* "Mr. Higgins, I'll take last night's and this morning's
evidence."

"Right, sir."

[ 166 ]

# FOUR

# 1

Brian Galgay walked across town from his hotel to Lexington Avenue and entered Grand Central Station. He fished the storage-locker key out of his vest pocket, having destroyed the envelope in which they had sent it to him. The Monday lunchtime mob had thinned, but the floor of the vast hall still swarmed with people. He found the dead-drop in the wall of lockers past the escalators to the Pan Am Building, opened the door with the key, and looked in—at emptiness.

He felt the chill in his groin a second before he felt the presence of the two men behind him. Enraged, he slammed the door shut, spun, and began walking away, practically right through them. Words that had begun as near-whispers turned to near-shouts after him: "Mr. Davis!"

Brian headed for the Stock Exchange booth, but it wasn't crowded enough. Nor, he could see, were the lines to the Off Track Betting windows. He moved to his left and joined a queue to a railroad information agent in the center of the terminal. He felt the two men line up behind him. He was thinking, *The swine! The idiots!* but kept his lips still, his face normal—if the contact was being photographed, by his own people or theirs or anybody, he would appear obliviously innocent of their existence behind him. A voice in his right ear began again: "Mr. Davis, we want to speak with—"

"Next train to Brewster?" Brian asked the clerk, and was told the time and the track number. He nodded and moved away swiftly. In all the din he could make out the two sets of feet pursuing him. He longed to stop, turn, and kill them. Or to break into a dead run. Instead he paused at the newsstand and bought a *Daily News*, perused the headlines blindly, then walked on toward the bright cluster of public phone booths, pretending not to hear: "Davis! Stop! We—"

Insulated inside the booth, he dropped in a dime and punched numbers at random, keeping his back to the door. He lucked out and got a busy signal on some stranger's line. For the benefit of the cameras, which he was all but positive didn't exist, he spoke aloud: "Hello, this is Davis, they're trying to throw a scare into me. God knows why. And I am, scared, right. Good. Okay, then . . . they're just dirt, though, just dogs. . . ."

It occurred to him that the pair might have pulled this unthinkable breach on their own thick-headed Russian initiative, and mentally changed the call now to somebody real and specific: their superior, the Englishman: ". . . and I want their balls for this! How dare you!" Yes, this was better; if they could lip-read, let them read: "You want to end it? That's fine by me. This ends it, then. You've fucking blown it sky-high this time, you scum! You've just lost me!" Then he slammed the receiver back into its cradle, and yanked the door open. In the narrow corridor they appeared from both sides, wearing stupid winter suits, blocking his exit. One said, "You're behind in your payments, Mr.—"

Swinging his heavy case forward like a club, Brian moved between them as if they were ghosts from another dimension. He went left to Forty-second Street. Outside the doors, he caught a cab immediately. "Just go, and fast," he said. "Go up Madison." Riding, he let the shock and fear finish their passage through his system, and let the sweat come.

Then, free of the tremors but still tightly wired, he thought, Either the Englishman ordered it, or he didn't. If he did, he's getting reckless . . . but I can't blame him—it might have worked. It nearly did work. But then he reasoned: If the Englishman did not order it, then it had merely been the Red underlings' own bright idea; typically brutal, typically stupid, typically Russian. He hoped sincerely that the latter was the case. If so, then when the Englishman heard of it, he would be nearly as outraged as he himself was—and this might very well buy him an extra grace period, some additional badly needed time in which to come up with something he could pass to them.

Brian let himself feel better now, almost glad that it had happened: if it had bought him some more time, then it had been well worth the shock and disturbance. "Anywhere in here, driver." He paid and got out, looking up to see he was at Fifty-ninth Street. He walked west a block to Fifth and tried to hail another cab. The downtown traffic here was three cars wide and solid. For as far as he could see north, it didn't contain one free taxicab. Deciding to walk, Brian slipped into the safe-feeling river of bodies flooding the broad sidewalk.

His hotel was the Royalton, on West Forty-fourth Street, opposite the Algonquin. It was an old-time place, once fine, now relatively seedy, but well kept up. Although it had neither bar nor dining room, a lobby door connected it to a coffee shop that provided room service. He had a one-bedroom suite at the end of the hall on the sixth floor. He unlocked its heavy, solid door and stepped into its anachronistically large sitting room. Before he could stop it, *"God damn it!"* shot out of him loudly.

Just as startled, the four Latina chambermaids flew to their feet. They had been eating their swing-shift lunch around his large, round coffee table. Their chirping, chattering apologies and attempts to explain while escaping went unheard beneath

Brian's uncontrollable shouts of *"Vamos! Pronto! Pronto!"* He even flung a vicious *"Conyos!"* at the head of the last one out the door, to let them know that he did not share their amusement, which he conveyed at once to the desk clerk by phone: ". . . and I mean this—if *anything* like this is ever allowed to happen to me again, you and everyone concerned will be in for some very serious trouble!"

Slamming the receiver down, he noticed the half-eaten sandwich left behind on the table in its square of aluminum foil. It wasn't until he had crunched it in his hand and was about to pitch it into the empty fireplace, that his rage lifted and his control returned, as suddenly as it had left him. He was breathing loudly and hard. He stepped slowly and methodically to the doorway of the bathroom, and dropped the soggy wad into the wastebasket. He never admitted to actually needing a drink, but felt assured now that the Scotch he poured into the heavy old hotel tumbler had been earned and would be good for him.

Wanting to pace, knowing he should sit, he stayed just standing there in the middle of the suddenly silent living room. He could hear his heart. He waited for it to calm down, brooding, What the hell had happened? What an absolutely foolish, careless reaction! How could he ever have exploded in rage like that, without one second's warning, over nothing? It scared him. If his accosters at the dead-drop trap had set out to shake him, they evidently had succeeded very well.

He put the drink down and undressed, hanging the gray tie and the blue suit in the closet, stuffing the socks and underwear and white shirt into the hotel laundry bag. He swallowed a Benzedrine, then showered and shaved for the second time that day. Feeling better, he pulled on the trousers from another suit, poured a new slosh of the Dewar's into his glass, then sat down at the desk at his portable typewriter. He intended to write the final paragraph to his running agent's report on the suspected General. But his hands seemed unable to move. He sat staring at nothing for a long time.

[ 172 ]

At last he got up and moved to the sofa where two of the chambermaids had been illicitly sitting. He picked up the phone and began dialing his home number in Maryland. He hung up after the area code, and sat staring for several minutes into the black-painted, unworking fireplace, swallowing Scotch, and thinking, *Evelyn, Evelyn, you bitch.* He snapped out of it, fetched his case in a burst of forced activity, took out the General's dossier, scanned it once again, then tossed it, not quite angrily, back in on top of his other material.

Brian leaned back heavily then, looked at the sandy white swirls in the ceiling, and reflected. He knew very well why they had leaned on him. The quality of his merchandise had been poor nearly to the point of fake for the last several drops. And this was their hoodlum way, and maybe even the Englishman's way, of saying that they knew it and were displeased.

He didn't like responding to their pressure like this, but he couldn't help himself. He was forever afraid of irritating them too severely, knowing it was not he himself but Anna who would suffer the real punishment if they chose to inflict it. All along his main dread had been the day when they might demand more than technical documents from him. Sitting still in the hotel room suddenly felt wrong and dangerous. He threw on his coat and left.

Outside, he walked for blocks and blocks aimlessly. Traversing the crowded, hurrying sidewalks, he felt desperately all alone in the world.

But he wasn't.

As he was returning to the Royalton, a woman was browsing the shop windows, strolling casually between the Bar Building and the hotel's entrance. When Brian passed, she stepped away and walked beside him, just close enough to be heard, just far enough away for an observer to decide she was alone. "Mr. Davis."

"Yes."

They passed the hotel. She said, "Left at the corner."

"What is it?"

"We must have a meeting."

"Why?"

"I know nothing. Only that there is serious distress. I am only to agree on a time and a place for the meeting."

They turned onto Sixth, the Avenue of the Americas—Network Boulevard farther uptown, but here only a drab suburb of SEX ACTS LIVE ON STAGE, Times Square a block west. By the Azuma store, the woman said, "The place is easy to remember. The old World's Fair site in Flushing. By the Unisphere. Can you go there today?"

"No."

"Why not?"

"How dare you—what is your name?" He looked at her then for the first time, dartingly. Any Queens or Brooklyn housewife in to shop at Alexander's.

"Then noon, a week from Thursday," she said.

"All right." He turned in to the Longley's Coffee Shop on the corner. He sat up on a counter stool and ordered eggs, sausages, and coffee. To surveillance the only possible discrepancy might be his having passed the other coffee shop, hard by the Royalton's entrance: a very faint question mark at worst. He was much more worried about the people behind the nervy woman. Serious distress. Mother of God, what could they mean? With his last drop, a manual, and a veritable coup in his estimation, he had expected satisfaction at the very least. And perhaps even a reprieve of a month or so from their demands on him. Instead they were coming down upon him.

His food came. He barely remembered having ordered it. He poked at it with a fork. He wanted to get out of there, but at the same time he wanted to put off going back to his hotel room. He could feel the Benzedrine wearing off. He knew he wouldn't be able to resist phoning Evelyn if he went back. But he had so much paper work to attack, the final report on the

[ 174 ]

General, the transcribing of the Burke interview, the . . . *Oh, Jesus, don't let it be something too terrible!* he prayed. *Keep them from going too far with me!*

Burke's surprisingly clear recollections had sucked his own mind back to those years, and burned away the clouds that time had put over his visions of Anna. Now he was beginning to see clearly again the pure, straight line of her slender nose, and the skin of her torso, pale and taut as bleached driftwood. In bed her body had smelled faintly like bread. She spoke German like a Russian, but English like an Englishwoman with a Berlin accent. She had made him laugh. She had fussed over him. Across from him in the choir, Anna had sung with the voice of one of God's own angels, but alone with him she had made plans like a jewel thief. She whistled.

He knew Anna was thirty-seven or -eight now, but he couldn't picture her beyond her early twenties. If a miracle brought her back to him tomorrow, he knew he wouldn't care how she looked. Still, it grieved him to think, sometimes, of what those years might have done to her. Those cruel, archaic, shriveling Russian years of semicaptivity. He had no words vile enough to describe his hatred of Anna's keepers. He drank his coffee, wishing she would return now to what she had been for him so long—more of an idea than an actual, living being.

In morbid lapses such as this he would wish Anna dead. So that they might both be finally free of it. But that wish hurt, and frightened him. To prevent it he jumped off his stool and went to the cashier. *Work!*

# 2

Again he found it impossible to concentrate long enough to add even one sensible sentence to his report. The hotel room felt no less dangerous and entrapping than it had before. He had to get out of it. He considered fleeing to his bedroom at the stakeout apartment, but rejected it. It would be safe enough, but now that their work was done, he didn't want to even go near it. He knew he had to go home to Maryland soon, but not yet; he wasn't up to that yet. He opened his notebook to the page where he had written Deborah Ormay's address and number. He had the strange feeling that it was not his own handwriting that he was looking at. Nor did it seem to be his own hands using the phone.

Her answering service referred him to a photographer's studio. A voice there told him the best they could do was take his name and number. Waiting, he sipped straight Scotch and paced. The phone rang within an hour. By then Brian was convinced it would not be her, but it was. She said no, she wasn't free for dinner. He said, "How about just drinks, then?"

"Okay, but it'll have to be fast, do you mind, Brian? This thing is going to go at least until six—maybe another night would be better."

He realized he didn't want to wait one minute before seeing her again. He told her he had to leave town the next day. She agreed to meet him at 6:30, and chose the Russian Tea Room.

He was there at six and ordered a martini at the small bar in the front. He looked around and felt very out of place, like something dark and heavy put inside a glass-lace Easter egg. But the bright, brass revolving door kept spinning, and he was soon lost within a crush at the bar, and he felt better.

When she entered, she caused heads to turn. It wasn't just the long mink coat: she wore full facial makeup, and her hair was blown out like a black sunburst. She spotted him while he was still in the process of recognizing her. He left too much money behind him on the bar and followed her inside to a table. There, she surprised him again—when she opened the coat and let it drop back over her chair, he saw she was wearing an old gray sweat shirt and jeans. He said, "You look . . . fabulous."

"Thanks." A waiter was already at her side, waiting. She said, "A tequila gimlet, please. What were you having, Brian?"

He ordered another martini. "I guess you only have vodka when there's a fireplace handy, that right?"

She hid her bafflement behind lighting a cigarette. Then she remembered the night in Derby. "No—I drink vodka only on my wedding nights."

"How was your Sunday? I'm still sorry I had to leave so abruptly."

"It was lovely. I hated to leave, myself."

"Did you see Nick Burke again in your travels?" He couldn't believe he had actually said it. It was exactly what he most wanted to know, but the last thing in the world he wanted to bring up with her. She didn't answer him at first. Her elaborately colored face looked as still as it would on the page of a magazine; he could read no expression in it.

At last she smiled. "No, Brian Galgay, I did not see your Mr. Nick Burke after he left us Saturday." Her instincts had told her not to see this married government man again, at least not so soon. What she took to be the rudeness of his question made her sorry she had come. She told him, "I played with the idea of giving Nick a call, actually."

"But you didn't?"

"No."

Their drinks came. He sipped his, liking the smell of the gin. "Why not?"

[ 177 ]

She sighed. "Because I was afraid he'd tell me to get lost."

He thought she was joking, and laughed.

"What's funny?"

"You. I can't imagine any man ever telling you to get lost."

She reached back and pulled her coat up to cover her shoulders. Its collar brought much of her hair inside it. She shrugged. "Well, one learns to sense things about people."

"What do you sense about me?"

The black mascara and rust-red eyeliner did not conceal her squint; they exaggerated its sharpness. "That you're presumptuous, if you have to know."

His stomach began to ache. He was spoiling it with her, just as he had feared he would. Yet he couldn't seem to stop his tongue from running on, so at odds with his thoughts. "How am I presumptuous?"

"You act as if we've known each other a long time. As if we're old buddies. And we're not. You were in the Army with him, remember, not me."

"With who?"

"With Burke."

"Burke who? I don't think I ever knew anyone named Burke."

Deborah laughed. Maybe there was some hope for this bird after all.

Brian drank more martini. He had apparently redeemed himself with her, but wasn't sure how he'd done it. His brain felt totally out of control over what his mouth chose to say. Next it was saying, "Why the sweat shirt?"

"I'm starting a trend." She smiled. "No—I was modeling clothes all day. Into one outfit right after another, zip, zip, zip. It's like—"

"And you're going to dinner like that?"

Her smile went away again. Could he be so used to cross-examining people that he couldn't quit? She had known a lawyer like that, briefly. She lowered the temperature of her voice: "No. I'm going home first, to change. The coat."

"When can you have dinner with me?"

"I don't know. How long will you be away? This is the frantic season, Brian. I can't make any long-term plans. Call me when you're back, and we'll see. Now I really have to scoot." She drank off her gimlet, so as not to leave him looking at a full glass.

He gave her enough time to catch a taxi, then paid and left. Fifty-seventh Street was a tunnel of bitter winds from both rivers, clashing. He pulled up his coat collar and thought of calling Nick Burke. *Maybe he wouldn't mind having some dinner with me and trying to remember more about General Ewing's past. Or maybe we could just talk, like friends. But no,* Burke was working nights still.

He walked down Sixth to the Royalton. He packed two suitcases, one with his own clothes, the other with the films and tapes and records of the stakeout. The latter he checked at the baggage room at Grand Central. He went outside to the corner of Park and Forty-second and waited for the bus to LaGuardia, a recently learned economy—he could put in for a taxi on his expense sheet and save about ten dollars. Spare change like that would come in handy, he thought, if he was going to start trying to show Deborah Ormay nice times, like tonight.

# 3

Grant Evans was staring sorrowfully out Nick's office window. "I just want us to get *cookin'*, Nick," he said, "that's all."

"I know, bud. And we will. Eventually."

"So what do we do, hey?"

"We keep faking it and wait," Nick said. "We come in mornings early and we stay late nights, but we don't do anything real yet. We can't even try to work up a package on the sly. They're going to kill everything until the last possible minute. Parkinson's Law."

"We can try."

"No. I know I'm reading it right this time, Grant." He was telling his partner the truth. He was simply omitting the fact that, personally, he was relieved that the Jingo situation was going this way. Grant did not have to know about his own impotence; it would only make him more rattled. It was 9:20, and they had just come upstairs from the morning Jingo session to begin their normal work, feeling that they'd already put in a day's headaching labor.

Grant left to see a photographer's portfolio. Nick opened his coffee, relieved to remember what he had to do this morning. He spoke into his intercom: "Erica, hold all calls unless it's Resnick or Katz. Even Grant, tell him I need—"

"He's got that insert shoot later anyhow."

"That's right, too. Tell him I'll catch him back here at the end of the day, then." He shut his door and took off his jacket. He opened the three bulky envelopes and spread their contents across his desk and couch. This was raw Jingo material from all departments concerned, and what was wanted was a white paper, a "think piece," collating and condensing it all into a plain, simple . . . Well, Nick thought, into an Intelligence Summary, actually.

He was delighted that it had been given to him to do. He could do it with his left hand, practically. It would fill the rest of the day, and it would pass for a real contribution from his corner. He picked up the market research pile and began reading, yellow pad under his poised pencil. Suddenly, sexy glimpses of Deborah Ormay began flashing again. He forced them to go back into hiding, but felt saved by them.

He retrieved his pad and pencil and forced himself to concentrate totally and myopically on the Jingo material. Slowly he began to elicit facts and key statements from it onto his yellow pad.

At five he handed the sheets of his "think piece" to Erica. "Okay, flying fingers, do your stuff. I'll skip proofing it, just get the original and twenty copies down to Katz by six, okay?"

"Okay, but I'm not on the late shift tonight, you know."

"Then put in for overtime."

"Oh, I didn't mean that, Nick. I meant I'd *like* to get on it, *every* night. I could use the bread, you know? And I mean, like I don't have anything else to do, you know?" She finished the rest of her message with her upturned, lonely-kid-in-the-big-city, I'm-on-the-pill eyes.

He considered the sweetness filling her sweater, and for a blink had her naked in his bed. He had a rule: "Never anyone from the office." Besides, Grant played her *Yiddische papa,* and would never forgive him for, ha, taking advantage of her. He told her, "Let me see what I can do. I'll talk to the lady running the pool."

"Oh, I don't want the pool, Nick!"

"*Type!*" he yelled, and left for the men's room, thinking, Still, it'd be a pretty nice cushion for the long day's fall.

---

He went down to the 6:45 Jingo meeting. Sam Katz was presiding, waiting for the room to fill. He asked, "Hi, guy, you okay?"

And Nick said, "Yeah, I'm okay," knowing he was, at least for tonight, having delivered the white paper at six.

Madeline Donavan arrived, with four other girls behind her, two from her group, two from Ira's. Sitting, she slid a card across the table to Nick. He read it, an invitation to a party, and slid it back. "You kidding, Maddy?"

"I just thought you might . . . I mean, even if I could get out of this Dachau, I couldn't go." She flicked the invitation back.

He took it to end it. "Thanks for the thought, anyhow, Mad."

Katz opened the meeting: "Good evening, or good morning, or whatever you want. Okay. First—those pristine sheets in front of you are the latest poop from group, as we say in the military. We want each of you to read them carefully, and don't, please, let your copy get away from you, even inside the agency. Consider it classified information.

"Again, it's to help you, not to hinder you. If you come across anything that seriously goes against any idea or any campaign you've got faith in, don't automatically kill the idea—bring it to Jerry or I, and we'll see which alters which. . . . We're not afraid to go to them and say, 'We know *that* is true, but we want you to do *this* anyhow!' I think they'll respond to that kind of gutsiness." He smiled and lit a cigarette from someone's pack on the table. "Now, you all know that *we* know how hard this is on you, personally." Then he removed the smile: "But don't start feeling too sorry for yourselves. I don't want to prolong this now, there's too much work to be done. *But*—and you all know this yourselves, and you know how pissed Jerry is getting—you haven't even *begun* to start putting out on this thing! You're all still fucking off, thinking *somebody else* is gonna do it! Well, there ain't no somebody else. And I don't even want to be shown any more stuff that's *like* something else, dig it?

"*Sam! You're gonna love it! You know the fritzback campaign? Great, right? Well, this is like that!* . . . Next one that does that to me is out the door, and I mean it. Now, I picked each and every one of you for this, but so far . . ."

Nick looked up from his doodling every now and then, to erase Kelsey's laughing face, and to pretend he was paying attention to Katz's usual tirade.

". . . I don't play that way! That kind of creative director you can get at B and B, Bates, or Thompson or some other fatcat faggot place, but not here, not from me. When I first became creative director here, I . . ."

It was all autobiography anyhow. If tested, Nick could improvise and pass; he knew the whole story by heart. But tonight the guy threw a change-up pitch, and it captured his complete attention.

Katz said, "I . . . I mean, it isn't that the stuff so far is that bad. Some of it's pretty good, and shrewd. But you haven't left the predictable. I mean, open the heads up, get into the guts of the thing—we *got* the Yankee Doodle and the Give me liberty or give me death! . . . We *got* the nigger staring at the radar screen! . . . We *got* the draft scare and the Depression scare! Okay. But maybe it's someplace else altogether. Maybe it's . . . I'm just winging this now, this isn't it, let me do it bad for you, just to open you up, maybe it's—*Civilian Life is Deadly!* Maybe it's, Jesus, quick, *escape!* If you don't move your ass now, you're gonna have the *wife,* and the *job,* and the *kids,* and the fucking *mortgage,* and the fucking *lawn,* and the fucking two weeks at the *lake,* and you're gonna be fucking *smothered* to death before you're twenty-five!

"Know what I'm saying? Now, I don't know how you do something like that without going to jail, but maybe there's

[ 183 ]

some words or some graphics that say it without saying it, that say, 'Hey, fuck it, guys, the military gets you *out* of all that, it . . .' "

As Katz ranted on, Nick scanned the faces for reactions. Ira, eyes lowered, wore his perpetual, noncommittal grin. Madeline's face couldn't decide whether to go pink or chalk. If Grant were there, he thought, he'd choke to death trying to pretend his idol wasn't saying what he sure as hell was saying to them. Embarrassed, Nick lit a smoke and thought that after this he could use the word *insane* literally. What depressed him all the more was the sight of all the little hands around the table taking eager notes. He wanted to go home and take a shower. He doodled on his pad: "Fuck the Family."

Even Katz realized that he had gone too far this time, and ended the rally quickly with his favorite joke: "So just remember, children, it's a dog-eat-dog business, but it's the people who make it worthless." The children of all ages there burst into laughter. Nick kept his face as straight as he'd kept it through the antidomestic rant. He and Ira Schenker exchanged furtive, knowing glances, then met outside the door.

Grant was popping off the elevator just as they reached it. The three of them went up to Ira's conference room, where Ira immediately began taking orders for food. He wheezed, "Me and the guys were thinking of doing pizza tonight, you and Grant like pizza?"

"Get me something female from the Erotic Bakery."

"That's not nice, Nick. Pizza okay, or not?"

"Call Katz and ask him what we should fucking eat!"

"That's really not nice, Nick."

"Ira," he laughed, "I know you have to do it, but do you have to like it?"

"What's not to like about getting food? You don't want pizza, just say so!"

"Pizza's fine, I don't care—Grant?"

[ 184 ]

"I'm gonna skip. Get me a coffee."

"*Skip?* You? Hey, gumba, you sick, or—?"

"I'm all right," Grant snapped, "I just don't want anything to eat, that's all."

"That's it," he told Ira. "Grant and me are going out."

"Where?"

"To a restaurant, for real food."

"Aw, Sam'll be up, Nick, you know he will. . . . What'll I tell him?"

"The truth. We went out. We'll be back before nine."

"He goes whacko, Nick! You know how he—"

"Let him. Tell him we're brainstorming someplace, inspired by his paranoia."

Down and out on the empty night sidewalk, Grant said, "Knickers? Goose and Gherkin? Griff's? Where?"

"Someplace more expensive."

"Haw!"

"I mean it. We'll go to Christo's."

"You're crazy! They'll shit!"

"Nah, when they see a big bill, they'll think we were really doing something." At Christo's he ordered two steaks, and Grant frowned. "I think we're making a big mistake, Nicko."

"Ah, it's about time somebody shoved them back a little."

They ate and went back. Katz, they learned, hadn't made his early strike tonight. Nick felt relieved, but disappointed as well, realizing that he actually had wanted a confrontation. He and Grant proceeded to help Ira move theme lines and stacks of roughs around on his cork wall, lending him suggestions for tightening, for expanding, again eliminating none except the most obviously poor.

Sam appeared at 11:15, but didn't sit for his usual verbal critique. He just said, "Lemme take the whole works down with me, guy, my ass is dragging, I couldn't recognize a good thing tonight if it put its tongue in my mouth." Then he left.

[ 185 ]

Cleaning up, Nick grumbled, "Shit. Now we're all supposed to feel *grateful* for getting out of a flogging!"

Ira giggled. "Nick, why don't you go home before you start beating up on people you like?"

In the Village he dropped down into the Lion's Head and ordered a beer, to bring him down enough to sleep. The place must have been busier before he came in, he thought: blue-gray smoke swirled and floated everywhere. A clutch of men and women talked low at the other end of the bar. The sound was calming. He prayed no ass would play the jukebox. He sipped his beer slowly.

"Got money in the bank, heh, Johnny?" came a voice.

He looked at the drunk leering at him from the corner. "What?"

"Yer lips was movin'!" the drunk laughed. "Then the twitches start, ya know. Watch out for the twitches, Johnny."

"I will. Thanks." He laughed, paid, and left. When he got home, he stripped and collapsed into bed. His legs began to twitch.

To relax he used a trick Kelsey had taught him: he tensed every muscle in his body, then untensed them one by one, beginning with his feet and moving up, meanwhile trying to make his mind think only happy thoughts. He was going to try to steal away home again Thursday night. He'd run on the beach. He'd go to the dump. He'd shoot pool with the gang at Perry's. He'd— Then he fell asleep, and, sleeping, he watched the Circus Tent breaking down to move.

He and Kelsey took a jeep and went to Graf for a shower and *schnitzels à la Holstein*. A waitress brought them a letter, addressed to both of them. They saw it was from Brian Galgay, in Berlin. He didn't want to open it, but the Kelse said to go ahead. He slit the envelope with his bayonet, and a snapshot fell out. It was the picture of a very pretty girl. He looked and looked, but couldn't make her face come clear. Her hair was very, very black.

# 4

Home in his house in Maryland, drying his face after shaving, Brian Galgay pondered the thing in the wastebasket beside the hopper. Finally, he bent and reached it out from among the discarded tissues, Q-Tips, and toilet-paper cores. He unwrapped it just enough to see the red stains of flow absorbed by it. Evelyn was telling him the truth about that, at least. He could remember when not even the mightiest torrent would stop them, times when they wouldn't even pause to throw towels under, Evelyn exulting, "They're only sheets."

Now when she told him she was "out of commission," he pretended disappointment, but inwardly felt relieved, almost indifferent. She said she was sorry, but he doubted it. All this was new. In his times home before, even after his suspicions had germinated and begun to grow, his very jealousy seemed to fire his desire for her to new intensities, and increase his potency to match. It didn't amuse him to think how losing her love had so dramatically improved their lovemaking: the new pleasures seemed very poor payment at best. And now they no longer had even that. At least he didn't.

He dropped the bloody husk back into the basket, the soft

paper-crash sounding to him like the noise his passion for her had made when it died—almost unheard. His blackness was now deep enough to let him think, She's being careful with the son of a bitch anyhow. Sparing all of us *that*. He still wished he could believe that Evelyn had begun her affair before her abortion, two years back. If so, he could perhaps deflect part of his pain by believing, or trying to believe, that the lost child had not been his own. But he was pretty certain that the "jiffy fix" had happened before her infidelity started. He had long since dismissed the idea that the operation itself might actually have been a cause of her changing. Because that seemed to suggest some fall into promiscuity. And he didn't want to believe that of Evelyn. It had to be that she had fallen in love with the bastard.

He went down for dinner.

The boy greeted him. "Dad! Look!"

"A quarter! Where'd you get that?"

"The Tooth Fairy left it!"

"Fantastic—I'll give you a dime for it."

"Oh, no, that's only a ten, this is twenty-five!"

"Aren't you smart. How're you doing, Evelyn?" kissing Evelyn's neck from behind at the stove, where she stood turning hamburgers. She wore slacks and a red angora sweater and had her blond hair swept up into the loose French roll he liked so much, wisps and strands of buttery gold falling toward her temples. She turned her head, kissed him by the ear, and said, "You'd better start the car now and let it warm up."

"Right. We ought to start thinking about turning it in for a Rabbit or something."

"Even they're about eight grand now—can you believe it, for a Volkswagen?"

He went out to the garage and started the Buick. He'd wanted to sell the house and move to New York, but she wouldn't consider that. At the time, he'd believed her reason:

"These are the first roots we've ever had, Brian. And you know how filthy it is up there."

The Buick stalled. He tried it again; this time the automatic choke took hold. A new car—future projects like that now flooded his heart with a mixture of false hope and bitter sadness.

He stood in his driveway a moment in the early twilight. It was starting to spit snow. Their street was one of the inner rings of a large bull's-eye of identical development houses. He'd noticed it from the sky many times. He liked it well enough, and it wasn't an unreasonable commute to the District, but he'd never thought of it as a place to establish roots until she'd said it. Of course, now he knew that she had much more tangible reasons for not leaving. He jogged back inside. "Better bundle up, Ev, it's starting to get a little snow out there."

"Yeah? Oh, wow!" Tim ran to the window.

Evelyn said, "Don't get your hopes up, the radio said it'll turn to rain during the night. It won't affect your plane tomorrow, Brian, will it?"

"No. I can call a cab, you know, if the driving—"

"Don't be silly." She set his meal at his place and he sat.

"Can I go out in the snow, Dad?"

Brian seemed not to have heard him.

Evelyn said, "Go ahead." She helped Tim get into his quilted parka, and he ran out.

"You using the bible again tonight?" he asked.

"Absolutely," she said.

Evelyn was active in a local ERA chapter, and her speciality was addressing groups of service wives, using as her text *The Army Wife*, the traditional reference book and general guide for women married to career military men. One of its classic tenets was that of the wife being *in* the Service, versus only attached to it through marriage, supportive but not secondary. Evelyn had expanded this and similar lines of pre-existing doctrine into

[ 189 ]

a persuasive set piece designed to raise consciousnesses.

She brought her coffee to the table and sat opposite him. "I'm sorry you have to go tomorrow. It seems you only just got home."

"I was lucky to get even this much time."

"Does Thanksgiving at least *look* okay?"

"So far, yeah, if nothing happens. Did your parents decide, I meant to—?"

"Yes, no—she says they just can't afford the airfare this year."

"That's too bad."

"Yeah, well, it is a lot, just to—"

"I am sorry I wasn't free to put in for leave at the time, it would've been nice to go out there this year. I just couldn't see that far ahead, then. The thing could've gone on for—"

"I know, Brian. I do, you know. Hey, I'd better get a move on, or I'll be late."

Brian put his coat on. From the door he said, "I would take the retirement, you know, but . . . I mean, do you know how many guys there are out there right now, all looking for some kind of industrial-security jobs or—?"

Evelyn lit a cigarette. "Don't do that to me again, all right? I know. Nobody's asking you to retire."

"Well, I just wanted to . . . Okay, let's go."

Tim was trying to catch snowflakes in his mouth. The three of them got into the car. Brian drove, thinking he should tell her now about being passed over for lieutenant colonel on the new list. It was possible that she'd already heard it, but that was like her, she'd wait for him to tell her. He had started to, a few times, but just couldn't seem to get it out. He guessed he was afraid to see her reaction. He calculated the time between their house and the meeting and decided he'd do it just before he dropped her off: short and sweet.

He told her.

Evelyn sat looking straight ahead through the windshield and let a few beats of silence pass. Then she said weakly, "Oh, Brian."

"You didn't know, then?"

"No."

"Well, there's always next time."

"Sure."

She was surprising him. She was either a better actress than he'd thought, or else she was truly disappointed. In any case she wasn't doing what he had most dreaded, wasn't pouring forth layers of comfort and reassurances and salving balms. Which would only have been, to him, further proof of her wanting the status quo to continue. The promotion would have meant, most likely, both a desk job and a transfer. He himself wouldn't have liked the first, but wouldn't have minded the second at all. He added, "Good-bye, raise."

"Do you have any idea why? Your efficiency reports have all been excellent."

"Who knows. It's peacetime, they're cutting back. . . . Just straight computer justice, I guess." He had never told her of his tunnel incident in Berlin.

"I don't care," she said. "They're bastards."

"Well, they—"

"It's just not fair, Brian. You're too damn dedicated for them to—"

"Nothing's fair in love and war, Evelyn."

"Oh, Christ, I hope you don't say things like that in public. And it's all's fair!"

"Same difference. Thanks anyhow, Evelyn."

"For what?"

"For being angry about it."

She gave him a sharp look of disbelief. "Angry's hardly the word for it."

"I didn't realize the promotion meant so much to you."

"It doesn't!"

He wanted to question her on that, but she had opened the door. She kissed the boy and told Brian, "I'll be back around eleven. Don't wait up. I know you're tired." The door slammed shut behind her.

By 11:30 Brian began worrying. Evelyn still hadn't returned. He had sent Tim to bed at nine and had been drinking Scotch ever since. He went again to the living-room window, parted the drapes an inch, and looked out. The snow had turned to rain. A single car stood by the curb. It hadn't been there before. Its lights were out, its engine breathing thin, white smoke out its exhaust pipe.

He slipped out the back kitchen door and stood for a moment in the driveway, watching. *My God, I'm catching her at last!* He walked along the hedges to the car. His hand grabbed the driver's door handle. The first sound he heard through the opened door was his wife's voice: *"Oh, my God! What—?"*

The guy was balding and bearded and came up and out from behind the wheel in Brian's grip as lightly as a kid or a woman. Slammed hard against his car, he yelled, "Don't! Wait! Take my money! I'll give you my money!"

Brian palmed his face hard, then backhanded it harder, holding the man by the front of his zippered wool parka.

Evelyn threw herself across the front seat, screaming, "Help! Stop it! Help! Police!" Then she saw him and gasped, "Brian! Jesus Christ, what are you doing?"

He openhanded the face again. This time he felt blood come wet onto his fingers. Pinned, the guy was swinging, but his fists kept landing no higher than Brian's upper arms. Sniffing and choking, he pleaded, "Hey, man, what's the matter? What's—?"

"Brian! Are you crazy? Stop!"

"Hey, Brian," the man echoed her, "come on, man, let's—"

"Hey, man!" Brian mocked him. "Hey, man!" He drove his right fist upturned into the man's soft, small paunch, keeping his left arm stiff to prevent the sleazy bastard from doubling over. "Hey, man!"

Evelyn was out of the car and close beside him on the street now. Her voice came cold and level into his ear and surprised him. "Stop now," she said.

He felt her hand then. It had somehow gotten through his clothes and was on the grip of his pistol in its small holster on his belt. He knew he could knock her across the street with one swing of his arm. He also knew that if she had the trigger she could shoot his balls off.

"Let him go," she said.

He released the man and stepped back. The desire to be deeply asleep crawled itchily across the skin of his face. The man had brought out a handkerchief and was bending his face down into it. Evelyn was at him, in front of Brian, saying, "No, put your head back, Reverend, that's it." She took the hankie and wet it from the beads of rain atop the car roof, then cleaned the man's face with it. Brian heard her say, "Get out of here, Brian. Go into the house."

Brian went.

The man said, "Will you be all right, Mrs. Galgay?"

"Yes, yes."

"You're sure?"

". . . tomorrow" was the last word Brian heard. He went back inside his house and sat down at the kitchen table.

In a while he heard voices again, then the front door slammed. He looked up. Evelyn was standing in the kitchen. The glare from her bright yellow slicker irritated his eyes. She seemed about to speak, then didn't. She went to the electric coffeepot on the counter, removed its innards, and plugged it in. She swung her leather shoulder bag over the mudroom doorknob, took off her coat, and hung it outside. She took a mug down from a cabinet, poured it full of coffee, placed it on the table beside his glass, and said, "Drink the coffee. Do you want something to eat?"

"No." He couldn't seem to move; he felt compelled to stare at the steam curling from the coffee in the mug.

She was drying something with a paper towel at the sink, her back to him. "He's a minister," she said, her voice thin with fury. "He runs a drug rehab center where we have our—"

The noise made him look. She had dropped a heavy cup into the stainless-steel sink. It had bounced but didn't break. She was staring down at it. The red of her angora sweater seemed to jump like fire. He shouted, "Go on! What else?"

"No more," she told the sink. "I'm sorry I said that much."

"This priest—" he yelled, much louder than he intended, "is he the one you've been fucking?"

She came around slowly. Her eyes were slits, and her mouth wore a strange, hard smile. She folded her arms into a shelf for her breasts. She seemed not to be breathing. She said nothing.

He stared hatred at her through bulging eyes. It was out in the open at last and it felt sweet to his soul. "Well," he demanded, "you think I'm a fool?"

"Yes," she said quietly. "No wonder they won't promote you."

He felt shot.

She saw it on his face and said, "This is all about hurt, isn't it, Brian? Fine. You want hurt, I'll give you hurt."

"You already have!" he blurted. "You're very good at—"

"Shut up." She said it so quietly that he had to. "I only hope that you're not too drunk to forget this tomorrow." Her eyes had come fully open. They looked very wet, yet oddly calm. "Yes, he's one of the men I've been fucking, if that's what you want to hear. Anything else you want to know? Just tell me. I'll admit to anything. And for Christ's sake take your jacket off."

"I just want the truth!" He knew he'd slurred the word, but pretended he hadn't.

"You don't want truth; you want a confession. So, I confess. I did it. Anything. Everything. Every chance I got! With . . . with niggers," she went on. "With hippies and degenerates, and other women, even. Sure. With *enlisted men*, Brian! And with other *agents!*"

He sat, watching her mouth. He expected her to break out laughing. She didn't. As carefully as he could he said, "I only want the truth, Evelyn."

"No," she sighed, "you mean you want me to say that I'm innocent, and I won't give you that. How dare you."

"Because you can't." He sipped some coffee. "Because you aren't."

"Fuck you."

"Nice. Classy." He lifted the mug and drank more of the coffee. He raised his eyes without lifting his head. She was still just standing there, staring at him. He couldn't identify the look in her eyes, but was fairly sure it was neither anger nor fear.

"Believe anything you like, Brian," she said. "Whatever turns you on. I don't care one way or another anymore."

His hand came free of the mug and got the cigarettes from his pocket. He lit one and dropped the match into the coffee.

"My God, don't tell me even you can have vices!"

He remembered with a jolt and said, "Would you have really shot me?"

She didn't hesitate. "No."

Hope stirred. "Why not?"

"You were his problem, not mine. My life is mess enough without getting into lawyers."

Hope died. "Oh." He got up and walked into the living room, returning with an unopened bottle of Scotch. Behind him the swinging door clicked on its hinges like the works of a large clock. He emptied the coffee and match into the sink, rinsed the mug, broke the aluminum seal on the bottle loudly, and poured warm whiskey into the mug.

She waited until he had sat down again and said, "When did you start that, anyhow?"

"Starting now," he said and drank.

"You'd better be careful, Brian," she said, leaving the room. "You're getting human."

# 5

At eleven o'clock Thanksgiving Day morning, Brian drove through the Midtown Tunnel and onto the Long Island Expressway. Traffic was at a near standstill. The fast lane was closed to infinity by barrels and MEN AT WORK signs, though none were. He had given himself ample time to spare, but still it was maddening. Ahead of him the high red apartment houses of Lefrak City straddled the highway like massive walls.

He had the radio on, but he couldn't seem to find any music that didn't start steel whips thrashing inside his brain. He couldn't escape Evelyn's voice. He had waited until only two nights ago to call and tell her that he wouldn't be able to be home for Thanksgiving after all. He had expected disappointment and even rage. What he'd got instead was still shocking him: "It doesn't matter, Brian. Tim and I won't be here, either. We're flying to my parents tomorrow." Then she had hung up.

He kept trying to call her back, but the phone wouldn't answer.

The traffic inched forward, then stopped again. Again Evelyn's calm, icy words attacked him. Again they made him think, What if he hadn't called her at all? Or what if, at the last moment, he had been able to get free today? He would've found his house empty! How could she do this to him? He spun the radio dial wildly. Still no peaceful places. He cursed himself for not having brought cigarettes. The traffic started to move; he accelerated, and in the movement his mind at last found a thought that did not threaten him. Deborah.

She had begun appearing in his dreams; nothing lewd, simply there, smiling out at him through the glass of her astonishing beauty. She made him feel good, that he was a good man. Giving Deborah all his thoughts soothed and encouraged him but also troubled him: was this how Evelyn thought of her lover? If so, then it was simple—she should be free to go to him and have him whole and openly. Yet the very idea brought new rage: Why was it no longer himself whom Evelyn felt for in this soul-quickening way? What shame. Divorce.

When he reached the exit to the Grand Central Parkway, he wound down and around it, then left it almost at once for the side street. He locked the car and walked across the footbridge to the huge hollow globe of steel, the Unisphere, still standing in the World's Fairgrounds. A gaggle of Japanese businessmen stood photographing it. His contact sat on a bench, perusing a *Sunday Times Magazine*. It was the Englishman. As much as he hated the limey, he was relieved that it wasn't one or more of the Russians this time.

Teen-aged boys in ponytails were playing Frisbee football on the stubbly grass area behind the benches. Brian stood watching them as he spoke. "Why here?"

"Hello, Mr. Davis. Because I'm quartered not far from here."

"The Unisphere. Jesus. And let me tell you something

[ 197 ]

right away—if this is anything like the last time, I'm walking."

"Ah, yes, the Grand Central fiasco. I heard."

"I don't have to take that shit."

"Please accept my apologies. Our . . . colleagues do get a bit heavy-handed when they're upset."

"They're pigs. They could have blown me."

"I'm sorry you're agitated. Tell me, did you *see* the World's Fair when it was—?"

"No." He'd been in Vietnam, but the other man knew that.

"Pity, it was quite stirring."

The kids were good. They could both catch and throw from under their legs—even, two of them, from midair leaps. Brian wished he were them. "The Unisphere! Cameras all over the place, out in the open! Where the fuck were you trained any—"

"Perhaps I'm having this photographed, Mr. Davis."

Brian fell silent. "All right, get on with it."

"Well, this is actually merely part two of the Grand Central meet."

"Then you didn't get my new package yet. It's hardware. It's good." The truth was, he never could tell what they considered good.

"Oh, yes, we got it. And were awfully disappointed by it."

Brian took a breath. *Oh, God.*

The limey turned another page of the newspaper. It made a sad sound in the chilly wind.

Brian recovered: "You know my level of operations, goddamn it."

"But there's the rub, isn't it. You'd be amazed at what you think we know when we don't. The manual was a noble effort. But, really. Nuclear submarine sonar systems. So old-hat, Davis. Even you must—"

"It's the best I can do."

"Your quantity's been far short of the mark too, you know. For quite some time now."

[ 198 ]

"Yeah? Well, it's also been *quite some time* now since you've given me a sign. How do I know?" Brian demanded. "I haven't had a sign in—"

"I'm well aware. By happy coincidence, I happen to have brought one for you this very day." The Englishman handed Brian an unusually heavy box of Rothmans cigarettes. "Keep the lot."

Brian opened the flip top and saw not a letter this time, but a tape cassette. Excited, he took one of the cigarettes, lit it, and inhaled. He saw a kid intercept a Frisbee pass by getting one finger under the spinning disc and sending it straight up. His heart felt likewise spun aloft as he pocketed the box.

"If I may say so, Mr. Davis, you appear in need of a holiday. Not burning the candle at both ends, I hope. Now, then. We have once more kept our half of the bargain. Consider the screw turned, Davis. This will be your last chance, I'm afraid."

Anna's message, when he heard it at the hotel, was painfully brief. He replayed it again and again. Sometimes he listened to it at very low volume with the speaker held close to his ear. Then he would turn it up to top volume so he could walk around the room listening to her. He still wore his suit jacket, and was drinking Scotch and smoking the Rothmans cigarettes. Some of her words made him smile; others brought tears.

She began with a girlish, self-conscious clearing of her throat. He noted that her voice seemed to have deepened with age, but he had no trouble seeing it coming forth from her strong, lovely face. *"My dearest Brian,"* pronouncing it *Bree-an* as she always had. *"Goddamn, this is a cheesy machine they give me to use!"* This made him giggle each time he heard it: this was her code, assuring him it was truly Anna speaking: "Brie is a cheese," he used to tease her. "Are you calling me cheesy?"

*"Oh, Brian,"* Anna went on, trying, Brian was sure, to con-

[ 199 ]

ceal it when the words caught in her throat, trying to remain cheerful for him. *"I only hope this is easier for you to listen to, than it is for me to say. I can still see you clearly, my darling, my brave one.*

*"I am well.*

*"Because of you.*

*"And also you should know, they . . . they do not treat me badly. They leave me alone.*

*"I often wish I could hate life, Brian, and stop caring, and die. But I can't. I'm sorry, my Brian, but I cannot. And I know that you don't want me to stop wanting my life, unhappy and incomplete as it is without you.*

*"I am still teaching at the academy. But did I tell you that in my letter? Yes, but . . . oh, and I have a child this year who I think and pray may be truly a grand voice one day. I shall have to pass her on, soon. Her potential is beyond my limits . . .*

*"They gave me the snapshot of you, in case you were doubtful. You look wonderful. Your hair looks better longer like that, better than your funny old whiffle. But you know how much I liked your hair cut short, too.*

*"I am still as vain as ever, of course, and I exercise, and I wear makeup."*

Silence for six seconds. He was sure he could hear her weeping. But then she came back briskly.

*"They say I must end this now. Perhaps there is a shortage of cheesy tape!"*

He laughed aloud. They were far from getting that feistiness out of her. Good girl!

*"You know, my Brian, my love. . . . You know that there will be a time of my thanking you, beyond the veil, in another place. You know that. There I will thank you for my life!"*

Then came the final black pause, followed by: *"After a while, crocodile!"*

He rewound it, then set it playing again.

# 6

Nick headed for Grant Evans's office, eager to see how far the art director had progressed in visualizing their concept. They were into December already, but Nick's block had finally lifted, and he'd written a campaign at last.

Grant was bent busy over his drawing board, humming along to a tune from his radio. Their ads and posters and television storyboards hung on his wall, each concealed by opaque sheets of paper. They were developing Nick's idea in secret, showing it only to Ira Schenker, who upon seeing it for the first time had wheezed, "I love it. It's big and clean. I love it. Boy, Nickie, you had me worried for a while there—it sure took you long enough, you getting old, or what?"

He shut off Grant's radio and played the head of the musical presentation tape they were putting together. *America, the Beautiful,* his theme line said, *She Needs You Now.* Ray Charles's voice entered the room, singing the song. They also planned to use José Feliciano, and The Band. Grant dove into a stack of scrap photography he was pulling from every source he knew. "Nick! Wait . . . oh, baby, wait'll you see what I got for ya!"

It was a close-up photograph of the faces of an old man and a baby. Nick said, "Perfect. That can be 'America, the Young.' No, better—'America, the Hopeful.' "

[ 201 ]

"I was thinking maybe 'the Vulnerable.' "

"Possible."

"That's something we can let Sam and Jerry *fix* anyhow, right?"

"Ha, right."

The second, *She Needs You Now*, part of the concept was what he and Grant called "a flexible flyer." This meant that it was open-ended, or modular, as in the poster Grant showed him next. The picture showed Soviet warships at full steam, and the message read, *America, the Threatened. She Needs You Now. In Uniform.* Or, they could tack on *In the Far East.* Or *In Europe.* Or *To Get Your Act Together*, or practically any other specific desired.

He knew that Sam Katz would see the *She* appeal as Freudianly shrewd, but consider the overall approach too lofty an attack, too soft-sell. He figured, however, that at least for the purposes of the presentation, Resnick would appreciate it as a sound piece of emotional theater. The marketing team would likewise vote to take it all the way.

The trickiest part now was to expand and polish it, without leaking it. If it got exposed too soon, he knew so well from past experience, the experts downstairs would "fix" it beyond recognition, to death.

That night he again had his beer in the Lion's Head, then crossed Seventh Avenue and took West Fourth Street across for the first few blocks. One lit window he passed displayed framed World War I and World War II posters, all the campy rage, *Loose Lips Sink Ships.* Farther along, a queer shop was selling combat boots, Air Force jackets, jumpsuits, web belts . . . war surplus gone swish. How he wished Waltzie Cooper were around to see this and explain its significance to him.

He reached Perry Street and turned south, feeling almost too exhausted to walk. Snow had begun to fall. The December wind off the river had a backbone of deep winter in it. It all suddenly felt like Operation Snowsword to him. He was just coming off shift again, slogging his numbed but still excited body toward the sleeping tent . . . except there was no Kelsey waiting with snow-cold Jack Daniel's to share. Kelsey. Christ, where the hell was he anyhow? The longer he went without hearing from him, the more Nick had begun to wonder if he'd actually met him at the Hilton, or had only imagined it.

At 7:30 the following morning he signed his office building's security register, and took the elevator to twelve. He stepped off to the bing of the bell and went left. Ira Schenker, in his gray suit trousers, pink-striped shirt, and gray tie winding over his belly like a road over a mountain, was, as usual, already ensconced on the black sofa in the dim light. His Styrofoam coffee cup shone white on the receptionist's immaculate desk.

"Geez," he said, "you must get up at four, Ira! How do you always beat me in? You know, I'm thinking of moving my bed into my—" He shut up: Ira's eyes were closed, his pudgy, manicured hands folded loosely together in his lap. Nick grinned, took off his winter coat, perched himself upon the desk, pulled his own coffee out of its bag, ripped two sugars in, stirred, then sipped.

He crumpled the bag loudly into a ball.

Ira didn't even twitch.

He pitched it loudly into the empty wastebasket.

Nothing.

He cleared his throat raucously.

He was about to speak again when he noticed the belly: it wasn't moving.

"Ira! . . . *Studs!* . . . *Ira!*"

Without touching him, he put his ear to Ira's nose and mouth. Then he stepped back and looked. His eyes welled with liquid that stung. He grabbed the phone, pushed the button for the after-hours outside line, dialed 911, reported the death, and hung up. He gave Ira one final look, took his coffee, coat, and carrybag, and went back down to the lobby.

"There's a man dead on the twelfth floor," he told the security guard, "right in the reception area." He didn't tell him he had already phoned for help. He just left.

Some pull drew him downhill, toward the river, sipping the warm coffee in the cold air as he went. At Second Avenue he dropped the container into a litter basket, then crossed. At First he went right and walked downtown until he reached the United Nations. He wanted to walk through the grounds to the railing by the East Side Drive that overlooked the river. But it wasn't unlocked yet.

He crossed back to the wide, cobblestoned pedestrian mall along Forty-seventh Street, where demonstrations were held and where trees grew. He sat on a bench, rested his forearms on his knees, and spat between his legs into the snow on the ground. After "God, take his soul and give him peace," he couldn't make any more prayer words come.

He sat back straight and lit a cigarette, confused to realize that he was thinking not of Ira Schenker, but of Waltzie and Julia Cooper. It came to him finally, and just as unexpectedly, that he had never mourned Waltzie and Julia right.

Even after Susan and his kids had gone, he still had wished and tried to live life the way Waltzie and Julia had begun to show him. Remembering so keenly and so weirdly now that they were still dead, he thought again of what a mystery and maybe a sin it was for people like them to be killed, while self-absorbed rejects like himself were let live. Would they be Ira's age by now? he wondered, then figured, No, they'd still be only in their early fifties.

He wiped his eyes on his sleeve, and looked up through the naked trees at the giant seismographic chart that the avenues of skyscrapers made against the overcast sky. Would even

Katz and Resnick be saying now with the others how *young* Ira was to die? Some man's voice yelled, *"Who'll take the supper orders tonight, you greedy pissants?"*

He realized that it had been himself shouting aloud, and it jarred him. He looked around: there was no one, not even a drunk, to see his lips moving. He could bay like a dog for all anyone would care. The roar of traffic from First and Second avenues reached him with its sound of a river running far away.

He got up, knowing what he was going to do. He was going to eat eggs and bacon and buy a paper and come back here and read it. When they unlocked the U.N. gate, he was going to walk through the snowy gardens to the railing and lean out over it and watch the river for a while. Maybe there'll be a lot of boats today, he thought, and helicopters, and seaplanes.

Then, maybe, he would go and do what Waltzie and Julia would do—he would go and find music playing someplace and listen to it, for as long as he damn well felt like listening to it, until he didn't have to listen to it anymore.

# 7

"Don't move, Deborah!"

She wore only a scarlet, half-cupped brassière, and a scarlet, translucent half-slip over scarlet bikini panties. All the skin of her face and body looked as bloodless and egg-white as marble. She wore a spiderweb-thin silver chain around her sucked-in midriff, her rib cage showing like pentimento. Smoke curled, as from a cigarette, out the end of the pearl-gripped, silver-plated pistol in her hand. She seemed to be attached to the black enamel radiator behind her without touching it. Fog flowed in through the open window. A split black-and-white test pattern glowed on the small television screen. A man's bare shins and ankles and feet, toes down, lay on the end of the bare bed. The mattress ticking under him looked as greenly soiled as if it had spent decades in a cheap Montmartre hotel.

"Don't move!" the voice ordered her again.

She stayed still, petrified.

"That's better."

She blinked.

"Don't move!"

*Will you just take the goddamn shot,* she thought, letting none of it into her goggling, frightened, trapped eyes.

"*Now,* Deborah darling! Move! *Give* it to me!"

She started moving, strobe light pop-flashing like a police car's spinning beacons, left profile, right profile, front, gun-hand up, gun-hand down, but "No swirling!", no movement of the hanging hair or of the lingerie: staccato moves. "Triumphant now, darling, you're glad, you don't care if you're caught. No, that's a leer! Some fury, some hate—*that's* better."

*Hate's easy, schmuck.*

"Gorgeous! All right! Got it! Adrienne? Are you ready? Thank you, Deborah! Change fast, now, darling! Jimmy! I want the bathroom, now! Everyone to the bathroom! Strike the bed-room, and we'll want the— What? Seymour, what comes after the . . . ? Right, we'll want the no-seam, the thunder-gray no-seam, with the antique surgical light hanging down!"

"That with or without the leather table?" Seymour asked.

"I don't know! How will I know until I see it, for Christ's sake? God! Where is my lighting for the *bathroom*? Those tiles have to match the tiles this morning at the public baths! How many times do I have to say it? Do I have to do *everything*

myself? Jimmy! With the bidet, then without the bidet, right?
Jesus! Somebody tell me that's not a *duck decal* I see on the
shower glass—Jimmy? Seymour? Where the *fuck* is Eileen?"

She ran into the makeup room, stripped out of the scarlet,
and handed it to the wardrobe mistress, who gave her two pow-
der-greasy towels to wrap herself in. She sat at the table and lit
a cigarette. Rico fluttered onto her, brushes and pencils and
puffs working. "You're fabulous, you're looking incredible—but,
listen, he's feeling your hostility, I know he is. Please, Deborah, *cool* it!"

The girl next to her was eighteen, a blonde with boy-short
hair, brown doe-eyes, and siliconed breasts. "Gee, real kinky
stuff for undies, huh? Far out, really."

"It's been done."

"Deborah! Will you please be quiet?"

"Well, I'm just so sick of these assholes acting as if they're
*creating* something!"

Rico tch-tched, in pain.

"He is fast, I'll give him that—what's this, six hundred set-
ups so far?"

"At least. Please—be nicer with him."

"Balls. When you're stealing you ought to admit it."

"He's not stealing!"

"Oh, Christ, if it isn't this, it's lifting scenes from old movies! Gee, just like Hedy Lamarr!"

"What's the trouble, are you having your you-know?"

"No, I'm not having my you-know!"

The blonde shed her towels and squeezed into lemon-yel-
low, lacy no-bra bra and bikinis. Deborah asked her in the mirror, "What are you going to do, choke a canary?" The younger
girl reached across her for something on the table. Deborah
said, "If you're looking for your ass, it's in my face."

The wardrobe mistress draped a white slip over a chair.
"He says nothing at all underneath, dear."

"Ask him if hair's okay."

[ 207 ]

"No, don't!" Rico pleaded.

She and the wardrobe mistress laughed.

"All right, go ahead," Rico huffed, brushing her shoulders. "Get yourself on another one's blacklist, I don't care!"

"I'll be nice. I will. For you, Rico."

"You're just tired, that's all."

"Oh. Meaning the old bag can't hack it anymore!"

"It's been a long day for everyone."

"He's ready for you, Deborah."

"Ready, Joey." She let the towels fall and slid into the slip. Rico followed, brushing her hair as they went.

As she was leaving at around seven that night in her flowing Blackglama mink, a pinch-faced secretary in the studio's reception area looked after her and whined, "Do you know how many animals *died* to make that coat?"

She heard and shot back without stopping: "I know *one* who did, honey!" Adding to herself: Me!

# 8

Brian Galgay had been waiting alone in the trailer since six o'clock.

An immense steel skeleton soared above him, twenty-odd stories up into the snowy sky. Around the half block of its base ran a wooden fence. Inside the fence, near the foundation, stood the construction company's trailer-office. On his periodic official visits Brian would usually wait inside it while his crew of men went up into the massive bones to electronically sweep the two floors that would eventually house the organization requiring such security precautions.

Tonight he had cleared his use of the site with the proper parties, and had alerted the watchman to stay clear of the trailer until its lights went out. When the trailer began to heat up, he had removed his overcoat. Now he put it back on to go outside.

He stood for a while in the slow-falling snow, looking up at the squares of vast emptiness overhead. Promptly at nine, gloved knuckles rapped on the door in the wood fence and he opened it, turning away immediately to prevent the man from speaking.

When they were both inside the trailer, he again removed his overcoat, and again took the bottle of Scotch from his attaché case, this time bringing out the second glass. He poured a double shot into his own glass, then held the mouth of the bottle over the second, asking.

"If you please," the Englishman said, unstrapping and unbuttoning his Burberry. He lifted the glass and offered "Cheers," but Brian was already drinking. The Englishman straddled a draftsman's stool and sent Brian his cold smile. "I do hope all this isn't just to bargain for more time, or something of the sort."

Brian reached to the floor and brought the package up onto the wide working ledge.

The Englishman cocked a brow at it. "Something we couldn't trust to the mails or a dead-drop, I take it?"

Brian took the manila envelope from his case and handed it to the limey. As the man opened it and began perusing the papers it held, Brian's teeth chewed the inside skin of his left cheek viciously. At first he had considered confronting the General himself with the evidence and with the ultimatum of becoming his source, or else. He had agonized over this option for many torturous hours in several sleepless nights before finally dismissing it as too risky—as well as too great a burden, he had to admit, for his own nervous system. He couldn't help it—this was the better way, in the long run, for all concerned, and that's all there was to it.

The Englishman sighed brightly. "My, my. Mr. Davis, you seem to have outdone yourself this time. My congratulations."

"I . . . I haven't given him to you, yet."

"Nor have I said we even want him, yet. I take it that the parcel contains damaging particulars. I also assume that said particulars were not found by happenstance in somebody's dustbin."

"That's no problem," he said. "It's in my hands totally. There were no corollary investigations of the subject, and there won't be any questions asked." He glanced at the package holding the films and tapes from the stakeout. "I can either write him clean, or send the bullet into his head."

The Englishman smiled and lit a Rothmans without offering one. "So the first thing you want," he said, "is for us to lead the good General to believe that we got onto him by ourselves."

"Of course," Brian said, expecting nothing of the kind.

"And, of course, that's out of the question. Why were you put onto the gentleman in the first place, eh? No, I don't like it, I don't like it one—"

"Then fuck it," Brian said. "Get out. It's off." He grabbed his coat and threw an arm into one sleeve. "Tell your superiors they know how to reach me."

The man relented. "All right, all right, there's really no need for our fencing, I suppose. I do apologize. I will take receipt of your, uh, latest contribution, and pass it on for evaluation."

Brian finished putting on his overcoat. "I want—" He gagged. Nausea churned in his belly.

"Yes, what *do* you want?"

"I want this to be all for a while." He faced the other end of the trailer. Trying to stay lucid, he read the names on the hardhats aligned along the tops of wall lockers there. "I want you to lay off me. For a long time."

"But that will depend on—"

"That's my deal! It's big, and you fucking well know it! Either you let me off, or it stays with me, and tonight never happened!"

The Englishman got into his coat and cinched its belt tightly. He put the envelope into his case and picked the package off the ledge. "If everything is as you say, I expect your terms will be no problem." His voice turned almost friendly, and he added to Brian's turned back, "If I may say so, Mr. Davis, if you do win some, uh, relief, please use the time wisely, will you? At your rate of decline, you'll soon be of no use to anyone. I do mean that kindly, old man."

"Just get out," he rasped without looking at him. When he heard the door shut, he counted to twenty and lunged for it. Outside, he retched violently onto the thin strip of gravel along the base of the trailer. Empty, gagging and coughing, he kicked snow over his vomit and climbed back inside. He swirled whiskey around the inside of his mouth, then swallowed it. He poured more into his glass and stood there alone, sipping it.

Someone from the construction gang had left a solitary cigarette in a bent pack. He ripped it free and lit it. *It's done,* he thought. *It's over.* He had finally done what he had vowed from the start he would never do: he'd given them another human being—another soldier. "May God forgive me," he prayed suddenly, and just as suddenly felt his whole system quicken with the sharp, overwhelming need to be with somebody.

He threw the trailer back into darkness, locked its door, then the one on the fence behind him. The snow was whipping south down the avenue. He went with it along several blocks of

[ 211 ]

closed shops and open bars. Finally he came to a corner posted with pay phones. He dialed her number without having to look it up. She had to be there, he thought. If she wasn't, he didn't know what he could do. The prospect of returning to his hotel room alone made his heart stutter with panic. He was afraid to stay alone with this awful, secret, evil act of desperation—still in the process of being committed, he realized, being forever and ever committed by him, without end.

She was there. She answered his call. She was the only good thing he had left in his life, and she was speaking to him. Like poor, damned Anna, Deborah was only a voice in his hearing now, but unlike Anna, she was not eternally disembodied. He could get to where she was.

He broke from the booth in a dead run, heading west. As he went, he had a hard time remembering not only what she had said, but if he had actually made the call to her at all.

# 9

The ringing phone had brought her out of the shower into the harsh, dry air sooner than she wanted. It had been Brian Galgay and she'd told him abruptly, "No. I'm sorry, maybe another time, but there's someplace I have to go tonight and I'm rushing to—"

"Please. I'm not far, and I'll only stay a minute."

She'd told him okay. Something oddly boyish in his voice touched her, and besides, it was easier to relent than to argue.

Her gown for the party lay spread on her bed, but she pulled her jeans and sweat shirt back on. Then she regretted it: the gown would prove she was telling the truth and help send him on his way faster. She began to change, but her lobby buzzer stopped her. *Christ*, she thought, *he must've called from the goddamn lobby.* "Yes, Julio," she said into the wall speaker. "It's okay, he can come up."

She heard the footfalls stop at her door and opened it before he rang. His condition stunned her. "My God," she cried, "you look awful! What happened? Come—"

Brian rushed past her into her apartment and walked all the way to the fireplace before he stopped, as if he'd been there hundreds of times before instead of never, or as if it were a totally vacant room.

She followed, full of dread. She should never have let him come up. He sank to the edge of her sofa, looked up at her darkly, then eased back against the cushions. She thought of offering him a drink, but was afraid he'd accept.

He mumbled, "You told me you had to go out someplace!"

She ignored the accusation. She moved closer, regarding him more carefully. His eyes were rheumy, but that could be from the cold outdoors, or the liquor she smelled on him. His chest had been heaving, but now was gradually calming down. She knew he'd feel better faster if he removed his coat, but she didn't want him to do that.

He said, "Deborah. Oh, Deborah, I need you so badly." He groaned, and rolled forward, cradling the top of his head in both large hands. "Christ, Deborah, I really did it this time. I've just done the worst thing imaginable. But it was my only way *out*! I—"

"Ssh, Brian, don't say anything more."

His hands suddenly closed hard on both her elbows. His

[ 213 ]

black remorse seemed to be turning into something else. "You're hurting me," she said flatly.

He seemed not to hear. "I love you," he said harshly. "You've got to let me stay here with you tonight!" He pulled her down against him.

She cracked her shin on the edge of the table. She tried to resist without actually fighting him. She kept twisting her face away from his searching mouth.

"You want me, I know you do!" he said into her neck, into her swirling hair. "Be like you were at that inn! I've been going crazy, thinking about you that night! Please, Deborah, please! I'll do anything in the world for you! God, I—"

She held herself tense as steel, though her eyes were tearing from pain and outrage, and she longed to punch and swing her legs, shriek and tear at his face.

Finally his mouth caught hers. His kiss felt like a punch. His lips were chapped scaly. She clamped her own lips tight, but could still taste and smell from his nose the sour fumes of his breath. She damned her own breath for passing so raspily through her nostrils. It was her lungs fighting for air, but she could feel the prick mistaking it for the sound of passion. His tongue was ramming and prying at her lips now, trying to force entry. She thought of letting it in, then biting it, but feared what worse violence this pitiful bastard might do to her.

His legs opened beneath her. She fell between them. His knees gripped her hips like ice tongs. Her shirt had ridden up, and the feel of his raging cock against her bare skin reminded her of the gun she'd held in the photographic shooting earlier— was it some violation like this that had presumably happened to the girl in the scarlet underwear before the opening of the lens? Her neck seemed about to snap at the nape. Numbness tingled in both her forearms. On purpose, her body abruptly gave up.

She went limp as a corpse. Powerful as they felt, his hands couldn't support her dead weight. They didn't release their grip, but she felt them gradually begin to lower. His tongue lunged inside her, scooping and searching, but like a cop smashing his way into an empty, airless room, it soon stopped, still and baffled. The last image her eyes saw before they closed was that of his eyes, coming open. He withdrew his head. Hers fell forward. Her forehead hit off his chin, then landed on the coarse, wet lapels of his overcoat. "Deborah!" he gasped. "What's the matter?" He thought she had fainted.

Staying dead, she felt the pain recede and life return to her limbs. He lifted her hastily off himself and onto the sofa, at last freeing her arms of his hands. She felt him stand and swing her legs up onto the cushions.

"My God, oh, Deborah," he was panting, "I want you so much, I love you, Deborah, I love you! I *need* you! Don't . . ."

When she felt his hand fall upon her chest, she was about to give it up and explode into wildness—scream and attack his square, red, fleshy head with the brass fire poker. But she realized in time that he was only feeling for her heartbeat. She breathed deeply, as in sleep, remaining otherwise flaccid. At last she felt him move away. Then she heard him hiss, "You bitch!" He knew what she had done.

Fear opened her eyes and led her to tell him, "You're not yourself, Brian. Please go away now, will you?"

He nodded, agreeing.

Her eyes shut again.

He left.

She listened to his footsteps, heard him retrieve his case from the floor, heard him open her door, heard it close solidly. Then she sprang to her feet, ran, and sent the chain-lock home in its catch.

She ran to her bathroom and inspected herself. Her elbows, she saw, were practically infrared photographs of Brian's fingers. She patted a bit of blusher onto her cheeks, to imitate the color the ordeal had drained out of her. A glaze of fresh lipstick made her mouth look less bruised and swollen. She practically threw the gown and her coat on. If she lingered for even a moment, she knew, she might never move again. And thank God, now, for that stupid party.

# 10

At the place she leapt out of the yellow Checker and made her shaky way along the awninged, outdoor-carpeted lane to the glassed entrance of the elegant new building. Like millions of other New York-watchers, she had seen it rise for a year, as she had later watched the silver X-acto pencil of the Citicorp Building rise farther south. This chocolate glass-and-steel needle housed wealthy tenants for its keep all the way up. But tonight it seemed a solid, fifty-story pedestal erected solely for the purpose of supporting the stucco-sided, triplex eagle's-nest penthouse at its very top, where the party was.

One joker leaned precariously over the iced railing of one of the penthouse's many floating catwalks, and yelled to the sidewalks miles below, "Hey, Vinnie—spaghetti night!"

Parapetted terraces and balconies defied gravity on all sides, offering vertigo-inducing views around the compass. Inside all was concrete, bare, gray and raw, pitted with evenly cut holes and niches meant to hold planters, sinks, cushions for seating. People walked up steps to go down and down steps to go up. Capped piping and rainbow wiring projected every-where, stalactites and stalagmites of aborted power. Tonight, bodies and a generator provided heat and light. In imitation of Max Pollikoff's famous "Music in Our Times" museum-concept of music, four different bands played in different corners on dif-ferent levels. Guests moved from dixieland to string quartet to marimba to disco, carrying the drinks they received from one or more of the five bars, or from the roving waiters in white jackets and black bow ties.

The gin was Beefeater and Tanqueray, the Scotch Pinch, the vodka Stolichnaya, the bourbon Wild Turkey, the beer Hei-neken, the quinine Schweppes, the soda Canada Dry and Per-rier. Jack Daniel's was there, and Old Grand-dad. Liz Smith, Suzy Knickerbocker, *People* magazine. All had flacks, hawks, and photographers there. Working Broadway and off-Broadway stars had to pose and run, saying they hoped to return later if they could. Reindeer of ice. Christmas trees of pâté. Camera-men-directors in suede and denim talking as if they were in the advertising business, or movies, depending on who was listen-ing. Writers, art directors, stylists, fashion coordinators, agents, and secretaries of same—all floating like fruit in brandy, sink-ing, surfacing, the corridors of talk among them alight with models aglow, smiling, moving, listening:

"*Bullshit! Simon stole* Odd Couple *from* The Honeymoon-ers, *that's where—*"

"*Christ, go back to the Greeks, if you're going to go back that far!*"

She swam through the throng, gulping a stinger.

"*Cyril, everyone in the business has to write* Take a Bite Out of Life *and* No Matter How You Look at It *at least once, to get it out of their system. It's endemic.*"

"*Yeah, but the trouble is, somebody's starting to run them!*"

She passed another model who side-mouthed, "Wanna hold hands and make news?"

"No, I mean it, Ira Schenker's dead."

"Don't be too sure, it's a funny business."

"He's dead!"

"I've heard that before about a lotta guys. Don't ever write anybody off!"

"He's dead, I'm telling you! Gonzo! Kaput!"

"Listen, they said that about me when I left Wells Rich, and look at me now. Ira Schenker, I know Ira Schenker! I mean personally. We go way back. That guy's an infighter, baby. Our wives know each other! Years, I'm talking. Guy's like a fucking brother to me. Sat with him at the Clio Awards last year."

"He's dead! He died this morning! His heart physically stopped, I'm trying to tell you!"

"No shit, I didn't hear that."

She stepped outside. Her breathing refused to return to normal. Dark had fallen and the lights of the city had come on. Snow still fell. She stared straight down and wondered if it was true that when somebody jumped they always died before they hit the ground. She decided that her thoughts were too morbid and the air was too cold to bear, and went back inside.

"Aah, it's all animatics now—how can you expect to do anything special or new if you have to make a goddamn cartoon of it first, so some droid can go out and ask other droids what they think of it?"

She wandered, listening, showing a glassy smile.

"Yeah, but one thing about animatics, Lillian—they sure put a lot of dying illustrators back to work."

"Who cares? Let's hit the groaning board and call it dinner, okay?"

To keep from screaming, she went to the disco area and danced with two men.

"Beautiful is easy; beautiful that can also speak, that can read two goddamn lines is something else."

"Oh, God, I know, my entire life is voice-over!"

[ 218 ]

She went to the ladies' room and did some coke. The crowded room sounded like a ward for head colds and generosity prevailed, but she used only her own.

"*I said, Christie . . .*"

"*I said, Jodie . . .*"

"*I said, Pam . . .*"

"*I said, Lauren . . .*"

"*I said . . .*"

"*I . . .*"

She took her stinger to a dark, vacant corner on a window ledge near the string quartet, and sank down, tired.

Watching, she realized that the party's rhythmic flow was suddenly breaking and starting to funnel toward and away from something happening on the dixieland floor. She left her drink and moved through the crowd reacting to whatever disorderly event it was. Then she heard, "It's a fight!"

Nearing the center of the storm, she jumped up to see over the barrier of heads, and came down shocked. She had seen Nick Burke. She began elbowing her way through the mob. "One side!" As she reached its edge, Nick was being punched backward into the trumpet player. His falling body jarred the mute out of the horn and stopped the music. Blood ran red from his split eyebrow. He got up. The other man was short and dark and well built. He looked less drunk than Nick did, but was staggering from the recoil of his own thrown punch. His face when Nick kicked him in the balls showed that he'd thought it was over. Nick stepped back into a crouch and cocked both fists, waiting for the guy to recover, at least enough to bring his face up into the open again.

She screamed, "Stop it!"

But the guy's face came up and Nick hit it with his right fist, three times fast in a row, all in the left eye. A cry came out of the man and he went down. Nick pounced, trying to peel the man's hands and arms away from his face. Voices wept, "Oh, no, don't!" A waiter made the mistake of approaching from the side. Nick came up and backhanded him in the throat in the same motion. A smarter, bigger man, a guest, grabbed Nick from behind, trying to lock his arms behind him. But he was halfhearted about it, and took Nick's left elbow in his kidney. Free, Nick spun and started his knee moving upward toward the peacemaker's lowered chin, but by then she reached him and he recognized her and stopped.

"Oh, Nick," she said. "What—oh!"

The first man's date had found an empty punch bowl and was lifting it to bring it down upon Nick's turned head. Deborah stepped forward and stopped her with an angry right hook. People milling behind instinctively caught the crumpling girl, but not the bowl. It hit the concrete and smashed.

He said, "Hi," and walked her fast through the crowd, pausing only to get their coats. The elevator took them away. In the lobby he grabbed her hand and yelled, "Run!"

They ran east through the falling snow. Slush started soaking through her snakeskin shoes, and she slowed, protesting, "Stop! My feet! I can't—"

"Run!" He laughed. "They're coming! They got sticks and everything!" But he had stopped, too, and was smiling at her.

"You," she said, "you're not drunk at all!"

"Aw . . . that mean we can't run in the snow anymore?"

She laughed. The sight of her teeth thrilled him. Then he noticed the slush streak on her coat. "Oh, jeez, I'll have to buy you a new one!"

She jumped back. "No, don't try to wipe it! Let it dry!"

He popped his eyes at the whole coat then and said, "My God, it's *real*, isn't it. Never mind, I'll just get it cleaned for you."

"No, really, it's all—"

"Oh, you want money, is that it?"

She swung her shoulder bag against her chest. "I want to

[ 220 ]

get out of this goddamn blizzard before I get pneumonia, that's what I want!"

He was inside her apartment for some time before the reality of it registered in his assaulted mind.

She had marched him straight into her bathroom, snapping light switches on the way. She had a large, oval antique mirror, and he watched her in it as she bathed the dried blood from above his eye, then swabbed Isodine into it with a Q-Tip. "Be still, now," she said. "It doesn't sting at all."

"I'm quiet as a mouse."

"Oh. Then yell yikes, or something. It's really ugly, you probably ought to go get a couple stitches."

"Just pinch it tight and slap a Band-Aid on it."

"I know what I'm doing. Hold it closed while I get the Band-Aid—are your hands clean?"

He obeyed her.

She applied the bandage. "There. Now I'm going to change. You can wash up if you want, just throw your coat anywhere," she said and disappeared into a room off the hall.

He went back to her living room and draped his coat and his jacket over hooks on a chrome tree behind her front door. Then he noticed the place and admired it. Framed prints, posters, and paintings leaned on narrow ledges along the pale walls. A freestanding shelf unit held books and stereo equipment and broke the long, spacious room in two. He walked back to the window end, to the wall fireplace. He balled a few pages of an old *Times* left in a wicker basket on the raised hearth and shoved them under the grate. He added some kindling, and reached for a log. It was then that he was struck aware that he had been brought into the privacy of her home. He put the log down.

She appeared in jeans and a T-shirt and huge black bunny slippers. The jeans were cut low at the waist, and when she walked the shirt flared a little, revealing quick glimpses of her nearly vertical navel. He was surprised to feel his distant-seeming sex instantly begin to rear, trying to make an erection for her. When she stopped, the crescent of her belly went away, but his beginning hard didn't. She said, "Well? Where's my roaring fire?"

He returned to the task.

She watched him for a moment, aware that he was making her feel safe. In her kitchen she plugged the coffeepot in to perk and arranged a tray with cups, snifters, a bottle of Rémy. She wished she could get rid of the vision of him fighting the guy at the party. The guy, in her memory, kept taking on Brian Galgay's face. It made her feel queasy and kind of scared, the way pro hockey games affected her, and boxing, and the time she'd witnessed a man being mugged by two hoods in the shadows of an alley near her building. She sneaked a peek inside at Nick squatting and blowing on the kindling.

Joe the parakeet had begun trilling along with the bubbling of the coffeepot. The pot stopped now, but Joe stayed happily lost in song. She whistled to him and he answered. She poured the strong coffee into a covered pitcher, and carried the works in, hoping she hadn't made any too serious mistake in pulling this Nick away from his brawl. It was too late now in any case, she decided.

She placed the full tray onto her low glass coffee table. He didn't turn, as she'd expected him to, but stayed staring into the high-jumping fire. She said, "A cuppa java for your thoughts."

He came around without standing, saw the stuff, and said, "Oh, great. Thanks a lot, Deborah."

"Sugar, Sweet 'n Low, cream, brandy, help yourself."

He sat cross-legged on the rug and added a splash of the Rémy to his black coffee. She held a snifter out and he turned an inch of the pungent liquid into it. She swirled it into a small whirlpool and said, "Well?"

"Well what?"

"What were you thinking?"

He looked down into the cup as he sipped. "I don't want to embarrass you."

She lowered herself from the edge of her chair to the floor. "Say it."

He looked at her and said, "All right . . . I was wondering why I've been blocking you up to tonight. And I decided that it was because I had you tied with Galgay, whom I don't like very much, and because I'm put off by your looks."

She heard nothing after "Galgay." The very word made her flinch. "Did you now," she said weakly.

"Did I what?"

"Decide all that."

"Yeah."

She swallowed some cognac and chased it with coffee. "Since we're being so candid, maybe I should tell you that I'm a bit frightened by you." As she said it, she realized how untrue it was.

"Oh, hey, Deborah, don't," he said. "I'm nobody to be scared of."

"Tell that to the poor guy you were beating up."

"Oh, that." He lit a cigarette from a twig out of the fire behind him. "I'm sorry about that. He really pushed me to it, though."

"How?"

He sighed. He suddenly felt very tired, as well as warm, and safe, and imposing. "A friend of mine died this morning," he told her. "I guess I never realized how much I really liked him until he was just gone, all of a sudden. Then this dope at the party . . . he pulled one of those I-know-he's-dead-but-I-have-to-be-honest raps with me, then started telling me what a hack my friend was."

"For that you hit him?"

"I explained myself first," he said. "I really did. I told

[ 223 ]

him at least twice . . . that he was making a big mistake."

"Why didn't you just get away from him?"

He stared into his coffee for a moment, then admitted, "Because I wanted to take him out. If it wasn't him, it probably would've been somebody else."

She looked at the vial and spoon in her hand as if someone else had taken them from her jeans pocket. She watched her hands unscrew the top and scoop out a hit, then heard her voice tell him, "Here—lean over."

He didn't move. "No thanks, you go ahead."

She hesitated, then poured the cocaine back into the tiny bottle. She replaced the top, put the thing onto the table in front of her, and sat looking at it.

He said, "What's the matter?"

She sipped more Rémy and shrugged. "I don't know. I feel this odd compunction to follow your lead." Then she arched herself up until she was sitting on her heels.

He said, "Wow," feeling his erection rise another notch.

"All right—I'm my wonderfully composed self again. Time in. Tell me about your friend who died."

He hunched his shoulders. "That's it, lady, that's the only explanation I've got."

"But we have to find something to talk about, don't we."

"Then let's talk about you."

"All right, but you first."

"God, you make it so hard," he said, laughing to himself at the pun. He wondered, If she knew, would she feel scared again, or complimented?

From her new, higher perch she had by now observed his physical condition. She decided that it was probably only an effect of the fire, blazing so close to his back, plus the coffee and brandy. "I was involved with some violence today, too," she said. "Tell me, why did you feel you had to fight somebody, just because somebody else died on you?"

"Ah, I don't know, Deborah. I'm hardly happy about it. In fact, I think it stinks. I'm too old for that kind of— I don't know, I've been strung out for too long a time at work, I had your pal Galgay giving me the third degree that day, then Ira died. If I were normal, I'd just get drunk and let some time pass, but—" He turned away to throw a new log onto the fire. Now that she'd forced him to think about it, he'd had to think of Waltzie Cooper again, too, and suddenly felt an unfamiliar, deep need to tell someone about it. He was aware, too, that his numbness had gone. So he told her: "It felt very loony. I started getting this Ira all mixed up in my head with this other guy I liked, a hundred years ago. He died, too. Him and his wife. They both died, in a car crash, and I don't know, it happened right in the middle of a whole bunch of other shit I was buried in at the same time, and . . . His name was Waltzie, his wife's name was Julia, and he was a shrink. Ha! I just hope he isn't listening to me now!"

"Maybe he is."

"Yeah. This'd be right down his alley. See, I've never forgotten them, I've thought about them a lot ever since, but . . . Ah, this is bullshit, you know? I mean, I *know* the school solution, at least my brain knows the answer. I never buried them properly, right? Old Aztec slogan—must mourn slain warriors!"

"But now you're feeling it, Nick."

"Yeah, but it's not what you . . . it's not nice, Deborah."

"My mother died when I was fifteen," she said. "I hated her for it for a long time."

"How did you stop?"

"I think I just finally gagged on the taste."

"Yeah," he said, "it sure doesn't taste good. But I also feel like I'm always disappointing them, you know?"

"No."

"Well, like today. Waltzie and Julia, anytime something

bad was coming down, they'd run off someplace fast and listen to some music. If they couldn't—well, once she went out and bought a little accordion, and started learning how to play it. And I tried that today. I went to some record shops, then I went home and listened to the radio. The only reason I went to that dumb party was I figured there'd be some music there."

"There was."

He stared at her for a long time. She stared back.

Finally he said, "My God, you're a beauty."

She dropped her eyes and lit a cigarette. "Don't change the subject."

"I'm not," he said. "I didn't mean your looks."

"Which put you off."

"Less and less."

"Good for you. You're pretty fragile for such a tough guy."

"It'll pass. Want to go back to being frightened?"

"I'm hungry, how about you?"

"Wow, she's even going to feed me."

"I'll feed you on one condition."

"Name it."

"Admit it—slugging that guy made you happy."

He finished his coffee. "Sure—there was something clean about it. Good enough?"

"For the moment."


He followed her to the kitchen.

She emptied a container of frozen chili into a frying pan on the stove and turned on the gas. She took a spoon and began hacking at the block of beans and meat. He approached her from the side. She turned her head to look, and he kissed her.

Just as he felt her begin to kiss him back, she stopped and pulled away. She was crying. "What's the matter? Jesus, what's the matter, Deborah?"

His voice didn't let her stop crying, but it let her drop the spoon, turn, and collapse against his chest. His arms wrapped around her and held her tightly. It was the comfort she had been seeking, but she found she had to fight her body's urge to recoil from him, frightened by the undiscerning memory of her nerves. She let herself weep. Sobbing, she told him of her ordeal. She felt him stiffen and heard his voice say "Galgay?" twice, into her hair, astonished as if he had never heard the name before.

Holding her close to him, he kept repeating, "Ssh, ssh, it's okay now, you're all right." After a while he released her and studied her eyes. "You okay now?"

She took a handful of his sweater. "Yes." His face continued to look inordinately worried and confused.

Then he said, "Why did he—why would *anyone* ever treat you like that?"

She tried to sound lighthearted and tough. "It happens. He was just drunk and horny, I guess. And kind of out of his skull. But God takes care of the working girl."

"Fucking *Galgay*. I can't believe it!"

"Forget it, Nick," she whispered. "It's over. It wasn't all that bad." She shut off the gas and left him. She walked to the other end of the room and turned on the radio, loud. Nick came after her. She said, "Any favorite stations?"

"Yeah, RVR."

She found it. Jazz saxophones flowed over them. She opened her arms to him. "You were looking for music?"

His arms opened too and they danced. In a while they kissed, still dancing, and kept doing that, kissing and dancing, long and slowly, until they quit dancing and melted like a candle to the floor.


Gently, he realized his wish of seeing her T-shirt hiked past her navel, then her ribs, then her breasts. These he hungrily kissed and licked and sucked upon, first one then the other then back, finally closing them together with his hands into one exotic fruit, covering both edible stems with his lips.

Feeling safe with him in her mind, she let her body go. She explored his back, his belly and his chest with her hands beneath his sweater. At length, she sent her right hand between them and unlocked the metal snap of her jeans: her ultimate signal. He responded by moving his face down toward the source of the sound, his fingertips replacing his lips upon her twin erections. His mouth kissed and tasted the skin of her concave stomach, the well of her navel. Then, he exposed her lower belly and rear to the light and to his lips. She worked his sweater upward. He removed his face and hands from her just long enough to pull the sweater free.

It crackled in the air above them as it went flying behind the sofa. Feeling him resume his loving, she sent both her hands to play in the hair of his head. She expected to feel her bottom clothing yanked clear. But instead, he was peeling it down piecemeal, like one body stocking, not uncovering the next strip of flesh until he had thoroughly kissed the one above. Soon after passing her venus his head lowered beyond the reach of her arms. Eager to keep touching him, she thought of sitting up but decided to luxuriate in the attention, and stretched both her arms back behind her in an arrowhead of abandon. He kissed the tops of her thighs and then her knees. Her clothes seemed to recede on their own like the tide, making way for his deliciously busy mouth. She was glad she'd had her legs waxed again, she wanted not even bristles to come between his lips and her . . . Her eyes flew open. He had stopped.

"Good God, Deborah," he said, "what did he *do* to you?"

She raised her head and saw that he was kneeling upright, looking down at her shin. She felt his fingers trace a line across the ridge of her bone. It stung, but she said, "Oh, that's nothing. I must have bumped into something."

[ 228 ]

"Like hell, that's a real gash!" He got up and left her.

She sat up and inspected the wound. He was right, it was worse than she'd thought. The skin had torn and bled. Her first thought was of tomorrow's job, hoping no close shots of her legs would be needed. Then he was back. She was charmed and surprised to see that while he walked, he had stripped. He was carrying the Isodine, a facecloth, and Band-Aids, and knelt once more at her feet.

She made her voice smoky and cooed, "I'm very impressed!"

He saw where she was looking and blushed. "Oh, himself? You can take all credit or blame for him."

"Glad to. Ow!"

"You're the one who said this stuff doesn't sting. It's just a little cold, that's all." He dabbed it into her wound, covered it with two large Band-Aids, then slid her panties and jeans the rest of the way off. "How'd he do this, Deborah?"

"I forget. It looks worse than it feels."

He put the first-aid gear onto the floor and sat back onto his heels, regarding her. The fire felt warm on his back and bathed her in red dancing lights. He said, "How about the top?"

She shed her shirt, then leaned back seductively on the heels of her hands.

"My God."

"Thank you," she said. "That's where it all came from."

"I could look at you forever."

"Don't."

A black-voiced singer sang of how it had used to be with her and her lover-man. Trapped air popped free from a flaming log. Their right hands met in the air between them and joined. He bent and kissed her knuckles, then tasted the berry-red tips of her fingers, one by one. Goosebumps tingled up her back, but she didn't shudder. When he got to her small finger, she

[ 229 ]

hooked it gently behind his bottom teeth and pulled him toward
her.

After the initial soft shock of actually being in her he whispered, "I wish I could reach your head."

She said, "You're there."

It wasn't until they moved inside to her bed that he noticed
the dark bruises on her arms, around the elbows. Winding the
clock under the small night lamp, she said carefully, "They
could have come from the rug." She had been kidding him
about the "washboards" on his knees from her carpet.

He stretched across her sheets and looked closer. "Fucking
Galgay!"

She rolled sideways into the bed with him, put her arms
around his back, and began kissing his neck and chest.

He said, "I want to know."

"Why? It's all in the past. Now it's now."

"That animal—what the hell's his number, anyhow?"

"Why?" she teased. "You want to call him?"

"Call him? I'll kill him."

"Oh, I already know how tough you are. Big deal." She
continued to mouth his tense shoulders. Her hand found his
recovering phallus and began milking its shaft gently. The vein
started to swell, but his distracted voice above was saying,
"Why would that bastard want to lean on you?"

She let go of him and sat up. "All right." She bristled with
impatience. "He wasn't leaning on me, he was trying to come
on to me, okay? I mean, Jesus! You're the one who's here,
aren't you? What else do you want? It isn't even any of your
damned business, if you—"

"Yet."

"What?"

"Say, it isn't even any of my damned business *yet*." He
made a wide grin and pointed at it. "See? Chastised. Sorry.
Ingratiating. Contrite. Uh . . ."

[ 230 ]

"Forgiven."

He said, "Do us all a favor and don't see him anymore, all right? That's not being too childish of me, is it?"

She said, "Don't worry. My life just started about thirty minutes ago."

He swallowed hard. "Boy," he said, "that's the most beautiful thing anyone ever said to me."

"Good," she said. "Because I've never said anything like that to anyone before."

# FIVE

# 1

It was late Sunday evening, the night before the presentation.

Sam Katz kept walking and talking.

Nick sat sprawled across two conference-room chairs, praying for the man to be struck dumb. To keep his eyes from shutting altogether, he stared at the long thin slit of glass in the back wall. The dark lenses of the film and slide projectors felt like guns pointed at him. He looked over them at the big clock inside the projection room. When he watched the spinning red second hand, it seemed that midnight was rushing at him like a railroad train. But the black hands seemed to have stayed still for hours. December itself had been going just like that, he thought. Flying and crawling at the same time. Deborah was the fleet red hand; the other parts of his life were the black. *Shut up and let me get out of here,* he was dying to yell at Katz. *This is all unnecessary.*

But Katz kept haranguing him, "coaching" him with stuff Nick had mastered his first year in the business: ". . . then, in the meeting itself, you find the guy at the table who has the power, right? And you direct the sell to him. Straight into his guts. Only you do it in such a way that the others think you're including them in it as equals! Otherwise, if they catch you playing to the big man, they feel neglected and go negative on you later!"

Nick moved his eyes to the heating vents. He swore he could hear Ira Schenker's wheezy laugh coming through them to tease him. Sure, he could make the presentation in Ira's place. And he could sit now where Ira should have been sitting. But otherwise he could not do for Katz what Ira could have done so well—he couldn't bring sweat to his brow, couldn't hang on Katz's every word with nervous eyes, couldn't nod ponderously, couldn't utter the profound grunts of feigned agreement and understanding.

"See the nuance there, Nicky? Think you can pull that off tomorrow?"

The sudden lull snapped him alert. Katz wanted an answer. He said, "Yeah, I can do that, Sam."

"But the stuff, like I said before—the stuff itself you present with equal enthusiasm across the board. *All* the work is our favorite. You're in love with every campaign on the table."

He had heard this particular "nuance" several times earlier, during the formal rehearsal, and let it pass. Now, however, with "H-Hour" of "D-Day" only about nine hours away, he balked. "That's bullshit, Sam."

"What is?"

"I don't know how to do that, Sam."

Katz squinted and automatically smiled. "You don't think all the work's great, Nick? You wanna push just 'America the fucking Beautiful,' right, guy?"

He tried not to show Katz his hard eye. He knew Katz had been glad to get the campaign, but personally resented it as a last-minute, grandstand play on Nick's part. God, he hated the position Ira Schenker's death had forced him into. One of the Pentagon's guidelines stipulated that the final presentation be made by those personnel who would actually be servicing the account should the agency be awarded the business. Top management could participate only in an advisory capacity. Jerry Resnick had fingered him to replace Ira, and Katz didn't like it. He sidestepped the favorite-campaign trap and said, "Sam, I've got a great idea—swap jobs with me for the day. Make me creative director on paper, and *you* make the goddamn pitch."

"Resnick said no," Katz said.

Nick laughed out loud, even though he was sure that this time Katz was dead serious. There was the real catch: Katz wanted to run the show *through* him. He had to do it, but wasn't free to do it in his own, natural style. "Sam, look," he said. "Let's say they stop me right in the middle and ask for the agency's recommendation—what do I say?"

"Let Jerry or I field that one for you."

"Dammit, that's amateur time. All time—what if I lay it all out even-steven, and they start yelling eureka over the straw man?"

"Then that becomes the agency recommendation."

His stomach turned; the other man's anxiety was infecting him after all. He lit another cigarette.

Katz stopped pacing and leaned on the table. "But I thought I made it clear, Nick. There is no straw man!"

He finally said it: "That *Gung-Ho Army* campaign sucks and you know it, Sam."

"No. I don't know that at all. It's . . . it's a lame horse, maybe. I'll give you that. But what can I say—Jerry really likes it."

"Nah, he's just afraid to only go with two."

"It ain't that bad, Nick."

"We're crazy to go in without a recommendation. *Gung-Ho's* a straw man—it's almost exactly what they're running now! *America,* and *Get It On* are at least different directions. We oughta put our money on one of them, and sell the hell out of it." He was about to add, "I know how these guys operate," but Katz was already stepping on his words.

"Listen, Nick, don't get carried away with yourself. You give good mouthpiece, good song-and-dance—and that's all you have to worry about, huh? You let Jerry and me move the tanks and the planes, baby. We're talking forty, fifty million bucks here, and, man, you're just one little tack on the map!"

Nick held a straight, stoic face. "Yeah, but I'm still the one who has to talk to them, Sam. And how the Christ can I sell anything if I have to sell everything?"

"You'll do fine, Nicko. Don't sell anything. Think of it that way. Yeah. Just present, Nick. Just lay it all out and walk them through it, nice and easy, nice and *clear*. But with enthusiasm. Trust me, Nick, you know?" He reached over and laid a hand on Nick's wrist and gave it a manly squeeze.

He said, "Okay," knowing the full, threatening implication of that "Trust me." Early this morning, when Katz had first told him that Resnick had picked him to replace Ira Schenker, his first reaction had been black panic. He had just two sources of hope in his world. Deborah in the city. And his days of sanctuary in Derby. This seemed to endanger both. The Army account, if they won it, would demand full-time supervision, full-time meaning virtually total commitment, half his life in Washington, the other half on shooting locations. He had blurted, "Aw, shit, Sam, I'd love to work on it, I'd *really* love to work on it—but just as a writer. I don't want to *run* the goddamn thing."

"I know your problem, Nick." Katz had winked. "Not to worry. If we don't get it, no sweat. If we do get it, then, Jesus, you can buy and fix up a dozen fish shacks. Trust me, huh, guy?"

Meaning bite the bullet. Which Nick was still trying to do, caught, as he was, between the rock and the hard place. He didn't trust Katz an inch. If they didn't get it, "no sweat" would hardly be his prevailing attitude. Yet how could they ever get it? Every instinct in him said that Katz's way was doomed to failure. And these weren't just his advertising faculties warning him.

"Another thing," Katz was saying, "I don't expect you to salute these robots, but remember—we're super respectful."

"They put their pants on the same way we do, Sam."

"Bullshit they do."

"That's an old Army saying."

"Where, on the rock pile?"

"I know it sounds hokey, but they like you to have the courage of your convictions." He was dying to shout, "This is the military we're going up against, and I know how to do it! Ask Kelsey—you present the big picture, you clarify, you elim- inate, then you *specify!*" He could still hear Kelsey teaching him the G-2 briefing: *Don't say the Soviets could come through Fulda or Hof, even though that's true. Say they're damn well gonna come through Hof, 'cause that's where our ass is at.*

Katz pressured his wrist again. "You're overthinking it, Nick. Just do your thing. Be yourself—only don't get too flip with them, that's all I'm saying. No funny stuff. They'll take it as we're not serious enough."

So he shut up. And quit listening, too. It was a business of imagery; appearances were everything. He could never tell Sam Katz of his experience as an officer, or his feelings for the mili- tary. It would only make Katz doubt his credentials as a creative talent. He watched him walk to the projection-room window and peer through. For Katz the clock behaved realistically. "Geez, after midnight already, we'd better go get our beauty sleep."

# 2

Hungry for air, he got out of the taxi at Benchley's and walked the edge of Abingdon Square toward his street. The wind was cold but not bitter and carried a tang of muskiness from the river. He let it clear away all his thoughts except those of Deborah. No matter how the Jingo pitch went, they could go on stealing their lunchtime moments together at her place. And there might not be all that much night work, even if they won the business. He and she could start having dinner together, beginning their delicious nights in the early evening. Exhausted and harassed as he was, thinking of her excited him. He walked faster.

As he approached his doorway, he sensed the presence of somebody waiting in its shadows. He slowed his gait, then paused near the stoop, making a fist. Before he could speak, the figure stepped forward into the light. "Howdy, son."

"Kelse!" His fist unclenched, but his heart kept thudding. "Jesus Christ, man! This is New York fucking *City*, you know— you don't go around playing Harry Lime on people!"

Kelsey laughed. "Scared you, huh? Sorry 'bout that."

"Bullshit, scared me."

"Ho. Well, anyhow—hi, howya doin'?"

"Fine." His heartbeat slowed to normal. "So you're back— I was beginning to think I just dreamed it all up!"

"Oh, no, it's real enough. I'm back. Ready to talk?"

"Sure."

"Good. Let's take a walk."

They moved back up the quiet street to noisier Eighth Avenue. Everything was still wet from the day's drizzle and glistened in the lights. Kelsey said, "So—you think about it? You feel up to taking an assignment from us?"

[ 240 ]

"Christ, Kelse. I guess so. I mean, what can I say? I don't even know what it's about. What's it about?"

"It's about Brian Galgay."

He almost stopped, like a black clock hand. His eyes shot up to Kelsey's face and held there.

"He's what you're being recruited for, Nick. The cocksucker's selling to the other side. We've traced him for quite some time. Now we have to get somebody in close to him."

His neck felt paralyzed; he had so many feelings, he didn't have any.

Kelsey's misleadingly light voice went on: "It can't look like us, or anybody doing work for us. It has to happen out of nowhere."

*It!?*

"An accident, suicide, maybe even natural causes," Kelsey said. "We need somebody very special. Somebody up to it, but invisible, before and after. I recommended you, Nick. You're perfect," he told him again. Then he too went silent and lit a cigarette.

Nick certainly felt invisible enough at the moment. His voice came from some part of his body that he was disconnected from: "Why?"

"Why what?"

"Why does he have to be—?"

"Hey—we're talking *treason*, Nick. The man's a traitor. If he were an ordinary soldier, he'd get a court-martial first. But he's not an ordinary soldier. He's Corps. He knows the rules. Don't worry, he knew what risk he was running."

The voice asked, "Then why *can't* it be somebody who does work for you—you mean professionals, right?"

"Right. Because they're known. We know theirs, they know ours. With Galgay, I can't even let it look like they did it. I'm not sure they always do the same for us, but . . ."

He had been telling it to the city; now he looked back, and Nick saw something new begin to glow in his eyes.

[ 241 ]

Kelsey continued, "It was one hell of a problem at first. The biggest and hardest assignment of my career. I even tried to get out of it, on the grounds that I once served with the bastard. But that didn't mean a hoot to them. Hellfire, Nick, but it looked totally unsolvable for the longest goddamn time!"

Maybe that's it, Nick thought, he's pulled a coup and he's proud of himself, but doesn't want to sound it, so it goes to his eyes.

"It got to where I was praying God to strike the fucking Judas dead in his sleep."

"I wish He answered you."

"Then ol' Ewing surfaced, and I thought of you! The perfect man."

"What's Ewing got to do with it anyhow?"

"Nothing, really, far as you're concerned. Just gave me the way to move Galgay to you." He seemed to know exactly what was happening to Nick's ambushed system. "Just take it in for now, son," he said. "Let it stay as simple as you can. The man is hurting us bad and has to be stopped. I'm gonna give you the whole ballawax, fast. You're already worrying about how you could do it, but don't. I'll give you the how and the when later. And you don't have to say anything tonight. I'll give you some time to think on it. Not much, but enough. Then you'll tell us yes or no, and that'll be it. Either way will be fine."

Listening, he thought, *He's right. I was thinking about how, already!* His will seemed to have jumped right over "if," to "how." But he was again thinking the word that Kelsey hadn't used: *kill.* My God, they want me to kill a man.

"On the logistics," Kelsey was saying, "you'll be offered some pretty grand recompense. At first you'll think you'll want to decline it, but believe me, it'll be best to take it. It'll save you from any possible psychological problems afterwards. The personal freedom you'll be able to buy for yourself should remind you of the kind of thing you've earned for others. Call it

[ 242 ]

back pay from when you got out, or well-deserved gratitude, or anything you want." He flicked his cigarette into the air. The river wind took it away into a sewer.

Nick plodded on, glassy-eyed.

"Oh, yeah," Kelsey sort of laughed. "There's even a bonus, just to make your day. You being with one of the outfits going after the Army's ad business was pure coincidence, Nick. But we can guarantee you that, too, if you say so."

Kelsey looked at him again. "So. You okay?"

All he could manage to say was, "Yeah." Below the St. Luke's complex, he led Kelsey across the broad avenue and started walking back on the other side. He felt they were leaving the awful reality of it behind them. It felt almost academic to him, and he said, "You want it to look like you weren't on to Galgay, that it? And who is it, the KGB themselves or—?"

"I'll tell you anything you ask me, Nick. Not yet, though. Later. But think about this—the less you know, the better. Ever. You'll have every right, I'm not saying that. As a friend, though—as my best friend, let me tell you. Keep it as simple as you can. It'll make it a lot easier to get through, believe me." Then, anticipating what had to be reaching the top of Nick's consciousness now, he said, "Galgay—did you like him?"

Instantly, Nick split Brian Galgay into two men. One was the agent from the past who had interviewed him in Derby. The other was the asshole who had molested Deborah. Obeying Kelsey's warning to keep it simple, he wouldn't mention the second one, wouldn't confess that ever since that first night with Deborah he had been dreaming of doing great harm to that son of a bitch, had daily been fighting away fantasies of catching Galgay alone and beating the shit out of him, even, yes, blowing his head off with a gun.

He spoke only of the first one: "I don't know, Kelse. I mean, he stayed pretty much all business with me, it's not like I got to know the bastard very well. He never was my kind of

[ 243 ]

guy, we both know that. And he's still got that arrogance about him. Condescending fucker. Comes on like he's God's younger brother, same as years ago. But to tell you the truth, he hit me as more boring than anything else—just one more tight-ass in a suit, you know? Jesus, I'd never guess it from looking at him, I'll tell you that."

"That he went over?"

"Yeah. How the hell did he—? Never mind."

"The how's easy enough, Nick. It's the why I can't tell you. There's nothing in his trace to indicate he's a believer, but who knows? Then, Christ, career management sure did treat him like shit ever since that tunnel fuck-up of his, way back in Berlin."

"Yeah. He talked about that a little."

"So maybe he got pissed and went for some revenge against the organization. I doubt it, though. From his record, I read him as a stronger character than that. And he might even *be* a believer, behind it all. He was a very strong Catholic at one time, and—"

"Jesuits?"

"Maryknolls. But those roots have a way of finding new soil, you know? It happens. Personally, I'd say it was just the money, though. It's almost always just the money. And the relative safety of it, at his level. It's hard to get caught, is the truth."

"Then how did he? Is he dumb?"

"No, he's anything but stupid. He went too far, got himself into some real deep waters. Galgay's gone way over his head now. As it stands, we can't tell for sure if he's gettin' set to run, go over altogether, or just come apart. Short fuse, any way you look at it."

The *come apart* jumped for Nick. *Out of his skull,* Deborah had said. Maybe he should tell Kelsey that part of it after all. It was moot: he found himself unable to speak.

[ 244 ]

They came to the corner of Nick's street, and Kelsey stopped them. "Anyhow, that's why you, Nicker." He gave him a card from an inside pocket. "Call me at this number when you make up your mind, roger? You got seven days."

He read the typed 800 number, and slipped the card into his billfold. He was aware that his stunned face burned with fear, shock, doubt, and vulnerability. He showed it to Kelsey anyhow. A whisper trickled out: "My God, Kelse."

His friend's eyes turned soothing. "Just this, Nick—maybe we don't know exactly why Galgay's doin' it. And maybe even he doesn't know why. But if you do this for us . . . you'll know damn well why." He smiled thinly, firmly. "You think hard on it, my friend, and call me. Okay?"

He nodded his head okay.

"One way or the other, Nick—you can feel very proud for the rest of your life after this." He hugged him briskly and walked away.

Nick headed for his building. *Feel proud* kept repeating itself in his mind. It sounded to him like doors slamming. FEEL PROUD, he remembered, had been one of the campaigns that had come out of Ira Schenker's group. Sam Katz and Jerry Resnick had eliminated it. The current market, they said, was not ready to respond favorably to such an old-fashioned appeal.

# 3

Deborah was wearing his huge blue bathrobe. She had been curled in his easy chair, reading. She greeted him with a hug and kiss, but said, "You creep—you forgot I was here, didn't you!"

"No, I didn't. I—"

"That's worse. Why didn't you call? I was worried sick. It's after *one!*"

*Christ. Less than eight hours to go.* "I'm sorry. It went a lot later than I thought." It shocked him that he could not ever tell her about Kelsey. "You should've gone to bed," he said. "It's almost time for you to get up."

"I'll sleep on the plane."

Deborah was leaving in the morning for a photographic shoot in the Bahamas. She'd be gone for the rest of the week, until Sunday. Before, he had been glad of it—with her away, he'd be free to concentrate on the Jingo presentation. Right this minute, though, still reeling from Kelsey, he wanted to weld his body to hers and beg her to stay and never leave. He longed to just spill all of it to her. He put down his bag and took off his jacket.

"What is it, Nick?"

"What's what?"

"There's something. I saw it in your eyes."

"It isn't anything."

"An *it* is something. Tell me."

"It's the pitch, that's all. It's at nine o'clock, and I'm tired and uptight, that's all." Having it be Brian Galgay made it even worse. Even if he could tell her, which he couldn't, the minute she heard it was Galgay, she'd climb all over him on his motives. He could just hear her: *Traitor, schmaitor, you want vengeance! He-man go kill now!* He'd never be able to sell her the purity of his real motives. He moved around his living room as if he were looking for something.

She kept trying to catch a glimpse of his eyes again, but he kept averting them. She said, "I didn't hang around here all night to watch you withdraw, you know."

He sat where she had been; the cushions were still warm from her. He had come from Kelsey to her too fast. Stalling, he said, "How about making us a nightcap?"

Deborah's left eyelid lowered with suspicion, she said okay and went into his kitchenette. This was not how she had pictured their rendezvous. She felt silence beginning to build up. To stop it, she called, "Really bad, was it, Nick?"

"Yeah. Awful." At Fort Holabird they had given them a brief survey course on covert operations. "You have to learn to lie," the instructor had said, "and to lie well. The morally squeamish may choose to consider it acting." The instructor's voice came to him from Sam Katz's mouth.

She handed him his drink, then stayed standing there a moment above him. She wanted him to ease her down onto his lap, but he didn't. She considered just plopping herself there on her own, but decided not to take the chance. She moved away a couple of steps and perched on the coffee table.

He risked a full look at her. Her eyes were cast down. It saddened him. Then an inspiration flared: If I decide *not* to do it, I'll be able to tell her all of it! He was tempted to force the issue immediately, rid himself of it, and win her back.

She sniffed the liquor's vapors but didn't feel like tasting it. The worst was, this was his true self. The eleven-day honeymoon was over. She fought accepting that. She looked up. His eyes were upon her face, watching her softly.

[ 247 ]

"For tonight," he said, "can we just go to bed?"

"God, yes," she said. "Let's just go to bed."

Pale and wintry as it was, Monday morning's first light woke him. He reached and found her gone. A note was pinned to her pillow. It said, *Deborah the departing. She needs you now! . . . Love and lotsa luck.*

It wasn't yet six, but he couldn't fall back asleep. He got up and turned on the shower. There was no hot water.

# 4

The black hands of his watch said 8:55. He knew he was in serious trouble. He and the rest of the presentation team crowded a small anteroom outside the agency boardroom. Waiting, the others chatted amicably. He stayed still, silently fighting the urge to bolt.

He could see now that Kelsey's timing couldn't have been worse—*Idiot, why didn't you wait until this was over? What kind of superman do you think I am anyhow?*

What he couldn't do was get his system back to where it had been before Kelsey intruded. He no longer felt that he knew better than Katz. He had stage fright and he had it bad— bordering on paralysis. This was new for him. He was always being told how he could lose his creative talents tomorrow and still make a living just on his selling ability. *People don't buy things, they buy other people. You sell yourself.* He'd known that for years. Now he was learning how it felt to run out of self.

He thought of the board of officers he'd soon be facing beyond the door. *I'm one of them. I'm one of their kind. I'm one sharp, young full-bird colonel who—* It wouldn't take. He tried falling back to who he truly was. That seemed even worse. *Jesus, get me out of this!* He couldn't care less now about any of it. They could all go to hell.

A Signal Corps major opened the door and summoned them. Jerry Resnick went first. The others funneled in behind him. Just as Nick moved to step over the threshold, Sam Katz whispered into his ear, *"Remember!"* The voice had only fear and threat in it; he had no idea what the man meant. Remember what? *Sell but don't sell? Let you or Jerry field everything? These guys respond to gutsiness?* The fever that he'd been feeling in his face seemed to spread throughout his whole body. He stacked his materials behind the two metal easels standing near the windowless wall. He sat down, wishing he could close his eyes and sleep.

The agency faced the Army across the conference table. A brigadier presided, flanked by two bird colonels, the major, a captain, a master sergeant, and a warrant officer in civilian clothes. Introductions were made briskly. There was no small talk. Resnick turned the meeting over to Braddock, the marketing director, who stepped to the easels and uncovered the first of his many charts. Creative would go second, then Media. Katz would give the summary, then Resnick would end it by asking for the business.

Nick turned to face Braddock, but his eyes kept sweeping the line of military men opposite him. The dark side of his floundering mind made one of them the Nuke Colonel Ewing. Another became the suicide investigator Major Archie Sprague. A third was Brian Galgay. The rest all strange new enemies.

They'd waited a long time for this, his shameful return.

Any minute now they'd have him where they wanted him, exposed at last—empty, unprepared, a phony . . . totally unworthy, even for woman's work.

His better instincts lunged for the only handhold left, Sam Katz's *"Remember!"* Desperately he decided it meant the injunction not to sell at all, just to lay the stuff out and guide them impartially through it. With that, he felt his mental faculties leave him completely. He'd have to fly blind. His body would have to do it all by itself.

His ears and eyes caught Braddock's cue. His spine straightened. His legs got ready to stand and walk. He rebuttoned the jacket of his suit, and buffed the toes of his shined shoes against the backs of his trouser legs. The indifference would be the hardest part. His dull, heavy, pervasive indifference.

# SIX

# 1

Near noontime of the day after their meeting with the Army, Nick sat in Sam Katz's office. It was like trying to have a conversation with a telephone switchboard operator, he thought, watching Katz let his phone buzzer once again scissor his sentence in the middle. The first couple of times it happened, Katz gave him the courtesy of a curse, or a sorry. Now he just segued straight into "Yeah."

"Norman Eliot in Mexico," said his girl's voice through the black plastic box atop the Early American table that Katz used as a desk.

Talking to him, Katz had been wearing that small, shallow dish of a smile that Nick had come to associate with men who were about to utter terrible things. Now, on the phone, his mouth burst into heartiness. "Normie! *Hola! Comestar?!*"

It had been like this with Sam Katz ever since Nick first went to work for him, and it had never much bothered him before. It was odd: Sam would always tell his secretary to hold all calls, yet she would always buzz him, and he would always answer. Usually Katz's phone conversations were totally uninteresting, leaving Nick to patiently daydream while he waited, cheering himself with the thought that he was being paid for his time regardless of how it was occupied. Today was different.

Today he had the scary inkling that he was there to be personally abused, or worse.

After their Jingo presentation Katz had withdrawn into a dark brood and stayed ominously silent. Nick had replayed the meeting over and over. From his point of view it had gone as well as anyone could have realistically hoped. Unemotionally efficient and complete.

When Katz's mouth came back from Mexico, Nick leaned forward and flicked his cigarette ash into Katz's ashtray, a hammered-copper bowl.

Sam's foreboding smile returned. "Okay . . . we know each other, Nick, so I feel gutsy enough to give it to you straight, right up front. I'm still amazed that you and I were able to meet each other in this scumbag business, and make friendship happen. But that's how I am, and that's how you are. All right—you did it different. I said, I'm gonna *go*, I'm gonna do it, all the way to the top, and I did it. When all the rest of the schmucks were still whining over trouble in frame three!

"You—you said the hell with the power and glory, you wanted the beach house and all that, you wanted to stay the wild-card hired gun and stick to the making of the stuff. And you still do it better than any of them, huh, guy? I mean it, and I'll tell the world *that*. But what you and I know is—"

*Buzz!*

"Yeah."

Nick shut his ears and slid his eyes away. He scanned Katz's office. The walls were covered with the skins of a thousand artificial reptiles, and God knew how many Halston jackets had had to die to cover the two long, suedey sofas. Potted trees and hanging plants effused their sappy greenness as obscenely as those on any Tennessee Williams verandah. It occurred to him vaguely that he might work the guy's face over with his fists when the time came. An enormous new copper kettledrum stood against a wall, a gift from some production company. Sam was always saying he was going to give it to a school band, but there it stayed.

It seemed less anachronistic than anything else in the room to Nick, and he felt a sudden urge to go pound hell out of its immaculate white head. Its sticks seemed to be missing, though. It was clearly wider than the doorway, and he wondered again how they had ever gotten it in. Maybe that was it: Katz just didn't know how to get it out, and would never ask.

*The little prick might very well take me,* he thought. Katz played a lot of tennis. Most other incredibly young men who had achieved Sam's level on the pyramid tended to bloat, to look almost stunned by the continual gratification of their senses. Katz wasn't like that. Nick could never write him off as "just another materialist," as he did so many others of the ilk. It was one of the things that kept Sam interesting to him; it was also one of the very few things that sometimes made him wonder if, as Sam had just been implying, he'd made a mistake in jumping off the up escalator early. He knew better, though. The fact was that Nick had been an associate creative director twice before in his life, once before he was thirty, and had hated it both times. The Peter Principle, pure and simple: he hadn't been any good at it. He didn't want to supervise, he wanted to do. They had discussed it in letters, and Kelsey had told him that it was generally the same in the Service, but added the taunt that Intelligence was different: you could move up and keep doing at the same time.

Katz rang the caller off without a good-bye. He looked at Nick again. "What you and me know, Nick, is *we* got our bellies up to the same table, in different ways, but at the same high-stakes table. And we played the cards as they came. We let all the others stand back, away from the dangers, huh? Maybe making a few little side bets at the most, when they felt *really* lucky and brave.

"Nick, you're a star. I made you a superstar here. We

understand the business. We understand each other. And you understand better than anyone what kind of creative director I am, and what kind of creative director I'm not. Nick—superstars get *no* strikes."

This, at last, was something he actually did understand. It was coming. He was really going to do it. Ira Schenker had been fond of philosophizing that you weren't a pro in this game until you'd been fired. If true, then he was finally going to turn pro. It did not feel consoling. He said, "How about Ruth, Williams, Mantle? They struck out as often as they—"

"When they struck out they got traded."

Jesus, he sighed, if the maniac didn't know baseball, how could he pretend to know anything else? "What the fuck is this, Sam?"

"You blew it, Nick." Katz took an opened pack of Camels from the drawer, punched one out, and lit it.

"Blew what?"

"Forty million bucks, maybe fifty."

The Camels had sprinkled bits of tobacco onto the surface of the table. Nick felt an oddly strong urge to study them. "They aren't going to announce their decision until March."

"I know now."

*You know shit*, Nick wanted to say. *I've got that fifty million on the tip of my phone finger, you schmuck.*

The phone rang again.

He tamped his cigarette out in Sam's bowl. He held his eyes on Katz talking, but wasn't seeing him. It was as if he'd just taken several swift hits of cocaine or strong pot: his head inside went hollow, and he felt lifted, one dizzy remove away from reality. In this state there seemed to be no good reason for doubting the message he received: just as he claimed, Sam Katz did know. Katz was right. He'd caught the indifference.

No ordinary man, no general or consultant, no agency president or staff member, could have possibly detected it. But shaman Katz had, and Nick couldn't now deny him that.

"I wish we could trade in this fucking business, Nick," Katz had come back saying, "but we can't. I want you to start looking, huh, guy?" He smiled that dish of a smile. "You're out. After this, I can't sell you as my superstar anymore, dig? Everyone in the joint sings your praises to high heaven, but after this they'll all flinch a little when I say I'm putting you on their business. I just can't afford those little flinches. I know you understand what I'm saying. Okay, Nickie?"

Listening, he had been sifting his options. One was to simply ask Katz to wait the few months, which would of course soon become a few weeks if he told Kelsey yes and made the prompt awarding of the account one of his conditions. For forty or fifty mil, he knew, Katz would learn to swallow a hell of a lot of little flinches, and like it. The other option was the one he took. Still smiling, he shrugged, stood, and said, "Sure."

Sam Katz stayed sitting. "Thanks, guy. Go see Polly, she'll take care of severance pay and dates and all that shit. And tell Yoko on your way to set up lunch or something with me later in the week. We'll get together and decide on what story we'll put out that'll make us both look good, huh?"

He passed Yoko without a sideways glance and headed down the cream-colored halls toward the creative personnel manager's office. He'd already known that Katz was leaving at the end of the day for a week's holiday in Florida.

Humming, Nick played: Should I let them have the account or not, if I do it? What a nice irony, for them to get it after firing me for blowing it. Then again, to withhold it from them would make Katz look right on even the reality level, and he wasn't sure he wanted to indulge the little prick that much. Maybe, even if he said no, he could still get Kelsey to pull some strings and fuck Katz out of it . . . or, again, give him it. What a nice, pretty problem to have, he thought, and buried it for future needs. The problem consuming him now was anything but nice and pretty.

[ 257 ]

Polly Sargent looked up and said, "Oh, Nick, I'm sorry. Tons of us tried. Even Jerry's against it, we—"

"Sam made an emotional decision, Poll. He's not open to rational arguments."

"My God, you're cool about it—you're letting us down, luv, we were all listening for the A-bomb to go off in there!"

"Grace under pressure," he said toughly.

"Then say good-bye, Gracie," Polly cracked. "I don't know what he told you, but he's not being exactly generous, Nick. You're to be physically out in three weeks. Last paycheck the fifteenth. You were up for only three weeks severance, but I can fake some vacation time and get you five. Full vesting for profit sharing is five years, and you'll just fall short of four, so you'll only get . . ."

When she finished, he said, "I'll be physically out in three minutes," and left for upstairs. In his office he looked out his windows to say good-bye to his view. It didn't seem to be his mystical foreign city out there any longer; merely the bridged river, Queens, Brooklyn, Nassau to the east, the Sound to the north, Coney south. All looking splendid enough in their own right under the midday overhead winter sun. They were just themselves, and it somehow felt okay. Their regained reality was just fine—better, even, and, in a way, a relief.

Grant Evans bounded in. *"True?"* The skin of his face and head was gray, with blood-red highlights.

"Yup."

"You putz! You asshole! You don't learn! You knew what to do to turn him around and you didn't do it, right?"

"Right." Nick wanted to hug him.

"Aw, God, aw, shit—you were great, Nick. Everyone said so. Sam's gone fucking nuts this time. Go back down, Nick. Do both of yourselves the favor. Say you know what he's talking about. Say you're sorry. Tell him—"

"That I somehow let *him* down, personally."

"Exactly!"

"That I was worried about my long-lost *kids*. My *parents* were dying, again!"

"Oh, that's not nice, Nick."

"My God, Grant, you said that just like Ira."

"That's it!" Grant snapped his fingers. "Tell him it was Ira. You were . . . Ira's death knocked you out of whack. Made you go cold, or whatever he thinks you did wrong. And listen—Ira'd be telling you the exact same what I'm telling you, Nick! If he was here, God rest his soul."

He wasn't so sure that was so, but let it go. The only thing of his in the office that wouldn't fit into his carrybag was the Steinberg blowup. He lifted it off its wall hook and carried it past Grant into Grant's office. He leaned it against the drawing board. "It's yours."

Grant sighed, and turned totally practical. He went to his print files. "Okay, tell me what you want laminated. Fuck 'em, they can at least pay for that. I'm assuming you've kept your goddamn reel up to date."

"Sure," he laughed. "But you pick them for me, will you? Don't go back more than two years, except for the perfume stuff." He saw no point in telling his erstwhile partner that he had no intention of updating his portfolio of ads or reel of commercials. How could he ever explain that he had too much work to do to take a job? "I'll come up and get them when they're ready."

"What, come up? He didn't give you a get-out, did he?"

"No, I gave me a get-out. I don't want to hear the words or see the looks in the elevators." He took a long last look at this guy. They'd see each other again. They'd talk on the phone, and meet sometimes for lunch. It would never be the same, unless they got to work together again. Which wasn't impossible, either, he forced himself to think, so he could walk away clean.

Back in his own office he packed his carrybag to roundness, and still had several books, stacks of correspondence, and the like left over. Behind his door leaned the large leather portfolio case still holding the *She Needs You Now* presentation pieces. He unzipped its top, slid in the rest of his belongings, and left the building carrying it and his shoulder bag, figuring he'd return the case when he came back to get his laminated samples from Grant. The campaign he'd keep, for old times' sake or revenge or something.

He weaved his way through the Tuesday lunchtime swarms along the sidewalks and descended the wet steps of the Fifty-third Street subway. Inside, he walked down the slow-moving escalator. An F train rattled in behind a wall of dirty tunnel wind, and he took shelter behind a riveted steel post, wondering, *Is Kelsey counting this as Day One or Day Two?* It didn't matter. He'd have to force himself to come to a decision soon— tomorrow, maybe.

An E train came and he got on. There were plenty of empty seats, but he went and stood at the window of the front door, next to the driver's closet. He pressed his face like a kid's to the glass, watching the train's long lights reach ahead into the narrow dark hole, all rock and steel. The next station came into view almost at once, Fifth and Madison, floating in light like some futuristic platform hung in space. Flying in, watching the faces and bodies of leaning, waiting passengers flick past, he recalled the recent rash of pushings he'd read about in the papers. Awful, anonymous shoves, straight-arms out of crowds, hurtling innocent people to maimings or deaths. Feeling the brakes squeezing against the speed, he thought, *The driver must feel the same thing as the victim!* The shock, the helplessness, the inevitability . . . and afterward, what? Regret? Innocence? Probably both. *Gimme more than a goddamn beer,*

[ 260 ]

*Marie, I had one today. Some fuckin' loon got me. There was nothin' I could do.*

And how many killings were as mindless and random as they seemed, he thought, resuming speed into the next black hole, and how innocent the victims? Would Galgay be something like that? He turned away and leaned against the driver's closed door. That kind of thinking was stupid, he knew, and the opposite of helpful. He had to keep remembering: "Keep it simple, Nick." *They'll do it for me,* he told himself. *They'll do it through me. I'll only be like the driver of the train. Except I'll know it's coming.*

He remembered that he had just been fired. One week before Christmas. How classic. None of that seemed real, either. At Fourteenth Street he ran up the stairs. The day was mild for winter in New York, and here in the relatively fumeless Village, invigorating. He stepped out smartly, knowing he had no need to hurry but wanting to anyway.

He crossed Greenwich. The little park, swept of winos and junkies, held only a young mother watching her two-year-old miniature Michelin Tire man push a yellow toy lawnmower over the thin snow. He passed down to the end of Eighth Avenue in a semistrut, seeing, for once, the daytime places and people. To be a shopkeeper. To know the other keepers of the other shops in one's block. To lock one's door with a BACK IN AN HOUR clock and step out into one's known, cobblestoned neighborhood. To take lunch at the Village Den. To worry only about rent and inventory. Maybe that's what he ought to do next with his life. If he decided to do what they wanted, and if he accepted their money for it.

He crossed to Hudson. High in the sky's milky blueness ahead, a silver 747 swam between the towers of the World Trade Center, diving for Kennedy or LaGuardia. He wished it was carrying Deborah back but knew it wasn't. Not until Sunday, she'd said.

[ 261 ]

He kept his eye on the plane. From up there, he thought, all this down here was one huge, living photograph, and me just another dot moving along a slot. No. *Being* moved felt more like it.

At his door he heard his phone ringing. He stepped inside and answered it.

"Is that you, Nick?"

"Yes." It was Brian Galgay.

"Good. This is Brian Galgay, you weren't at your office, and I thought . . . Uh, Merry Christmas."

"You too."

"Listen, they've reactivated your case. When can we meet? I'm in Maryland, but I'll be coming to New York tonight."

"I'm splitting for the beach. I was fired."

"Oh. I'm sorry to hear that. I can come down there. When would be a good time?"

"I don't know. Not tomorrow. You want to come Thursday?"

"Fine. Any particular time?"

"No. I don't know. Whenever. I'll be there." *Yes, fink, come Thursday. By then I'll know.*

"Okay. Uh—you all right, Nick? That must have been a shock."

"It's okay. Listen, I've got to—"

"Right. Me too. I'm swamped. It'll, er, be good to see you again. I'll be seeing Deborah tonight, I'll say hello to her for you."

"You do that."

"Right."

Nick hung up and stood staring at the black, still phone for a moment. His hand moved to pick it up again; he stopped it in midair. The place was unbearably hot and dark. He went and screwed shut the valves of the radiators, silencing their hissing and spitting. He folded the blinds back and opened the windows, letting sunlight and air in. In his bedroom he grabbed the extension phone and dialed Deborah's number. It wasn't her answering service he heard, but her recorded voice, saying she was out of town and to wait for the beep before leaving a message. He hung it up before the beep sounded, feeling ashamed for having made the call.

He brought his overnight bag from his closet and set it open on his bed. He opened his armoire to get socks and underwear, and saw her slip where she had left it, hanging by its straps from his tie rack. He remembered: the last time she was there, she had come in a dress and left in jeans. She was the first woman since Susan whom he had not, nicely, asked to leave nothing personal behind in his apartment. In fact he'd even told her: "I usually say I've got a madly jealous cleaning lady who thinks she's my mother and burns anything female she finds." The slip was pale yellow. He brought it to his face and breathed of it deeply, hearing her voice again: "I'd say I've heard that one before, but then you'd think I sleep around a lot."

He found himself throwing in some city sweaters on top of the socks. He wanted to fall across the bed and stare at the ceiling. But he had to keep moving. Why had he bothered to come here at all? He certainly had enough clothes in Derby. He took Deborah's slip, and folded it into his bag. There—the detour was justified. He closed and shuttered the windows and left the apartment. A strange feeling crawled up his back. The place was not vanishing. He was only walking away from it. It was there, and would still be there if and when he ever came back.

Struggling into the narrow backseat of the Dodge taxi, he realized he had taken the cumbersome portfolio with him. He gave the cabbie the address of the garage. The thrust of the cab

[ 263 ]

gunning off forced him back against the seat. *You'd think I had stolen their goddamn money and was running to Panama, for God's sake.*

He got his car from the garage, and headed out of the city. In the tunnel the Triumph's radio went dead. He thought: *All those lines I thought were parallel seem to be coming to a point.* He burst forth into the cold sunlight, as if he had just shot through some infamous black hole.

The Triumph held easily at sixty-five. The city station began to fade. A noise like an elephant's scream sounded, close behind him. His eyes shot to the mirror and saw the bottom of the immense chrome grille of a trailer truck. He had to push the Triumph to near eighty to steer clear of the stampeding rig. Passing, the enormous machine blasted its horn again and thundered on. *Wouldn't that have been terrific. To get killed when I wasn't even there. The black hole to end black holes.*

Air returned with a shudder that rocked the car. With it came the ability to at last acknowledge the reality of Brian Galgay's call. No, it was not sinister of Kelsey, he decided, to send Galgay back into his life before his decision. It was only shrewd and logical. "I'll be seeing Deborah tonight," he heard Galgay's voice say again.

He grabbed a cassette and clicked it into the player. Music came, without static. He didn't want to feel hatred. Hatred would only cheapen the whole idea of doing it.

# 2

The treetop angel's body was only a paper-covered sugar cone. Brian opened his hand from around it, and watched brown bits of it fall into the ornamented and icicled branches. He slid it off the top and backed down the stepladder with it. The face that the boy had drawn on its round foam head was still smiling, but the aluminum foil wings had been crushed, too. It resembled a dead bird in his hand. He dropped it into the throwaway bag, thinking, If the kid were here, as he should be, it wouldn't have happened.

He went back up the ladder and began moving bulbs from limbs to the boxes of nests he'd laid open on the ladder's top three steps and on its paint shelf. First the bulbs, then the tinsel, then the lights, he repeated to himself, in his own father's voice. Of course his own father, he realized, would never have been in this situation, taking a tree *down* two weeks before Christmas. Only two days after putting it up. But to hell with his own, dear father. In those days mothers didn't pack up and leave, either. Didn't take their children with them back, "for a while," to the homes of their own fathers and mothers, far away.

He reached from the ladder and lifted his glass of straight Scotch from its coaster on the fireplace mantelpiece. He sipped and said aloud, "Well, now's now." He put the drink down and reached for the next bulb. Its hook caught and he had to tug a bit, which caused the tree to shiver and send off a loud sprinkle of needles onto the floor and nearby sofa. He could already see the trail he'd make carrying the tree outside to the sidewalk. He'd be sure to vacuum it all clean, though, before he left for

New York. It wouldn't be fair to let Evelyn find any unnecessary work to do if and when she and the kid ever returned.

He sighed patiently, thinking, She can't keep the boy out of school too long. I doubt if she'd try to put him into one out there. No, she'll be back. Hell, she said it herself: her roots are here. And so's her fucking boyfriend, let's not forget that. He backstepped clear of the ladder and lifted the filled boxes to their covers waiting lined up on the seat of the sofa. Then he moved the ladder out of the way. He could reach the rest from the floor now. If I wanted to be mean about it, he thought, I could say it was all just a big phony-baloney act on her part, that her loverboy was going to be in Nebraska a while too, and that was really her reason for running out there like some hysterical dame. Whether it was that jerk in the car that night or whoever. Her and her spoiled-brat silent treatment! As if she didn't realize that all her refusing to deny it was the same as admitting it outright! For a brainy girl she could be so dumb, sometimes.

Bulbs done, he replaced the ladder and started on the icicles. This year he'd bought the kind that came in wide strips. They stayed connected at the tops and were easier to save for use again next year. He used his left hand like a clothespin, holding strip upon strip of the icicles that his right hand was taking off the branches. Moving lower on the tree, he tried to speed up his rhythm but found he was starting to tear the tinsel. To do it right he could go only so fast and no faster. He began again to feel the twinges of guilt for performing such a personal task on a duty day, and again defended himself to some imaginary challenger—I called the office on time. I made the Burke contact, as ordered. Subject unavailable until Saturday, earliest.

He had intended to proceed to New York directly, but then he hadn't been able to reach Deborah, and then he'd remembered the tree he'd just put up and suddenly knew he couldn't leave while it was still standing in the vacated house.

Done at last, he carried the ornaments and lights in their boxes and bags to their shelf in the cellar. He started to take the tree out to the sidewalk, turned and carried it to the garage. He vacuumed the living room, then drank off the last of the Scotch and took the glass and coaster into the kitchen.

He pushed through the swinging doors, which ticktocked behind him, looked down the quiet long hallway to the den and the bedrooms, and thought of the tunnel years ago in Berlin. You went after what was Right and True, that's all, and damn all their picayune rules and regulations. And you suffered the consequences, but so what. Anna had, and so had he.

He walked to the den and looked in to make sure he had folded away his pillow and blankets. He headed for his and Evelyn's room for his luggage. Outside the bathroom door, he stopped abruptly, listening to the house. He felt his heart beating in his ears. After a few moments he identified the single sound as only the refrigerator, humming so softly that it might as well have been outside the house and down the street someplace. He could hear no clock ticking, no faucet dripping, no furnace rumbling. He stood still as a lamp, not wishing to disturb such deep, total, overwhelming absence of sound.

A strange feeling of being a young boy again suddenly landed upon his body from the silence and passed through him like fever. It ignited something furtively sweet in the pit of his stomach. He stepped into the bathroom stealthily. He looked at his face in the mirror. He decided to brush his teeth. He couldn't quite believe that he was going to do what he was going to do. But at the same time he knew he was going to do it. And for proof, there, he had picked up the handle of the electric toothbrush and had set its tiny engine vibrating without attaching his brush, the yellow one, to its tip.

The tip jiggled in the air. He draped his penis not upon it but upon the plastic hood of the handle. He stayed facing the mirror but now his eyes had closed and showed him the merging faces of Anna and Deborah. Soon all that was left of Anna

[ 267 ]

was her voice coming from Deborah's lips, saying good-bye again to him from the tape cassette he had destroyed. Then her voice quit altogether.

He clenched his teeth against the urge to cry out. His spasms came and went in silence.

Brian slept the flight away. He endured the long, slow, late-rush-hour bus ride from LaGuardia to Grand Central. At the Royalton he took a very hot shower, then a very cold one, unpacked, dressed, and called Deborah again. Still "out of town." Where? he wondered. For how long? He put on his suit jacket and overcoat. To stay here now was dangerous.

He turned up Fifth Avenue, but stayed on it for only a block. The broad, deserted street was filled with a mean wind bearing the first sharp points of new snow. A few taxis and cars crashed recklessly southward within it. They looked to him like pairs of running men, carrying flashlights, in a tunnel.

He traveled with no destination, yet something drew him eastward, a few face-stinging blocks at a time. He went inside the Waldorf-Astoria when he reached it and passed through its Texas-accented lobby. Near the foot of the escalator at its Lexington Avenue exit, a furred woman he thought was waiting for a cab looked into his eyes.

Outside, he walked harder into the wind and came to the Citicorp Building, rising bright and silver against the black night. A cascade of concrete steps dropped gracefully from the sidewalk. He descended them dizzily, holding onto the bannister. Inside the sleek, modern arcade he passed the closed florist's shop and bookstore. Ahead, the Atrium suddenly opened.

There was a French bakery, a Greek café, Italian, Hungarian, Swiss restaurants. He walked, amazed, around the perimeter of the underground oasis. Above, an electric sun shone down through glass upon people sitting at tables, just talking, smoking, reading, as if it was Berlin and the Kurfürstendamm. He went inside the Swiss bar and asked the bartender for a martini to take outside to a table. The man said it wasn't allowed. Brian slipped him a ten and the drink was given to him in a paper cup. He found a chair at an empty table near the middle of the raised terracelike space. He looked up at the inleaning tiers of balconies overhead, all draped with delicate, pretty green ivies.

What a perfect place to bring Deborah. We can meet here for breakfasts, and for lunches, maybe. Other men would gawk at her, and he wouldn't mind, only feel proud—no, not so much proud as grateful, very grateful. The martini tasted so good he tried to merely nibble at it. The guy probably wouldn't want to stretch the rules twice. He looked around again at the other people. Some were alone, but more were in couples. It felt nice not to feel angered by them.

My God, he marveled, when your mind starts working well and clearly again, it sure makes it a lot easier for the rest of you to feel good, and calm. An ice cube slid and hit his upper lip. The drink was gone. He went up to the bar in the Hungarian place and opened his wallet. There seemed to be too many bills missing. He tried it with a five this time. "Okay," the barman said, "but you didn't get it here."

He returned to his boulevard seat. Maybe Nick and I could meet here too, sometimes. No—Nick would probably rather go to bars. Someplace ad guys go. I wish he liked me. Because Nick *knows*. That was it—Nick had been there then, in the same place, at the same time. And he remembered how it had been for them. Nick will understand everything perfectly. He'll say, I would have done the same thing in your place, Brian, the exact same thing.

Nick and I will get to be buddies. He'll have to like me, when he sees how alike we are, really. And only he will be able to see how incredibly tough it was for me to have the other, on top of all the rest! To carry. To handle. To keep so balanced, all those years. Nick'll say, Well, hell, they had her *life* in their hands, for Christ's sake—what else could you do?

[ 269 ]

Not at first, probably, but he was sure Nick was sophisticated enough to grasp how the end result of his situation had been actually a *gain*, and not a loss. Paradoxical or not. Once he'd heard the whole story, Nick would say, I get it—by holding the girl's life and freedom over your head, all they were really doing was helping you remember how *evil* they are . . . making you, automatically, that much sharper in your work against them. In a way, your constant, clandestine contact with them helped keep you from ever getting too soft and sloppy as an agent, right? That wasn't quite the way Nick would put it, maybe, but the point was valid—Nick would see the real truth of the matter.

Again, ice cubes slid and struck his mouth. The cup *clopped* when he put it down on the table, but nobody noticed. He yawned. He felt a lot better now, about everything. He stood and put on his coat, heavy with moisture. It registered that he had become slightly drunk. It was a feeling he hated, but, walking away from the Atrium along the corridor between the Swiss bar and the Hungarian bar, he forgave himself the slight indulgence.

He ascended the stairs by the English pub to Third Avenue, plunging again into the wind storming down the tunnel avenues of the city. He had known all along where he was heading. Now he was able to let himself accept it.

There, he walked down the ramp into the underground parking garage and found the freight elevator. He stepped in, pushed the button, and it took him up to her floor. He walked down the hall to her door, knocked on it, rang the bell, then picked the locks with tools from his kit. Inside, the parakeet made a curious, croaking sound at him. Brian snapped on the lights and stood still near the closed door, scanning Deborah's apartment with slow-moving eyes. It felt a little like being alone in his own vacated house in Maryland.

He removed his coat, hung it upon a hook on her coat tree, and stepped into the living room. He looked at the quiet, dark fireplace and heard the merry castanets of glass breaking against brick. We're Russian, she said, fooling. My God, he thought, as if she knew.

He went to her kitchen, pulled open the cabinet door, and found a bottle of Stolichnaya vodka staring him in the face. He felt like grabbing it and smashing it onto the floor. Beside it on the filled, round tray stood a fifth of Seagram's gin. He took it down and poured some into a glass, fetching ice from her freezer. The bird was chirping away madly now.

As usual, moving felt better than standing still. He prowled around her large, clean, simple place, sipping his gin. He said aloud, "A new bottle of expensive gin'll be one of the first gifts I'll buy her," then regretted intensely having spoken here. If they for any reason had her bugged, his words would have activated the equipment, and they'd have him.

He felt himself sweating profusely. Spinning on his heel, he hurried into the dark of Deborah's bedroom. He did not switch on any light. He found the bed with his shins and sat down upon it, resting his back against the pillows. This was better. Here he could get things straight.

*I am not hiding.*

*Although, if I were, this would probably be about the smartest place in the whole city.*

*But I'm not. I have no reason to. I'm okay. From both sides.*

*I just want to see her, that's all. Whenever she comes in, I'll say I got here just five minutes before. She'll love it. It'll show her how serious I am about her. She'll love it, and she'll laugh.*

*I only hope she comes before Thursday. Thursday, I have to go see Nick.*

# 3

In Derby, Nick lay in bed in the dark, trying to clear his mind for the night, willing the diver inside him to plunge straight for the dark bottom. Nothing but solid, black, cleansing water. It didn't work. His sleep all night flashed with menacing glimpses of guns, knives, hatchets, always in his own hand. Sometimes directed away from him against some formless enemy, just as often pointed back at himself. When he woke Wednesday morning, he did not feel refreshed.

But when he looked at his clock, he felt encouraged. The alarm in his mind had sounded exactly a half hour before the clock's, just as he had willed it to. His systems were working. He threw aside his covers and swung out onto the cold wooden floor. He pushed in the pin on the back of the clock and went to his single, small window, folding open the louver shutters. He had hoped to see first light break, but all he saw was snow, whipping small-flaked and angry against the glass. He could hear it hitting the shingles of his slanted roof low over his head, and recognized it as the same hissing noise he'd been vaguely conscious of all night. Before, he'd assumed his gun-nightmares had come with their own soundtrack.

He showered, and was dismayed to realize that the strange heat he was feeling was not being rinsed away by the water. He was running a fever. Shaving, he cursed his flushed face. He hated having anything physical go wrong with him; even the slightest cold or toothache made him feel betrayed by his body. He took two Anacins and an extra vitamin capsule.

Downstairs he filled the electric percolator to ten cups and plugged it in. He decided against turning up the thermostat and instead made a fire in the kitchen's small woodstove. Waiting, he lit a cigarette and walked to his sunporch. Its glass walls were loud and awash with the swirling, curling snow. Every now and then he caught a fleet glimpse of the bay waters beyond the dunes. He had expected them to be white-capped and boiling, but they lay strangely calm and submissive under the raging storm. He scratched breakfast. Whether it was "starve a fever" or not, he had no appetite for food.

He opened the door to his cellar landing and took his big sheepskin coat off its hook. He pulled his watch cap from its pocket and pulled it down over his head until it covered his ears. A heavy sluggishness was beginning to make its weight felt, but he fought it.

Outside, he had to pull hard against the wind to get his door closed. Head down, he walked around the side of his house, crossed over the wide dune, and reached the winter-narrow beach. The snow was icy. More than an inch of it was already clinging tightly to the land. Beneath it, the crusted sand broke under his boots. Reaching the tideline, he turned parallel to the surf and began to jog. The snow-laden wind at his back helped him push his jog into a heavy-footed run sooner than usual.

His thoughts flurried, eager to start, but he held them off. The fever made it hard for him to gauge the timing of his reactions—he seemed to be breathing deeply earlier than normal, he was certainly starting to sweat long before he usually did. No matter. His nose dripped and his eyes watered until he felt like the snowstorm had entered him. That didn't matter either. This was necessary. This was something he couldn't scratch. What mattered was holding off his mind until he'd got his body properly beaten down.

He reached the last jetty, the one at the far end of the fourth beach. Breathing loudly through his open mouth he slowed to a walk, turned, and began the trip back. Eyes fixed on the sand, he saw kelp and stones and slippershells, the carcass of a dead gull.

He came to a length of wood, half-buried. It looked good for use as a staff, to help him hold his momentum against the snow. He hefted it and saw that it was smooth and strong, but too heavy, really, for . . . *Christ!* His right hand had reflexively port-armed the long, straight limb hard into his upraised left palm—it felt exactly like a rifle. Lighter than an M-1, heavier than a carbine.

Walking faster, he forced the stick into use, driving its end into the cold ground ahead, leaning into it as he walked past it, then driving it forward again. But it was too late. The connection had been made. He had become, at least for one blazing moment of recollection, a soldier in the snow. Rushed by Red Alert to the border. Discovering not only that he was willing to kill, but that he wanted to.

He let go of the wooden rifle and walked on, letting it fall behind him. The memory had flashed not as a picture but as a feeling, an emotion so strong it had startled him—it had felt *great!* This was what his intellect had feared most all along, and it hurried in now to remind him: *The snow . . . the Kelsey reality . . . the feeling of gun—it was a setup. You couldn't help it! It didn't mean anything!*

*Maybe,* he answered, walking, *but I know what I felt. I can still feel it, a little. And feelings tell you things.*

Back in his house, he hung up his clothes, kicked his boots off, stuffed them with old newspapers and set them near the radiating woodstove, which he fed. He assumed that the downstairs, at least, was beginning to heat up. His fever made it hard for him to tell. He drank fresh coffee, smoked, and checked his mental list: next came the bags.

He took his overnight bag upstairs to the washer-dryer in his bathroom, picked out the socks onto the floor, and dumped the underwear and towels into the washing tub, added detergent, and set it churning. Down, he carried the agency portfolio case from where he had dropped it in the living room into the small spare room off the kitchen, which he used as a study.

He piled his office books on his desk, then he slid out his and Grant's Army campaign. He had intended to just stash all the pieces in the back of his closet, and did so with the enlarged TV storyboards. But seeing the mounted, acetate-covered print ads and posters gave him a new idea. He thumbtacked them up at eye level on the corkboard-covered wall, stood back, and looked at them. AMERICA, THE BEAUTIFUL. *She Needs You Now.* AMERICA, THE FREE . . . the vulnerable, the young.

He sat in his chair and studied the pictures again. He remembered defending them at the agency. If soft drinks could show a kid tumbling with laughter under a litter of puppies, if bus companies could show a young girl running from a farmhouse to throw her arms around the GI arriving home, if hamburger chains and breweries could go for your heart with images of good people loving their lives, their work and each other, "Why can't we?" he'd demanded. "Who's got a better right to go for the gut?" To show a grandfather holding a baby, brothers opening a hardware store, a black girl getting a diploma.

He felt right, inside. He left the study and went back upstairs. What the hell. He'd do it. Just so that later he could never say he hadn't tried everything he could think of. He slid his footlocker out from under the bed in his guest room, opened

[ 275 ]

it, and brought forth his fatigues. Long ago, he had raided it for the faded, epauletted khaki shirts he'd worn on active duty, and which he still wore often now, with their sleeves rolled up and fronts unbuttoned at the top.

Putting on the fatigues, he had a brief self-conscious thought that maybe he ought to go lock his door, but ignored it. Nobody would be coming by, especially in this storm. And what the hell did he care what anyone might think anyhow? The uniform was a bit tight around the middle and at the butt, but it still fit him. He laced up his combat boots and bloused his trouser legs over their tops, using the ball-bearing-filled rubber tubes for weight. He'd kept it all. The belt was there, and he uncoiled it but didn't run it through the loops yet—its buckle was too tarnished.

He snapped the camouflage scarf around his neck and set the hard-crowned, Johnny Reb slanted cap squarely on his head, the baseball-curled visor forward over his eyes. The fit was snugger than years ago, when his hair had been crew-cut. His First Lieutenant insignia on the cap and collar, made of cloth, were still bright. His Engineer castle was still a clean gold. In the kitchen he cleaned the brass buckle with silver polish, reattached it to the belt, and slid the belt on. He buffed the boots with a potholder, and was done.

He went into his office and looked at himself in the full-length mirror on the closet door. He didn't laugh. If the louie bars were colonel clusters or birds, he thought, this is how I'd look, and I'd look pretty fucking good. He stayed standing, studying his ads again, pulling up the old, sweet feelings. He remembered he was indoors and removed the cap. Turning, he caught his reflection in the mirror again, then immediately looked away, shaken. This was suddenly feeling like nothing he had intended. This was feeling a little crazy. Maybe it was the fever. He rushed upstairs and returned his uniform to its locker. *Come on. You aren't trying to decide whether you can or not. You're trying to talk yourself into doing it.* Back in his sweater and jeans he felt better and lighter.

# 4

Deep inside the tubular canvas cabana that same Wednesday, Deborah sat reclined upon a wooden lounge chair, alone, playing a game of defiance with the rainstorm. As she watched, the mass of solid-seeming lines of rain moved faster and faster across the back of the sea, leaped the tops of the jungle trees on the cliffs below, raked the already hysterical hotel swimming pool, and once again roared on over her head, strafing the canvas, and firing yet another burst of water in at her. Once again even the farthest reaching splashes landed way short of her bare feet. She laughed, but nervously.

She wore her terry robe over her bikini only for modesty. The tropical winds blew as warm as the heat from an open oven door. No one could claim that the place hadn't delivered the warmth, if not the sun. Until today, when she discovered the rainstorm game, she had found it impossible to do anything besides think of Nick. She wished their last night together had gone easier.

She watched the storm regrouping itself at sea for its next assault. A man's figure appeared at the bottom of her vision. He wore only white bell-bottoms, and ran around the edge of the pool toward her, mindless of the downpour. If only it was Nick, she thought. God, to love him in this cave in this rain! But of course it was only the photographer, Jake. He came in, red-skinned and drenched, white moustache dripping. "Hey."

"Hi." She threw him a towel.

"Thanks."

Jake's voice was one thing she'd always liked about him: even in crises, it stayed very light and friendly. She said, "So?"

Jake took a small metal case from his pants pocket, sat next to her left leg, and opened it. It held a pile of cocaine and a glass straw. He jiggled the case to make the crystals thin and spread. "Thought you might be sick of rain and like some snow."

"Nah, that's okay."

He shrugged and did himself up both nostrils. "Geez, Deborah, you don't wanna get high, you don't wanna ball with me and the Dirdle sisters, you don't wanna do anything anymore!"

She laughed. "Dirdle sisters! That's perfect." He meant the two youngest of the four other models there for the shoot. "Come on, Jakie, you know I'm too old for that stuff—I'm almost nineteen!"

He grinned. He was known for his penchant for extremely young girls.

"The summit meeting getting anywhere," she asked, "or are we still on the phone to New York?"

"Deborah, I'm worried about you, off all by yourself like this. You okay?"

"I'm happy enough, Jake."

"That's great. Why?"

"Keep a secret?"

"Nope."

"Because I'm getting married!"

"No fooling. When?"

"I don't know. I haven't asked him yet."

"I see. He in New York?"

"Yeah."

"Then I got good news for you. The job's a wrap. We're going back."

Her heart fluttered but her sense said, "But that's nuts! We're all here, for Christ's sake. Why don't they just give up on this place and move us out of the storm?"

Jake took one of her cigarettes and lit it. "What can I tell you? I told them that Monday, told them it yesterday, just said it again five minutes ago."

"Never go back without the pictures."

"They're new and scared, Deborah, they don't know that yet."

"Jesus, I feel old."

"Yeah, you *better* hang it up and get married or something."

"Fuck you."

"That's more like it. Listen—some of us are talking about staying on through the weekend on our own, have some fun."

"Sounds like indoor fun to me, Jake."

"Whatever. Interested?"

"Listen, if it's really a cancel, I'm on the next plane home."

"Well, it's a cancel all right," he said, "but listen, hon, what the hell, this might be your last chance to—" He jumped. The rain had barreled up and shot its wad at the cabana again. "Jesus! Holy! That—" His right hand had shot to the taut, hairless skin over his heart.

She hooted. "Ha! Look at you! It's only rain, Jake! And you were soaked already!"

Half-calmed, he chided her, "That wasn't funny, Deborah. I don't think I like you anymore." At the mouth of the cabana he turned back to her and winked. "Go on back to rancid civilization, then. See if I care."

She grinned. "Ah, the Valium's working."

He brightened and turned back inside, raising his right hand toward her.

"Oh, God," she said, "he's going to lecture me again. Please don't start wagging that finger at me, Jake." She knew him well enough: he was taking her declining of his offer to stay as a rebuke, and felt the need to justify himself to her. Such a boy.

The blast of rain had scared the cigarette out of his hand. He sat back down and lit another. "You know how great you're looking, don't you, toots?"

"Am I?"

"Mm. The weather's a shame. We could have got some really incredible pictures of you. Love, huh?"

"Yup."

"Yeah, love'll do it every time." He sighed deeply and looked where she was still looking, out at the storm sweeping in upon the land from the sea. After a moment he said, "You're right, Deborah, this is jerking off. I think I'll send them all back, and split for Cuba."

"Cuba!"

"I went there, a couple years ago, on a tour. Just after they opened it up again. I was with the second or third group to go in."

"I didn't even know they had opened it. How was it?"

"It was . . . I don't know, kind of fun," he told the storm. "Different, anyhow. It was sad to see Havana. In the fifties, when I was first there, Havana was *the* sin city, you know? Really hot. Casinos, bordellos . . . Now it all needs a coat of paint. Commies cleaned it up, but it only looks dirty. They schlepped us around on these buses. They'd point to a tree and tell you how in a couple of months it was going to be some terrific factory, employing thousands. Meantime, they're all on food stamps."

"Sounds depressing, Jake. I don't think you should go back."

As if he didn't hear her, Jake went on. "We saw this ancient Indian village being restored by this sculptress. They got black, Spanish, and Indian cultures going there, you know? The Indians are extinct, but so people will know how they lived, they're reproducing this . . . Ha! I walk into this tent, this cement or something tepee—and over there's where they sleep, and here's their fire, and there's this brave kneeling in the middle of the floor. I look close, and he's got this straw going from his nose to this little heap of stuff in the palm of his hand!

"I ask the tour guide what he's doing. And I mean that cat is *snorting*, you know? But I want to see how she'll explain it. She gives me some Indian name for it, and I say yeah, but what does that mean? You know what she says? She says they called it *'reality'*! Freaked me out, you know, Deborah?" He turned his pale, twinkling blue eyes back on her. "These freaking old primitives, man, they *knew*. They weren't checking out of reality when they turned on, they were checking in! Over *there* was reality!"

She said, "No wonder they're extinct."

"Christ, what's this guy you're in love with anyhow, a *narc*?"

She felt the blood rush to her face. Silence filled the cabana, warm as the air. It struck her: Jake, too, had been thinking of Nick all the while, even though he didn't know even his name. Defensively, she cracked, "What's the matter, Jake, jealous?"

"Sure," he said softly. "Everyone's jealous when somebody else is in love. They all want a piece of the glow. It's why we all hate you for hiding out for three days."

She blushed fully and hotly.

He let her off the hook. He patted her knee and smiled. "Except me, of course. I know it's good for business. Accessibility defeats allure, right? It's why you're a star, Ormay, keep it up." He stood. "If you'll excuse me, I think I'll go back to the gloom, fear, and self-pity. It's a lot safer."

[ 281 ]

"Good luck with the Dirdle sisters, Jake."

"You too, Deborah, and your narc."

"He's no narc, for God's sake!"

"I know. He's another drummer with another rock band."

"Right."

He reached the end of the cabana again, turned back, and said with hardness in his light voice, "Christ, it's all just penises and vaginas anyhow—what's the big deal?"

She only glared.

He left, curling forward and breaking into his light, graceful, barefooted trot through the rain, back around the simmering pool to vanish behind the corner of the hotel's porch. She watched his image diminish and disappear. Her anger went away as well. *No, it's more than that, Jake. It is a big deal.* Maybe Nick, like Jake, thought that the only way he had to go was solo. With all his deaths and secrets and looking away from her. But Nick's solitude had a crack in it. She had seen inside it and knew—he needed her. He just hadn't admitted it yet, or at least didn't act it; in fact he still acted the opposite, as if she needed him. Which was also true enough.

She wanted to be with him again now as quickly as she could. She swung off the chaise to her feet, scooping up her lighter and cigarettes into her robe pocket. She lingered just inside the cabana's mouth a moment, wishing to time her exit just right. Waiting, she experienced an emotion new to her. This was no crush or whimsy this time; this was real. *I love him.* She looked out at the pool, the hotel, the sea. The sky was so low she could touch it. She thought, This is reality. And wherever he is, that's reality, too. But neither reality will be complete until we're together again.

"Now!" she said and stepped outside, away from the cabana. She loosened the bow of the cinch, letting the robe blow open, and took the storm's newest blast full force upon her hair, face, and body, rising on tiptoe and arching belly-out. She half-expected to be blown back inside the canvas tunnel, but she prevailed, cutting through the fierce wind and water like the blade of a knife.

In the sudden, calm wake she closed the robe around her once again, bent as Jake had, and ran for the hotel. As she went, she felt a twinge of pity for Jake—he had nobody waiting for him back in New York.

Running, drenched, she exulted, "But *I* do!"

# 5

*All I know for sure is Fincher.*

Nick meandered aimlessly around the first floor of his house. Coming again into his sunporch, he willed himself to stay put. Maybe standing still here, safe amidst the chaos of the snowstorm blowing outside the glass, would help him regain some calm. *Get psyched!* He had gone into this day of retreat and solitude in search of an emotion. He wanted to *feel* something. *Well, what did you expect. A blinding vision?*

"Shit," he sighed aloud.

He laid the back of his fist against his forehead. *This damned fever!* If it wasn't for Galgay, he thought, what a pleasant day this might be. To be here in my house in the snow, truly alone, free to anticipate simply the pleasures of Deborah's return. And the days and maybe weeks ahead of feeling free of the city and jobs, at least for the time being. The life he'd been living prior to Kelsey and Galgay suddenly seemed less onerous.

Yet Galgay had brought him Deborah, and Kelsey had brought him this . . . *What the Christ is it anyhow?*

"Keep it simple," he heard Kelsey remind him.

"Up yours," he replied, his frustration approaching rage. Why can't *you* do it? All right, so you can't use a pro, but "Why me?" he finally blurted out, and thought he was going to puke. All his life, he had hated no words the way he hated those two.

His windows with the snow at them suddenly snapped into clear focus. He felt cooler. He knew it was not murder. He had no problems with the act itself. The man was a traitor. Treason demands the death penalty. Not even the traitor would deny that. "The man's hurting us bad, and has to be stopped," Kelsey had said. And that man was coming here tomorrow.

*But all I know for sure is Fincher.*

That was the closest he'd ever come to the real thing. He'd braced and aimed and fired that .45 and seen that crazy, poor kid's guts and head go exploding off into the ammo dump night. This was about killing, and about death, and all he knew for sure was Fincher.

He would. If something ever put him back to twenty-four or whatever years old again and back in the Service, he would, he'd do the exact same thing—he'd fire that gun and still refuse to take even the hint of a rap for Fincher's dying.

Then it hit him—did Kelsey think that Fincher was enough? *He knows I did it once. Does he think I can do it again that easy?*

"Oh, Kelse, you bastard, I love you, but—" He felt his chest's reflexes strain to block it, the sigh threatening to slide deeper and deeper, down and down beyond the end of his breath into some black, waiting void.

He failed to stop it. He felt the hot tears well and then spill

out of his burning eyes onto his face. He sat, thoroughly bemused. He was crying. He didn't know why, but the painful
tears had come, and were still coming. He didn't feel like weeping over anything, yet here he was, weeping, anyhow.

He let them come, and soon the feelings followed and he
knew—as he wept at last for Waltzie and Julia, he was finally
crying for Fincher. I'm sorry, he prayed behind his tears, I'm
sorry. I had to shoot, but I'm sorry you died.

At length his tears stopped, and when they did, Nick
wiped his face dry with his fingers.

He put the old worn record on his turntable and set it playing. The needle cut its way through the first grooves of static.
He replenished the fire, then sat and listened. His dear dead
Bobby Darin sang "Mack the Knife" one more time. "Oh, the
shark, babe . . ."

At the end he went and lifted the needle back to the start.
The first time too many echoes had come shoving in. It came
on him that he'd kept playing this song so often all these years
especially to hear those echoes: the merry, raucous voices of
Kelsey, Big John, J.J., Scotty, all the wives and women, Waltzie and Julia, Billy Hogue, D., all the flyboys . . . all of Baker
Barracks itself belting out that one same song to racket off the
mountain and go ringing down the misty Fils Valley.

He played the song through a third time, listening hard to
the words. The echoes of the voices of all the Army people he
had known got fainter and fainter. He started to sing, then, and
to bop along with it. He began feeling up and high and excited
and hip—*recharged*.

He stopped. What *was* this new-old jazzy feeling?

He recognized it. Yeah. This was the way that song had
used to make him feel. The feeling of this song, like the feeling
of the soldier in the snow—it rang so true. He loved it.

He went to the player, lifted the old record off the turnta-

[ 285 ]

ble gingerly, and slid it into its paper sleeve. *Waltzie was right, in more ways than he knew. Him and Julia. Always go to the music.*

*All right.*

*First, check out Kelsey's system.* He walked to the kitchen phone and dialed the number Kelsey had given him. Kelsey's recorded voice said, "Hello, son. Just make your drop at the tone, and I'll get back to you soon as I can." That was all. When the tone sounded, he hung up.

*All right.*

*Next, sleep. Then—call the Kelse and tell him yes.*

He lay upon the couch on his back and covered his eyes with his left forearm.

# 6

Deborah rapped on the door and shoved it open at the same time. Sleeping, Nick didn't stir. She waited, then coughed sharply. He stayed dead to the world. She swung out of her fur, shedding snowflakes, and realized how chilly it was in here, and eerily dark. From outside, through the falling snow, the one light burning in the kitchen had looked much brighter than it was.

She went to the fireplace. Her anger had stayed hot all the way on the plane up, and then driving here. She knew it would keep a little while longer. She sat on the hearth, to catch some heat and watch him at the same time. Normally she was a sucker for anything asleep, but now she thought, You bastard, how come you *never* look defenseless? A queer sound caught her ear. It was his turntable, spinning empty. She went over and shut it off. The click woke him.

He sat up and swung his feet onto the floor. His eyes popped when he saw her. She growled, "Nice. I rush all the way from the equator, and he can't even stay awake for me."

He palmed his eyes. "I'm dreaming, right?"

"Wrong."

"I've died and gone to heaven?"

"You'll wish it."

He fell back, opening his arms. "Well, you just gonna sit over there?"

"Yup."

He sat back. "How the hell did you get here anyhow?"

"I came straight from the airport. My job got canceled. When your apartment didn't answer, I knew you were here. I rented a car."

"I might have just been out eating or something."

"I knew you were here."

"I got fired yesterday."

"I know, your buddy Grant told me."

"You were nuts, driving in all that snow."

"Sure."

Flickers of reality were beginning to reach him and bring him back. He said, "What, did you try to get me at the office?"

"I just told you that."

"Did you call here?"

"No. It didn't seem necessary—or welcome."

"What the hell time is it?"

"Beats me."

He finally put it all together and marveled at her. "You

mean, you came from the islands, didn't get me there, and came here, just like that?"

"Just like that."

"I had something I had to do today."

"What was that?"

Her tone brought him fully awake. "I can't tell you specifically, but—"

"You'd better tell me specifically, or I'm back out that door in two seconds."

She was serious. He felt puzzled, "I'm sorry, babe, but really, it's something I just can't tell anybody."

Her anger sent her prowling around the room. "Sorry! You're sorry! Everybody's always so fucking sorry! Well, I'm sorry I ever met you, how's that? Why the hell couldn't you call me?"

"Hey, Deborah, what—?"

"Shut up! Just shut up, will you? You can't say anything *specifically* anyhow, so don't try to tell me anything. Go ahead, stay by yourself. Curl up and suck your thumb—hey, I broke into your precious goddamn house, did you think of that? Should I say I'm sorry about that?" She swept in and out of his kitchen. "And oh, it's cute, Nick. Nice and snug and tight— nothing can get to you here, no, sir! You're safe here, all right— you prick!"

"What's the *matter*?"

"Nothing! Everything's the matter, that's what's the goddamn matter!" She had stormed into the sunporch, met the outside storm at the windows, and turned back. "You didn't even think to leave me a message, did you? I come back and you're gone. Just *gone*. Well, that ain't the way it works, man—not with me, anyhow."

"But you were away, I knew you were—"

"They have phones everywhere in the world now, Nick. You just dial a number and talk." She got cigarettes from her coat, lit one, and sat down again on the hearth. Her rage had found a cold steadiness. She aimed her fierce gaze directly at his scared-looking eyes. "Admit it—I never even crossed your mind. Just what was it, Nick? What was so bloody important that you had to do today? Besides lick your wounds?"

He swallowed dryly.

"Oh, forget it." She sighed bitterly. "I don't want to hear it. You wouldn't think of me until you felt like screwing me again." Tears filled her eyes. She looked away into the fire behind her. "I don't know why I should be so upset," she said. "It's certainly nothing new."

Silence fell between them.

He sat, staring at the veil of dew that had begun to glisten in her hair. He knew that she was trying to keep from crying, and he wanted to go and comfort her, but was afraid she might explode and he'd lose her. When he couldn't stand the tension any longer, he risked her wrath and spoke. "I've had some serious troubles to deal with, Deborah."

She stayed looking away. Her voice came low and tired. "That's just all the more reason, Nick. To call me. You told me you loved me. That's what it means."

"They want me to kill a man."

Her head snapped around. She studied his face. "You serious?"

"Yeah."

"My God. Who?"

He didn't think about it, he just told her: "The Counterintelligence Corps. They caught one of their own agents passing stuff to the Russians. He has to be stopped, and they recruited me to do it." She didn't speak, but her whole face softened; her eyes went dry and brightened, seeming to reach out to him, full of questions. So he told her, specifically, all of it—except the identity of the traitor. ". . . and I had to be alone, to make up my mind."

When he finished, she whispered, "Oh, babe."

"You're right, though, I should have at least let you know where I was." The next was harder to say: "I kept trying *not* to think of you, is the truth."

"Why?"

"I'm not sure."

"No. Nick, think about it—why?"

He dropped his eyes to the coffee table in front of him.

She knew he wasn't going to be able to answer, and said, "You've decided to do it, haven't you?"

He nodded yes. "I was going to call and tell Kelsey when I woke up."

Lighter than a whisper she said, "*Was* going to?"

He fell back against the couch. "Now I'm not so sure. I don't know what I think anymore."

"Fuck think—how do you feel, Nick?"

"Feel," he repeated after a moment. He made the word sound like *shit*.

Her heart was pounding. Words came before she thought them: "My real name is Moore," she said.

"What?"

"Moore. Ormay is just pig latin for plain old Moore."

She moved and sat on the couch with him. She told him: "I was never let have feelings. One Saturday when I was around twelve my mother sent me to the store. But I had my hair all done up in these rags—you know, for those big, fat curls? And I told her I was afraid. I knew all these bigger kids would be hanging out around the store, and they'd make fun of me. She made me go anyhow. As if I hadn't said anything. And I remember passing this older kid, I don't know now whether it was a boy or a girl, just that it was an older kid, and whoever it was said, 'Nothing can be that bad, girlie!' So you can imagine the look I must have had on my face. But all I learned from that was, Never show your feelings."

He looked at her gravely.

"Your turn, Nick—tell me something secret."

He said, "I . . . okay—I think I've spent my whole god-damn life trying to please some institution or other, from my mother on. School, country, outfits I worked for. I never saw myself as doing that, though. I always felt the opposite—oddball or offbeat or unique, or something like that. But now, now I think it was always still inside *their* fucking walls, you know?"

She edged closer to him on the couch. "I used to think," she said, "that I had to think every thought that came into my head, and never feel any of the feelings. But now I . . ." She stopped. Then she added softly, "I feel very good with you, Nick. I want to know everything about you."

He said, "I hope you know I love you."

She jumped him.

He wrapped his arms around her tightly, buried his face in her neck, and wished he could press her until she was inside his own skin with him.

Kissing his ears and cheeks, she told him, "I love you. Oh, Nick, I love you, I missed you so much, it hurt."

He sucked her collarbones and throat. "I love you, Debo-rah, Christ, do I love you!"

They kissed and rubbed, embraced and stroked each other, losing themselves in it. They undressed each other, then re-sumed, looking so close into each other's eyes that neither could see. She said, "Oh, now," but he whispered, "Wait."

He plunged his mouth there and fretted her steadily until she began arching and crying out. Then, in their first perfectly synchronized unspoken agreement, she pulled his head upward at the precise moment it was rising on its own and together they broke through to find what it was like there, beyond all the body business.

They tried to reach cigarettes and recuperate without com-ing apart, but had to give it up and separate. He got up and fed the fireplace. She fetched her coat and returned to the couch, draping it over her nakedness like a great fur blanket. He moved toward her, but she said, "Make your call now, Nick. Get it over with."

He turned and walked to the kitchen. She held her breath and prayed, watching him. He dialed the phone ten times.

Once again Kelsey's recorded voice said, "Hello, son. Just make your drop at the tone, and I'll get back to you soon as I can." This time when the tone sounded, he said, "Kelse, this is me. I'm sorry, partner, but it's got to be a negative. *Wiedersehen.*"

Going back to her, Nick started to speak but Deborah hushed him with a finger to her lips. She lifted the coat, let him in, then closed it around his back.

# SEVEN

# 1

An abrupt silence woke Nick, but not completely. He did not
open his eyes. He and Deborah lay nestled like spoons beneath
the coat-blanket on the couch. He assumed the silence he'd
heard had been the snow stopping, and imagined that he could
see the day's sun coming out to set, like a single Kilroy-was-
here eye, into the fence-top line of the horizon.

But then he heard something real. And realized that it had
not been silence that woke him, but rather another, earlier
sound, similar to this one. His body had already quickened, so
he couldn't tell himself that he hadn't heard anything. He tried
to will this dark intrusion away. He listened, but heard nothing
but his own breath and the light feather-brushing of Deborah's
sleeping. He remembered the evil little creak once again. Nothing that belonged to his house could have made it.

He wished it would sound again, and prayed to God that it
wouldn't. Trying to move as little as possible, he opened his
eyes, slid them across Deborah's hair, then raised them one
click. A blue-black handgun extended by a dull gray silencer
was staring back at him.

His first stunned thought was only that none of the guns in
his killing-dreams of the night before had appeared with si-
lencers. He'd never seen a silencer before, except in movies.

So the sight of Brian Galgay there behind and above it oddly made him feel more disappointed than shocked. He actually thought of saying, "You stupid, cowardly bastard, what are you afraid of? Who's going to hear you here?"

His body had already begun to move, swiftly bringing him up and sending his left hand back to hold Deborah down. This woke her. He held her still with his hand, and stared up at the glaring, silent Galgay. Clear of the fur coat, he involuntarily began to shiver. From behind him her muffled voice cried, *"What is it?"*

Brian Galgay stood wearing his heavy overcoat, unbuttoned over a suit. His face looked shiningly, redly shaved, but he still seemed strangely derelictlike, looming there over them. Some huge mistake was happening, or else some event that would soon be explained away.

Brian's words finally came in a roar that contradicted the silencer. "What are you *doing* here? You *traitor!*"

She squirmed like a beached sandshark. "Get away from us! Get out! Go away, you . . . geek!"

"This is my house, Galgay. Get out." The normality of his own voice astonished him. He felt abject fear and despair pierce his soul. He leaned back on Deborah, wishing to keep her shielded from the gun and from Galgay's vision. But the action made him feel weirdly disloyal, as if he were trying to help her attacker. *Why is he after her?*

In a new, softer voice Galgay told Deborah, "I waited for you! You never came home!"

Nick noticed that while Galgay's eyes left him for some point to his side, the eye of the silencer stayed fixed upon him. He found its stare almost irresistible. He had seen a weasel mesmerize a rabbit into fascinated, fatal immobility before lunging for its throat. This was how the rabbit felt.

"Why are you here?" Galgay was pleading. "You're supposed to be gone away someplace. Now, look where I find you! My God. Why did you—?"

"Are you crazy? You're crazy!" she yelled.

"Ssh!" Nick tightened his grip on her shoulder.

"*You!*" Brian accused, and slashed the side of the silencer against Nick's left temple.

Nick forced himself to spring back upright. His hand had flown to the pain. A little blood ran wet and warm there, but the slash had surprised more than hurt him. He heard Deborah say, "You bastard!" in a much louder and clearer voice, and realized she had turned around behind him. He also realized that it was not she who was in danger of being seriously harmed here. *Jesus*, he thought—*does Galgay know?*

"I don't care, all right?" Brian said to Deborah. "Just get out of there and come with me, now. We'll go away. It'll be okay, it'll be good."

She heard her own breath hiss through her teeth, inhaling. She felt her hand biting into the flesh of Nick's bare hip and released it. Then she said to Brian, "All right." She felt Nick's "No!" rumble through her body, and took another handful of his flesh, trying to signal him to stay quiet. "I will," she told Brian clearly, propped up on her palms now and facing him over Nick's shoulder. The rheumy glaze in Brian's eyes reminded her of the night he had pressed himself upon her, and of the awful anger he contained. Matter-of-factly, she said, "I'll have to get dressed."

Brian felt his head begin to waver on his neck, which hurt inside and out. His throat was so dry it pained him to swallow. His eyes stung, and his inner vision threatened to desert him, playing malicious tricks with his control of things—Deborah was herself now, and talking sense. But she might twist into Evelyn, or even into Anna again. Anna would be worse. With Evelyn it would only be that jerk from the car, caught in the act at last. But with Anna he had no idea, no image of what sort of man she might be with.

Nick was nothing. Another minor disappointment and no surprise. It had been his own slip that let him imagine Nick might be capable of understanding anything. If killing him would make Nick disappear, he'd blow him away right this minute. But it wouldn't. It would only make him dead—a mess that might upset Deborah and make her act foolish again. "Yes," he said to her, "get dressed. You," he told Nick, "get away from her. Let her up."

Under cover of his hand, Nick blinked his eye furiously to make it unblur. The bleeding had stopped and was drying. He wanted to just leap blindly at the loon, but knew that was suicide: just the guy's nerve endings would stop him in midair. He didn't know what to do. When he felt Deborah's hands nudging him to move sideways, he gave up and obeyed.

Brian had a flash vision of the General sparring with his lover. He spat at Nick, "Turn around, you! Faggot! Who wants to look at you!" He moved the tip of his pistol the inch to the left needed to keep the guy pinned, then looked back at Deborah. It hurt him to see that she had covered herself with her coat. "It's all right." He smiled at her. "You're safe now, Deborah."

*My God,* she thought. Maybe this wasn't such a sensible idea after all. If she bounced up and threw on her clothes too swiftly, he'd take it as a put-down and might start doubting her intentions. Yet it couldn't look like anything too willing, either. She remembered his hands on her elbows and his cock against her belly. If he was as far over the line as he looked, he'd be liable to flip out altogether, shoot Nick and do God knows what to her. She stayed sitting on the couch, trying to stare as blankly at him as she could.

Nick said, "You fucking voyeur!" He was convinced now that the man was psycho enough to kill him, but watching the creep gawking at her enraged him. "What's this all about anyhow, Brian? What are you doing here? You said you were coming tomorrow, remember? To do more interviews." He had to keep himself believing that Galgay did not know that he knew

[ 298 ]

the truth about him. *He couldn't know!* "Why are you here, man?"

Brian looked at him. "Stay where you are. She has to get dressed. Just be quiet, and you'll be all right."

Nick wanted to challenge him, You're not taking her! Instead he heard himself say only, "This is my house."

"Your house, your stupid little house," Brian exploded. "People are starving, people are dying! Whole families could live in this house, not just you!"

Nick stared at him, shocked. *Jesus. Kelsey ought to know this. Maybe this baby is a believer.* Then a worse thought came: *Maybe he's found out! And he wants her as a hostage!*

Brian knew some of the things he had to do—render Nick helpless, kill the phone, disable the two cars outside, and get her and himself to where he had hidden his own car in the woods. But he still couldn't think clearly past that point.

But that was okay. Once they were away and driving together, a plan would make itself known to him. The sight of Nick fingering his eye reminded him of having struck him. He didn't regret it. It had been necessary. Still, an odd softness enlarged spongily in his chest, and he admitted, "I can't blame you, you know, Nick. She's really something. A woman can really take you over. I know. Believe me, I really do know."

Nick just stayed looking at him; he seemed to be waiting for something. Feeling strangely compelled, Brian explained, "I didn't expect any of this, either. But her cleaning woman came! And started cleaning the bird cage!" He swung his next words pointedly at Deborah: "Finding a man there *didn't* seem to surprise her!" To Nick again he said, "So I figured I'd come see you early. Get you over with. But you lied to me. You *both* lied to me!" He stopped speaking. His throat felt as if a razor blade had lodged in it. He forced stern authority to return to his voice. "Burke—make us some coffee to take—and some food, too. And I need a drink. Show me where it is. Get it for me!"

Nick didn't move.

Deborah whispered, "Do what he wants."

Nick put on his clothes, resisting the impulse to hurry. Then he walked into the kitchen area, to his liquor rack on the counter.

Brian followed him. He went to the wall phone and ripped the coiled receiver wire out of its base. From here the pistol had no more than two inches to move between Nick and the woman, so he stayed put. He felt sweat leaking beneath his shirt collar, and took off his overcoat, draping it over a chair back.

Nick pulled out several bottles and stood them on the counter.

Brian said, "Pour some Scotch and some ice in a glass, then put it on the table here, and the bottle." All that mattered now was relieving the pain in his throat, easing the pressure in his head, and calming his mind.

Nick fixed the drink, then backed away from the table.

Brian picked up the glass and took one long swallow of the whiskey. "Now—the food." He could feel the medicine begin to work. He turned to Deborah. "Get dressed!" Keeping the pistol on Nick, he watched her bend to pick her things up off the floor. He sipped more Scotch, then poured more from the bottle, darting his eyes up and back.

Nick opened the refrigerator door. He moved things from its inside to the counter, and opened a drawer.

Brian said, "No! No knives. Shut it." Deborah had begun speaking, but he didn't look at her until he saw both of Nick's hands come clear of the closed drawer.

She held her clothes in one hand; the other held the coat bunched in front of her. "Can I go upstairs, or in the—?"

"Do it right there! You show yourself all the time to anyone who's looking! But not to me?"

Nick hung helplessly over the pile of food, looking out the window over the sink. He saw only his and Deborah's cars parked out there—Galgay must have crept up to the house on foot. The snow had turned to rain before it stopped. What little of it remained lay scattered in sparse, dirty-looking streaks and splotches on the ground. The air was thick and bleak and gray. He heard Deborah's coat land heavily on the couch, and began to turn. Galgay was looking at him, his voice seeming to come from the hole in the silencer, still leveled at him: "Eyes off her, Burke—you've seen all you're ever going to, now! I want that food!"

She made no attempt to conceal anything. She didn't even turn sideways, just stepped into her panties, then sat straight down on the coffee table and began working the body stocking on over her feet and up her legs.

Brian had intended to take deliberate pleasure from seeing her nakedness. Why not, he'd earned at least that; she'd been manipulating and keeping him at a distance for a lot longer than any normal man would be expected to tolerate. Yet, now that it was happening, he found himself pointedly keeping his gaze upon Burke's back at the sink. A sense of something had seized him; he couldn't tell if it was honor or shame or pity for her sudden vulnerability. He backed away slowly, holding the gun on Burke. When she was ready, he'd turn and she'd let him comfort her in his arms. He asked her, "All right, Deborah?"

"Almost."

He turned. She already had her jeans and sweater back on, and was pulling her boots onto her feet. He stepped close to her, reached down, and stroked her hair. "You'll see, Deborah, I'll—"

Nick had spun and run straight at him.

Brian heard and swung around. The back of his closed fist caught Nick squarely on the ear and sent him sprawling.

Barking from the new pain, he crashed down into the small table holding his receiver and turntable. He just lay there, heaving. Within the deafening ringing inside his skull he thought he could hear the distant thuds of other voices yelling.

"You prick! You animal! You—!"

"Stay where you are, Deborah! He made me do that!"

She ignored him and went to Nick.

Galgay shouted, "Stop that. Don't touch him anymore."

But she didn't listen. She kept on rubbing and stroking Nick's leg, through the rough denim. Her other hand was hidden beneath her down-hanging hair, squeezing her temples with her fingers to make it all stop and go away and be a nightmare from which she would awaken and find Nick peacefully locked with her, asleep.

Galgay opened up into his full standing height again. "All right, Deborah. It's up to you, now. Don't let this get out of hand again. Nobody has to get hurt. Get up. Go fix us some food to take. Don't bother making sandwiches, or anything. Just put it all in a bag, that we can fix later. Take as much as he's got. He's not going anywhere. We—" The sight of her stopped him.

Her head came up and turned toward him. She cleared her hair away from her face with her free hand. Her huge eyes glistened. She drew her lips into a small hole, but only her head was making the word, as she slowly shook it back and forth: No, no, no, no . . .

Brian sighed. He couldn't remember now why he'd thought taking food was so important. He regretted all of this very much, but knew it was useless to try to tell her that yet. It would take a long time, probably, and a lot of kind handling and explaining before she would become able again to believe him and love him. He stepped to the table, emptied the glass of whiskey, downed another, then set to work.

The garbage bags were just where he thought they'd be, under the sink. He opened one and arranged his hand so it could keep the pistol aimed in their general direction while holding the sack open. With his left hand, he dropped the stuff from the counter into the bag. Then he moved to the refrigerator for more. Done, he set the sack of food near the chair holding his coat, and reached out his wallet. He estimated that thirty dollars would cover it all. He laid three tens flat under the salt and pepper shakers on the table, and heard a new sound.

At first he thought it was only in the back of his brain. The hum of an engine, the crackling of gravel. His eyes shot to the window. It was a car, clearing the woods, entering Burke's parking area!

The driver killed the engine and got out. It took Brian a moment to recognize Kelsey; he had been only a signature on telexes and orders; his memory had to fly back twenty years. He spun around, grabbed Deborah's arm, and pulled her from Nick. "Open the door before he knocks on it—*just* before!" He stuck his gun into the hollow of her waist.

All of it was nothing but faraway, incomprehensible sounds to Nick. He lay wedged between his armchair and coffee table. His turntable was sticking into his belly. The receiver had slid off the small of his back. The broken halves of the small table lay on either side of him. He forced his hands against the floor, and pushed until he could hook his left elbow over the top of the coffee table, where Deborah was no longer sitting. Then he swung up his right arm limply. He collapsed there, exhausted, on his forearms, fighting unconsciousness.

"Now!" Brian shoved the pistol deeper into her side.

She opened the door.

Joel Kelsey's right hand froze in midair. Seeing her, he began to smile.

"She's a dead one, Kelsey. Bring up the other arm. . . . Good. Close your eyes. . . . That's it. All right—step up inside, two paces. Turn to your left in place, then to your left again. Move."

Brian shut the door, and shoved Deborah away, pointing the pistol at Kelsey. "Lean forward against the wall, Colonel— on the tips of your index fingers only."

Kelsey performed the drill. "You're making a mistake, Galgay! Where's Nick?"

"He's hurt!" Deborah cried, back beside Nick, who was on the table.

"Silence! You, too, Kelsey—keep the mouth shut. Bring your feet back a few more inches!" He frisked his prisoner, found his weapon, and disarmed him. He broke the cylinder, shook the bullets free of their chambers, and pocketed the pistol. Then he backed away and resumed his post at the archway to the kitchen. From here he could shoot them all, if necessary.

On their own, Nick's groping fingers found the old LP on the coffee table behind Deborah. He coughed convulsively and cracked the record in his hands. Now he had a weapon. The trouble was, he was still too weak to use it. The best he could do was slip it to Deborah.

"Get your coat," Brian ordered, "we're—"

"We can't leave Nick like this! He might hemorrhage!"

"I didn't hit him that hard." Brian looked back at Kelsey. He knew the colonel was enduring excruciating pain by now, went up behind him, and brought the leaden butt of the revolver down upon the base of his skull. Kelsey's tall, inert body toppled forward, then crumpled to the floor. There. But what was Kelsey doing here at all? "What's he *doing* here?" he yelled. "*What the hell is Kelsey doing here?*"

She looked up. He was moving, wild-eyed, toward her. "I don't know! Nick . . . Nick called him on the phone!"

"When?"

"I . . . a few hours ago, I guess."

"Why?"

"I don't know!"

She was afraid he was going to crush her under his big, heavy body again like the night in her apartment. But he stopped, reached down, and grabbed her shoulder, trying to pull her to her feet. He was too strong. She rose from the table. As she did, her arm lashed up and out like a whip.

At first Brian was aware only of a tiny pinpoint of pain on his left cheek near his ear, like a bee sting. His fingers found the puncture and began tracing the wire-thin cut; he had been slashed nearly from ear to chin. Even his lips had been sliced. Following the slow, amazed touch of his fingers, the awful pain came streaking out of the pinpoint and across the skin of his face with the blinding heat of a welder's arc.

Deborah watched, praying for him to faint. She had dropped the piece of record and grabbed his gun. She'd thought it would weigh a ton, but it was light.

His hand opened beneath his eyes. It looked as if he had touched wet, watery, crimson paint. He realized that the pain in his back had come from slamming into the corner of the doorway to the kitchen. He saw that the woman was still over there, across the floor near Burke.

He couldn't make out her features. She was just an amorphous form, pointing at him, a Provo border guard with a gun materializing out of the gloom of the tunnel beneath the wall.

# 2

Brian turned and ran. At the sink he tore off handfuls of paper towels, soaked them under cold water, and held them hard against his slitted face. He was aware of his sudden helplessness but had no fear of her. He was sure she'd never actually shoot him. He turned from the sink to face her again. He was only mildly surprised to see that it was Nick holding the gun on him. He had somehow come to.

Nick said, "You're a dead man, Galgay." His right elbow rested upon his right thigh. He held his right wrist steady with his left hand, pointing the pistol just below where he gauged Galgay's heart to be.

Brian leaned back against the sink. "It's not in you, Nick. Don't kid yourself."

"Wrong."

"She's not in any danger from me, if that's what you're thinking. And neither are you, so you can't call it self-defense, or—"

"Like hell!" Nick's body stayed rigid, but inside he wavered. Insane or not, Galgay was reading his mind. He felt his motives melting one by one.

"Give me the gun, Nick."

"Fuck you. Get out."

Brian made no move. "I want Deborah."

"Get out or I'll kill you."

"You haven't even got the safety off."

"Yes, I have." He knew Galgay wasn't going to back off. He played his final card: "I've been recruited, Brian. You're a fucking double, and they know it."

The shock made Galgay go gray. He actually reeled back a full step.

Nick pushed his advantage: "I was going to do it tomorrow anyhow," he said.

Brian's lips had begun to bleed again. His thoughts teemed like snakes in a pit. His words trickled out feebly: "You're lying!"

Nick felt Deborah's hand grab his shoulders. As much for her benefit as to convince Galgay, he said, "No, I'm not, Brian, and you know it. Remember Joel Kelsey? He's running it. You helped set me up yourself."

"Kelsey's *here*, Nick!" She finally got it out.

"Where?

"On the floor. He's unconscious. He—"

"Then, Jesus, go help him—bring him to!" Sure. Fucking Kelsey. Not about to take no for an answer. He was *here*! Thank God. "Use the Scotch," he yelled to her.

Brian lifted his blank gaze from the floor. "Ask not what your country can do for you, huh, Nick?"

"Don't give me any of your shit, spook."

"Oh, *why*, Brian?" Deborah suddenly cried, administering to Kelsey.

"You tell her, Nick. Why do they think I did it?"

"Money."

Brian let out a sad "No."

"And they think you're probably a believer."

Brian stared down at the floor, straining desperately inside to regain his wits before Kelsey came around. "I'll tell you why. It's funny . . . I was thinking of telling you this anyhow, Nick— sometime. Thought you'd understand. They got to you first, though. Yeah, I can see it now—you're perfect. Boy, they love to find guys like you out there. God knows there's enough of you, still running around with half a hard on."

"Why, Brian?" she asked again softly. Kelsey had begun to make noises in his throat and chest.

Brian brought up the sleeve of his jacket and blotted his mouth. Then he told them: "I had a girl in Berlin. Anna. I was

[ 307 ]

going to bring her out, after the wall went up. Through a tunnel. But the night she was there, it was a trap and we had to run. She was a Russian, they took her back, then later found me here and said if I didn't play the game they'd throw her in a camp for life or kill her."

"Oh, Brian!" Deborah said sadly.

Nick tried to fight the wavering he felt. "That was a hell of a long time ago, Galgay!"

"*You* were a hell of a long time ago, Nick!" He knew he had given Kelsey a good slam; he wouldn't be brought out of it all that easily. Testing Nick, he dared to turn casually away, pull down and tear off a new length of paper towel, and poke at his face with it.

Deborah was blurting, "My God, Nick! They can't just go killing a person for that!"

"Leave it alone! The fucker broke in here! He hurt me, he hurt Kelsey, he—listen to me—get yourself out of here. There's a Shell station about two miles down the road, to the right. Go call the police from there."

Brian said, "That's a mistake, Nick. The Corps . . . Kelsey won't like that."

Kelsey had snapped awake. He looked across at Nick and Galgay and said, "Do it, Nick. Just *do* him. Now."

Nick kept his eyes nailed to Galgay's heart. He could not speak. The only part of his body that he could move if he had to was his finger upon the trigger.

"I said do it, Nick!" Kelsey had stood up.

"Jesus, Kelse, lay off."

"For Christ's sake, Nick, just drop him and be done with it, will ya?"

Softly, Galgay said, "It's okay, Nick. You're right—it would be wrong for you to do their dirty work. You're not one of us. It's too late for you."

"Be careful, fink. Don't push me." He was almost wanting to actually do it now.

[ 308 ]

"Shoot that fucker, you asshole!"

*Asshole?* "You be careful too, Kelse." He tightened his grip on the gun, and tried to pretend he hadn't heard that eerie loosening, that threat of panic in Kelsey's voice.

"*Careful,*" Kelsey mimicked him, then blew: "Shoot! God damn it, just fucking do it, Nick! Jesus, what's happened to you?"

*My life happened,* Nick thought.

Then Kelsey crossed the line: "Where's your balls, Nick? You lost your balls, didn't you! Damn. Another one. Just another de-balled . . ."

Nick didn't dare move his gaze from Galgay to Kelsey; he didn't want to see the face these new words were coming out of.

Kelsey finished. ". . . all your goddamn woman's work, for you! Christ, they got you, didn't they!"

"Yeah, they got me, Kelse," he said, and turned both his gaze and the gun away from Galgay and onto Kelsey. He tried to smile. "And you know what, Kelse? It's a life. It's what I got, and I like it—I'm letting this poor bastard go. Move out, Brian."

"Give me the gun, Nick!" Kelsey reached Nick's side. "Give me the gun! I'll do it!"

"No. . . . Take off, Brian."

Kelsey went for the gun. Nick hit him with it.

Deborah shouted, "Brian, you idiot, *run!*"

Galgay ran.

Interlocked, Nick and Kelsey rolled off the coffee table. The gun came free and went sliding across the floor. Kelsey tried to pull loose and retrieve it, but Nick held him back by his coat.

On his feet again, Kelsey pounded down at Nick's head and face with both fists. Nick just held on, buying Galgay time.

Deborah kept waiting for Nick to come up and start hitting the guy, the way he had at that party. When she saw the truth, she started screaming, "Stop it! Stop it!" She looked around for something to hit Kelsey with. She raised the fire iron in both hands. Kelsey swung back and hit her. She ran and got the gun. She pointed it at his back and pulled the trigger.

It hit him in the right shoulder. As he fell, Nick let go, then pushed himself clear of Kelsey's groaning, cursing body.

Nick looked over at Deborah, and held out the palm of his hand. Dazed, she walked over, flopped the gun onto it, and collapsed onto the couch. He emptied the bullets out, got the other ones off the floor, went outside, and threw them into the dunes. He came back and went to her. She was shivering, unable to speak. He sat and put both his arms around her.

Kelsey got to his feet. Gasping for breath, he said, "Always was pretty sure I could take ya, son."

"You call that taking me?"

Deborah said to Kelsey, "Get out, all right?"

Kelsey grinned, still clutching his shoulder. "Okay, lady, I'm goin'."

"Galgay," Nick said.

Kelsey shrugged. "We'll get him—but what in hell was he doin' here *today*?"

"I thought *you* knew. Isn't that why you came?"

"Christ, no. I got your stupid call and came down thinkin' we'd get drunk and have us another long talk, that's all."

Nick said, "Well, you had your talk. You heard her, Kelse. Get out."

# 3

He said, "I guess we'll have to sell this place now. That's too bad."

She loved his "we." She looked at his face. "We don't have to sell anything, Nick." One of his eyes was closed to a slit, yet she felt she could see them both, fixed clearly and steadily upon her own.

She walked across the room. He had three lamps. She lit them all. Then she lit all the lights in the kitchen. Finally she went to the radio. A station playing music came in through the night. "There," she said, "the joint's been exorcised."

"Now I know why I love you."

"Took you long enough."


Outside, the light through the windows carried farther than the sounds of the music and their voices. Sometime later, the lights in the downstairs of the house all went out. There was a moment of total darkness, then one thin upstairs window suddenly shined forth yellow.

The music played on.

CPSIA information can be obtained at www.ICGtesting.com
Printed in the USA
BVOW03s1559180314

348030BV00001B/48/P